A *Regency* Collection

CHRISTINE MERRILL — A Regency Virgin's Undoing

LOUISE ALLEN — A Regency Rake's Redemption

ANN LETHBRIDGE — A Regency Courtesan's Pride

DIANE GASTON — A Regency Gentleman's Passion

ANNE HERRIES — A Regency Lord's Command

CAROLE MORTIMER — A Regency Lady's Scandal

MARGARET McPHEE — A Regency Captain's Prize

SARAH MALLORY — A Regency Baron's Bride

AMANDA McCABE — A Regency Duel's Awakening

CARLA KELLY — A Regency

ISABELLE GODDARD — A Regency

ELIZABETH BEACON — A Regency Rebel's Seduction

A
Regency
Rebel's
Seduction

ELIZABETH BEACON

MILLS & BOON

Published in Great Britain 2016
by Mills & Boon, an imprint of Harlequin (UK) Limited,
Eton House, 18-24 Paradise Road, Richmond, Surrey, TW9 1SR

A REGENCY REBEL'S SEDUCTION © 2016 Harlequin Books S.A.

A Most Unladylike Adventure © 2012 Elizabeth Beacon
The Rake of Hollowhurst Castle © 2010 Elizabeth Beacon

ISBN: 978-0-263-91771-0

052-0716

Printed and bound
by CPI Group (UK) Ltd, Croydon, CR0 4YY

A Most
Unladylike Adventure

ELIZABETH BEACON

Elizabeth Beacon has a passion for history and storytelling and, with the English West Country on her doorstep, never lacks a glorious setting for her books. Elizabeth tried horticulture, higher education as a mature student, briefly taught English and worked in an office, before finally turning her daydreams about dashing, piratical heroes and their stubborn and independent heroines into her dream job: writing Regency romances for Mills & Boon.

Chapter One

Wondering if she could still climb like a cat, Louisa Alstone
swung her feet out of the window and eased into the spring
night; considering the thought of marrying Charlton Hawberry was unendurable, she supposed she'd find out soon
enough. His purloined breeches shifted about her lithely feminine legs as she flexed muscles she hadn't used properly in
six years and did her best not to look down. She'd certainly
changed since the last time she had chased through the London streets, or scampered across rooftops above them, but
she fervently hoped she hadn't forgotten all her street-urchin
skills.

She should be far too much of a lady to consider such a
desperate escape now, but silently prayed her agility hadn't
deserted her as she tried not to shake like a leaf in a high
wind. Her brother, Christopher, or Kit Stone as he went by
in business, was off with his best friend and business partner
Ben Shaw, too busy having adventures on the high seas, so
there was really no point waiting around for them to rescue
her. Since she'd rather die than wed a man who would happily force her up the aisle after she had refused to marry him,

she let go of the window mouldings and edged out along the parapet.

This would work; she refused to think of the swift death awaiting her if she fumbled. She boosted herself across the next window and blessed the builder of these narrow town houses for insisting every shutter fitted so neatly no hint of her passing outside would shadow the closely barred wood. She still breathed a little more easily when no one stirred within and felt for her next shallow grip on Charlton Hawberry's house.

If she managed this, then where was there to go next? No point asking Uncle William and Aunt Prudence for help when they were calluding with Charlton. Uncle William would sell his soul to the devil for a good enough price and Kit's growing wealth hadn't endeared him or his sisters to their uncle, especially since her brother made sure their uncle got as little of it as possible, which left only her sister and brother-in-law to turn to. Maria and Brandon Heathcote would be deeply shocked at Charlton's appalling behaviour and give her sanctuary, but how could she bring scandal down on their comfortable Kentish rectory when neither of them deserved such notoriety? Then there was Maria's ridiculous soft-heartedness to contend with and Louisa grimaced at the thought of her sister feeling sorry for lying, cheating, facilely good-looking Charlton Hawberry.

You must learn to be less extreme in your opinions, my dearest, Maria had written in reply to Louisa's last letter, in which she announced she'd rather die than marry the wretched man after his third proposal in as many weeks. *And why not consider Mr Hawberry's proposals a little more seriously?* she had continued. *For all you persist in believing you will never marry, he sounds well enough looking and genuinely devoted to you. Being wed is so much better than dwindling into spinsterhood, my love, and I really think you should try to find yourself an agreeable husband, rather than regretting becoming an old maid when it is too late to remedy.*

Louisa no more believed in that love of Charlton's than she did in her own ridiculous persona of lovely, impossibly fussy Miss Alstone, Ice Diamond of the *ton*, rumoured to have rejected more suitors than most débutantes imagined in their wildest dreams. Louisa knew her resistance to marriage would make her a curiosity to the bored gentlemen of the *ton*, so she'd made herself treat them coldly from the outset. Now her carefully cultivated aloofness was in ruins and, if she escaped Charlton, she'd be besieged by suitors and would-be seducers. In truth, neither Maria nor amiable, optimistic Brandon had it in them to stand up to Charlton for long and Uncle William and Aunt Prudence wouldn't even try, so her reputation was already gone—a lost cause she couldn't bring herself to mourn deeply. Perhaps it would persuade Kit to let her keep his house and help in his business, she decided, an old hope lightening her heart as she edged along the ledge, teeth gritted against the compulsion to look down into three-storeys' worth of shadowy space.

'I'd sooner starve,' she'd told Uncle William truthfully when Charlton brought him into the unappealingly luxurious bedchamber she was imprisoned in to show how compromised she was only an hour ago.

'As you please. I won't have a notorious woman under my roof, so you can go back to the streets we took you from as far as your aunt and I are concerned,' Uncle William had replied with a Judas shrug and added, 'If you don't want to wed Hawberry, you shouldn't have run off with him in the first place.'

'He abducted me from that wretched masked ball Aunt Prudence insisted on attending and you know very well I hate the man. Won't you send me to Chelsea to await my brother's return, even if you won't help me in any other way?'

'I'm done with you, madam. I wish I'd never taken you into my home when your return for my foolishness was to ruin your cousin's chance of making a good match by stealing all her suitors.'

'I couldn't do that if I tried. I've no idea where Sophia gets her looks or her sweet nature since it's clearly not from you. A normal brother would have helped us when Mama died out of compassion for your orphan nieces and love for your only sister, but *you* had to be paid a king's ransom to house us once Kit was at sea mending all our fortunes,' she told him bitterly as she saw the weasel look in his eyes and realised he'd known about this horrid scheme all along. 'Don't worry, Uncle William, I wouldn't spend five minutes under your roof now if the only alternative was the workhouse.'

Which seemed unlikely since her dowry was substantial, thanks to Kit's efforts; if she could escape Charlton she'd live on that if Kit wouldn't let her share his new bachelor home in Chelsea. A share of her fortune would fill Uncle William's coffers very nicely, of course, but while her uncle and aunt had clearly plotted against her, could her cousin Sophia have known what was afoot? Louisa shook her head very warily and decided to trust one of two certainties in this shifting world that she suddenly seemed to have stumbled into. Cousin Sophia was far too amiable and feather-headed to be party to such a plan. She wondered how Uncle William came to have a sister like her lion-hearted, stubborn mother, and such a sweet widgeon for a daughter. Deciding the mysteries of heredity were unaccountable, she crept on along the façade of the hired town house, still trying to block the killing drop to the flagged pavement three storeys below from her thoughts.

Louisa didn't intend to marry; now the man she didn't want to marry most of all was threatening her very soul, she wished she'd never agreed to give the marriage mart another try to appease her brother and sister. Her heart hammered against her breastbone as she took an unwary glance into the street below and fancied Death was creeping along the ledge behind her, his cold breath on her neck and bony fingers clutching a ghostly scythe. Since she'd rather die than wed Charlton, she crept on, keeping her thoughts busy with what came next.

Could she evade her uncle and Charlton until her brother came home to dismiss their antics as the farce they ought to be? Her brother's house would be the first place anyone would look for her and his minions lacked the authority or power to repel her enemies. Not quite true; one of Kit's employees had both and she recalled her encounter with Kit's most notorious captain as she ghosted past the empty rooms on this part of the third floor inch by heart-racing inch. Captain Hugh Darke had made a vivid impression on her, but he was one step from being a pirate and the rudest man she'd ever met, so little wonder if the image of him had lingered on her senses and her memory long after the man had left her alone in Kit's office.

Considering she'd spent mere seconds in Captain Darke's darkly brooding, offensively arrogant company, his abrupt insolence and the satirical glint in his silver-blue eyes shouldn't haunt her as they did. She fumbled her handhold on the neatly jointed stone at the very thought of explaining this latest misadventure to sternly indifferent Hugh Darke and had to swallow a very unladylike curse while she scrambled for another and terror threatened to ruin her escape in a very final way.

'Confoundedly inconvenient, ill-mannered, cocksure braggart of a man,' she muttered very softly to herself as she inched round the corner of the Portland Stone–faced building and finally reached the drainpipe to cling onto until the rapid beat of her heart slowed while she thought out her next move.

Better with solid-feeling metal under her clutching hands, she decided to go upwards, since she'd got this far and risked being seen on the way down. Better to wait for solid ground under her feet after she had reached the last of this terrace of genteel houses, where there was less chance of being discovered clambering down from the rooftops of a stranger's house, than if she swarmed down this one like some large and very fearful fly. The idea of meeting Charlton's bullies again made her shudder with horror and she forced herself to forget their jeering comments and greedy eyes as she crept across the rooftops of Charlton's unsuspecting neighbours.

She reached the quiet and blissfully sleeping house on the end of the row and wasted a few precious moments debating whether to risk the roofs of the humbler mews that ran alongside the high town houses and reluctantly decided against it. Night had made courts and alleyways, relatively safe in daylight, into the haunts of the desperate and dangerous, but there were too many leaps into the unknown to spring across uncharted voids and risk the slightest miscalculation bringing her crashing down to earth.

Slipping very cautiously to the ground at last, Louisa blessed Charlton's love of the macabre for the ridiculous suit of black she'd found in a chest he'd thought safely locked. She grinned at the idea of him clumsily creeping about in the dark in some half-hearted imitation of Francis Dashwood's infamous Hell-Fire Club of the last century and refused to even consider what Charlton got up to in his other life. His dark clothes had helped her escape and made her hard to see in the dark, so she blessed his secret vices for once and crept on through the chilling night.

Kit's house was the only place that offered her immediate sanctuary and access to the store of money he'd once shown her, in case she was ever in dire need of it and he was away from home. How prophetic of him, she decided, and at least she would be safe until dawn. Apparently six years of dull respectability had taught her to fear her native streets, so she launched into the fuggy darkness with her heart beating like a war drum and prayed she'd find her way in the dark before she aroused the interest of the night-hawks.

Captain Hugh Darke woke very reluctantly from the nice little drunken stupor that he'd worked hard to achieve all the previous evening and peered at the ceiling above his head with only the faint, town-bred moonlight to help him work out whose it was and, more importantly, why some malicious elf was jumping about on his mysterious host's roof and waking him from the best sleep he'd had in weeks.

'And now I've got the devil of a head as well,' he muttered, much aggrieved at such a lack of consideration by whoever owned the bed he was currently occupying.

An insomniac clog dancer, perhaps? Or an iron master with a rush order his unfortunate founders must work all night to fulfil? Although that didn't work; even he knew no iron founder would carry out his sulphurous trade anywhere but on the ground floor and there'd be smoke, lots of smoke, and flaring furnaces belching out infernal heat, and, if anything, it was rather cool in here. In a moment of reluctant fairness, he forced himself to admit it was a very quiet racket, furtive even; he wondered uneasily what bad company he'd got himself into this time. He shrugged, decided he wasn't that good company himself and concluded there was no point trying to sleep through it, reminding himself he'd faced down far worse threats than an incompetent burglar before now.

Not being content to cower under the bedclothes and wait for this now almost-silent menace to pass him by—if only he'd bothered to get under them in the first place, of course—he decided to find whoever it was and silence them so he could get back to sleep. If he went about it briskly enough, perhaps he could avoid succumbing to the best cure for his various ills that he'd ever come across—a hair of the dog who'd bitten him—and spare himself an even worse hangover come morning. He'd long ago given up pretending everything about his life he didn't like would go away if he ignored it, so he swung his feet to the floor; even as his head left the pillow it thumped violently in protest, as if the elf had gotten bored with dancing on the ceiling and come into his room to beat out a dance on the inside of his reeling skull instead.

'Confounded din,' he mumbled and, liking the sound of his own voice in the suddenly eerily quiet house, he roared out a challenge in his best hear-it-over-a-hurricane-at-sea bark. 'I *said* you're making a confounded din!' he bellowed as he stamped through the doorway into a stairwell that looked vaguely familiar.

'Not half as much of a one as you are,' a woman's voice snapped back as if he were the intruder and she had a perfect right to steal about in the dark.

Her voice was as low and throaty as it was distinctive, so Hugh wondered if she was more afraid of drawing attention to her peculiar nocturnal activities than she was willing to admit. Yet the very sound of her husky tones roused fantasies he'd been trying to forget for days. Her voice reminded him of honey and mid-summer, and the response of his fool body to her presence made him groan out loud, before he reminded himself the witch was Kit Stone's woman and would never be his.

He cursed the day he'd first laid eyes on the expensive-looking houri in his friend's fine new offices dressed in an excellent imitation of a lady's restrained finery, with an outrageous bonnet whose curling feathers had been dyed to try to match the apparently matchless dark eyes she had stared so boldly at him with. Such a speculative, unladylike deep-blue gaze it had been as well, wide and curious and fathomless as the Mediterranean, and he'd felt his body respond like a warhorse to the drum without permission from his furious brain. It had seemed more urgent that Kit never discover his notorious captain lusted after his mistress than handing over the report of his latest voyage his employer had demanded as soon as he'd docked in person, so Hugh had left the expensive high-stepper alone in Kit's office with a gauchely mumbled excuse and a loud sigh of relief.

She'd responded to his gaucherie with a few cool words and a dismissive glance that made him feel like an overgrown schoolboy, instead of a seasoned captain of eight and twenty with an adventurous naval career behind him and one in front as master of a fine ship of the merchant marine. Since he was done with reckless adventures, he did his best to avoid the enemy nowadays, as well as his old naval brothers-in-arms, who thought it quite legitimate to hunt down ships like his in order to steal his crew of experienced mariners and press them into the navy. It was a second chance that Hugh valued, so somehow he'd kept his eager hands off his employer's whore and returned to his ship and the relative peace of his cabin to await Kit Stone's summons to discuss this last voyage and plan the next one.

Now Kit had gone off on some mysterious mission known only to himself; and the other half of Stone & Shaw was probably in the Caribbean by now, while Hugh Darke was drunk, in charge of Kit Stone's house and business and fantasising over his doxy. There'd be hell to pay if Kit heard so much as a whisper of them being here in the middle of the night together, him stale drunk and her... What exactly was the high-and-mighty little light-skirt doing here when her lover was absent, and in the stilly watches of the night to make bad worse as well?

'Did you hear me?' she demanded from far too close for comfort.

He swayed a little, then corrected himself impatiently as he wished the annoying witch would stop nagging and let him think. 'How the devil could I avoid it, woman? You're yelling in my ear like a fishwife.'

'I'm not yelling, you are,' she informed him haughtily, 'and where's my b...?' She seemed to hesitate for a long moment.

Which, even still half-drunk as he was, Hugh thought very unlike the headlong siren who'd so tempted him with her ultramarine come-hither gaze that day in the city. Confound the witchy creature, but he'd had to drink out of the island to get a decent night's sleep all these weeks later because she had haunted his dreams with the most heated and unattainably alluring fantasies any female had ever troubled him with in an eventful life. He couldn't have her, had told himself time and time again that he didn't really want her and it was just a normal lust-driven urge that drove him to dream about her, given he was a normal lusty male and she was very definitely a desirable and perhaps equally lusty female, given her profession. Then he'd gone on to reassure himself that she was nothing like the almost mythically sensuous creature he was fantasising her to be.

In reality, the rackety female was probably coarse and calculating under all that lovely outer glamour and fine packaging. Far too often he'd reassured himself she was just a Cyprian, told himself he'd only have to know her to learn to despise her for selling all that boldness and beauty to the highest bidder. Somehow, now she was so close to him again and he was so lightly in control of his senses after all that cognac, the sensible voice of reason was in danger of being drowned out by the hard, primitive demand of his body for hers, as the very sound of her husky feminine tones rendered him powerfully, uncomfortably erect the instant they loomed out of the night and wrapped her toils round him. He fervently hoped her night eyes and well-developed instincts weren't honed enough to tell her what a parlous state he was in and he bit down on a string of invectives that might have shocked even such an experienced night-stalker as her.

'Where's my bad, bold Kit?' she finally managed, secretly horrified at what her very correct and stern brother would have to say about her various deceits, if he ever found out about them, of course.

'No idea, he's his own man and goes his own way,' he told her absently, wondering why she wasn't much-better informed about Kit's whereabouts than he was, considering her supposedly special status in his life.

If she were his woman, he wouldn't let her out of his sight long enough to even look elsewhere, let alone allow her to roam about in a dark and virtually deserted house in the middle of the night, tormenting a poor devil like him who didn't much care whether he lived or died at the best of times. Yet with her here, the scent and elusive shadows of a playful moon and its lightly concealing clouds playing with her face and form, and the night cool and silent all around them, suddenly the threat of Kit's wrath wasn't the deterrent it ought to be. When they had first met, his youthful employer had sobered Hugh up from a far worse carouse than this one before recklessly trusting him with the command of one of his best ships when nobody else would risk a rowboat to his sole charge, for how could a captain control his ship when he couldn't control himself, or even care that he'd fallen from master of nearly all he surveyed headlong into the gutter?

Until this dratted woman sparked all these unwanted urges and one or two wickedly tempting fantasies that made him recall his other life and all the bitter betrayals it had contained, he'd been doing so splendidly at sobriety as well. He'd almost been in danger of becoming a useful member of society, until something occurred to remind him how useless he actually was; but, he decided with a cynical twist of his lips that might have passed for a smile in a dim light, it would have been a fine joke on society if he'd only managed to bring it off.

'Drat him for not telling me, then,' the major cause of his latest downfall muttered at his gruff disclaimer and there wasn't light enough to see if she looked as defeated and desperate as she sounded, before she seemed to recall another option and asked in a brighter voice, 'Has Ben gone too?'

'I dare say Captain Shaw will be in the West Indies or even Virginia by now. So at least *he*'s out there earning us all some money, whilst I'm stuck on shore sailing nothing better than a desk and your Kit's off on some wild goose chase all of his own that I would have expected you to know about far better than I do.'

'Aye, Ben's proving himself the best of us all as usual,' she said, affection very evident in her husky voice, and Hugh frowned fleetingly at hearing her so neatly avoid his implication she wasn't as close to her protector as she hoped she was.

Then he forgot his doubts about that position himself as he pondered the possibility of her maintaining intimate relations with Kit's business partner as well as Kit himself. He silently cursed the blond giant for apparently taking shares in his best friend's doxy, especially when Kit could have shared her with him instead.

'So why are *you* still here? You could easily have gone to sea in Ben's stead, and I doubt very much anyone would have missed you,' she informed him irritably.

Which was perfectly correct, he allowed fairly, even if it was brutally frank and deliberately tactless. Once upon a time, when he'd gone by another name and still possessed a relatively innocent soul, a number of good people had cared what became of him and some had even claimed to miss him sadly whilst he was away at sea. The few who were left to recall the blithe young idiot he'd once been probably welcomed the disappearance of the cynical sot he'd become from their lives with unalloyed relief, when he finally had the good manners to remove himself from polite society and the place he'd once thought of as home.

He reminded himself sourly that the past was dead and gone and he'd resolved to live for the day when he became Hugh Darke, a man who congratulated himself on caring for nobody, just as nobody cared for him, except somewhere along the way he'd come to value the good opinion of his rescuers. Still, at least he'd been able to tell himself that he'd never again be the gullible, arrogant young fool he'd been back then, before his world fell apart and everything he'd thought solid and safe melted away like mist.

Memory of the wanton havoc a careless and selfish woman could create in the life of a so-called gentleman should make him turn away from this one and barricade himself into his borrowed chamber until she gave up on him and went back into the night as swiftly and silently as she'd come. Unfortunately, she fascinated him far too much, even when he was sober and responsible; now he was three-parts' castaway, he was much too forgetful that whatever sort of woman she was, she certainly wasn't his, for all his driven wanting of her.

'I've been ordered to stay ashore and run things here while they're both busy playing on the high seas, or wherever Kit Stone happens to be hiding himself just now,' he admitted gruffly at last.

His ruffled feelings about his part of their current mission were too apparent in his aggrieved tone and he hated to hear that faint whine of discontent in his own voice. From what he could see of his unexpected visitor's face through the shadowed gloom, she looked quite tempted to push him down the stairs and have done with him for good. A part of himself he'd almost managed to smother in drink and duty would almost be glad if she could put a period to his worthless existence as well, but he shook off the deep sense of melancholy he suspected had a lot to do with returning sobriety and wondered how soon he could drown it in brandy again. The sooner he got rid of the confounded woman and got back to this useless excuse for a life the better, he decided bitterly, then frowned fiercely at the intruder, which made it a crying shame she probably couldn't see in the dark how very little he wanted her here.

Chapter Two

'So you're playing at being in charge of Kit and Ben's business ashore, whenever you manage to stay sober enough to care if it sinks or swims for the odd half-hour you can spare it, whilst they're both busy risking their lives to make your fortune for you?' the intrusive female asked Hugh, condemnation heavy in otherwise dulcet tones.

How irresistible her voice might be if she ever found anything to like about him, he mused foolishly. As it was, her question echoed about his head like knife blades and he wondered if she'd been sent to torture him with her nagging questions and the haunting scent of her, the ridiculous sensuality of her very presence in the same room with him when it was too dark for him to see the outline of her superb body. A vital, unignorable here-and-now allure that somehow reminded him with every breath that she was a very human woman and not a haughty goddess after all. A woman well used to satisfying a man's every fantasy on her back—as long as that man had enough gold in his pockets to pay for the privilege. And, thanks to Kit Stone and Ben Shaw, he had more than enough gelt to buy a lovely woman for their mutual pleasure nowadays, and keep her in comfort while he did so. How unfortunate that the one he wanted at the moment belonged to a friend he already owed so much to that he must leave her as untouched as a vestal virgin.

'I mind my own business—would I could say the same for you, madam,' he informed her sharply, in the hope she couldn't read his bitter frustration at her unavailability or discern his ridiculous state in this gloom.

'Kit and Ben *are* my business,' she informed him impatiently and confirmed every conclusion he'd already reached about her, which really shouldn't disappoint him as bitterly as it did somehow, especially considering he already expected the worst of her and most of her gender.

'Not at the moment they're not, since there's a few hundred leagues of ocean between you and their moneybags, so you'll just have to ply your trade elsewhere until they return,' he drawled as insultingly as he could manage.

'That's it! Out you; go on, you get out of this house right now, you verminous toad!' she ordered as if she had every right to evict him from the house Kit had told him to treat as his own while he was away.

'Firstly, you'll cease your screeching, my girl,' he ordered as he grasped her arms in a steely hold, in case she started scratching and biting in retaliation for being thwarted as was the habit of her type—bred in the gutter and inclined to revert to it at the slightest provocation he decided unfairly, considering he'd long ago concluded nobody could help where they were born, mansion or hovel, and that he preferred hovel dwellers over their better-off neighbours nine times out of ten.

'Damn you, I'll screech as long and as loud as I choose to,' she snapped back and he shook her in the hope it would rob her of breath. Her noise and her closeness and the elusive, womanly scent of her as she fought his grip with a determination he secretly admired was making his head pound again.

'Secondly, you'll get out of my room,' he went on doggedly.

'We're not in a room; even if we were, it wouldn't be yours.'

'Irrelevant,' he dismissed and felt something strange under the controlling grip he couldn't bring himself to make a punishing one, despite his disillusionment with her sex and the urgent need he felt to be rid of her before disaster struck, something besides warm, soft, tempting woman. 'And what the devil are you doing running wild about the place dressed in a man's shirt and breeches and not just asking for trouble but begging for it, you idiot woman?' he demanded harshly, quite put off his list of demands by that shocking discovery.

At least he wished fervently he really did find her unconventional attire shocking, instead of far too sensually appealing for comfort or safety as his exploring hand on her neat *derrière* made her squirm even more determinedly against him and curse him with an impressive, if far from ladylike, fluency while she was doing so.

'How I choose to dress is none of your business and never will be,' she informed him sharply at last, but if she could still blush he was almost sure she was doing so from the sudden increase in body heat under his exploring fingers.

'No, it's clearly Kit Stone's or Ben Shaw's business, and therefore mine in their absence,' he asserted, senses sharpening despite the brandy, as he felt a terrible threat to his jealously guarded aloofness in that demand for more information and carried on all the same. 'Come on,' he urged recklessly, making her obedience irrelevant by tugging her after him all the way downstairs and into the kitchen, where at least a fire was still burning faintly, even if the manservant Kit employed was snoring in the porter's chair in the hall, more drunk than Hugh had managed to become so far despite all his efforts before this confounded woman came along and spoilt his chance of a decent night's stupor.

Now, he supposed bitterly, he'd have to endure his usual nightmare-haunted sleep replaying a past he'd so much rather forget, if he was to be allowed any rest this night at all, which currently seemed doubtful with Kit Stone's woman actually here in the flesh rather than in spirit for once and making sure he had no chance of resting, even when he wasn't dreaming about her writhing under him, moaning out her desire and then her lusty pleasure as he satisfied every single one.

Setting a taper to the dying fire, Hugh lit a candle, decided he didn't believe his eyes and lit a whole branch of them. He wasn't often rendered speechless nowadays, but he couldn't think of a single word to say as his eyes roved over this extraordinary night visitor with numb astonishment. Numb because all the blood and feeling he still had left in him rushed straight to his loins and stopped there to torture him with the mere sight of such blatant allure. It should definitely be a crime for any woman to go about dressed like that, he decided bitterly. A felony carrying with it some sort of severe but not deadly punishment that would put her off taunting poor devils like him with her goddess's body and those endless, neatly feminine legs. An amateurish attempt at binding her breasts had only made them seem all the more worthy of a sensual exploration and as for that sweetly rounded *derrière* of hers... If she didn't realise what a temptation it posed to any red-blooded male who set eyes on her, then she ought to be locked up for her own safety until he'd taught her to know better.

'What the devil are you doing strutting the streets at night dressed like a female resurrectionist or an undertaker's apprentice?' he finally managed, faintly surprised, until they came out of his mouth, that he'd got that many words left in him.

'It's nothing to do with you what I choose to do, or where I decide to go while I'm doing it,' she told him and wrenched her arm out of his slackened grip at last so she could fold it belligerently across her body, trying her best to look as if she'd every right to go about dressed in black breeches and a dark shirt with a black cravat knotted about her slender neck. Her crow's-wing dark locks suddenly cascaded down her back, like the wickedest promise he'd seen in a long time, when she shook her head defiantly at him and her neat black-velvet cap finally gave up trying to contain so much dusky luxuriance.

'You just made it a lot to do with me, Witch,' he informed her hoarsely and let his eyes rove as they pleased over the very feminine body he'd reluctantly fantasised over since the black day he'd found her waiting in Kit's office, looking as if she had every right to be there and he was the intruder.

'Men!' she condemned impatiently, as if his sudden fascination with her long slender legs and those neatly rounded, womanly curves, so blatantly on show, was entirely his fault and nothing to do with her unconventional garb or extraordinary behaviour at all. 'You're all the same.'

'Now there you're almost certainly mistaken,' he lazily informed her, making no attempt to disguise his wolfishly thorough appraisal of her well-displayed charms, for if she aspired to meet some impossibly gallant chevalier who'd be so overwhelmed by her sensual beauty that he'd offer her anything she demanded of him during her peculiar night wanderings, she should never have embarked on a career of selling herself to the highest bidder in the first place. 'We're all different, but we *think* alike when presented with nigh-irresistible temptation, such as you pose any red-blooded male by going about dressed like that.'

'On the contrary, it seems to me that you don't think at all,' she muttered darkly and frowned at him as if she had the right to find his blatantly sexual scrutiny of her outrageously displayed body ill-mannered at best and deeply insulting at worst.

Hugh wondered how she expected any red-blooded male to actually *think* while she was standing there displaying her assets so generously that he'd soon only function on pure, or impure, instinct alone if she wasn't very careful.

'You could be right,' he told her with a wickedly unrepentant grin as he forgot his headache and began to enjoy himself by living down to her expectations. 'At the moment I'm too busy fantasising about the feel of your magnificent body writhing under me as you desperately beg me to take you to paradise to waste much of my energy on rational thought, my darling.'

'I'm not your darling and I'm prepared to bet you don't know the first thing about what would truly transport a woman to paradise,' Louisa snapped back, wishing she felt as cool as she sounded as she stood in front of this outrageous, drunken and dissipated man in her shirt sleeves with everything going wrong with her wonderful plan of escape, even now she'd finally got away from Charlton.

She'd shed her jacket and been forced to leave it behind when it had been caught on a spike put there by an inconsiderate neighbour of Kit's to prevent the stealthy and desperate using their roof for nefarious purposes such as hers. Doing her best not to remember how terrified she'd been then, swinging between safety and a forty-foot drop to her death by one hand as she had wrestled the inextricably trapped coat undone so that she could finally wriggle out of it and haul herself to safety, she shivered in the unreliable light of those untrimmed candle wicks this sot had lit to inspect her by.

Until her brother or Ben came back to put the world right for her, she might still be discovered and marched up the aisle so fast the vicar wouldn't have time to ask what she'd been up to that she deserved this and why she was protesting every step of the way. She reassured herself that could only happen if she was caught and resolved to stay in this scandalous disguise for the rest of her life if she had to, rather than endure such a fate. So she did her best to glare defiance at the wretched man while she convinced herself even his company was preferable to roaming the streets now she was grown up and vulnerable, open to the use and abuse such a reckless female might attract from rogues like this one, if she wandered about even more freely dressed in what was left of Charlton's fantasy disguise.

'Aren't you willing to add me to your stable of lucrative lovers then, my darling doxy?' he suddenly asked as if he had every right to insult her.

He'd only set eyes on her twice in his life, for goodness' sake, and she doubted he even remembered their first encounter now, given the reek of brandy on his breath whenever he came near her. Not knowing her at all, he somehow thought he had every right to eye her like a starving dog slavering over a juicy bone—surely he couldn't know a visceral, wayward part of her was inclined to look at him the same way and only made the rest more furious.

'Firstly, I'm very particular whom I allow to even call me darling, Captain Darke, and secondly, I certainly wouldn't take a man like you to my bed, even if I wasn't,' she informed him haughtily, kicking herself for letting him know she'd been fascinated enough to find out what his name was after that first sight of him in Kit's office.

'You put such a high price on your charms, then?' he asked as if he was surprised.

She had to bless his consumption of brandy for fogging his wits that he hadn't even noticed her *faux pas*, even if it fuddled him into mistaking her for Kit's mistress rather than his sister. After all, she didn't want him to think of her as his employer's close kin, did she? No, of course she didn't. If he knew who she really was, he might ruin everything by handing her back to her temporary guardians, so it was far better if he thought her no better than she should be and let her stop here for the night.

'A very high one indeed,' she assured him with a toss of her head, which she hoped told him it was beyond anything he could pay, if he had anything left of his share of the last cargo after buying enough brandy to inebriate even him.

'How's a man supposed to know if a woman's price is worth the paying when he's not even been permitted to check the quality of the goods? Strikes me you're asking a man to buy a pig in a poke, my dear.'

Good heavens! The appalling man really thought she was a streetwalker, casually selling her body for a bed and food in her belly as well as the clothes on her back. More of a roof-walker, her sense of the ridiculous reminded her, and the past years of suffocating respectability threatened to fall away under the liberty of his wild conclusions about Miss Alstone, spinster of impeccable birth, if not exactly unimpeachable upbringing. Maybe Aunt Prudence was right and she'd never be the proper lady she should have been since birth, if only said birth hadn't taken place in a rundown lodging-house, so perilously close to the rookeries of St Giles it was almost a part of them.

She'd never know now how differently she might have felt about the world if she'd come into it at lofty Wychwood Court, a vast Tudor mansion in the county of Derbyshire that was the Alstones' ancestral home. A house she'd never been invited to visit and doubtless never would be now, since her Alstone cousins seemed intent on ignoring any relations low enough to run the streets for most of their childhood and then lower the family name still more by taking to trade in order to make up their lamentable lack of the proverbial penny to bless themselves with. Reminded how little she'd enjoyed a life of cramping propriety, she made herself meet this monster of depravity's sceptical gaze and match his cynical scrutiny with one she hoped he'd find just as difficult to meet.

'The customer always has the choice not to buy,' she said boldly, as if she fended off such outrageous provocation every day of the week and reminded herself that, if not for Kit and Ben, she'd probably be exactly what this poor apology for a gentleman thought her right now. 'And I can take my pick of those who want to do so whenever I like.'

'The most readily caught fish doesn't always taste sweetest.'

'But if you throw them back, I've found the little ones often live to grow up and learn a lot more, which makes catching them again into much better sport.'

'I'll have to be the one that got away, then, for hooking me would prove a challenge even to the most cunning enchantress, let alone an amateur angler like yourself, Miss… Confound it, whatever is your name, woman?'

'Miss Confoundit? Now why didn't I think of that?'

'I'll just make one up to call you by then, shall I?'

'No, it's…' Louisa racked her brains for something suitably exotic, something an aspiring Cyprian might use to intrigue ardent gentlemen with plenty of gold in their pockets, if not rude and probably impoverished sea captains. 'Eloise La Rochelle,' she invented on the spur of the moment and decided she rather liked it.

Nobody would dare drive Eloise La Rochelle to such desperation that she'd risk climbing out of a second-floor window to escape her uncle's machinations and her importunate suitor, she decided whimsically. Indeed, Eloise would doubtless have far less respectable gentlemen than even this one climbing up the creepers to her scented balcony in their droves of a night-time to beg for her nigh-on legendary favours instead.

Would she accept any of them? she wondered, as she slipped deeper into the dangerous fantasy of being a very different female from the one she was in reality, or make them climb back into the night? Charlton could go back the way he came as fast as gravity could take him and she hoped it would teach him a salutary lesson, but Hugh Darke? Daring, dashing Eloise La Rochelle might just let him stay for a while, because he amused and intrigued her, of course, and to enchant him into parting with the dark secrets that lurked in those ironic grey-blue eyes of his, until he finally laid even his cynical heart at her feet. Then he could take his brooding gaze and his warrior's body down the stairs when he left, to scandalise and intrigue passing dowager duchesses with his disreputable looks and piratical charm and make them long to be as young, bold, stunningly beautiful and irresistibly seductive as the notorious Eloise La Rochelle of such scandalous fame even they couldn't pretend never to have heard of her.

No, she revised her story, he wouldn't be *able* to leave. He'd demand, then beg, then sell his soul to stay with her, if he still had one. Infamous Eloise La Rochelle would spoil him for every other female he ever met and in return he'd satisfy her as extravagantly as she would him, or be banished to decline and fall alone as a punishment for his sensual failure.

'And I'm the Queen of Sheba,' he responded sceptically to her exotic *nom de plume*, bringing her back to here and now with an unpleasant jolt, as she struggled with the uneasy certainty that he wouldn't fail to pleasure her in such an encounter, even if she was a little foggy about what such sensual satisfaction would involve.

A very uncomfortable present it was as well, where he didn't look at all enchanted by her assumed name or shockingly displayed charms and probably wouldn't beg aught but peace from the likes of her, so he could broach another bottle and swinishly lose himself in drink once more.

'I suggest you act a little more regally from now on, then,' she told him crossly, turning her back on that ridiculous fantasy of him falling at her feet, tortured by passion and his searing, insatiable need for her as she searched the Spartan-looking kitchen for something to eat instead.

'Make yourself at home, why don't you?' he muttered ungraciously.

'Certainly I shall and you can build up the fire whilst I do so,' she demanded, wishing she could find something more appealing than a hunk of hard and cracked cheese and some pickled onions along with, of all things, a naval officer's dress sword, in Kit's larder.

'Coste sends out for food whenever we're hungry,' Hugh told her as if that explained everything and, since they were both men, it probably did.

'On the rare occasions either of you forsake the brandy bottle long enough to bother to eat at all, I suppose?' she asked sweetly.

'Whatever our domestic arrangements may or may not be, we certainly didn't invite you here in the middle of the night to see if they were up to scratch,' he mumbled gruffly as he bent to stoke the fire.

'Which is just as well, considering you clearly don't have any,' she informed him disgustedly as she chewed valiantly on the hunk of cheese and wondered if even she was hungry enough to indulge in a pickled onion or two to force it down with, as she could see no sign of anything else remotely edible or drinkable.

'We don't need them,' he informed her defensively, looking endearingly sheepish even as he did so. 'Neither of us wanted a female nagging and criticising and poking her nose in everywhere it wasn't wanted when we can manage very well for ourselves.'

'No, you can't. I can assure you that you and Coste really, really can't manage anything more refined than a sty, Captain Darke,' she told him fervently, as she finally gave up on finding anything else remotely edible in the dusty larder and purloined his branch of almost-gutted candles to make a more thorough tour round the dusty, dirty, unused room and the once-pristine scullery on the other side of the kitchen that turned out to be piled with every glass, tankard and mug Kit's house possessed. All were dirty and looked as if they'd been so for too long. 'And wherever have Mrs Calhoun and Midge gone off to?' she asked at last.

'Kit's housekeeper wouldn't stay once he'd been gone awhile, nor let Midge stop here without her. She said we lived like swine and she'd no mind to go on mucking out a pigsty every morning, so you two obviously have a lot in common.'

'How very sensible of her, but wherever did they go?' she asked and when he didn't reply, she walked back into the kitchen to find him watching her as if he wished she'd conveniently disappear as well.

Oddly hurt by his clear preference for her room over her company, she frowned and tapped an impatient foot as if waiting for his answer, when she suspected both women would be at Brandon and Maria's rectory in Kent, awaiting the return of their master before they deigned to come back.

'She just said Kit would know where to find her when he wanted his house made civilised again,' he drawled unrepentantly.

'How insightful of her,' she said with a scornful glance round the room.

'I'll borrow a few deckhands to clean up next time we unload a ship.'

'In the meantime you intend to go on treating my br…brave Kit's house worse than a stable? At least a well-run stable is mucked out every day, but this place has obviously been going to rack and ruin ever since he left.'

Was Captain Darke actually blushing? Louisa wondered. Her half-guttered candles were flickering annoyingly and refused to illuminate him properly, but she was surprised he'd even heard it could be done, let alone learnt how to do it himself.

'He said I was to treat the place as my own,' he excused himself gruffly.

'And you truly think so little of yourself, Captain?'

'Yes, Miss Eloise so-called Rochelle, I do, and this is all I want or need of any place I lay my head nowadays,' he rasped harshly, as if she'd stepped on to forbidden ground by even asking that question.

'Why?' she asked, biting back a ladylike apology for intruding on his private thoughts and opinions.

'Because… Devil fly away with it all, woman, what right have you to break in here and interrogate me like some long-nosed inquisitor? While we're on the subject of the devil, where's Coste hidden the rest of the brandy, so I can get back to my previous occupation when you leave us or at least stop your infernal nagging?'

'Inside himself from the look of it,' she answered impatiently and watched him with an implacable look Kit called her I'll-find-out-if-it-kills-us-both stare.

'Selfish bastard,' he grated in a much-tried voice and tried to look as if he didn't know he was being inspected by his unwanted night visitor and found wanting.

'You probably have enough left in your system to inebriate a goat.'

'I never saw a drunken goat, but what an interesting life you must have lived to have done so, Miss Le Havre.'

'Yes, I have,' she informed him truthfully, or at least she had until she'd been hauled off to learn respectability at the age of thirteen, much against her will. 'And it's not Miss Le Havre, but Miss La Rochelle, if you're capable of remembering your own name, of course, let alone mine, which I sincerely doubt just at the moment.'

'I know that too well, but I dare say you could tell a tale or two about that life, could you not?'

'I could, but I won't.'

'Yet you expect me to tell you my entire life story, whilst you reveal nothing of your own? You're an implacably demanding, as well as an insensitive and intrusive, female footpad, are you not, Miss Rockyshore?'

'You really have no idea, Captain Darke.'

'So, *is* that how you keep your lovers under your slender little thumb?' he drawled in his velvet-rubbed-the-wrong-way voice. 'By dragging their darkest secrets out of them when they're drunk, then holding them over the unfortunate idiots?'

'Nothing about me is so very little, sir, I'm above average height for a woman,' she parried coolly, ignoring the urge to counter the rest of his accusations as beneath her notice.

Trust him to take her words as an open invitation to let his silver-blue eyes rove over her boldly. He was good at defending his privacy, she mused, as he let his gaze track over her until those eyes had all but stripped her bare. Then the renegade let that blatant stare of his rest explicitly on the secret centre of her and she had to fight not to press her legs together and visibly, physically clamp down on the fiery demand suddenly all too alive and wildly curious for more under his outrageous scrutiny. Kit and Ben hadn't fought battle after battle to preserve her honour in their youth so she could be secretly tempted to throw it away on a ne'er-do-well like this.

Yet that fully-formed temptation stopped her thundering scold and sharp exit in its tracks. If she let him take her virginity, then she'd lose all her value on the marriage mart the instant he did so. Not even a Charlton Hawberry would take another man's leavings, so deeply ingrained as it was in a gentleman's psyche that he must marry a virgin, or at the very least a virtuous widow—she would certainly be neither after a night in the ungallant captain's bed. It might be a desperate idea, almost as reckless as climbing out of a second-floor window at midnight, but she wasn't in a position to discard any possibility just now.

'So I see,' he said with a pantomime leer she almost applauded, but there was something deeper and darker than simple lust in his eyes as well. It suddenly occurred to her that the real Captain Darke, whoever he might be under all this dark and dangerous front he faced the world behind, could break her heart if she had one. Luckily she didn't and stared boldly back at him.

'That could change,' she warned, 'if you don't stop staring at me.'

'Me, Miss Rockisle?' he said, and his silvery-blue eyes were beginning to lose the haze of brandy and world-weariness that had clouded them until now. She dare not look lower to find out if his body was as blatantly aroused as his cocky smile and intent gaze argued it must be.

'Yes, you—we were discussing your total lack of ambition and self-respect rather than my height and frame, if you remember?' she said coldly.

'You can talk as much as you like, my lovely, if you have the breath left for it after I've finished with you,' he mocked as he sauntered confidently towards her.

'I know when a man is determined to shut me up at any price,' she blustered.

Suddenly it was very quiet in the house, echoingly empty but for the unconscious Coste, who she would have to swear to keep her identity from Hugh Darke, and two almost-adversaries, each determined to give no quarter. Louisa was too much a child of the streets to yield an inch in the eternal battle to make every choice her own, however wrong-headed and contrary it might be, and stood her ground while she wondered what that next choice would be.

'And I know just as surely when a woman wants me as much as I do her, my dear,' he said and stepped closer, silvery-blue eyes full of sensual challenge.

'I'm not your dear,' she argued and tried to tell herself it didn't matter.

'And if you're not, what do you care? In a profession where "affection" is traded for expensive jewellery, fine gowns and a rich man's protection, you can't afford emotions, can you?'

Chapter Three

Temper had always been her undoing, Louisa decided as she lost it spectacularly and did her best to punch him in the gut. The wretched, ungentlemanly Captain Darke countered her onslaught by engulfing her in such a tight hold there wasn't even a tissue of air to shield them from each other and it sparked a heat set burning weeks ago, when they had first laid eyes on each other and wondered 'what if?'. It was like a force of nature, fuelled by some terrible need she hadn't known could come so urgent it might tear into her very soul in order to make them indivisible.

She moaned at the shock of wanting more so desperately and should have been shaken instead of fascinated by the novel hardness of his rampant male member nudging explicitly, demandingly against her very core. Logic, scruples, reality—they could all wait. She needed to indulge, to learn, to luxuriate. His mouth took hers in an open-mouthed kiss that stole her breath and sent her straight into sensual arousal no real lady would feel for a lover, at least until he'd chipped away at her scruples and guarded heart for weeks, or maybe even months.

Louisa's heart kicked with a shameless thrill at being so easily seduced, so starkly introduced to rampant sexual hunger, to the merciless drive of one achingly aroused body for another. She was all too ready to lose herself in the heat and novelty, and didn't that prove her uncle and aunt had been right all along and she'd never make a proper lady?

Unable to resist the urge to explore him with every sense as he amply demonstrated his skills as a lover of passionate women, she lazily let the tips of her fingers take a census of his features. His chin felt as firm as if he chewed nails for a pastime, when not seducing very unlikely maidens, and it was intriguingly shadowed with fine, dark whiskers.

'I'd have barbered myself if I'd known you were coming,' he told her wryly in a brief moment of respite, then ran his index finger over her tingling lips as if they fascinated him as much as his did her, before kissing her again as if he couldn't help himself test their softness and their welcome.

The small part of her brain not occupied with kissing him back went on with her sensual exploration of his intriguing features. He'd broken his nose once upon a time, as she felt a slight twist in his regally aquiline nose, and she decided it made his wickedly handsome face more human. His mouth was all sensuality just now; his firm lips on her softer ones were a balm, the impudent exploration of his tongue an arousing, teasing echo of something deeper and darker at the core of her that throbbed and ground with need in shameless response.

Her breath sobbed when he raised his mouth enough to lick along the cushiony softness he'd made of her lush lips, to tease and tantalise their moist arousal with his tongue as if he couldn't get enough of her. Then it was his turn to groan as she darted her tongue inside his mouth, to chase and tease and put into practice all he'd just taught her.

Now wouldn't he be surprised if he knew I was only as adept in the amorous arts as he's just shown me how to be? she mocked herself silently.

He was a drunkard, a hardened cynic, and now she could add accomplished seducer of women to the slate against him. And he thought her barely one step away from a doxy touting for custom in the Haymarket. Even under the addictive spell of his kiss, Louisa managed to sigh. To him she was a willing mouth and an eager body and suddenly that was insulting everything there should be between lovers. If she were what he thought, she'd still have a heart and soul, however broken and damaged, and she wanted to be more than a reluctant itch to be scratched then added to a list of women he'd taken, then all but forgotten. He was more than that as well, for all he looked as if he didn't care to be.

There was a depth of sadness under all that to hell-with-you manner, what suddenly seemed almost a wasteland of loss behind his cynical self-mockery. If letting him take her to their mutual satisfaction meant no more than a quick tumble in the hay, then she couldn't do it even to evade a legion of Charltons. *No*, a mocking internal voice said, *because you want too much from this conundrum of a man for that, don't you, Louisa?*

The question taunted her as his large hands cupped her shamefully aroused breasts and threatened to incinerate other wants with the sheer sensual need for more. Her eager nipples pebbled under the wicked stimulation of his suddenly very sensitive fingers and she felt as if she might burst into spontaneous flames. Temptation tore into her at the very thought of learning more, of letting him take her and render her unmarriageable between one moment and the next, but she fought it. Those who loved her might hope she wavered because of proper, belated, maidenly shrinking at the irrevocable step between virgin and woman, but that was nothing to do with it. It was because he was too embittered to wake up next to her in the morning and make the loss of her maidenhead feel right to either of them that she couldn't take that step and walk him over a precipice.

It would solve so much, but then he'd know Eloise La Rochelle was as big a lie as the brilliant and icy Miss Alstone was to the *ton*. Perhaps she was the biggest fool in London to pass on seduction by such a master of the amorous arts, but she met Captain Darke's clearing gaze and knew her instincts were right. He could be all her tomorrows and her sensual fate, or just a regretted possibility, but she wanted more than a brief but blazing seduction that would probably haunt her for a lifetime. Did she hope for protracted and lingering seductions to come, perhaps? Not marriage—to her that was as impossible as fairy dust—but she couldn't kill whatever held her back by melting into his kisses and solving one problem with an even greater one.

'I see how you hook in your prey now, Miss La Rochelle,' he said with a shake of need in his deep voice that spoilt the steeliness of his would-be taunt.

'I don't hook them, as you so elegantly put it—they catch themselves, Captain, then I take my pick,' she lied.

'If you think to net me, then you've rarely been more wrong,' he grated out in a fine, frustrated fury.

'I'm a woman, Mr Darke, and therefore very rarely wrong at all,' she taunted him with a sidelong look at his still-heaving chest and the flush of hard colour burning on his high cheekbones. She wriggled her hips and boldly abraded his impressive manhood with her lithe body to prove it.

'In this instance you're so glaringly mistaken I'm surprised you can't find the good sense to admit it,' he informed her stiffly and snapped the spell their bodies were slower to relinquish than their minds by pushing her roughly away. Turning his back on the wanton sight of her, draped against the hard edge of the kitchen table, he groaned in unmistakable self-disgust.

Louisa stayed where she was, mainly because her legs were still shaking so much from want and shock that she doubted they'd hold her up if she tried to move. 'Yet you'll remember me, Captain Darke. Even if I was about to let you put me outside like a stray cat, you'd still take the fire we've just lit between us back to bed with you and burn mercilessly for me all night long, deny it as you might,' she taunted dangerously, recklessly prodding at his temper for some reason she couldn't even put into words for her own satisfaction.

Maybe part of her still wanted to goad him into seducing her until she forgot anything else. She wondered uneasily at her own folly and tried to look as if his revulsion at the very idea of ever touching her again couldn't possibly hurt her.

'I might well, but why draw back from a promising new keeper when you seem to be without one while my youthful employer is at sea, Eloise?'

'To make you more eager, of course,' she explained, as if it was perfectly obvious to any masculine idiot who hadn't pickled his intellect in brandy.

'Just how eager do you expect your lovers to be? Is seeing me so burnt up by the lure of paradise between your finely displayed legs that I'd have promised you everything I have, short of a soul I long ago sold to the devil, not desperate enough for you?'

'Obviously not,' she parried, doing her best not to blush at the thought of what they would probably be doing right now if she hadn't drawn back.

She imagined they'd somehow be striving for a fulfilment her body ached for with a merciless, hard knot of frustration at the centre of her that felt as if it might never relax on being denied what was natural and right between lovers. 'Lovers'— that was the key. It was what they didn't have—not one sliver of love flowed between them, so none of it would be right, however hot and needy they were for each other. Although she would never marry, she wouldn't let herself fully love a man outside it unless she really did love him. That seemed about as unlikely as Captain Darke falling at her feet and swearing undying, unswerving devotion to a woman he despised, for all he claimed to want her so hotly.

'What else *do* you expect of a man, then, if that's not enough?' he asked.

'Affection,' she told him rather forlornly, knowing she'd probably never gain it from this guarded, isolated man. 'And a little respect.'

'Very hard qualities for a female in your profession to find, I would have thought,' he mocked her almost angrily, as if no woman had a right to demand so much of a man she was thinking of taking to her bed, always supposing they managed to get that far.

'Hard ones to seek anywhere, Captain Darke, let alone on the streets,' she said, with what she knew would look like too much knowledge in her dark-blue eyes as she met his hard gaze.

'Aye, I'll grant you that much bravery, or should that be

impudence rather?' he said reluctantly and she didn't know whether to feel smug or guilty.

She reminded herself he was so drunk she could probably have pushed him over with one hand when he first staggered across the open door of that bedchamber and made her jump nigh out of her skin. If she'd pushed him away hard enough at any time during this surreal encounter, he would very likely have fallen in a heap and gone back to sleep as sweetly as Kit's watchman, and nothing they'd done in the last half-hour had caused a stutter in Coste's impressive snoring. The world ticked on and she and Captain Darke ticked with it and suddenly it felt as if their bittersweet interlude had been little more than a wicked daydream. She put a hand out as if to grasp it, but a picture of him ardent and wholeheartedly wanting her with every sense evaporated under her touch. Such fantasies weren't for the likes of them; she knew too much and he'd learnt too much for that sweet pipe dream to ever come true.

'I'd curtsy to acknowledge your extraordinary gracious-ness,' she told him in the hard, cynical voice she thought Eloise would use to protect herself from her enemies, 'but somehow I've forgotten to be suitably servile these last few years.'

'Aye, it's easy to grow accustomed to luxury and money. Harder than I hope you'll ever know to manage without them when they've become such a part of your life you can't imag-ine losing everything,' he said and she wasn't fool enough to think he was worrying about her future.

'I started out with nothing more than the clothes I stood up in, Captain, but you fell a lot further, I think?'

'You may think what you wish, but don't expect me to confirm or deny your fantasies,' he told her abruptly, the story of his sorry downfall obviously forbidden ground.

'I can pick out the nob in a crowd any day of the week, so don't try to pretend you're not one, Captain.'

'Then be content with being right and leave it at that, my dear.'

'Again, I'm not dear to you in any way, Captain Darke. Let's stick to the truth as often as we may.'

'And if that's as often as usual, it won't be heard much.'

She shrugged and reminded herself how little she wanted him to know her true self, even if she would dearly love to know his. 'So be it,' she said carelessly.

'Not much point in me asking what you're really doing here then, I suppose?'

'Not much,' she confirmed with a nonchalance she hoped masked her shudder at the thought of what she'd escaped to-night—and how she'd done it.

'Well, I suppose we're done with each other for now then, at least until morning.'

'Yes, I really suppose that we must be, Captain.'

'For good, if I had my way, Miss La Rochelle,' he informed her gruffly enough for her to know he still wanted her and bitterly resented her for it.

'Now your way would be downright boring and I make it a rule never to be so tedious that gentlemen of my acquaintance truly prefer my room to my company,' she fantasised cheerfully.

Perhaps from now on she would be herself, as she'd seldom dared to be while she had tried to move amongst his true kind as if she belonged—and blatantly did not. Whatever it cost her to be the girl who'd belonged nowhere in particular once again, that girl was who she was. And to be that person she had to sleep. At least she'd be safe from the predators who stalked the night-time streets, so until it was too early for Charlton and his ilk to be abroad, she could allow herself the luxury of sleep and hope she'd have resolve enough to take up her new life come morning.

She took the candles he carefully didn't offer her and lit a new one off them, after fetching some from Kit's dusty and unused drawing room, handing the guttering ones back to him and giving him a significant look she recalled her mother darting at her when she wanted her to go to bed and saw no reason to tell such a grown-up girl to actually go there. By saving herself the fact and almost the feel of his all-too masculine gaze on her nether regions, outrageously outlined as they were by Charlton's breeches, she had to watch his lithely masculine legs, narrow hips and lean body as he effortlessly scaled the stairs ahead of her instead.

She decided she was turning into some sort of female satyr and felt herself flush at the wicked thoughts the sight of his muscular form roused in her rebellious body. Tonight she'd felt powerfully male limbs so intimately against her own and not even wanted to flinch away; she'd known the astonishing novelty of actually yearning for the thrust and rhythm of that very particular man deep inside her, to show her what no words could ever tell her about the wild, sweet potential of it all. Never mind her unwanted success among the polite world, tonight she'd gone from schoolgirl to woman and never mind the physical fact of her virginity, still exactly as it had always been.

Tonight Captain Darke had taught her to truly want; even now part of her did so as she undressed in Kit's second-best spare bedchamber, did her best to perform a brief *toilette*, then blew out her candle and slid between cool linen sheets.

She shifted in protest against that unfulfilled need as she stretched luxuriously on the feather mattress and decided her terrifying climb to freedom had been worth every precarious step. Tonight she'd found out exactly why Charlton Hawberry wouldn't do as her husband, even if she wanted one. Now all she had to do was find out the Captain's quirks and qualities if she was to take him to her bed and maybe even her heart. That thought sobered her, as she considered the impossibility of Captain Darke ever returning so huge and compelling an emotion as love, even if she had no more desire to be trapped into marriage than he did.

Could any woman reach the last traces of gentleness and vulnerability that must still exist under all that armour of indifference and cynicism, or why would that armour need to be so strong? A colder, less ardent soul than the one he'd sought to bury under layers of pack-ice, or drown in a brandy bottle, would survive without the embittered shell Captain Darke had grown to survive, but could she get inside it if all she found out when she got there was how much he refused to trust his emotions? And how on earth would she ever persuade him she was worthy of his trust if he found out when he took her to his bed that Eloise La Rochelle was as big a lie as hard, embittered and dangerous Captain Darke?

Hugh woke reluctantly and groped for his pocket watch even as he bit back a loud moan at the brightness of a new spring day and the lying promise of a London sky washed clean of all its sins, until it besmirched itself again with the smoke and stink of a great city. He might be less cynical about the day, he supposed, if the sharp sunlight wasn't falling across his eyes unveiled by shutters or curtains, just as he'd so often fooled himself he liked it. Might be, but he doubted it, as full memory of the night before kicked in again and another shot of agony tore across his aching forehead at the very thought of Miss Eloise La Rochelle, who was very likely waiting to torture him over the breakfast table at this very moment. If she could find it under all the detritus he and Coste had deposited there, of course.

Rubbing an exploring hand over his villainously rough chin, he winced at the idea of having kissed even that intrusive and annoying gadfly of a woman in such an ungentlemanly state, even though he'd been drunk and driven by some unholy need he still couldn't fully comprehend by the light of day. She might not be a lady, might not have been accustomed to respect and good manners from her seducers before she encountered his friend Kit and decided to hang on to him with both hands, but Hugh had once been a gentleman so it was a matter of honour not to harm a woman of any stamp. He should have taken a second shave of the day to insure that he didn't hurt her soft skin, if only he'd known he'd be kissing such a wanton siren last night. 'Failed again, Hugh,' he scolded himself cynically. 'Proved yourself a rogue once more, as per expectations.'

Not bothering to even make the effort to cling to well-bred restraint in the face of so many failures, he hauled himself out of bed and gave vent to a heartfelt groan as his own heartbeat pounded fists of pain into his suffering brain at the sudden movement. Reaching blindly for the water jug, he gulped a lukewarm draught directly from it and groaned as he waited for the thundering in his ears to abate and the pain in his temples to dull to a bearable throb, then splashed water on to his face to try to relieve the ache behind his eyes.

'Damned petticoat-led idiot,' he castigated himself as he glared at his bleary-eyed reflection in the fine mirror his friend had furnished this guest bedchamber with, as he dried his face on the fine towel provided for more appreciative visitors than he was proving to be. 'And just what would you think of me if you could see me right now, my friend?' he speculated as he contemplated Kit Stone's outspoken disgust at the spectre he'd made of himself.

And that was before Kit could even begin on the subject of kept women and which of them was keeping her. Hugh shook his head, despite the fierce clash of pain it cause, frowned fiercely at his reflection, then realised he didn't even want to meet his own eyes in the mirror any more, let alone imagine holding his friend's dark and yet somehow steely gaze when he finally came home and took back his empire and his woman from such faulty hands as Hugh Darke's had proved to be.

'Abel Coste! Where the devil are you?' he went to the door and bellowed, in the hope his drinking companion of last night was in a better state of preservation than he was himself this morning, which would hardly be difficult, given that he felt as if he'd been trampled half to death by a herd of wild horses.

'Whatever is it?' his unwelcome visitor demanded impatiently from below.

'I want Coste,' he snapped back.

'Well, you can't have him, he's busy.'

'Since you certainly don't need a shave, I can't imagine how,' he mumbled disagreeably, but she obviously possessed hearing a cat would have been proud of.

'And if you were planning to let him shave you, then you must be even more addled than I thought, considering the sorry state he's in this morning,' she told him, as if she was some sort of stern maiden aunt rather than a brazen hussy.

She was still looking like a barbarian princess in her ill-fitting breeches and that ridiculous black shirt, her silken mass of dark chestnut hair falling down her back like a promise of all kinds of sensual delights. He knew she was no better than she should be, yet she made him ache to feel the luxurious wonder of her against his naked skin while he played idly with that wanton hair as they lay, momentarily sated, in each other's arms. The last thing he needed was this burning desire to make her scream with desire and passion such as she'd never known before, and now he came to think about it, a mild shout of satisfaction might well blast the top of his head off and do permanent damage to his feeble brain just now.

Damnation take it, he shouldn't even think of her *in extremis* like that. Not only was he in no state to pleasure even the most undemanding of houris, but he was also an ungrateful bastard who suddenly really wanted to at least try to drive her wild with mutual lust and see if such exquisite gratification could cure his hangover.

How could he even think of turning on the man who'd rescued him when everyone else had left him to rot in the gutter by trying to steal his woman? He'd better convince his baser self he didn't want the confounded woman as a matter of urgency, then at least he'd be ready to conduct Kit's business for the day instead of standing here fantasising about seducing his mistress.

'I wasn't planning on letting Abel or anyone else near my throat with a razor,' he drawled in a deliberate echo of the insufferably cocky aristocrat he'd once been, 'but to shave myself properly I need hot water and Coste is much better at lighting the range than I am.'

'You must be atrocious at it then, since he made such a sad

business out of it with all his moaning and groaning and constant "oh deary, deary me, but I don't feel at all well," that I found it a good deal quicker to deal with it myself,' Miss La Rochelle told him so disapprovingly he was reminded of his sister's steely-backboned governess in a particularly formidable frame of mind. He made the mistake of grinning over an image of his gadfly in breeches, instructing the daughters of the nobility in good manners and proper behaviour. 'It wasn't in the least bit funny to be expected to light your confounded fires for you as well as sober up the only help you seem to have left in the house in order to get some breakfast,' she snapped.

She then subjected him to a hostile glare that should reduce him to abject penitence. Wise enough to know it would be counter-productive to tell her that her ire was a boon rather than a bane to his aching head, he kept a grin from his lips with a mighty effort and did his best to look crushed. In his experience, the only way to deal with a female on the rampage was to agree with whatever she said and go his own way when her back was turned.

'Of course not,' he agreed. 'It's probably a disgrace as well—did you forget to tell me that or have my aching ears left out some listening?'

'Men have a very peculiar sense of the ridiculous,' she informed him with regal contempt, obviously not inclined to gratify him by rising to his baiting.

'And most women don't have one at all,' he let slip, then corrected himself. 'Except for the odd honourable exception, of course,' he told her with a would-be placating smile that must have come out as a mocking grin since she glared at him, before marching back to the domestic regions. He didn't even have time to muse on feminine unpredictability before she was back with a steaming jug.

'Here's your hot water and don't scald yourself,' she ordered him as she thrust it into his hands. 'I suggest you make your-self decent before you come downstairs, if that's not too much to ask of a man with trembling hands and a brandy-addled constitution like yours,' she told him before she rounded on her heel and strode towards the kitchen while he gazed owl-ishly after her.

'Managing female,' he muttered darkly to himself.

'I heard that!' she shouted back improbably and he amended her hearing up to bat-like sensitivity and resolved to tell the truth about her only when he was safely on the opposite side of London in future.

He kept trying not to smile as he shaved more deftly than he could have believed possible when he woke up this morn-ing, and had to force a suitable blandness on to his reflected features in order not to cut himself. Usually the sight of his own face froze any inclination he might have to smile, but this morning even that didn't seem as bitter a spectacle as expected. Last night he met a ladybird in the dark and now he was grinning to himself about her like a lunatic, despite a painful state he would prefer to deny existed that ought to be beyond a man in his condition. He reminded himself he couldn't have her, even if she wanted him to, and poured his cooling shaving water with its unattractive bloom of shorn whiskers and used soap back into the can.

Hugh set the jug by the door to take downstairs once he was dressed for a morning in the City, spent attending to his employers' business affairs and grimaced at the thought of the hours of checking tallies and reviewing accounts lying ahead of him. Somehow even the thorny task ahead of him couldn't blot out the dangerous sense of anticipation he felt at tangling with the woman downstairs one last time. He even caught himself whistling, before realising she would hear him. Eyeing himself—cravat decently tied and stockings and knee-breeches unwrinkled—he shrugged into a very sober waistcoat and gave himself a mocking bow. Today he was almost unrecognisable as the renegade captain of the *Jezebel* and resolved to avoid the haunts of the *ton* on his way to the City, lest someone recognise him even got up like a respectable cit. He shrugged off the prospect of being known for someone far less worthy, decided breakfast took precedence over old sins and let the smell of Miss La Rochelle's cooking lure him downstairs once more.

Chapter Four

'My guess is that you're a better cook than Coste or I will ever be,' Hugh observed as he strolled through the propped-open kitchen door.

'Which wouldn't be difficult, given the state of the saucepans and skillets left in the scullery,' the most unusual cook in England muttered irritably in reply.

'We never claimed to be domesticated,' he admitted with a casual shrug.

'You'd be arrested for fraud if you did.'

'Very likely, but where did you get all this?' he asked with a wave of his hand at the largesse spread over the end of the long deal table nearest to the closed stove.

Her self-imposed task had put an attractive flush of colour on her cheeks and he noted the surprisingly seductive scent of warm woman and the faint suggestion of a gloss of perspiration on her fine, creamy skin. Never having been the sort of man who preyed on his servants, he'd not subjected kitchenmaids to lecherous scrutiny in the past, but the sight of his employer's exotic mistress, dressed in her scandalous dark breeches with that absurd black shirt clinging to her

all the more because of the light bloom of perspiration on
her delectable body, was enough to make a monk ache with
frustration, and he wasn't a monk. Wrenching his eyes from
the spectacle of all he couldn't have, he made himself listen
to her reply to his question through the thunder of his own
blood in his ears and sought refuge behind the table until he
had his body in a fit state not to betray him.

'I dragged your fellow debauchee out of his chair and
pushed him under the pump until he stopped screaming like
a stuck pig, then told him if he didn't find me the makings
of a very hearty breakfast, I'd tell Kit what a useless excuse
for a man he still is, then hope he was sent straight back to
the gutter where Kit found him,' she explained, mercifully
all without turning round to turn those shrewd dark eyes of
hers on yet another faulty male.

Yet Hugh doubted she'd carry out her threat against his
brother-in-iniquity; her shoulders were hunched against
his scrutiny, but her very defensiveness argued against her.
'Where's Coste hiding himself now, then?' he asked, as he
dared to come out from behind his barricade and pick up a
slice of just-crisp-enough bacon from the stack keeping warm
on the side of the hob.

'He's probably still trying to find a couple of scrubbing
women willing to muck out the pigsty you two have made out
of this room and the scullery, and another couple to dust and
make good the rooms you haven't yet got around to spoiling.
He insisted that he wasn't ready to eat yet,' she said gruffly.

'He won't know where to start.'

'I told him where to find a reliable domestic agency and
sent a note along with him for the manageress setting out
my requirements,' she said, turning about at last to sharply
forbid him to take one more bite until it was all ready, oth-

erwise mercifully keeping her eyes on what she was doing rather than on him. His more-obvious state of arousal had mercifully subsided, but it was his body and he knew very well it was only waiting for the flimsiest excuse to lust after hers once more. 'I expected I'd have to force you into eating anything this morning,' she said with an ambiguous twist of the lips that might have been a smile and something told him she'd been looking forward to it.

'Sorry to disappoint you, Miss La Rochelle, but I have a very hard head.'

'Evidently,' she replied coldly, as if he didn't deserve such a mercy.

He strolled into the scullery to leave his used shaving water and was astonished to find that she had washed all the crockery and glassware he and Coste had left scattered about the kitchen. Such an excess of energy made him wonder if she'd slept at all and whether she had embarked on this whirlwind of activity to put whatever came next for her out of her mind for a while. What was bold, bad Eloise La Rochelle afraid of? he wondered, and why did he hate to think of her facing problems so insurmountable that they might leave her cowed and fearful instead of her usual bold and brazen self?

Given her daring method of arrival last night, she certainly wasn't naturally timid and many things that would make even a bolder-than-average female quake seemed to leave her unmoved. So had she got herself tangled up in something dangerous as soon as Kit's back was turned and should he be making it his business to find out just what she'd been up to? He eyed the racks of dishes draining over the sink with a preoccupied frown and went back into the kitchen for his breakfast and a more sober and detached assessment of his uninvited guest than any he'd managed to make so far.

'You've been very busy indeed,' he said on returning to the kitchen.

'I don't like to be idle,' she admitted and he thought he saw a shadow darken her deep-blue eyes, then it was gone and she was glaring at him as if he might eat with his knife unless sternly watched once more.

'There seems very little risk of that,' he said and tried not to fall on the food she'd cooked like a ravening beast. 'Can I pour you coffee?' he asked, reaching for the pot at the same time as she did, flinching as what felt like a shock of lightning jagged up his arm as their fingers met fleetingly, then fell away.

He took a deep breath and stared at his hands, unaware until he saw his knuckles whiten that he'd clenched them into fists to stop himself gripping her slender fingers as if they were his lifeline. He loosened his fists and made himself glance at the bright morning outside the window, still gallantly promising something more than the usual London haze. Today he could enjoy the blessing of a fine morning, a useful occupation and a full belly—what more could a man ask of life? Sighing at the thought of all he *could* ask for, but no longer dared risk wanting, he turned back to watch her with raised eyebrows and a cynical half-smile.

'I am perfectly capable of lifting a coffee pot for myself, thank you,' she said sharply and he wondered if she'd been as disturbed by that startling bolt of connection between them as he had.

'I don't doubt it, after viewing the evidence of your industry,' he said mildly and ate his way through a delicious meal as the headache he knew very well he richly deserved began to drum at his temples once more.

It was probably caused by the tension of wanting her so

urgently, but not being able to have her, he assured himself. An old familiar and purely physical burn that, as a captain used to months without female company, he knew all too well and had learnt to endure. This time, however, he somehow doubted that reading Shakespeare or studying his charts and plotting a series of possible courses to fanciful places would distract him from it, but at least experience had taught him that the sharpness of it would dull if he could find a sufficiently absorbing occupation. Yet could any distraction blot Eloise La Rochelle from a man's mind for very long?

'Thank you,' she said unexpectedly and sat and sipped her fragrant brew with what he guessed was feminine satisfaction in producing something edible when two supposedly strong men had been unable to do so between them. 'It's good to be busy once more,' she added and he wondered if a life of silken idleness had palled on such an unusual Cyprian.

'I'd be an ingrate if I failed to appreciate the fruits of your labour, even so,' he said as he laid down his knife and fork to pour coffee and add sugar to it.

'Should I pass you the cream?' she asked.

'No, thank you, I became used to going without it on board ship.'

'Don't most captains take a cow with them on long voyages?' she asked and he wondered if she'd studied the life of a sea captain because her lover often lived that life without her. The shock of pure venomous jealousy at the very idea of her pining for her lover brought him up short and made him glare at his own hand stirring his coffee as if it had mortally offended him.

'Sometimes there isn't enough room for luxuries,' he managed fairly normally.

'Oh, yes, merchantmen are carefully designed to make use

of every available inch of space for cargo, are they not?' she replied, setting off that demon of envy in him once more and making him even more silently furious with himself.

'Men-of-war are just as niggardly with every spare inch they can gain, having a goodly quantity of ammunition and unstable gunpowder to stow, as well as a vastly greater crew to accommodate,' he explained.

'It must be strange for you to go to sea as captain of a merchantman after commanding in the Royal Navy,' she mused, blasting his attempt at replacing the general with the personal out of the water. He sighed as he lay back in his chair to sip his coffee and met her eyes warily.

'I never said I'd been a navy man,' he argued, almost groaning aloud at the defensiveness in his voice. It was still a wound he hated to have probed, which seemed foolish in the extreme compared to everything else he'd lost.

'How else to account for the naval officer's sword in the larder, I wonder?' she said with a pretence at scratching her head. 'Was Coste a dashing captain at Trafalgar, I wonder? Or perhaps he's really an admiral on half-pay, when not pretending to be Kit's hall porter and supposed watchman? No, I think the sword must be yours, Captain. I doubt Coste rose above able seaman in his entire career at sea and neither Kit nor Ben have served in the Royal Navy.'

'It's not so very different,' he admitted because it was easier than arguing. 'The sea can only be read or even guessed at by good navigation and a weather eye on her contrary moods. It's still my job to decide if it's wiser to sail before the wind or ride out a storm in safe anchorage. And at least I have a sound, fast ship that isn't an easy target for any enterprising French frigate captain, eager to build a fine and romantic reputation as a triumphant sea wolf.'

'And did you once roam the seas looking for such prey yourself?'

'Of course, that's what the Admiralty expects of flag officers not on blockade.'

'And were you good at it?'

'Naval captains must prove worthy of their rank if they expect to stay at sea,' he said carefully.

'And some do so more easily than others, I dare say,' she said blandly, so why didn't he trust her smile?

'Perhaps,' he replied tersely.

'And you were one of them,' she said and he cursed himself for giving her a clue if she ever wanted to track him down.

At least the Admiralty hadn't ordered the breaking of the sword now resting in Kit's larder, or his speedy expulsion from the Service. He almost wished they had, so it couldn't follow him like a symbol of all he no longer was, but couldn't quite discard.

'Don't bother visiting the Admiralty to find out how and when they lost or mislaid one of their junior officers, will you? Their lordships don't encourage idle curiosity.'

'Who says it would be idle? And you're very defensive about a career you pretend not to care a fig for, Captain Darke,' she said shrewdly.

'Perhaps I hate having my life picked over for the amusement of others?'

'And I don't have time or inclination for idle gossip, Captain Darke.'

'Then you must be the most unusual female I have ever met.'

'Please don't think me artless enough to mistake that for a compliment,' she countered smoothly, yet he felt he'd annoyed her by lumping her with the more curious of her kind and tried to be glad of it.

'I don't think you in the least bit artless, I assure you, Miss La Rochelle,' he said with a cynical almost-smile she didn't bother to return.

'Clearly,' she told him, but he thought he saw a shadow of pain in her blue eyes before she gathered up their dirty crockery and bore it off to the scullery.

'You hardly need to be with so many charms already in your armoury,' he explained clumsily—why must he follow her into that utilitarian room when she'd given him an ideal escape route?

'Look what you've made me do now,' she chided fiercely as she jumped on finding him so close to her, splashed herself, then swatted angrily at the large wet patch plastering her dusky shirt to her torso with a glass cloth.

He did just what she asked and the cool scullery was suddenly close and stuffy as his gaze lingered on wet dark linen, clinging emphatically to wet woman and almost as closely plastered to her fine breasts and tightly furled nipples as he'd like to be himself. Hard and fierce and instantly emphatic, his painful erection would have informed him he wanted her any way he could get her, even if his hungry eyes weren't busy devouring her like a lover. Want flared hot and heady between them again, but on its heels came a dark memory of his younger self, home from the sea and pitifully eager for the woman he thought was his. At least his wife's betrayal had armoured him against mistaking lust for anything else. He assured himself that his annoying reaction to Eloise La Rochelle, or whatever she cared to call herself, was a physical thing he'd learn to ignore and nothing deeper.

'I wish you good day and expect you to be gone by the

time I get home, madam,' he informed her stiffly and turned to pick up his coat from the chair he'd flung it on to earlier, shrugging into it as he cravenly bolted for the front door and freedom from wanting what he couldn't have.

At least it should have been freedom, except he had to halt stock-still on Kit's doorstep to breathe deeply and steadily as he thought hard about desolate arctic waters and relentless storms at sea. At last he was respectable enough to proceed through this confoundedly civilised neighbourhood without his very obvious need for Miss Eloise La Rochelle and her magnificent body instantly causing a scandal.

Not just her body either, he couldn't help but recall as he marched rather blindly along the wide streets to his destination. She had that acute, questing mind and an unexpected sense of humour to render her almost irresistible as well. He let himself consider the unique charms of such a contrary, intriguing woman for a moment and would have been horrified to know an unguarded smile quirked his mouth as he did so. Most of the time she was as knowing as any street urchin, full of self-reliance and used to hardship almost from birth, then she'd astonish him with an eager enthusiasm for life and suddenly seem as coltish as any *ingénue*. No, he assured himself, he was long past being a fit companion for any sort of innocent, even if it was Eloise the buccaneer. Once again, he fought his overactive imagination as he pictured her in that black shirt aiming a pirate ship at his sturdy merchantman, and discovered how much he'd relish capturing and taming such an unlikely opponent when she failed to overrun him.

'Idiot,' he chided himself as he nearly walked into a lamp-post. A little restored to his usual stern self, he strolled towards Stone & Shaw's offices in the City, but was still too preoccupied with his eventful evening, sore head and un-wanted visitor to sense that he was being followed.

Louisa paused when he did and wondered why she'd impul-sively stuffed her cap on her head and shrugged into Coste's overlarge jacket, then ventured out in broad daylight to see where rude and disobliging Captain Darke was bound. She watched her own reflection in a shuttered window and tucked a giveaway strand of hair under the hatband of the silly hat she'd stolen last night. At least Charlton could live without his very odd suit of clothes, but she promised herself she'd replace Coste's jacket if she damaged it, then all her senses suddenly sharpened as she considered a wiry young tough who seemed as intent on staying on Captain Darke's tail as she was herself.

He was good, she grudgingly admitted that much to herself as she lurked in a doorway and eyed the innocuous-looking youth pretending to watch a street vendor chase off a starv-ing little would-be pickpocket. Luckily she'd trained herself to be even better once upon a time and felt her old skills re-turn as she fell into step behind both the Captain and his follower and neither of them even had a suspicion she was there. Spying a fancy footman, she was grateful Kit didn't in-sist on Coste going about in some fanciful livery, though, for she'd certainly attract attention if she'd been forced to steal a *chapeau-bras* and gold-laced blue jacket. She slouched to-wards the unfortunate dressed so ostentatiously and he gave her a pained snarl and shuffled his feet self-consciously, ob-viously believing her another annoying idler, silently jeering his ridiculous uniform.

Grinning at this confirmation that she looked nothing like fashionable Miss Alstone, or even Miss Eloise La Rochelle,

Louisa swaggered a little in her disreputable breeches and worn and ill-fitting coat and pretended to be absorbed in the noise and bustle of Cheapside as follower and followed moved onwards. Hands in her pockets, she sauntered along at a distance from Captain Darke and his shadow, keeping enough space between herself and them to look as if she was aimlessly passing the time until more promising mischief offered.

She mused on the quality of the Captain's enemies and decided the boy was very good, and at the next crossroads she cast a disguised gaze about her to see if she was being followed in her turn. All was clear and as innocent as London streets ever were, so Hugh Darke's foes weren't that canny. Suddenly she wished more fervently than usual that her big brother would come home. Kit would soon find out who was so interested in his infamous captain and she suddenly felt inadequate for this suddenly very serious task, as well as uncertain why it seemed so vitally important that Hugh Darke should not be hurt by his enemies.

She'd followed him on impulse, unable to think of another way to fill in her time until Kit came back without sitting tamely in his kitchen, waiting for Charlton or her uncle to come and march her up the aisle. Now her impulse had changed from a way of idling away the day into a quest to protect the ungallant Captain's back. She wove a cautious track over to the other side of the street and blessed Hugh Darke for being tall enough to stand a little above the crowd and show her the way, even if he was several inches shy of her brother's lofty height and Ben Shaw must tower over him like a giant, as he did over everyone else she had ever come across outside a fairground sideshow.

Now Hugh Darke was entering the quieter street where her brother and Ben had their offices and she had to walk past it and head down an ally to avoid being too noticeable to him or his pursuer. Anxious all of a sudden that the young tough would use the sparseness of the area to attack Hugh, she sped to the end of her alley and out into the opposite end of the street, only to skid to a halt and have to duck into a handy doorway to avoid the nondescript lad coming the other way, obviously off to report to someone that the target was safe in his office now and beyond following. Wondering even more at such an odd sequence of events, she leaned back against the heavily made door at her back and decided she must follow the young thug, rather than do as instinct demanded and stay to make sure Hugh Darke was safe if he ventured abroad again. Doubtless someone else would keep watch over Kit's offices for the next few hours, but for now she might get a clue about who was behind all this if she could track the young bully to his lair or his current employer.

At the end of the chase she was very glad Kit and Ben weren't in London after all, for they would surely have had fits if they knew where she'd been today. First of all to the cheapest of pie shops the City rejoiced in, where she managed to loiter and look hungry as well as penniless until chased off by the infuriated owner with a fearsome ladle. Then the boy sauntered through the noisome rookery she knew from her youth was the haunt of thieves and pimps of the worst sort; even high on the rooftops as she'd had to go to follow him there, she had to tread as if on pins to avoid discovery.

The houses might be rotten as a blown pear, but they were full of people forced into degradation and misery and every room and attic seemed to heave with human souls even at this time of day. That was what she'd conveniently forgotten from her childhood spent with one foot in the underworld and the other in an almost respectable street on the edge of Mayfair:

the stench and misery and hopelessness of poverty. It seemed criminal to her that anyone should be expected to actually live in such cramped, dank and stinking conditions, so close to one of the richest capital cities the world had ever seen. She ghosted across closely packed rooftops, jumped at leaning chimneys and soot-grimed walkways even the inhabitants appeared to have forgotten about and wondered at herself for ever being discontent with the well-fed and secure-seeming life she'd lived since she left all this behind.

Reminding herself she wasn't here to redeem her blemished soul, she followed the boy as he finally quit his native streets and again they were into quieter, wealthier areas and she wondered whether it might be better to come down from her unlikely perch and risk the broader streets with her now-sooty clothes and grimy hands and face making her remarkable in such a place. The apprentice tough ended the chase he didn't know he was involved in at a quietly respectable church, of all unlikely places. Louisa paused and watched with bafflement as the rough youth from the slums removed his apology for a hat and bowed his head, as he entered the church by a side door as humbly as if he really had come to seek salvation. Could she be mistaken about him after all, then? Was he really a lost soul in search of redemption, who just happened to have been going in the same direction as herself and the Captain this morning? Her once-honed instincts argued he was nothing so simple and she stayed to see if anyone else would come to such a sacrilegious meeting place.

Nobody went in or out until the boy came out and sauntered down the street looking singularly unrepentant. Torn between wanting to follow him and staying to watch for his confederate, Louisa tried to decide which would gain her more, then the door opened again and a soberly dressed gentleman stepped out of the church.

Something about that clerical-seeming figure below seemed wrong and she didn't know why the hairs on the back of her head rose in warning at the sight of him, but this was clearly a more important rogue than the one she now had to let go. Louisa eyed up her possible routes and hoped the man wasn't about to cross the wide square the church was set in, as she would either have to scramble across a good many rooftops to follow him, or climb down and risk being seen in the open.

Luckily he headed towards her rather than away, so they were soon in the maze of service streets and wide roads that made up the most exclusive part of the capital. Louisa's mind buzzed with possibilities as the sober figure finally entered one of the most prosperous squares through the mews behind it, then she scrambled to follow along the more generous roofs and was only just in time to see him disappear through French windows giving on to a town garden, as if he knew the house very well and could stroll in and out as he pleased. She pondered the man's position in such a household and wondered what to do next. No scruffy idler would gain access to such a house and how would she find out anything about the owner and his connections from such a humble position even if she did?

Marking the house on her internal map for future reference, she waited until a genteel bustle of activity made her realise it was the fashionable hour for visiting and any trail the man had left was about to be wiped out. He could have left in any of those coaches in whatever guise he usually wore, he might be someone she'd met at a ball or some soirée he couldn't manage to escape, she could even have danced with him in her other life. Horrified by the idea of being so close to a man who clearly wished Hugh Darke no good, she finally left very cautiously indeed and travelled a few streets at her lofty level before descending. She could find out nothing more just now, so she headed for a dealer in second-hand clothing that she knew from experience was the least likely to leave her scratching and cursing at someone else's parasites when she wore their wares.

By mid-afternoon Hugh had ploughed through his mathematical duties and was secretly relieved to get an urgent summons to the enclosed dock his youthful employers were having built to cut down on the organised pilfering of their cargoes. Hugh frowned as he pondered that pilfering and told himself it was normal, all owners suffered from the problem, which was why the East India Company had already built a closed dock and were probably planning more. Like Kit, he thought there was something more than chance behind their own heavy losses. It was all of a piece with the loss of one of his ships and the murder of its crew not already corrupted by whoever organised the infamous scheme a couple of years ago.

It had taken a deal of hard work and scrupulously fair accounting to repair the damage to their reputation and persuade Lloyds that Stone & Shaw were not behind the fraud. Rumours that the *Mirabelle* had not gone down after all, but was sailing under another name with an entirely different crew, had horrified her young owners and sent Kit on a quest to discover the truth and Hugh knew his friend wouldn't give up until he had every detail of the infamous scheme at his fingertips. Having an implacable yet invisible enemy of his own, Hugh knew how that constant but intangible malice ate away at a man's soul. At least he knew his foe was probably one of his late wife's legion of lovers, determined to make him pay for the unresolved crime that ended her life, but Hugh couldn't solve it and prove he wasn't a wife killer, so it had seemed better to take a captaincy from Stone & Shaw and stay out of the idiot's way rather than fight for his good name—a lost cause if ever there was one.

Chapter Five

Hugh frowned blackly out of the window of the hackney he'd summoned to get to Stone & Shaw's dock as fast as he could and wondered at the elaborate route the jarvey was taking. About to tap on the roof and inform the driver he wasn't the flat he probably looked today, he jolted in his seat as the hackney veered abruptly and threw him forwards with a jarring thud. Hugh was still rubbing his bruised temple and trying to reassemble his dignity when the door was thrust open and a familiar voice demanded he get down immediately and follow her.

'Why the devil should I?' he snapped back crossly.

'Because it's all a sham and you're being kidnapped,' Eloise informed him shortly, tugging ineffectually at his sleeve. 'Please, believe me. I'm not sure how much longer my diversion will hold up,' she added desperately and he believed her, despite all her secrets and lies.

'I'll come, but only because this is the most unlikely route to my destination.'

'Good of you, now hurry up,' she urged impatiently.

Hugh took a swift glance about him and suppressed a grin

as he took in the quality of her helpers. A one-legged sailor was sitting in the road, scrabbling for his wooden leg and loudly bemoaning the losses from his spilled apple cart in terms that must make even the assembled urchins blush, while an old woman berated him for a drunken and careless old fool. The urchins were wriggling about under the cab for the fallen and bruised apples and tangling up the traces as they darted nimbly out of the way of the jarvey's whiplash whenever he tried to fend off the sea of bodies suddenly surrounding his battered vehicle.

'Hurry,' Eloise urged and he gave her a long, distrustful look before deciding she'd gone to such a deal of trouble to get him out of that cab, he might as well humour her, if only to find out exactly what she was up to.

This time she was dressed in layer upon layer of disreputable clothes like a rag-picker's daughter, carrying as many of his wares as she could on her own back. It certainly hid her fine figure a lot better than her last disguise, he thought as he followed her into a maze of courts and alleys and had to concentrate hard to recall the way back should he need a hasty escape from her toils. Sensing his resistance, she tugged on his hand impatiently and drew him on as swiftly as she could. He could sense her apprehension through their locked hands as he felt a prickle of awareness shiver over his own skin and knew they were being watched from dark doorways and darker rooms. Unwillingly caught up in her drama, he made himself as silent and wary as he could and hoped he managed to seem the over-eager client to Eloise's part-time whore, although he wondered how such a client would know what delights lay under her false bulk.

He knew, even under all that ridiculous cover that must be making her sweat like a racehorse under her burden. Just the thought of her long, elegant legs under so many layers of hampering fabric—her dangerous allure threatened to slide under his guard once more and draw him into her net. He sweated himself now as she reached more commercial areas, full of workshops and small factories, and upped their pace as fast as she could without everyone coming out to watch them pass. It wasn't their speed that made his breath come short, it was the incendiary thought of finding a space where he could be alone with her to finally slake this feral passion for her, once and for all, that had him almost unmanned with longing. Stupid, he railed at himself—undisciplined, ill-starred and just plain stupid. She'd turned him into a lust-led fool in less than a day after haunting him waking and sleeping for three weeks before that. She always seemed to affect him as fiercely as water did baked lime and he wished he'd never laid eyes on the devious jade.

Now that they were closer to the river and among the warehouses where he was probably far more familiar with their surroundings than she was, he pulled away from her. Letting her take the lead only so he, too, could be sure they hadn't been followed, he sharpened his senses, made himself forget her as a woman as far as it was in him to do. Knowing suddenly that she was leading him to the small warehouse Kit and Ben had hired, then bought when they first set up a small business hauling coastal cargoes, he let her dart into the cover of its ancient shadow and fumble for the keys under her many layers of clothing. He opened his mouth to demand them of her, then closed it again when she hushed him and slipped the key furtively into the lock and turned it as silently as she could with both hands on the doughty iron.

Shrugging impatiently at her silent pantomime, he followed her inside and turned to help her close and relock the stout side door and inspect the gloom inside. He summoned up his captain's senses and sent them to explore that semi-darkness and came up with nothing but a cargo of finest coffee beans destined for the breakfast tables of discerning northern households, not very fresh air still haunted by sugar and spices and other exotics, a hint of mouse and worse. Even his sixth sense could find no trace of another human being, although there seemed an unacceptable quantity of non-human ones, which reinforced his opinion that Kit and Ben should demolish the venerable old building and replace it with something a lot more vermin-proof and never mind sentiment.

'Right, there's obviously nobody here, so I'll go no further into this business of yours without an explanation, madam,' he informed her grimly.

'Very well then, this morning I followed you to work.'

'You followed me?' he demanded, suddenly distrusting those finely honed senses he'd always prided himself on after all.

'I'm very good,' she boasted unrepentantly and how could he argue when he'd sensed not a single hint of her behind him? 'But so was the other person tailing you through the City this morning,' she added; this time he wondered if he had any senses left to him to have missed two of them trailing after him like a procession.

'The other person?'

'I used to know a parrot just like you, Captain,' she mocked him, but must have seen the warning glint in his eyes, because she suddenly looked as serious as anyone could wish, especially a beleaguered and apparently rather simple sea captain. 'He was a well-trained follower and belongs to a villainous crew.'

'And how can I trust you to recognise such a man?'

'You just can,' she assured him and met his eyes unflinchingly, despite the dusty gloom thickening as daylight began to seep away from such dark places early.

'But can I also be sure of your motives, Miss La Rochelle, since you seem a little over-familiar with the workings of the London underworld?'

'You can,' she insisted steadily.

'For some extraordinary reason, I believe you.'

'Why, thank you, I'm suitably flattered, of course.'

'So you should be,' he told her dourly.

'Never mind all that now, we're in the devil of a jam and have to find the best way out of it.'

'I only have your word for that, so how do you conclude I'm in a pickle just because a man followed me to Stone & Shaw's offices in the City?'

'I followed him afterwards to a fashionable church where he met a supposedly clerical gentleman.'

'Which is odd, I admit, but perhaps the man is struggling for his lost soul.'

'And perhaps he's also raising flying pigs, because when they parted I followed the respectable cleric to a mansion in Mayfair and waited for over an hour before I got down off my perch to try to find out why he went into that house and departed arrayed in the height of fashion among his own kind.'

'Not a son of the church after all, then?' he asked whimsically, but his brain was whirling with ideas as he went over all the possibilities her story presented.

'Very far from it,' she said disapprovingly.

'You knew him, didn't you?' he suddenly realised, marvelling at her acquaintance with such fine gentlemen and instantly rigidly jealous of a man who could be a former protector of hers.

'Only later, when I realised whose house it actually was. I can't believe how convincing his disguise was, especially when he always seemed such an empty-headed fool when I met him at—'

She stopped, blank-faced and wary, as she bit back whatever it was she was going to say next. What a damned fool *he* was, he decided dazedly as he forced himself to assess Eloise La Rochelle anew. Her faultlessly unaccented accent, her unconscious elegance and that air she had of being a princess let out of her castle for a holiday and only pretending to be a female buccaneer, or even Eloise La Rochelle herself. An appalling suspicion crept into his obviously rather slow mind and he eyed her annoyingly calm countenance through the thickening darkness with hot fury clawing at his gut.

'You met him in polite society, did you not?' he asked coldly.

'How can you even think such a thing?' Louisa blustered, but ground to a halt as she met his steady, condemning gaze and decided the game was up. 'Yes,' she agreed stoically, trying hard to pretend having her clever disguise penetrated at exactly the wrong moment didn't matter in the least.

'Then you really are slumming it?' he asked stiffly.

'No, I'm looking for something real,' she told him in a raw voice that threatened to tug at his heartstrings, so Hugh hardened his heart against her and made himself re-examine the information he had about her and reach another startling conclusion.

'Say something unreal rather, Miss Alstone,' he said stiffly, trying to be cool and logical, yet struggling with hot humiliation, and a disappointment he refused to examine at the thought of her laughing up her sleeve at him. She'd deceived him every step of her way last night and again this morning.

'As far as I cared for anything or anyone in polite society, I gave Christopher Alstone's little sister the benefit of the doubt when I heard that you'd been named the Ice Diamond by the wags, my dear, but at least now I know how richly you must have deserved that nickname and can learn to pity your victims instead.'

'You never gave any fashionable female a second chance in your life,' she scoffed. How could he have not seen the haughty minx for what she was the instant she eyed him like an offended queen across Kit's office that first day?

'Now there you're more wrong than you'll ever know,' he said grimly, thinking of all the times he'd believed Ariadne, when only an idiot would take his wife's interpretation over the plain facts. 'I'm cured of it though, Miss Alstone, and if you made up this shameful tarradiddle for your own perverse amusement then I'll see you publically exposed and pilloried for it as you deserve to be.'

'I should have left you to your enemies, but oddly enough my sense of fairness wouldn't let me leave you to take your chance against such overwhelming odds. I'm rapidly changing my mind, needless to say,' she said, her face such a mask of polite indifference he couldn't read what lay behind it, and how he hated the mass of contradictions gnawing away at *his* supposedly stern composure.

'Good, I certainly need no help from the likes of you,' he snapped.

'You don't even know me.'

'I know enough.'

Hugh watched her lining up glib arguments to defend herself with and held up his hand to stop her. With his foul luck, and worse judgement, she'd be as convincing at it as his late wife had been. Ariadne had believed her own lies so steadfastly by the time she told them that she'd cheerfully swear to them, even when all the facts proved her wrong. Yet now she was dead and he was branded a murderer in all but proof. Dark grief, fury and shame threatened to swallow him up in the horror of that terrible crime once more, but he fought it back to hell where it belonged and hated this lying female all the more for showing him Hugo the Fool, the cuckolded husband, was still alive behind Hugh Darke's cynical disguise.

'I know you are the despair of your brother and sister, Miss Alstone,' he said coolly enough, for all that hot fury raged under his surface calm. 'Even I have heard that you lead half the otherwise sane men in polite society around by the nose with your beauty and various other perfections that elude me. It's just as well known that you don't care a snap of your fingers for a single one of them. You're a cold-hearted vixen who dismisses her suitors as if she's waiting for a prince or a king at the very least to decorate her cold brow with a crown, instead of the coronets you are apparently offered by the cart-load every Season. And rather than make your long-suffering brother happy by graciously accepting one of those lords or their foolishly besotted heirs, you dance and flirt and charm them for your own idle satisfaction the one day, then give them a very cold shoulder the next.'

'My, I *am* a bad woman,' she said with deceptive mildness and Hugh realised he'd let some of his fury with Ariadne for being a liar and cheat and a lovely, dead, fool creep into his verbal attack on Kit's little sister.

'I don't care what sort of a woman you are,' he lied, 'but I'll certainly manage without your help from now on. Something tells me you'll lead me further into the maze just because you can, rather than show me the way out of it.'

'Don't you want to know who your enemy is, then?'

'How can I believe you? No doubt you have one or two inconvenient suitors littering your path to glory whom you would be very happy to rid yourself of at no cost to yourself.'

'I get worse by the moment,' she said with flippant amusement that only made him more furious with himself for being taken in by her, for believing her because he desperately wanted to, and for still wanting her so badly her refusal to accept any guilt for her actions threatened to charm rather than revolt him.

He'd fantasised about her in her lying disguise—heaven forbid he start doing so in her real one—that one day Kit and Eloise might have parted. It had gone, and he didn't even want to think about the appalling pictures that set up in his mind now he knew who she really was. One day, Eloise might have turned to him for satisfaction and seduction; only now that that was impossible did he realise how deeply she'd tangled him in her devious web. Never having Eloise in his bed to laugh with, to live with and to come home to, knowing she would expect no more from a hollowed-out creature like him, cut like a knife to the gut and he wanted to be done with her, to be hundreds of miles clear of her before the pain struck and the fury stopped hiding his hurt at yet another betrayal.

'Who is he, then?' he made himself ask distantly, thinking how much he'd once wanted to know that very thing and now it didn't seem to matter all that much.

'Now, which of my discarded lovers do I despise the most?' she mused, silently counting off on her fingers as if needing them to compile the best list.

Hugh clenched his fists against the urge to pound the old walls in a roaring frenzy because she'd used him for her own ends and he'd almost trusted her, until she proved him an idiot all over again.

'The first one to come into your head will do,' he said cynically, wondering exactly how many lovers she'd managed to draw in under the very noses of the *ton*.

'Oh, well, that would be you.'

'I'm not your lover,' he said starkly.

'Only because I chose a disguise that held you back, Captain Darke, you being a pirate of such peculiar honour as to never take his employer's moll, however much he might long to. If I hadn't hit on that particular alias, we would have been lovers by now and you know it. Imagine it—us two being lovebirds, liars, then sworn enemies together all in one day.'

'This is not a joke, madam.'

'No, you're right, it's not,' Louisa said desolately, stiffening her backbone and forcing herself to meet the hostility in his starkly austere gaze. There was no point defending herself against such revulsion, no reason to believe he'd ever change his bigoted, second-hand opinion of her. 'But it's more of a comedy than a tragedy.'

'And if only you knew how close one can be to the other, you might stop wilfully creating havoc wherever you go,' he muttered furiously, seeming to retreat into himself, to brood on something apparently even worse than wicked young ladies like herself.

'Which is rich, coming from you,' she accused and suddenly had all his attention as he glared at her with acute greyblue eyes.

'What else do you know?' he demanded. As she flinched away from the steely purpose in his gaze and he stopped her retreat with a rough hand about her wrist, she doubted he knew it was tight as a trap on her soft skin.

'What else *could* I know, Captain?' she asked, doing her best to ice over her own eyes as efficiently as he had to stare at her as if he'd somehow scare everything she knew about him out of her by sheer force of will.

It was his gaze that fell and not hers, although she felt a sting of something she refused to analyse and blinked it back as she watched his eyes take in the tightness of his grip on her, before he unclenched his hand from her, then stepped back as if she'd stung him.

'I'm sorry,' he claimed hoarsely. 'I never meant to hurt you,'

'I expect you say that to all your women,' she responded bitterly, suddenly transported back to her childhood with a violent drunkard.

'Never,' he husked and despair and bitterness and something that might even be grief haunted his silver-shot eyes and that hard, dare-not-be tender mouth of his.

'Whatever have they done to you?' she whispered as she watched him fight back something terrible and felt helpless in the face of such horror and pain, despite all he'd just said and accused her of being.

'Nothing you would understand,' he scorned, protecting himself against any hint of pity. Perhaps it was his ordinary defence against shallow sympathy and spurious curiosity, rather than the deeply personal slight it felt like for a moment.

'Oh, of course not,' she forced herself to say as carelessly as if they were discussing an obscure subject outside the self-ish remit of such a vain young lady.

'Does it still hurt?' he asked huskily.

'You should know by now that Miss Alstone, the Ice Diamond, is untouched by feelings of any kind, Captain,' she lied lightly and silently dared him to take a step nearer and breach that fragile distance between them.

Ignoring her, he took that step and cradled her wrist in his large hand, the hardness and occasional roughness of his palm pulling her deeper under his sensual spell, if he did but know it, and she silently despaired of herself.

'Yet you're not as unbreakable as you pretend,' he muttered as if the words were forced from that sensual, cynical mouth, before he sank his head and kissed her slightly reddened wrist and made her knees wobble with a rush of stubborn need.

Stiffening them against the too-potent appeal of a man who hated her one moment, then soothed and seduced the next, while probably still hating her, she resisted the silly urge to raise her other hand and smooth the over-long and distinctly shaggy dark locks he wore so well into some kind of order.

'No, I'm not yet quite unbreakable, I'm sorry,' she answered with a wry smile meant to defuse the sensual tension suddenly so alive in the growing darkness scented with old cargoes and coffee beans.

'Don't be,' he counselled as if he couldn't help himself.

'It's easier,' she replied as if she understood, when all she could currently think about was the jags of heat and longing for more that were afflicting her, even as he probably despised her more deeply than ever.

'I know, but not necessarily better,' he told her with a look of untold wanting and infinite sadness, before he abandoned her hand and kissed her full on the mouth once again instead, as if he couldn't resist the temptation of it.

It was a fantasy, she told herself; cynical Louisa Alstone who didn't believe in love or marriage, or any of the comforting illusions that got her fellow young ladies through life, and angry, disillusioned Captain Hugh Darke, who didn't believe in anything much at all. It was impossible and they would tear each other to pieces. Yet it was such a sensuous, irresistible seduction of her senses that she stopped thinking and blindly took whatever he had left to give. It was so luxurious, so heated and all engrossing that it felt infinitely better than anything else she'd been offered. Moaning her agreement, she opened her mouth as demandingly as he'd already taken hers and let her tongue tangle with his, so they could take up where they left off last night. At least tonight he knew she was nobody's but his, just for now.

Acknowledging the transitory nature of anything they could be to each other, she strove to make her agreement to it even more emphatic, by letting her hands explore his strong neck muscles and up to muss his already unruly hair and run her fingers through the sensual silkiness of it. His groan of whatever it was—agreement, encouragement, or just downright approval—made her breath come short and her mouth even more desperate as he cupped her face in his strong hands and drew her closer. He shifted and the threat of losing even this harsh magic between them made her keen a protest, then ghost her hands down his neck and soothe along his throat as she silently acknowledged he'd made himself vulnerable to her in this much at least. And it was enough for her, would have to be enough.

Chapter Six

Louisa felt the mighty muscles in her ungallant captain's broad shoulders shift under her touch and it made her feel sensually powerful. To spark such an instantaneous reaction from this guarded soul made her seem very special to herself tonight. She revelled in the sense of being outside time and normal spaces, locked inside this cocoon of darkness as the spring evening closed in all round them. Then she felt the full force of the fire he'd lit in her last night streak through her and settle burning almost as bright as the sun at the centre of her being until she shook with need. Lost for words to communicate what she wanted, even if he allowed her mouth the freedom to do it, she made an incoherent sound—half-moan and half-imperious demand—and sighed her relief into his kiss as his hands sank to knead her neat *derrière* and draw her closer to his mightily aroused manhood. She did her best not to give away her awe and that furtive heat it sparked inside her at the very feel of what she did to him, but it was hard not to just sink into his arms and beg.

Typical, she managed to spare the time to think, as far as she could think with his mouth on hers and her body so fascinated by the proximity of his. *Typical that he is as deep in thrall to whatever it is driving us together, apparently against our wills, yet he still manages to hang on to his essential apartness while I must melt all over him like heated sealing wax.*

How could she want any man so much it blasted through her much-vaunted self-control and breached that cherished separateness of hers, especially this one? She sensed that the craving making her hands shake as she laid them against the warmth and masculinity and sheer nerve-singing fact of him was exerting just as strong a pull on him, if not even stronger, but he still had control enough not to moan with need or tremble with frustration and this bittersweetest longing. A curiosity burned within her to know more; one he certainly wouldn't believe she had any need of, now she'd let him think she'd managed to accrue a procession of lovers with the critical eyes of the *ton* on her, the hawk-like watch of her elder brother, even from afar, and her aunt and uncle's very critical eyes on her as they waited for a reason to denounce her and rid themselves of a charge they never wanted for aught but the money she brought with her in the first place.

The man was undoubtedly an idiot if he believed a word of that silly implication of hers. She could only suppose it was her inner demon of curiosity and the sheer sensual excitement within her that made her claim to be something she wasn't yet again and get away with it. He might hate her eventually if they went on, but he was the only man she'd ever met who made her want him mercilessly just by inhabiting the same space, whatever space, even this dark, comfortless, unlikely meeting place. A siren voice whispered that he wouldn't have been so easy to fool if he hadn't wanted to believe her and do this, so she let herself believe it for a space borrowed out of the real world. It was a chance that wouldn't come again—an interlude apart from the real Louisa and her unlikely lover. A chance she intended to take, then afterwards she'd somehow find a way to forget it and stick to her chosen course through life, even knowing what she'd be missing.

In the heat of this particular moment there seemed nothing to hold her back from following his lead and exploring the very different, masculine, grace of his leaner hips and round to learn how his buttocks differed from her own by being sparser and more taut with muscle. Now why had she never dreamt how arousing satin-taut skin over strong male muscle and bone could feel under her fingers as she dared to send them just that bit lower and search for the sensitive join of his leg to the pared-down curve above? Evidently he liked it almost as much as she had when he drew his teasing fingers along the lusher line of her feminine curves, before raising those wickedly knowing hands to soothe and rouse and tease her breasts into begging so shamelessly for his touch she could feel it, even through the layers she'd donned for this misadventure.

Torn between memory of how little he actually liked her, however much he might want her, and the promise of a lovemaking she'd never forget in all her long and spinsterly future, she abandoned the memory and embraced the promise and Hugh Darke. He would have delved under all those layers for buttons and access to her tightly furled nipples demanding his touch and his mouth as they remembered last night with a mind of their own. No, let him do that and she'd lose this. Let him think what he was doing for long enough to undo all the layers she was wrapped in and remember who she was, and she'd lose this one moment of enchantment among their usual disenchantment. It felt like an odd, mutual innocence at the moment and she even wondered at herself for thinking so.

She put thinking aside for later and whispered a demand for faster, a wanton command that he stopped wasting time and got on with it, as if all the worst rumours were true and she already had a pack of secret lovers and knew exactly what she was doing now. Trying not to dread that particular falsehood on his tongue, she pulled him closer to fit lush lips to his and felt need overtake reason as his kisses became even wilder and more arousing. He lifted her with one hand round her slim waist and the other beneath her buttocks until she was cradled into him like the most precious of beings, as he walked her towards those very convenient sacks of good Brazilian coffee beans. Wondering how he found his way so unerringly in the ever-deepening darkness, she felt him hesitate, begin to think about this, about him and her again and, even as he set her down on the lowest stack of sacks, pulled him down after her, to tangle him up in kisses before he stopped this wondrous banquet of the senses.

'I want you,' she murmured in a breathy voice she hardly even recognised as her own. 'Now,' she added with an instinctive, feminine demand that he seemed quite unable to resist.

'It's almost too late to stop already, but are you sure?' he managed in a husky voice she loved, because it revealed just how true his desire-rasped words were and added a layer of extra enchantment to their seduction of each other.

'Never surer,' she told him, stopping his mouth with quick, frantic kisses so heated and needy that he groaned into her mouth in response as she felt him bunch up her second-hand skirts and petticoats and then there was the cooling April air, first on her bare knees, then her smooth thighs and ever upwards to expose the betraying hot wetness at the apex of those thighs.

'Hot and sweet and all mine,' he whispered possessively in her ear as his teasing fingers found that unmistakable welcome and explored it until she let out an emphatic, very articulate moan for more and he rubbed and caressed and melted the until-now secret place he'd found, and to think that she hadn't even known she needed his touch there so badly until now.

'Yours,' she agreed recklessly as she felt pleasure almost beyond bearing pool and fight for release within her, but he removed his teasing fingers just before it became inevitable and took her word for it as he swiftly undid his breeches' flap with one deft hand whilst holding his weight above her as he stripped his nether garments off in a fluid shove, before smoothing her willing buttocks deeper into the oddly comfortable beans at her prone back and parting her legs a little farther.

Louisa felt the nudge of his fiercely aroused member against her aching, heated core and knew this was the last chance to go back to how she'd been until now. Separate, aloof, alone. No, it didn't sound in the least bit worth clinging on to in the face of being together, frantic and needy for each other. So she let her thighs fall either side of his narrow hips and lay a little farther back to bid him very welcome.

'Witch,' he murmured and his voice was a caress, even while it sounded as driven and latently powerful as the feel of him between her legs.

'Pirate,' she sparked back, imagining his face intent and intense above her in the late-afternoon darkness and somehow finding it even more seductive that they could see little of each other but shadows.

'Blissful, wonderful witch,' he added as he surged into her in one long thrust she knew was far too powerful to let him hesitate as he beat against the shock of her virginity. 'Devious, lying, idiotic, enchantress of a woman,' he gasped in protest as he tore through that slender barrier and centred himself at the very heart of her as if that was where he belonged, despite himself and her one-time resolution not to have this ultimate wonder in her life, before he loomed out the night and undermined it.

'I am now,' she said complacently, 'but I want more', and shocked even herself by riding the flash and burn of pain so determinedly that the novelty and fullness and sheer wonder of him inside her threatened to set her on the road to madness if he didn't move, do something to assuage this burning need for more that still rode her like the most exquisite goad of half-ultimate pleasure, half-heavy, almost painful need.

'You'll get it, but only if you stay still for a while,' he gritted, holding himself motionless with a mighty effort as he fought the primitive urge to slam into her until he'd climaxed and emptied himself into her as relentlessly as the beat of life itself.

Even then she flexed internal muscles around him experimentally, as if she hadn't even known she had them until now and threatened to enchant as well as unman him. Minx she undoubtedly was, but vixen as well? Somehow he doubted it as he felt her adjust about him with an almost trusting innocence, a giving in her usually steely composure and armour of humour that touched him a bit too deeply for comfort. Letting his awesome arousal overcome a need for something more than even this most sensual of couplings, he dared let himself move at last and let out a long groan of satisfaction as he felt her strive to match her rhythm to his.

Now, in the moment, he knew she was his as no other woman ever had been. He was her only lover, the only man who had ever moved inside her like this, striving against the beat and demand of outrageous desire in his head and heart to take her slowly, to ride her to the sweetest of oblivion. For now, all he needed to do was to make this wonderful for her, then it would be wondrous for him as well. He let her feel his desperately rigid manhood stretch and fill her and blocked out the silken marvel of her fitting him as if she was made for him alone. Not since he was a hasty boy with his first eager, just a little bit more experienced girl had he needed to fight his body quite so hard for mastery. Not with his mistresses and certainly not with his wife, but then, Ariadne hadn't been virgin any more than any of his other lovers had been, until now. Louisa Alstone was the first woman who'd ever allowed him to be first and he must guard himself against the privilege and wonder of that marvel, when he was rational again. For now he luxuriated in it as he felt her move with him, begin to breathe more deeply, to clench even more exquisitely about his manhood and, at last, he knew she was ready for more.

Breathing hard to keep that more from releasing him before time into his own selfish pleasure, he occupied himself with meeting her deepest of blue eyes in the darkness, although he could see only the quick shine of them in this almost-blackness as she opened her eyes in wonder and lure at the feel of him moving within her. Next time he'd make sure they had their eyes to add to the other four senses, so they could drive each other even more insane with how they were together. He blotted out the thought that there would be no next time by stroking harder and deeper into her as he felt her begin to spasm, felt the bow of her body even before he heard a deep heavy breath fill her straining lungs as she let it out, on a long wondering moan of delight. At last he could slip his tethers and he plunged headlong into the greatest, most satisfying completion he'd ever experienced.

Hugh felt his whole being spasm in ecstasy as she plunged into the unknown, then flew under him and their individual peaks of utter delight were as dangerous as they were giving. As he drifted into absolute release, complete satisfaction for what felt like the first time in his life, a part of him exulted and worshipped her, even as another woke up and groaned in disbelief. At their destination for a lovely, peaceful moment it felt generous, shared, too much to let go. Then let go he did and finally descended from absolute delight into almost complete horror when he realised exactly what he'd done by taking up her invitation to seduce her so eagerly, then failing to draw out of her before he climaxed and damned them both for a pair of over-lusty fools.

Coming back to her workaday self at last, Louisa allowed herself a delighted little wriggle and let herself be pleased he was still inside her, even after she knew that he'd experienced the ultimate release with her. He sank against her pleasured torso for a sweet moment and she let her arms come up to grasp him, then fall to her sides as he groaned as if in agony. Horrified that he wasn't as warmly delighted with life and his lover as she was with her only one, she suddenly felt chilled and all too distant again. He regretted what they'd just done and she wanted to cry so badly she had to clench her fists until she felt her nails bite into her tender palms. She'd grown too soft for this sort of disappointment; she fought not to expect anything of him other than what she'd already had and did her best to reassemble the Ice Diamond, before he could voice his misgivings. Suddenly she hated that brilliant, heartless creature with a passion even he might not be able to match, but it was an old familiar shield from a hurtful world and, at the moment, all she had.

'Thank you,' she made herself say, as if the most significant-seeming minutes of her life so far didn't matter all that much after all.

'Thank you?' the contrary monster echoed as if she'd spat poison at him.

'Yes. I shall never marry, you see, so you relieved me of a burden of curiosity I had no wish to carry for the rest of my life.'

'How useful of me,' he replied as if the words nauseated him.

'Yes,' she made herself say blandly, 'it was, very useful.'

Suddenly she felt so utterly vulnerable lying here, stretched under him like a wanton, and shifted restlessly, telling her body it had to let go of the glittering fantasy of ever doing that again, with anyone. Then he seemed to find a rampant need of her after all, when she'd thought him spent for the rest of the night and for ever done with her. She felt him roll his hips suggestively within the cradle of hers and, to her shame, something ravenous and desperate awoke in her as well. Breath stuttered from her lips before she could calm it and she heard his grunt of satisfaction, just before his mouth descended on hers in a kiss that allowed nothing for the tenderness of her bee-stung lips or the newness of sensations as his arousal hardened inside her once more.

Once more she drank in the scent of him, the abrasion of springy masculine hair against her clutching fingertips as she curled her hands into his heaving chest for want of any other purchase on his sweat-slicked body. Whatever he said, she heard the driven sound of his approving, then demanding murmurs as they climbed another summit when she'd thought herself at the top of this particular mountain. Every sense screamed for satisfaction as her eyes searched the darkness for a clue to his feelings when he made her shudder with driven desire, made her cry out for more as he rode her with a tenderness for her once-virgin body that made tears glaze her eyes and allowed her to be glad he couldn't see her after all.

She sank and rose and twisted and thrashed under him with need and this time she knew where they were bound and tensed for sheer delight as the warmth and golden release of body on body, heart on heart, overrode everything once more. Convulsing helplessly as he drove her mercilessly on and on, until she was left breathless and sobbing for breath and for sanity. He buried his dear, ruffled head in the curve of her vulnerable throat and let her feel his mouth open on a long, silent shout of rapturous possession.

'Was that useful of me as well?' he gasped when he finally managed to pump enough air into his lungs to speak. 'I'd hate it if you found your one, and apparently only, lover to be inept or unmemorable.'

'Don't worry, I don't suppose I stand much risk of forgetting that if I live to be ninety,' she murmured gruffly.

With a great sigh of goodness-knew-what emotion, he rolled away from her at last and rested at the side of her as if he didn't have energy to get himself any farther. *Not because he can't bear to forsake your arms, Louisa,* a hateful voice warned as he drew in long gasps of air and she felt his lungs expand, even as she had to grasp her hands tightly together above her head in order not to reach out to him. She so wanted to smooth his tense features, to linger over his mightily muscled shoulders and caress his labouring chest that only her own exhaustion stopped her springing up and putting the width of this shady warehouse between them.

'Nice to know something about me is likely to prove memorable.'

'There's nothing about you that isn't,' she reassured him before she'd even thought about it. 'Not that I could ever forget so objectionable a man,' she added hastily as she sat up at last, hoping he hadn't read something into her words she couldn't let herself admit, even in her own head.

'Of course not,' he said remotely, as his breath settled and she felt his powerful limbs tense for action.

Luckily he couldn't see the hand she held up in protest for the darkness that loomed between them. Still she knew the moment he stepped away and began to don his clothing, scrabbling in the dark for the odd garment she'd cast into the wider darkness in the heat of frantic desire. She reluctantly began the task of trying to reorder her own appearance, shucking off an outer layer of dull and overlarge garments because they wouldn't be needed now. It was too dark outside for him to need a disguise now and she doubted he'd consent to hide his undisputed masculinity under even so sketchy a veil as the extra clothes she'd kirtled about her waist.

'Even as I hope you're getting dressed and concealing yourself from me before you rouse me to insanity once more, you're undressing yourself, Louisa Alstone. What a very contrary female you truly are,' he commented out of the gloom and she had to bite back on a sigh of regret, for all that lovely intimacy, that wonderful forgetfulness of herself in him.

She smoothed down her remaining, nondescript skirts and wished that, just once, he could have seen her in her elegant evening finery. She'd be groomed to perfection, she let herself fantasise for a brief moment. Her hair would be brushed into immaculate disorder, every shining lock curled and pinned to show the fiery glow within its apparent darkness. Her gown would fit as only an exclusive Bond Street modiste could shape it and it would be made up of the finest cross-cut silk crepe to cling and lovingly outline her much-vaunted figure. Apparently she was not too tall or too short and would have been the epitome of elegance, if she wasn't so cold. She allowed herself a wry grimace for the rosy glow her brother's money cast over her as far as her needy suitors were concerned.

'The top layer was meant to be for you,' she managed to tell him when she could make it sound as if it didn't matter.

'For me—devil take it, woman, do you take me for a molly?'

'How could I?' she muttered under her breath, but he heard her all the same.

'You certainly know different now, if you ever did,' he confirmed smugly.

'Would you like me to provide you with a testimonial?'

'Thank you, but your brother would undoubtedly kill me, so I'll pass on that.'

'As well, perhaps, but the clothes were meant to be a disguise.'

'Good heavens, I think you really mean it. You really are the oddest female,' he told her as if he had more important things on his mind and she seethed in the darkness as she fumbled for the key under her skirts and then searched about for the wretched thing on her erstwhile resting place.

'Looking for this?' he asked, suddenly in front of her and she felt as much as saw the outline of the cleverly wrought key held out to her.

'You stole it?' she accused rashly.

'Just as you must have done,' he confirmed lazily. 'It's always as well to be prepared, as you undoubtedly know.'

'You took it while you were busy seducing me?'

'Not exactly while, more afterwards, and I dispute your definition, since you seduced me as surely as I did you. Don't try to denounce me as the despoiler of innocence when you begged to be deflowered. No—correction, you convinced me you were as experienced as the lovely Eloise and had nothing left to deflower. Which of us do you think anyone would believe, once they knew you kidnapped me and lured me here in a questionable guise, my dear Miss Alstone?'

'I have no intention of broadcasting my seduction, so if that's what you're worried about, Captain Darke, stop plaguing me with slanderous suggestions and be reassured that I'll never tell a living soul.'

'Yet Mother Nature has a way of catching out the most secretive of lovers. So what about any child we made tonight?' he asked all too seriously and her heart stuttered in its tracks at the bare idea.

'It would take more than that to make one,' she managed to say scornfully, even as part of her marvelled at the very notion.

'No, sorry,' he said with a fine act of light-hearted indifference, 'unfortunately I can't close my eyes to the fact that it often takes a good deal less than we just managed between us.'

'Well, there's certainly no need for you to sound so smug about it.'

'That's not smugness, it's resignation. We must marry, my dear.'

'Over my dead body,' she managed to whisper between gritted teeth.

'I admit it's not what either you or your brother would have wanted, but I'll not have a child of mine running about the place, blithely learning petty theft and fraud at its mother's knee.'

'I can't be a mother,' she gasped as if the very idea pained her, which it did, acutely. She let the insult pass her by as she stood horrified by the suddenly very-present possibility that he might be right.

'I think we may shortly find that you can, like it or no,' he mocked her.

'No, no, I mustn't,' she said, hugging her arms about her suddenly trembling body and trying not to come apart in front of him. 'No,' she whispered again in horror at the very idea as she sat suddenly back down on her much-maligned coffee sacks and rocked backwards and forwards at the desperate possibility of it.

'I've heard of being wise after the event, but this is ridiculous, Miss Alstone,' he told her. When she didn't reply, but continued to rock blindly, as if she'd forgotten he was even there, he moved to kneel beside her and hold her still.

He was almost tender as he soothed her and whispered meaningless words of comfort as he felt the dry sobs that shook her, for all her faint attempts to put the usual armour of indifference back in place.

Chapter Seven

'I can see how a lady like you might be horrified by the bare notion of bearing my child, but I promise it won't be as bad as you think, Louisa. We will contrive to look after it somehow between us, and even if I'm not the husband you would have chosen, I'll try to be an easy one on you and a good father to our children, whenever they should come.' Hugh Darke was promising her all the time she tried to take in what had happened and how stupid she'd been to make him think he had to vow anything to her, let alone marriage.

'You don't understand,' she wailed, ineffectually hitting a would-be fist against his rock-like chest as he tried to take her in his arms in an embrace of pure comfort that was so tempting she had to find a way to make him let her go.

'I understand that you're a lady and a very lately ex-virgin and I'm just a common sea captain, but I could say we've made our bed and now must lie on it, if only we'd ever got that far.'

'It's not that, and I'm not a lady anyway,' she said vaguely, for it seemed as if they were moving through a dream and she was looking much further back at a reality he couldn't even guess at.

'That you are—the whole world knows Miss Alstone is a Diamond of the *ton*, and only the highest born and most beautiful in the land gain that accolade.'

'The Ice Diamond, the Untouchable Alstone?' she scorned incredulously. 'You should be the first to pour scorn on that epithet from now on.'

'I'll call out any man who seeks to argue with your icy reputation in public, even while I'm enjoying the real, warm human woman in my bed,' he reassured her and if she hadn't been bound up in her own misery she would have surely relished his partisanship, as well as his apparent desire to revisit her bed, however makeshift it might prove to be.

'I never wanted to make my début among the *ton*,' she told him blankly, as if not quite sure who she was talking to and all of a sudden she felt him take her misery seriously and draw back to try to see her face in all this frustrating darkness. 'I certainly never intend to marry and did everything I could to make that fact clear to my family. I would not accept any gentleman's offer of marriage, could not,' she explained desolately as if she was in the dock instead of his arms.

'Since I'm in a very good position to know you were a very proper maiden lady, then why not, Miss Alstone?'

'Oh, for goodness' sake, call me Louisa,' she demanded with a sudden return to her usual forthright manner and, for a brief moment, she felt horror recede and the world rock back on to its proper axis for the first time in years. Then it was back again, that old revulsion at herself, the familiar, terrible worthlessness of what she'd done, so long ago.

'Why will you have no husband or child to love, Louisa?' he demanded imperiously and suddenly she knew he had easily as much noble blood pumping round his body as she could claim to have inherited from the Earls of Carnwood.

'I can't tell you,' she whispered, back in that nightmare. 'Whatever will you think of me if I do?'

'How can I say, until you actually tell me what troubles you so deeply? We can hardly say or think much worse of each other than we already have, now can we?'

'No,' she admitted hollowly, thinking back to all the names she had called him, all the harsh opinions he'd already voiced about her.

'Then what does it matter to you what I think of you? If you won't marry me and insist on bastardising our maybe child, then I'll certainly think far worse of you than you currently do of yourself, I can safely promise you that much at least.'

'How comforting,' she managed to say almost lightly and decided he might as well know the worst about her, if only so he'd agree to walk away and forget her.

'Tell me, it can't be worse than a secret I can't bring myself to tell you in return,' he soothed ruefully, but she couldn't imagine anything worse than her own dark misdeeds.

'It was back in the years before I became a lady,' she warned him.

'Before you were born, you mean? I can't say I approve of the axiom that the sins of the fathers are to be visited on the sons, or in this case the daughters, so I know that you were always a lady, my dear.'

'My father certainly had a full hand of misdeeds to hand on, even if that was all he left us.'

'So I have heard, but as I say, I can't see why that ought to blight you, any more than it has your brother and sister.'

'Only me,' she said so low he had to bow his head to catch

it and she felt him so close to her again that her heart seemed to ache over that last inch of space between them.

'No, you're an Alstone just as surely as they are. Your parentage is stamped all over the three of you for anyone to see.'

'Oh, my mother was ever faithful to him—despite his rages and his false promises and the hundreds of ways in which he didn't deserve her devotion. But once upon a time there were four of us children, and it's my fault that there aren't four of us any more.'

'How can it be? You must have been a child yourself when you lost your brother or sister, for I never heard of another little Alstone going to live with your aunt and uncle after your parents' deaths.'

'I was thirteen years old when Maria and I went to our uncle's house to be turned from little savages into proper ladies, at least according to him. Maria was sixteen and eager to please, as well as good and dutiful, so she found it far easier to be "civilised" than I did and settled to it without complaint.'

'Which you most certainly did not, Louisa, if I know anything about you at all,' he said with a smile in his voice that made her knees weak. Again she longed to breach that small gap and lean into the comfort he was offering, but somehow forced herself not to. 'You were a child and no wonder if you were rebellious,' he continued, her unexpected advocate. 'You're an Alstone when all's said and done, are you not? I never came across one yet who wasn't as proud as the devil and impatient of the rules—apart from your sister, of course. Even I can see that Mrs Heathcote is almost as good as she is lovely and perhaps provides the exception to prove the rule.'

Another man who had evidently fallen very willingly under her lovely blonde sister's gentle spell, Louisa decided with unaccustomed bitterness and hated herself all over again. 'Aye, Maria is the best of us wicked Alstones,' she said, 'and I am the worst—I carry my father's loathsome stamp right through me.'

'Don't talk such damnable nonsense, woman, you have the Alstone looks and believe me, they are quite spectacular enough for the rest of us mere mortals to cope with. There's a glorious portrait of the Lucinda Alstone rumour insists enchanted Charles the Second even more than usual in the Royal Collection and you can believe me, because I've seen it, that you're even lovelier than she was. It's lucky I found you before Prinny did, really,' he added and she almost smiled at the absurdity of his cocky reassurance.

'Oh, really—lucky for whom exactly?'

'Me, of course, since you're going to marry me. For him as well, I suppose, since I won't have to threaten him with *laissez*-majesty when I go after him with my horse pistols for leering at my wife, so long as he never has the chance to leer at you in the first place.'

'How do you know he hasn't done so already?'

'Has he, then?'

'Just a little, but he called me a pretty child and tickled me under the chin before Lady Hertford became restless and dragged him away.'

'Sensible female,' he approved smugly and she felt the comfort of normality he was trying to create for her and also a lurch of feeling she hadn't armed herself against. Dangerous, she decided with a shiver, and sat a little straighter, almost next to him as she was.

'They say he was once handsome and quite dashing,' she mused so that he'd hopefully forget he'd been trying to plumb her deepest, darkest secrets.

'According to my mother, he was as pretty a prince as you'd find in any fairy tale, until he became so fat and petulant you can't help but wonder if he'd have been better finding something to do, besides feel sorry for himself.'

'You know a lot about him,' she said suspiciously.

'Any Londoner in town when he was still Prince Florizel, and not fat as an alderman, could tell you that much.'

'But your mama wasn't just a London bystander, was she, Captain?'

'Never mind my mother, we were discussing yours.'

She sighed deeply and felt the shadow of the past loom until even the deep darkness of this windowless cavern seemed to be touched by it.

'She was far more beautiful than I am in her youth, but stubborn as any mule and somehow saw some quality in my father nobody else ever did. Mama never raged about her reduced circumstances or let us children think we were in any way less because we didn't have servants and fine clothes, or aught but a few second-hand books she managed to squirrel away from my father somehow or another. I deplore her blindness towards my father, for there was never a more selfish or ruthlessly vain man put on this earth than Bevis Alstone, but I can't bring myself to blame her for it, because she genuinely loved him. In the end I think she thought of him as a particularly naughty child.'

'How humiliating for him,' he said gently and she suddenly supposed it had been, so perhaps it was an unfortunate marriage on both sides and her mother would have been far better loving a better man and he a worse woman.

'He didn't kill her, though, I did that,' she finally said bleakly. 'And Peter,' she added as if purging her soul of all her bitter crimes at once.

'Of course you didn't,' he told her before she could add another word.

'How do you know?' she asked indignantly, almost as if she had to defend her right to the worst crime a human could commit against another of her kind.

'You haven't got it in you to harm a newborn kitten, let alone a woman you obviously loved and any kind of brother, even if he took after your sire in every vice available to him, which I doubt, since the rest of you certainly do not.'

'Well, he didn't, anyway. Peter was a dear, good boy; if he was a little slower than the rest of us, he loved more to make up for it. You never came across a more endearing soul than him and even the thieves and thugs in our near neighbourhood wouldn't have hurt him, although we only lived on the edges of a rookery and Kit and I would never have taken him inside for fear of what they would do to him there. He was five years younger than me, so Kit and Ben and I ran riot and played catch-me-if-you-can through St Giles while Maria and Peter stayed home with Mama and minded their lessons.'

'And Kit is five years older than you at the very least, so you were not running wild with him at thirteen years old, were you?'

'No.' She shook her head slowly, shuddering at the thought of what she'd done and why. 'He left for the sea when I was seven or eight, but whenever he was home I'd follow him everywhere. Even he stopped trying to prevent me doing so, once he realised I could climb like a monkey and run as fast as the wind from any pursuit, so there really wasn't much point in him trying to stop me when he knew I'd get out anyway, and find it all the more sport to track him and Ben down when I did. I hated the times he and Ben were at sea and how I hated my father for reducing us all to such straits that Kit couldn't go to school as Mama longed for him to do. I couldn't endure the thought that Kit might be lost at sea, while Papa gamed and drank and demanded good food and warm clothes, even if we had to go without so he could present a smooth face to so-called "good" society. I've since discovered anything remotely akin to society turned its back years before, but at the time I hated "society" almost as much as I hated the gaming hells for letting him in.'

'Understandable in the circumstances,' Hugh Darke said.

'I was worse than he was, easily as selfish as he was,' she condemned herself. 'Anything Mama asked me to do, I ignored. Any task I had to perform because we were too poor for any of us to be idle, I did with ill grace and escaped from the boarding house my mother ran as soon as I could. Then I went into the rookeries and the mean streets around them, so I could play at being all the things girls and boys my own age were forced to do in order to put food in their bellies.'

'In your shoes, I'd have done the same.'

'You'd have been off to sea with Kit and Ben and left me more alone than ever, in my own eyes at least.'

'Well, if I'd been born a girl I dare say I'd have followed in your footsteps, then,' he assured her with a smile in his voice she suddenly wished she could see.

'You're a better man than me,' she said on the whisper of a laugh. 'Make that a better woman,' she added; for a moment, none of it felt bad after all.

'Best make it neither. I'm very glad I'm a man and you're a woman, but I still know I'd have felt as frustrated and rebellious in your situation as you did, Louisa Alstone. You're spirited and clever and if you managed to survive alone in such a harsh world, then you're evidently extremely resourceful as well.'

'Don't make me into someone better than I deserve, Captain,' she cautioned.

'And don't make yourself into your own demon.'

'No need for that, I killed Peter and Mama,' she remembered bleakly and all temptation to take herself at his inflated value disappeared.

'How?' he asked and she marvelled that he didn't draw his arms away or try to set her at arm's length.

'Kit and Ben had gone back to sea again and I hated losing their company and the exciting adventures we had, so I ran off one day when I'd finished my daily ration of sewing and chores about the house. It was high summer and the nights were almost as light as the days, so I climbed out of a bedroom window and stayed away all night. I found a roof in Mayfair to sleep on and it was a good deal cooler and more comfortable than our bedroom under the eaves in a rotten old house that should have been pulled down half a century ago. Then I decided to run back through the streets before the world was awake, just for the devilment of it. Except this time I ran through the wrong ones and picked up the typhus fever,' she said, then stared blankly into the darkness as she finished her tale. 'It killed Peter first and then I don't think Mama could fight it for her grief at losing him. Maria was only ill for a couple of days and I recovered in time to know what I'd done and wish I hadn't. Maria and I bungled along somehow, running the boarding house as best we could with Mrs Calhoun and Coste's help, and Papa came home every now and again when he had nowhere else to go. Then Kit came home with his share of a cargo in his pocket and arranged for Maria and me to live with our uncle and his wife. So Kit has paid for our keep and education ever since and I stayed there and tried to make up for the terrible thing I did, but nothing could wipe out that particular sin.'

'You did nothing wrong, you idiotic woman. I can understand a grieving child taking on a terrible burden of guilt, but surely not even you are stubborn enough to cling to it now, in the face of all logic and mature consideration?'

She shrugged, knowing he couldn't see her, but they were so close she could feel the frustration come off him. It was both unexpected and kind of him to try to absolve her of guilt. It also confirmed he had all the instincts, as well as the upbringing, of the gentleman she now knew him to be.

'If I had only stayed at home as I should have done that day, Mama and Peter would probably still be alive today,' she said sadly.

'And if any number of things in history had happened in a different order we might not be standing here tonight, futilely discussing ifs and maybes. You know as well as I do that disease is rife in the slums of this city, especially in the summer, and anyone could have given them that illness. Would you expect the butcher or baker or candlestick-maker to carry a burden of guilt for the rest of their lives if they had carried it into your home?'

'No, but they would have spread it in innocence, not after disobeying every rule my mother tried to lay down for my safety and well-being and probably worrying her sleepless all night as well.'

'So you were headstrong and difficult—what's new about that, Louisa?' he asked impatiently and for some reason that made her consider his words more seriously than sympathy might have done.

'Not much,' she finally admitted as if it came as a shock. He chuckled and she kicked herself silently for feeling a warm glow threaten to run through her at the deep, masculine sound of it. 'I doubt very much those who love you would have you any other than as you are, despite your many faults,' he told her almost gently.

'But Peter's dead,' she told him tragically and if he couldn't hear the tears in her voice at the very thought of her loving little brother, now six years in his grave, she certainly could and bit her lip to try to hold them back.

'And just how do you think your brother Kit and Ben Shaw would have felt if they came home to find you or your sister gone as well? Such epidemics are no respecters of what is fair and unfair, Louisa. None of you deserved to die or to bear blame for deaths that happened because the poor live in little better than open sewers at the heart of this fair city. Blame the aldermen and government ministers who allow such abject poverty to thrive in what's supposed to be the most advanced nation in the world, but don't be arrogant enough to take the blame yourself. And don't you think your mother would hate to hear you now? It sounds to me as if she loved her children very much, so she'd certainly not want to hear you talk like a fool and refuse to bear children yourself, just because she's not here any more and your little brother couldn't fight a desperate and dangerous illness that can just as easily take strong men in the prime of their lives.'

'I still shouldn't have gone.'

'No, but all the other times you climbed out of your window and ran wild through the streets you probably should have been sewing samplers or minding your books. It sounds like the natural reaction of a spirited girl, denied the pleasures and luxuries of the life you should have had, if your father wasn't selfish and shallow and self-obsessed. Taking the burden of guilt for what happened when it clearly belongs elsewhere is

arrogant, Louisa. All you were guilty of was a childish rebellion that you would have grown out of, once your brother
was able to provide you and your family with the sort of life
you should have lived from the outset.'

'He was so sad, Hugh,' she confided with a sniff to hold
back her tears that he somehow found deeply touching. 'At
night when he thought Maria and I were in bed and asleep I
would hear him weep for them. Then Papa came home one
night, drunk as usual, and they argued and raged at each other
until Papa stormed off into the night and swore not to come
home again until Kit was back at sea. They found his body
floating in the Thames two days later and only my sister was
ever soft-hearted enough to think he'd drowned himself out
of grief for my mother, when he was so drunk he probably
couldn't tell the difference between high water and dry land.
Yet it wouldn't have happened if he hadn't argued with Kit
and I hadn't done what I did.'

'And no doubt Kit feels guilty about that as well, being
made in the same stubborn, ridiculous mould as you and the
rest of the Earl of Carnwood's rackety family. There's no
need for you to take on his regrets as well as your own, since
I never met a man more able to own his sins and omissions
than Christopher Alstone.'

'I suppose you could be right.'

'Of course I am. Now, kindly inform me what you were
planning to do to me once you had me guyed up in that ridiculous disguise and let's have done with your imagined sins.'

'That's it? I am to consider myself absolved? You should
have been a priest.'

'Maybe not,' he said with a laugh that would have been
self-mocking if he wasn't so busy mocking her. 'But nothing you did or didn't do in the past has made you unfit to be

a mother, Louisa. Probably just as well, since we're going to be wed and will doubtless bed each other at regular intervals, very likely before we get to the altar as well if you keep glaring at me like that,' he threatened half-seriously.

'How do you know I'm glaring at you?' she asked haughtily.

'Instinct,' he told her succinctly. 'I can't promise you much, but I will promise not to treat you as shabbily as your father did your mother,' he added gruffly.

'That would be nice of you, if I had the least intention of marrying you.'

'You will have to, my girl, since I refuse to spend the next three months or so not meeting your brother's eyes or hiding from Ben Shaw's mighty wrath while we wait for you to decide if I've just got you pregnant or not. Consider it the wages of sin and take that guilt on your shoulders if you must, but at least let's have no more Cheltenham tragedies while you wait it out as my wife instead.'

'So far I hear only what you want and nothing about me, but the answer to your question about the disguise is that I don't really know. I can't go back to Kit's house because my enemies will be looking for me by now, and I wanted to get you away from the man who's trying to trap you until we could defeat him somehow, which was all very stupid of me, I suppose.'

'Undoubtedly it was,' he agreed gruffly.

'You could probably go back there safely yourself,' she encouraged him and felt his suspicion on the heavy air as clearly as if she could actually see his frown.

'While you do what in the meantime?'

'I have plenty of plans for my future. It's you I don't know what to do with.'

'I think we just demonstrated that you know *exactly* what to do with me,' he said, sounding as silkily lethal as he must when examining any of his crew brought in front of him to explain their sins.

'And you dislike being thought fit for only one purpose as much as I do?'

'When did I imply any such thing, woman?'

'With every word you drawl at me as if you're right and everything I say proves how bird-witted I am.'

'Only when you're talking rubbish,' he muttered impatiently, as if driven to the edge of reason by addle-pated arguments, when she ought to accept his words as proven fact, then do as she was bid.

'It's hardly rubbish to say we're both unsuited to marriage and even more so to marrying one another.'

'Yes, it is. We'll do very well in our marriage bed, something we just proved to each other beyond all reasonable doubt.'

'So my doubts are unreasonable and that's all there is to marriage?' she asked with a theatrical wave at the coffee stacks she was quite glad he couldn't see. The very thought of them made her blush now they were discussing seduction and his peculiar idea that it automatically led to marriage.

'Ah, now I can see why you were truly so unsuited to the *ton*nish ideals of marriage *à la mode*. You, Miss Alstone, destined as you are not to be a miss for very much longer, are a romantic.'

Stung by the accusation, when she'd always thought herself such a cynic, Louisa was about to loudly dispute such a slur when she made the mistake of wondering if he could be right.

Chapter Eight

'I have never felt the slightest need to sigh and yearn over a man,' Louisa lied defensively, 'and least of all over you, Captain Darke.'

'Good, because I'm not worth wasting a moment's peace on,' he said curtly and a fierce desire to argue that statement shook her, but she fought it with an effort she must think about later.

'I'm not going to marry you,' she said as definitely as she could.

'You're such an odd mix of cynicism and vulnerability, my dear. I'll probably spend a lifetime trying to understand you,' he said, as if he hadn't heard.

'It will be a lifetime separate from mine,' she insisted for the sake of it more than out of any passionate certainty. She was so busy feeling hollow inside at the idea that the sounds she was waiting for from outside hardly seemed important any more.

'Why the devil is a ship docking hard by, Louisa?' he barked at her and she felt his frustration as he gripped her as if he'd like to shake her.

'It's come for me, of course—what's the point of having a brother with his own shipping empire if I can't call on it when I need to?' she replied coolly.

'You don't trust me to keep you safe, then?'

'It's not a matter of trust,' she argued uncomfortably.

'Now there you're so very wrong, Miss Alstone.' His voice was so low she did her best not to hear it as he turned to the master of the coastal brig she'd summoned here once the tide was right. 'What the devil do you want?' he barked when a shadowy figure unlocked the riverside door and stood outlined against the night.

'My sister,' Christopher Alstone replied grimly, opening his dark lantern and making Louisa blink. 'So what in Hades are you doing here?' he demanded.

'Kit!' Louisa exclaimed on a huge sigh of relief and confusion as she ran into his arms. 'I missed you so much,' she told him fervently.

'It's mutual, you confounded nuisance of a female,' he informed her abruptly, even as she felt at least half of his attention slide to Hugh Darke and his muscles stiffen like a fighting dog scenting a challenge. 'What have you done to my sister?' he ground out, as if he knew exactly what they'd been doing, but surely even her powerful brother couldn't see through walls?

'Nothing,' she said impatiently. 'And what are you doing here?' she asked, standing away from him to examine his deeply shadowed face.

'I asked first,' he said silkily, his eyes not moving from Hugh and she wondered if these two warriors were about to try to kill each other over her.

'And you're clearly as annoying as ever,' she sparked back,

determined not to be sidelined and silent while they decided her future between them.

'Clearly,' he agreed with that flinty lack of temper she knew from experience was his most effective weapon in an argument. 'An answer, if you please?' he demanded starkly and Hugh Darke moved Louisa aside to confront her brother.

'I was trying to persuade her to marry me, until you interrupted us,' he said, as arrogantly challenging as if he'd just thrown down a knightly gauntlet and fully expected to have it thrown back in his face.

'Oh, good,' Kit said mildly and Louisa felt her rage soar almost out of control at the exact moment his seemed to deflate.

'Good? Do you really want this idiot to marry me?' she raged.

'Why not? Lots of other idiots have asked you to do so and they only mildly annoyed you. At least this one seems to have found a way of holding your full attention while he puts the question, even if I don't like anything else about him being shut in here alone with my little sister.'

Drat him, but why did her brother have to be so uncannily perceptive? Because he was Kit Stone, she supposed: precociously successful, driven and even more stubborn than she was.

'Speaking as the idiot in question, I don't care about your ruffled pride and your reputation for icy detachment, Miss Alstone. I just want you to agree to marry me, so your brother doesn't have to beat me to a bloody pulp and we can all go home, before eating our dinner and getting on with our interrupted lives with no more of your infernal melodramas,' Hugh told her impatiently.

'Which is exactly why we should *not* marry, since your

dinner clearly matters to you a lot more than I do,' she said, rounding on him now that Kit seemed more an amused bystander than her avenging guardian.

If she let herself think about the volumes that detachment spoke about her brother's belief in Captain Darke's bone-deep sense of honour, she might start respecting the devilish rogue herself and she knew precisely where that would get her—marched up the aisle before she came back to her right senses again.

'On the contrary, I'm exactly the right husband to deal with your wrongheaded ideas and headstrong ways. Any other man would be driven demented by your starts inside a sennight.'

'He could be right,' Kit observed traitorously.

'And I'll be flying to the moon any moment now,' she scorned, but the idea of arguing with Hugh Darke for the rest of their born days suddenly seemed a little bit too promising.

'I'll take you there, Eloise,' he whispered in her ear and she wondered how he'd managed to creep so close behind her that she was all but in his arms once more, and in front of her brother as well.

She shuddered with what she told herself was revulsion, but he'd reminded her how it felt to soar in his arms, to strive for the very moon and stars, and she sighed in besotted anticipation of doing it all again.

'Not until you've put a wedding ring on her finger, you won't,' Kit warned as he eyed them very suspiciously once more. 'And what's all this Eloise business?'

'You really don't want to know,' Hugh said with a return to his austerely apart, piratical-captain look as he withdrew his warmth and strength from her.

Louisa shivered at no longer feeling him next to her—how could she know if her scent and sound and touch were as deeply imprinted on his senses as his were on hers? He was so detached all of a sudden it was as if she'd dreamt that feverish interlude in his arms when neither of them seemed able to hold anything back from the other. She was almost glad when Kit decided this was neither the time nor the place for such an important discussion and put aside that comment to pick over later and eyed her pale face with brotherly concern.

'I probably don't either, but let's get Louisa out of here. We can deal with Eloise and the details of your wedding in the morning.'

'No, I can't go home with you, I need to get away,' Louisa argued, an illogical sense that she needed to escape nagging at her even now she had two powerful protectors instead of just the one.

'Why?' her brother asked.

'Because Uncle William has been scheming to marry me off to a worm of a man, who probably offered to share my dowry with him, and both of them will be hot on my trail by now.'

'He'll answer to me for it, then, but why would that mean we can't go home?'

'The insect abducted me and kept me in his bedchamber for a night and a day and made sure my uncle and aunt saw me there, so they could exclaim loudly about my wickedness and their scandalised feelings. They forbade me their roof, unless I instantly married the repulsive toad, which I refused to do needless to say.'

'That need not worry you, Miss Alstone. He won't pollute the world for very much longer,' Hugh Darke gritted between his strong white teeth and, given the fierce look in his eyes, she believed him.

'How would your killing him help me? You would have to flee the country and I would still be the centre of a fine scandal, all the more so if I was stupid enough to have married you in the meantime. It would seem as if I ran off with you after growing bored with him.'

'She's right, Hugh,' Kit intervened as Hugh Darke rounded on her with his best master-of-all-I-survey glare. 'You need to leave the worm to me,' Kit added, offering that caveat to soothe the devil of temper so very evident in Hugh's furious gaze and stirring hers instead.

'No, he'll only dirty your hands,' Hugh gritted furiously, quite lost to reason, even if her brother only had more masculine folly to offer. 'What's his name, this insect-worm?' he asked fiercely.

'Do you think I'm fool enough to tell you that, when you will only add to the scandal already surrounding me by calling him out?'

His hands closed about her arms, as if he wanted to shake some sense into her and she condemned her senses for leaping to attention, even at his angry touch through her second-hand jacket and gown. For a betraying moment she swayed towards him, as if her body and her senses were begging for a kiss despite her growing fury.

'He must not get away with it, Louisa, I can't let him,' he gritted as if her lost reputation mattered to him more than it ever could to her. As surely as she knew Charlton would walk away if she was teetering on the edge of a cliff, she knew this man would plunge off it himself, if that was what it took to save her.

'Don't you think me capable of making him sorry he was even born, then, Hugo?' Kit said almost gently.

'I do, but it should be my job. No, make that my pleasure.'

'It can't be and you know why,' Kit said obscurely and Louisa's ears pricked up at the veiled curb in that short sentence. Then she felt the reminder bite into the man still holding her arms as if he didn't know quite what to do with her.

Hugh jerked away from her, seeming horrified that he'd ever laid hands on her in the first place and watched those very hands with revulsion, like a very masculine Lady Macbeth, after she'd driven herself mad with murder and ambition and couldn't wash the imaginary blood off them.

'I know, so how can I wed your sister? I forgot what I am in the heat of the moment,' he whispered and it was as if he and Kit were talking about something deeply important she wasn't going to be told.

'Whilst I suspect I don't want to know about the heat of that particular moment, we both know there's nothing to stop you marrying. The rub will come if you fail to make my sister happy afterwards and I'm forced to kill you,' Kit told him implacably, and any illusion she'd suffered that he was resigned to what had taken place between herself and Hugh tonight melted away like mist in the July sun.

'That would go quite badly with me, either way,' she muttered mutinously.

'Not as badly as you knowing the truth about me would,' Hugh said, looking glum about her predicted unhappiness and softening her heart, if he did but know it.

'I told you my tale,' she challenged him, and if Kit chose to think it was the one about her abduction and lost reputation, then so be it.

'And you think mine is that simple—just a few words and a rueful smile at how easy that was to get out of the way and go on?'

'As mine was?' she demanded, furious with him for brushing aside her fears and peculiarities as if they didn't matter.

'I didn't mean...' he blundered on.

'Never mind what you meant, never mind your secrets. I haven't got all night to spare for arguing with you. I'm tired and hungry and downright weary of rescuing ungrateful, lying, mistrustful idiots from their enemies. If neither of you intends to take me somewhere safe and warm and feed me, pray give me a hand up on to that brig of yours, brother mine, and I'll get the master to drop me off at the nearest port downriver where I can buy myself a bedchamber for the night and a decent meal.'

'Not in a hundred years, sister dear, and he's long gone. I thought half of London must know he was casting off and none too happy to be going in the middle of the night, given the amount of noise he made about it.'

'I didn't hear him,' she said stiffly and actually caught herself out in a flounce as she spun round to glare at her would-be bridegroom and dare him to comment.

'Neither did I,' he admitted meekly.

'Lovebirds,' Kit added sarcastically and Louisa wondered if she ought to kick one of them, even if it was just because they were men and couldn't help being infuriating any more than they could voluntarily stop breathing.

'What are we going to do, then?' she demanded.

'Go home,' Kit told her implacably and, since there was nowhere she'd rather be, she allowed him to bustle her out of the warehouse and along narrow streets and alleys he knew even better than she did in the dark, then out on to wider and marginally more respectable streets where he hailed a cab, then sat back to watch the night-time streets roll past as if they fascinated him.

'Where have you been, then?' Louisa finally asked her brother, remembering she ought to be furious with him for disappearing as he had.

'Here and there,' he told her shortly.

Simmering with temper because it was better than letting her tiredness and uncertainty take over, she put her mind to Hugh Darke's many mysteries as the little house in Chelsea and a degree of physical comfort beckoned at last.

'Just as well you didn't get back last night,' she muttered as they arrived and her brother helped her down while Hugh paid the jarvey.

'I'm not going to ask why not until I've had my dinner and a soothing shot of brandy,' he said as he ushered her up the steps and rapped sharply on the door.

'Hah! That's a lot less likely than you think,' she observed with a sidelong glance at Hugh that made Kit frown as Coste cautiously opened the door.

'Let us in, you idiot,' Kit ordered sharply.

'Didn't know it was you, now, did I?' Coste mumbled as he stood back to do so.

'You would have done if you actually made use of the Judas hole I had put in for once,' his employer informed him as he used Coste's candle to light those in the sconces round the cosy dining parlour they had got nowhere near last night. 'Is there anything edible in the house?' he demanded and put a taper to the fire laid ready in the hearth for good measure.

'Aye, sir. Miss Louisa gave me money for food and a couple of cleaning women. We've a good pork pie and a ham and all sorts of fancy bits of this and that. There's treacle tart, apple pie and gingerbread, too, but not so much of the treacle tart as there might be,' Coste said with a reminiscent grin.

'And you two somehow managed until now without my housekeeper and a kitchenmaid?' Kit asked mildly enough.

'Well, I was going to tell you about that, Captain...' Coste trailed off, casting a look at Hugh that begged him to take over explaining their misconduct.

'We two bachelors proved too rowdy to satisfy Mrs Calhoun's strict standards of behaviour and she took herself and her daughter off before there was any gossip about them being here with two rowdy bachelors like us,' he obligingly admitted, nodding at Coste to make himself scarce while he still could.

'I warrant she did,' Kit replied grimly. 'Don't forget to bring that pie and a pint of porter along with tea for Miss Louisa,' he urged his retreating manservant and watched Hugh with cold eyes. 'I trust my sister was not caught up in that rowdiness,' he added with such mild iciness that even Louisa shivered in her seat by the fire.

Hugh shifted in his chair as Louisa carefully stared into the flames and Kit sighed rather heavily. 'Later,' he said portentously and Louisa felt as if the two men were once more having a silent but fierce conversation she didn't understand, and that they had no intention of explaining any of it to her.

Hugh Darke wasn't in the least bit overshadowed by her powerful brother. Despite her captain's apparently subservient role in Kit and Ben's empire, he acted as Kit's equal and her suspicions about his true place in the world crept back and left her wondering why he took orders from even so compelling, and successful, a pair as her brother and Ben Shaw. She furtively surveyed her brother and her lover in turn, noting the similarities in their elegantly powerful builds and proud carriage. They were both dark-haired as well, of course, but that was about the end of any similarity between them and

Hugh Darke was certainly the more mysterious and contrary of the two, even judged on appearance alone.

He had that strong Roman nose that looked as if it had been broken at some point in his varied career; emphatically marked dark brows frowned above his challenging silver-blue eyes and yet his mouth could have belonged on a poet or a troubadour, if not for the stern control he kept it under. She knew how sensitive it could feel against hers now, but the containment of it argued he'd been through a very hot fire to become the steely-eyed captain he was now. A younger Hugh Darke would be almost too handsome and appealing for his own good; she imagined this complex and contrary man carefree and laughing, and was glad to be spared that pristine version of him, since she was far too impressed with the current one to need any more encouragement.

Louisa gave up on reading Hugh's thoughts and tried her brother's instead, seeing nothing but an austere lack of expression on his face that made him exasperating, even as she let herself realise how much she'd missed him. Grief and guilt had hardened her against loving anyone easily, but now she could let it go at last and remember her little brother as he was and it was as if her family had been given back to her. Kit was darker than the rest of them, of course, but Peter had looked so much like her it had hurt to look at herself in the mirror when he died. Who would ever guess that Captain Darke could give her little brother back to her as he was, instead of the reproachful angel guilt had painted him? She owed him a debt for that, which added to her confusion as they all sat in weary silence, carefully not discussing her eventful day.

Coste finally carried in a rattling tray, deposited it on the nearest table, then went back for her tea. It wasn't a very elegant repast, but they made short work of slices of pie and ham with the mustard and fresh bread and some pickles that looked much less ancient than the ones that had confronted her last night. After a while she refused anything more, sitting back to sip her tea and watch Kit and Hugh eat as if they hadn't done so for a week.

'The amount of food you gentlemen require to sustain life will never cease to amaze me,' she observed at last.

'Whilst we coarse males are continually astonished by how little a lady can maintain herself upon,' Hugh returned with an unexpectedly boyish grin that somehow managed to warm her more effectively than the now-glowing fire.

'Since I don't subscribe to the idea that ladies should eat before they dine in mixed company, so we appear to possess the most bird-like of appetites, Captain Darke, perhaps I'm not a lady,' she said with a shy smile.

'I've always thought that a true lady doesn't need to try to be one myself, Miss Alstone,' he replied and surprised her into blushing at his implied compliment.

'You'll be sipping ratafia and exchanging remarks about the weather next,' Kit interrupted impatiently and Louisa decided she'd much prefer to put off the conversation he wanted to have until morning, except then she'd toss and turn all night worrying, so it was probably as well to get it over with.

'Very well, what do you want to know?' she asked.

'So much I hardly know where to begin, but the name of your worm will do to start with. Then we can discuss everything else and what must be done about it once we've dealt with him,' her brother said grimly.

Louisa annoyed herself by looking to Hugh for support and he nodded as if he was only waiting for that detail before storming off into the night to wreak havoc as well. 'No,' she said and prepared to be very stubborn rather than let him risk his skin once again.

'All I need do is enter any fashionable lady's drawing room tomorrow afternoon and flap my sharp ears towards the nearest whispered conversation and I'll find out in five minutes,' Kit threatened and she knew he was right. Such a juicy scandal would not even be silenced when the lady's sharp-eared brother was in the room if the story really was running about the *ton* like wildfire.

'Promise me first that neither of you will try to kill him?'

'Does the man's safety mean so much to you then, Miss Alstone?' Hugh Darke said coldly.

'No, but my brother's does and even you are too good a man to soil your hands on a nothing like him,' she told him fiercely and it was more than he deserved after the icy disdain he'd just glared at her.

'My apologies, ma'am,' he said stiffly.

'His name, Louisa?' her brother demanded.

'First your promise,' she replied stubbornly.

'Very well, I promise he can live until morning.'

'Not good enough, I'll not have you banished for duelling or hung for murder either. I've already lost one brother and certainly can't spare another.'

Kit looked thoughtful at that reminder, then nodded reluctantly. 'I'll find another way to punish the wretch, Lou, but don't ask me to let him get away with what he's done to you, for I just can't do it.'

'And you, Captain Darke?' she asked implacably.

'And I what, Miss Alstone?'

'Are you going to promise not to chase my would-be husband down with the carving knife?'

'I have a perfectly good sword handy, as you no doubt recall.'

'There will be no swordfighting, no furtive and stupid duel with pistols at dawn and no pretend-casual encounter at some club or at a mill, or anywhere else for that matter. If you don't promise not to kill the man, I shall inform my uncle you two are on the rampage and the worm will be long gone before you get anywhere near him.'

'Justice can be swift indeed, Miss Alstone,' he argued.

'That's exactly what I'm worried about, you stupid man. Do you think I want any more deaths on my conscience, after carrying such a burden of guilt for so long?' she said and made herself let her pain at the very idea of losing him show in her gaze.

'I promise,' he murmured, his eyes silently telling her it was only because of that burden of guilt that he reluctantly gave in.

'And what exactly are you promising me, Captain?'

'To find another way to make his life hell,' he said with a grim smile.

'I don't mind that, then. Mr Charlton Hawberry abducted me and, since he made my life hellish for a spell, whatever punishment you come up with might at least stop him doing it to some other female.'

'Although I never heard his name before, he even sounds like the villain out of a melodrama,' Hugh exclaimed disgustedly.

'I told you he was a worm, didn't I?' she offered mildly.

'He sounds more like some obscure breed of fly that needs squashing. Will you give me that promise back so I may do so, Miss Alstone?'

'No, and need I remind you that I rescued myself from him,

which must have gone some way towards swatting the horrible man and will have to do for now.'

'I'd still dearly like to know how you managed it.'

'As would I,' Kit told her with a keen look that made Louisa wish she hadn't used her misadventures to divert them from their manly wrath.

'I waited for the right moment and got away from him,' she said airily.

'How?' Hugh barked as if he had every right to examine her.

'I found the only way to evade his bullies and his revolting company that he'd neglected to close off and took it.'

'Describe exactly how you did so, then,' Hugh said implacably, as if very near the end of his tether. She wondered fleetingly why Kit was sitting back in his chair and letting his captain interrogate her, then decided she might as well get the tale over as quickly as possible and it didn't matter which of them asked the questions.

'I climbed out of a window,' she admitted, because it could be any window, on any floor. She realised her mistake as soon as she recalled telling them she was imprisoned in Charlton's bedchamber, and they knew as well as she did that most of the narrow town houses hired for the Season had their principal bedrooms on the second floor, three storeys and a basement above the ground.

'With the aid of a rope of some sort, I trust?' Hugh asked roughly, as if the very idea made him imagine all sorts of terrible consequences in retrospect.

'Um, no,' was all she could manage as she shifted in her seat by the fire and avoided both their gazes as she recalled her truly terrifying escape.

Chapter Nine

'Devil take it, Louisa! You're not a wild girl clambering about the slums like some sort of human spider any more. You're supposed to be a lady,' Kit objected, which might have seemed bad enough, if Hugh hadn't gone as silent and lethally furious as a tiger grabbed by his tail.

'If I'd meekly sat there waiting for rescue, then I'd be well and truly wed to the insect-worm by now,' she defended herself rather half-heartedly, as she remembered that appalling climb across the front of a house with fewer handholds than a sheer cliff might fairly be expected to have.

'Not for long,' Hugh finally said with a hiss of pent-up fury that made her wonder if he was a gentleman of his word after all. Of course he was, she concluded as she met the barely contained rage in his icy-blue gaze, he wouldn't be so irate at having given it if he wasn't.

'You wouldn't have cared if I was wed to him or not, since you hardly knew me then,' she reminded him, but it didn't restore him to his usual cynical self somehow.

'I would have cared because you're Kit's sister, but it would be my pleasure to beat Hawberry to a pulp now. And adventurers don't start molesting females because it suddenly occurred to them, Miss Alstone, so I very much doubt if you are the first one he's ever used such despicable tactics against.'

'I'm not a victim,' she insisted fiercely.

'And I never met a female less likely to be anyone's dupe than you are, my Eloise. He chose his target very badly this time,' he asserted and at last she saw something in his silvered-blue gaze that could have been admiration.

'Eloise?' Kit asked as his sharp ears and even sharper brain picked up on that unfortunate nickname again. 'Who the devil is this Eloise?'

'I am,' she said as uninformatively as possible.

'Oh, good,' Hugh said irrepressibly and she glared at him.

'You keep out of this,' she demanded and her glare was even more furious as his smile became wolfish and his gaze almost molten with heat at the memory of Eloise and her bold ways and even bolder tongue.

'Spoilsport,' he muttered a little too intimately and, if he wasn't conscious of Kit's eagle-eyed gaze shifting between them suspiciously, she felt it acutely.

'Later,' Kit promised ominously and Louisa caught a typical masculine resolve to punch each other until they both felt better flash between them and was tempted to stamp upstairs and let them get on with it, but she didn't want either of them hurt.

It puzzled her how deeply Hugh Darke's well-being had come to matter to her in such a short time and she fought a fluffy reverie on the intriguing subject of how instantaneously she took fire whenever he was near. It was almost as if someone had laid such a strong enchantment on them that they were helpless to resist it, but she was such an unlikely heroine of a fairy tale that she reminded herself who she really was and glared at them both.

'No, you don't,' she insisted sharply. 'There's enough to worry about without you two pummelling each other bruised and bloody just for the fun of it.'

'You think we'd have fun?' Hugh said, so blandly innocent she was sure of it and decided she understood the opposite sex even less than usual.

'Yes, I do,' she replied and silently dared him to argue, 'and never mind Charlton, how do we find out who's behind today's plot against you, Captain Darke?'

'What plot?' Kit demanded.

'There was one, however he tries to convince you otherwise. I foiled it and your captain was most ungrateful at being rescued from his enemies by a mere woman.'

'Only because your sister thinks she's justified in taking intolerable risks with herself any time she decides to pry into matters that don't concern her, Alstone. A note to inform me of your suspicions would have done the job just as well,' he accused her, turning the full benefit of his angry scowl on her rather than Kit.

'There wasn't time,' she told him defiantly.

'Yet you found plenty of it in which to organise a rather showy ambush and procure yet another disreputable disguise for yourself, let alone an even more absurd one for me?'

'Would you have believed me?' she asked after a long moment while his gaze on hers seemed to demand an explanation she couldn't give, when she didn't really understand why she'd had to secure his safety so personally in the first place.

'Probably,' he finally breathed as if in response to a far deeper challenge.

'That wasn't good enough, you see, I had to be sure.'

'And if my lion-hearted sister decided you needed to be rescued, believe me, Hugo, rescued you were going to be,' Kit intervened with what looked astonishingly like an approving smile.

'Clearly,' he responded, looking a little dazed by the notion that he mattered to anybody.

'Don't you want to know who I rescued you from?' she demanded.

'You might as well ask her, Hugh. My sister seems to be a mine of unwelcome information tonight,' Kit said with a glance of fellow feeling at Hugh Darke that made Louisa want to kick some inanimate object and flounce out of the room, except that would only make them more smugly masculine than ever.

'I have a legion of enemies,' Hugh said wearily.

'You might have a new one,' Kit said, offering up cold comfort.

'New or old, he certainly puzzled me, Captain,' she said, wanting to comfort him for his surfeit of foes for some odd reason.

'He's bewildering me at the moment, because I haven't the least idea who he is, so why not part with his name, whoever you think he is, and let your brother and I add him to our list?' Hugh said indifferently.

'What list?' she asked.

'The one of all the people we're supposed to punish for their sins without actually laying a finger on them, remember?'

'And a very civilised form of retribution it will be, too,' she said virtuously.

'Tell him who it was then, Lou, so you can go upstairs and rest before you fall asleep in your tea,' Kit advised and suddenly she felt the weight of the last night and day's worth of adventures bear down on her.

'I racked my memory for hours afterwards, but I'm nearly sure I've finally managed to match the house to the man, although I still can't quite believe it can be right,' she told them.

'For goodness' sake, just give us your best guess and then go to bed,' Hugh demanded impatiently.

'It's not a guess,' she said with as much dignity as she could muster while battling against the after-effects of her demanding day. 'I tracked the man who met your follower back to a house in Grosvenor Square. When he ran down the front steps nearly an hour later I could tell he was one of the *ton* from his dress and that air of owning the world you aristocrats seem to be born with.'

'You should, since you have it yourself in spades. Now cut line and get on with your story, Louisa,' her brother said shortly.

'It took me a while to work out who he was because it's so unlikely, but I went to a ball there once so I'm sure it was the Earl of Kinsham's house. The man who had Hugh followed, Kit, was his lordship's son and heir, Viscount Rarebridge, and what earthly reason could he have to do that?' she said, barely able to believe it herself, so no wonder if they didn't either.

'The deuce it was!' Hugh exclaimed softly, taking her word for it, even while he visibly flinched at that name, as if the knowledge hurt.

'Why would a man like his lordship have you followed?' she asked.

'I heard whispers that he was one of them,' he muttered half to himself, 'but I never let myself believe it.'

'One of whom?' she demanded.

'My wife's lovers,' he explained bleakly and she felt her knees wobble with the stark shock of his words.

'You have a wife?' she whispered and wondered numbly how words could actually hurt on your tongue.

'What?' he asked, almost as if he'd forgotten she was there.

'Your wife?' she asked more firmly, rediscovering her temper under the goad of his impatience.

'What wife? Oh, that one. No, my wife has been dead these three years and more,' he replied rather vaguely, somehow not defusing her temper when he couldn't seem to grasp what he'd done to anger her in the first place.

'You have a lot of explaining to do,' she informed him haughtily.

'Later,' he said, as if she was bothering him with foolish trivialities.

'Now, unless you want me to march round to Grosvenor Square this minute and ask Lord Rarebridge why he's so intent on pursuing you myself.'

'That I don't, it would be most unseemly' he said primly.

'Then tell me,' she insisted, trying to look as if she was metaphorically picking out the right bonnet and gloves for the trip.

'My wife took lovers. I stopped counting after the first one I found out about and left for my ship,' he said so brusquely she knew he lied and every name on that list had hurt him. 'Unfortunately, my father wouldn't believe Ariadne anything other than the innocent she played so convincingly and she continued to live under his roof when I was forbidden it for slandering such a fine example of English womanhood. Better for her sake perhaps if she hadn't, since she died there next time I was home on shore leave and raging about the neighbourhood like a wild bull, telling anyone who would listen to me about the injustice of it all, while they no doubt considered my plight a rare piece of entertainment. Looking back at the rash young idiot I was then, he seems so young and silly that I marvel at my own folly.'

'How did she die?' she asked, certain from the shadow in his eyes there was far more to his wife's death than the blunt facts he'd told her so far.

'She was found strangled with one of her silk stockings and my elder brother lay dead outside her bedchamber door. He'd been shot in the back as if he was in the act of fleeing her bed and I, the wronged husband, was presumed to have found him there and murdered him in a furious rage. My estrangement from my wife and family was hardly news in the neighbourhood and I was the only suspect.'

'How could they even think it?' she asked, crossing the room to touch his arm and draw his gaze back to here and now; anything to take the stark bleakness from his blue-grey gaze and set mouth at the thought of that terrible night.

'If not for an old friend vouching for me, I would have hung, Miss Alstone.'

'Idiots,' she condemned roundly and he managed a half-smile before looking remote again and carrying on as if he had to tell her the worst before he faltered.

'I was so blind drunk that night that I'd collapsed in the taproom of the local inn and been left there to sleep it off for half the village to see. According to Dickon Thrale, the landlord and my childhood friend, he left me lying there in the hope I'd wake up and realise what an idiot I was making of myself. I recall almost nothing of that night, but he certainly saved my life. Yet, because Dickon and I ran wild together when we were young, many in the surrounding area refused to believe I didn't wake up, escape, commit murder, then crawl back to the inn to pretend I'd been there all along. Apparently there were signs that whoever did it must have climbed up the outside of the house to reach my wife's bedchamber, so eventually my inability to even stand upright unassisted that night was accepted and I was declared innocent, if stupid and dissipated. Even now I sometimes wonder if I did it and my friend lied to save my skin, so I can hardly blame the whisperers for persisting in their claim that I had got away with murder twice over.'

'You might fight with your brother, since you're a man and it seems to me that's what men do, and I'm quite sure you bellowed at your wife when you found out what she was up to with other men, but you couldn't hurt a woman or shoot a man in the back if your life depended on it, Hugh Darke,' she informed him impatiently, wondering how he could even dream he ever would.

'How could you know that?' he demanded equally impatiently.

'Because I know you.'

'You know Hugh Darke, or you think you do after a very short acquaintance, which has hardly given you enough time to plumb my darkest depths.'

'No, I know you. Whatever you care to call yourself, whoever you've been since you left your own home and old way of life, there is an essential core of honour and almost brutal honesty about you I would be a want-wit not to recognise.'

'How can you know anything significant about a man you met one day ago? Come, Miss Alstone,' he mocked as if her belief in him might become a danger in itself and therefore must be avoided at all cost, 'I'm quite sure that you, of all people, know better than to trust your first impressions of anyone. You know society presents a smiling face in public and it's really naught but a mask.'

'Would that insight be gained over the years I ran wild through the slums of this unfair city of ours, do you think, Captain? I admit the ones I spent with my so-called equals were a good deal less varied, but you're right in thinking they taught me to recognise a person's true nature, under all the pretty sham the *ton* use to disguise their power and ambitions, so I really don't follow your current argument.'

'Both your lives should serve to warn you I'm not a man to be trusted,' he said roughly, as if she were being obtuse and not him.

'Whether you're striding about your quarter-deck or in your cups, you're the man you've made yourself and, whatever else I might think of you, I'll never believe that man a murderer. I met one or two of those in my youth and you don't have either the heartless steel or the casual cowardice to make a good killer,' she assured him, holding his gaze as she stepped closer to make her point, matching his hard palm to her soft one in a silent declaration of her faith in her lover.

'I've killed for my country,' he told her blankly, as if he couldn't bear to be thought too much of, but he didn't remove his hand from hers.

'You were only there to offer and join battle with our enemies. Please don't take me for a fool, Hugh.'

'And please don't take me at all, Louisa, not now I've remembered who I really am and how little chance I'll probably have to pretend I'm Hugh Darke for much longer,' he asked, looking as if he truly regretted it when he removed the warmth of his palm from hers and retreated a step or two.

'Perhaps you consider I'm not a good enough match for Hugo Kenton, then?' she asked as coolly as she could, contrarily feeling as if the promise of their shared future was being withdrawn, just when she'd almost got used to having it there.

'Of course you were bound to work out who I really am,' he said bitterly. 'How many men are openly cuckolded by their wife, then accused of murdering her as well as their own brother? I should have known you'd soon pin me down, Miss Alstone, moving in the circles you do.'

'Yes, you should,' she said impatiently, 'and you're still innocent.'

'Only until I'm proven guilty, and no doubt Rarebridge is congratulating himself on getting one step nearer to doing that right now. He probably wants to examine me properly and disprove Dickon's evidence.'

'You believe every man your wife slept with to be innocent apart from yourself then, Captain? I'm not as sanguine about his purpose as you appear to be and it must be very convenient for the real murderer that you took the blame for his crimes on your own shoulders as if you deserved it. The men he set on you are not poor and simple souls, intent on making a little money by tracking down a renegade for a man with more gold than sense. They come from a gang who will do anything for money, up to and including murder.'

'Believe her, Kenton, my sister used to amuse herself by following the worst and most suspicious villains she could find, for the sheer daredevil challenge of staying on their tails without them knowing about it,' Kit said grimly and Louisa was surprised he'd known what she got up to when he wasn't there to check her wilder starts. 'I had to get her out of the stews for more reasons than the obvious one of not leaving my sisters in such a place once they began to mature.'

'At least physically,' Hugh said sceptically, his gaze hard on her as he realised what dangers she'd run, now and then.

'Never mind that—do you believe me about the nature of the company his lordship is keeping?'

'I believe what you say is worth a clear-headed investigation.'

'How very flattering of you, Captain, I'm almost overwhelmed.'

'It is, if you did but know,' he said with a rather weary smile. 'I promised myself when Ariadne died that I would never listen to another woman swearing she was telling me only the truth, when my wife lied as compulsively as she breathed. Now I'm considering a man I once called my friend could want me dead or be willing to let me hang in his stead, all on the say-so of a lady.'

'How very remarkable of me to persuade you of anything so vexatious, being a woman and all,' she drawled, hanging on to her temper by a hair's breadth.

'Clumsy of you, Hugo,' Kit observed. 'And loathe though I am to part you two lovebirds, it really is high time my sister went to bed. Climbing out of windows, scaling three-storey buildings, carousing with rogues like you and tramping about half of London at a dizzying height must take it out of a woman, even if she is my intrepid sister. Are you sure you can match her, Kenton?'

'Quite sure you'll insist I do, whether I want to or not,' he replied with a withdrawal of all emotion that made Louisa feel very weary indeed, and resolved not to wed the man, child or no, if he couldn't make a better fist of wanting her.

'We'll see,' she told them both, with a militant nod as she quit the room with a cold look for Hugh and a warning one for her brother ordering him not to follow her.

* * *

'That certainly told us,' Kit said ruefully as the door snapped to behind her.

'Little firebrand,' Hugh replied with a wry smile.

'And if you ever manage to persuade her to marry you, my sister will be as true to you as honed steel for the rest of your mutual lives. She doesn't know how to be anything but loyal to those she loves, confoundedly restless little minx though she is.'

'Who said anything about love?' Hugh argued, although the very notion of gaining Louisa Alstone's suddenly seemed infinitely desirable, rather than the cursed trap it ought to be to a man with his history.

'If you don't propose even trying to love my sister, I might have to kill you after all, Kenton,' Kit warned him, with none of the drama and fuss a lesser man might put into such a threat, and all the cold purpose it would lack on such blustering tongues.

'What man lucky enough to have even a chance of winning your sister wouldn't fight his best friend for her? If he had aught to offer but a filthy scandal and a sword of Damocles hanging over his head, of course,' Hugh made himself answer just as coldly, feeling as if he was bidding farewell to an impossible dream he would regret losing for the rest of his life.

'Then it's high time we got on and cleared your name, Hugo. This limbo can't continue much longer, under the circumstances.'

'And do you think I haven't tried to do just that?' Hugh responded gruffly.

'Not hard enough, or those damned rumours would have died a natural death the day you were declared innocent by the magistrates. Louisa is right—while you half-believe you could have done it, there's no reason to probe the matter more deeply. Are you going to honour her belief in you and do what you should have done three years ago, man? It would help the rest of us if you weren't more interested in finding oblivion in the bottom of the nearest bottle while you're about it, but if you insist on turning aside from your obligations, no doubt my redoubtable sister will continue her crusade to clear your name anyway.'

'God forbid!' Hugh said with a shudder, easily picturing Louisa Alstone doing exactly that. His frown softened into a silly grin as he considered the extraordinary outcome of his latest attempt at losing himself in a brandy bottle.

'When I found you drunk and disorderly in the gutter all those years ago, you hadn't shared too much with my sister,' Christopher Alstone warned him austerely. 'You'll fight your demons this time, Hugh Kenton, or you'll fight me.'

'How did you know?' Hugh asked unwarily, his thoughts on the extraordinary intimacy he'd shared with the so-called Ice Diamond, which proved what a pack of witless fools the beaux who misnamed her so in their cups truly were.

'Don't be ridiculous; even if it wasn't written all over your faces when I arrived, I recognised you two were lovers the instant I saw you alone together. Why else do you think I sent the *Kindly Maid* on her way in such a hurry, before the crew got the slightest drift of what the two of you had been doing while my back was turned?'

What could he say to the man who took him in and gave him work when the rest of the world turned their backs? God, but Kit Alstone must be regretting his kindness now, and how could he blame him?

'I'm sorry, Alstone, there's no excuse for what I did. It was the act of a villain and a braggart and all they say of me under both my names I have just proved all too true. I can't seem to keep my hands off your sister and the devil's driven me from the instant I laid eyes on her, and I'll confess to you that I've dreamt about her night after night, like some mawkish youth, until I tried to drown the very thought of her in brandy and still failed. She only made it worse by materialising out of the night when I was several sheets to the wind, looking like a pirate queen and the embodiment of every idiotic fantasy I ever had about her. I've no excuse for how I behaved, not even when the very sight of her makes me forget every last scrap of honour and integrity I thought I still had.'

'When *did* you first lay eyes on her?' Kit asked, suspicion sharp in his dark eyes once more, and Hugh could hardly blame him, since he'd made it sound as if they'd been carrying on a clandestine affair for weeks while his back was turned.

If anyone laid his greedy hands on his sister, he'd take him apart with his bare hands. So why was Kit Alstone watching him so keenly, instead of slamming his fists into his face and making him regret the day he was born? He'd not be able to offer any resistance when his employer had every right to beat him to a bloody pulp for taking his sister's maidenhead, then threatening to walk away and leave her to deal with any consequences of their heated, hasty coupling alone.

'When I docked three weeks ago. I found Miss Alstone alone in your office, glaring at me with those extraordinary indigo eyes of hers and looking like every unattainable fantasy I ever dreamt after too long at sea, and she was quite evidently there to see you and not me.'

'And she encouraged you to think she was my lightskirt, I dare say?'

'How could you know that?' Hugh was surprised into asking before he realised he'd just confirmed Kit's suspicions about his wayward sister, when he'd been doing his shabby best to protect her from the worst of her brother's wrath as well.

'She's my sister, don't forget. Louisa has been a delight and a challenge to the rest of us from the day she was born and has more steely determination in her little finger than you'd find in half a legion of proper young ladies in pursuit of a peer's coronet. My sister hates to be thwarted, nearly as much as she dislikes being left out of any mad adventure that's brewing. It's only because I know what devious schemes and tall tales she's capable of thinking up that I'm not dismembering you slowly and painfully at this very moment.'

'That's something for me to be grateful for then,' Hugh said solemnly.

'Did you still think she was this mysterious Eloise when you...?' Kit's voice trailed off and Hugh saw a tinge of hot colour on his cheeks that matched the one he could feel burning across his own at the very thought of what they were discussing. For a moment he was tempted to lie and say yes, but he owed Louisa more honesty.

'No, I'd smoked her out shortly before that.'

'Then why the hell did you do it, man? You knew very well she was not only a lady, but my little sister by then, so even if she somehow misled you about her virginity, which is the kind of ridiculous lie I wouldn't put past her if it suited her, you must have known I'd flay you alive, then use your worthless hide for a waistcoat if you didn't marry her very soon after being fool enough to take her at her word.'

'I couldn't *not* touch her,' Hugh finally admitted in a rush of baffled emotion, as if the very words had been racked out of him along with the inexplicable feelings behind them. 'I can't keep my hands off her, or my mouth or… No, you don't want to know. I admit that I lose control of my senses and my mind and my very self when I'm alone in the dark with your sister and let's leave it at that, shall we?'

'Yes, let's,' Kit said with suspicious geniality. 'Which will give us so much more time for planning your wedding, don't you think?'

'I'm a nothing, who can't even use the name I was born with. Do you really think your sister would be better off wed to a potential murderer than bearing a bastard alone, Alstone? I'm not sure I do, especially when I could be taken up for murder and hung if Dickon and the villagers recant their story, or someone manages to cast enough doubt on it in order to justify a trial. Better if Louisa went off somewhere anonymous to have my child in secret, if there is one, then later adopt it as some obscure little orphan cousin, rather than marry a dangerous brute like me.'

'When are you going to explain all this self-pitying drivel to her then, Hugo? Just so I can quit the scene and leave you to take the furious edge of her tongue because, by God, you'll richly deserve it. I don't say it's what I wanted for her; I won't even lie and tell you the idea that you might prove the ideal man for my feisty little sister had ever occurred to me before you made it a *fait accompli*, but now your marriage is imperative, at least I'm more hopeful about it than either of you seem to be.'

'She deserves a better husband.'

'True, so make yourself better, unless you want to be slowly dismembered after all?'

'If only it were as easy as merely wanting to deserve her,'

Hugo said, sadly shaking his head over how very far from the ideal husband he would always be.

'It could be simple enough, if you'd only get on and fight for your reputation and the life you should have led these past three years, rather than lying down for everyone to trample over as if that's all you deserve.'

'And that's supposed to be easy?'

'When you consider the alternative of telling my sister you're not going to marry her, even though you might have got her with child, I think you'll find that it is. You are innocent of murdering your wife and brother, Hugo, but clearly you lack the courage to prove it—so what exactly do you expect Louisa to say when you explain to her why you can't marry her after all?'

'Put like that, the whole business appears much simpler,' Hugh admitted.

'Because you fear the rough side of Louisa's tongue?' Kit asked coolly.

'No, because I hate the way she squares up to take the next blow on her stubborn chin without letting anyone see how much it hurts her. I don't know why you thrust her into society when she clearly didn't want to be there, Alstone, but the *ton* doesn't seem to have done her any more good than it ever did me.'

Somehow Hugh sensed that he'd said something right, purely by accident, and some of the tension left his friend's lean frame and the atmosphere in this now-stuffy room seemed a little easier all of a sudden. Perhaps he could make a success of himself after all, or at least enough of a success to give Louisa the sort of life she richly deserved, if not the husband he would have wished for such a fiery, loyal, misjudged lady as his Eloise had proved herself to be.

'That's because neither of you ever learnt how to handle them, Kenton,' his future brother-in-law was telling him and it behoved Hugh to listen if he really wanted that unlikely future with an equally unlikely bride. 'My sister is far too proud to admit she needs anyone's approval, let alone that of a pack of finicky strangers inclined to look down their long noses at Bevis Alstone's brood, and it strikes me you're not a sight different to her. I know you were lionised as a hero even before Trafalgar and your captaincy came along to make you even more bigheaded, so falling from such dizzy heights was harder for you than a man like me who never had much grace to lose in the first place. Now you're so wrapped up in living down to your dark and desperate reputation that you can't see there are good people among the *ton*. I'd probably include you in those honourable exceptions, by the way, if you hadn't sunk to being one of my ship's masters through your own inaction.'

'What a spineless fellow I am, to be sure.'

'No, but you probably need to prove to yourself and my sister that you're not, if you're ever going to be happy together. I trust you do intend making Louisa happy, by the way?'

The question was suddenly sharp and Hugh reminded himself exactly who he was dealing with and how ruthless Christopher Alstone could be, as he considered that question as soberly and honestly as he had it in him to manage at the moment.

'I would be honoured to wed your sister, if I thought she wouldn't suffer by such a close association with me,' Hugh admitted cautiously, not willing to look deeper into his feelings whilst it seemed such an unlikely outcome.

'Good, I'll let you live until morning so you can ask her

properly then,' Kit said casually and held open the parlour door so that Hugh had no choice but to take the candle thrust at him and go up to bed as well.

Chapter Ten

Louisa awoke the following morning in the bedchamber that was fast becoming familiar and wondered what Mrs Calhoun would have to say about that state of affairs, once she arrived back at her post to find Louisa living in such close proximity with dissolute Captain Darke. Not quite sure what to make of it herself, she climbed out of bed and found a can of cooling hot water on the washstand she only hoped her brother had brought in, instead of the man she must learn to think of as Hugo Kenton. Somehow the idea of Hugh seeing her asleep and unguarded made her shiver and she told herself it was because she wasn't yet so committed to the man she wanted him to know how she looked first thing in the morning, either asleep or barely awake.

The Kenton baronetcy went back a good deal further into history than the Alstone family earldom and, since she recalled hearing that the current baronet only had two sons to his name to begin with, Hugo Kenton would be a baronet one day, whether he liked it or not. Or he would if he was cleared of suspicion for his wife's and brother's murders, since no murderer could gain from his crime. She didn't feel like the future wife of a potential baronet. She didn't feel much like daring, mysterious Captain Hugh Darke's bold and brassy lady either.

Except for the odd twinge of soreness at her most intimate core, she didn't feel much different from the Louisa Alstone who'd risen from this very bed only yesterday morning. Yet she knew deep down that she was drastically different all the same and not just physically either. As she washed and dressed in garments much more suited to a young lady than Charlton's silly dressing-up clothes or the cast-offs she'd bought yesterday, she considered that difference distractedly. What if she was in the process of becoming a mother at this very moment? Could the tiny seed of a new human being, hers and Hugh's child, be growing in her belly right now?

She rubbed a wondering hand over her flat stomach and felt awed by the very idea of taking responsibility for something so much greater than herself. The idea of a tiny being, partly from her and partly from its potent father, was too much to even think about when it might only be alive in her imagination. Yet the possible product of that hasty, driven coupling between her and Hugh Kenton might dictate her future—all their futures. Odd that love and consideration for a being that might not even exist should drive two such unlikely people into marriage. But what if there really was to be a child and she refused it a father as strong and brooding and torn by ridiculous self-doubts as her impossible, piratical lover?

Pushing all such possibilities and questions aside for consideration later, she wound her hair into a simple knot on the back of her head, decided she was as neat as she'd ever be without the help of a maid and went downstairs to find out if she had to cook breakfast again this morning.

Apparently she was to be spared the task as Mrs Calhoun

had miraculously reappeared, obviously from somewhere much closer than Maria and Brandon's rectory, and was directing operations with a long ladle in her hand, as if she fully expected to conjure something remarkable at any moment.

'You two can go and sit in the breakfast parlour and wait for Miss Louisa to join you like a pair of civilised gentlemen for once,' she scolded as Hugh repeated his trick of the morning before and stole a piece of crisp bacon from the dish she was preparing for what looked like a formal banquet rather than a simple breakfast.

Louisa felt a clench of something dangerous squeeze her heart at the intimacy of coming to know her lover in so many ways other than the obvious. A smile she sincerely hoped nobody saw curved her mouth while she wondered what it would be like to learn as many of his odd quirks and habits as he'd ever let anyone know as his wife. If he didn't feel any more for her than a passing lust and a guilty conscience at having seduced an over-eager virgin, then she was never likely to know more about him than she did right now. The very idea of that brutal separation from a man who was already beginning to mean too much to her killed her smile before she hardly felt it on her lips, ready to betray her.

'No need, Mrs Calhoun,' she said brightly enough as she stepped forwards, 'I'm already here, so why can't we all eat together as we did in the old days?'

'I know what's due to a lady, even if she doesn't seem to have the least idea herself,' Mrs Calhoun informed her sternly.

'And if we agree to take that old argument of yours as a given, dear Mrs Calhoun, why should we three sit apart from the rest of the household like a trio of bodkins? If you're intending to tell me Kit sits in lone state whenever he has no visitors to entertain, then you must have become a lot less truthful since last we met,' she told her mother's one-time cook-housekeeper with an affectionate smile.

'You're as bad as that one yonder,' Mrs Calhoun told her with another wave of that expressive ladle of hers towards Hugh, who did his best to look innocent and failed, as well he might.

'Oh, no, I challenge anyone to turn your kitchen into a midden quite as quickly as Captain Darke managed to do when you were gone,' Louisa said with a militant frown he pretended not to notice.

'There you are, Master Kit, I told you he was a heathen.'

'Did I argue with you?' her employer asked as if it was nothing to do with him what went on in his own household, so Louisa scowled at him as well.

'No, but only because you know I'm right. Just as I was right to take Midge away for a while as well, for all he'd not lay a finger on her, even when he's in his cups. I wasn't having a lot of nasty-minded gossip about my girl doin' the rounds, just because she's not as clever as she might be and his nibs is as handsome as the devil and almost as bad.'

'Why, thank you, ma'am,' Hugh said with a would-be modest smile. 'I thought you were immune to my charms, but you know very well that you will always have my heart,' he added with a soulful look and his hand theatrically over the place where it ought to be, if only he had one.

'My cooking has your heart you mean, you black-hearted rogue, you. Now get along to the breakfast parlour like I told you to and take Miss Louisa with you, for I've no time to put up with either of you under my feet this morning when Midge and I already have more than enough to do getting this place set to rights again.'

'I can help you,' Louisa offered.

'That you can't, young lady, and it strikes me as how you've got more important things to do than pretend to be a house-maid this morning,' the formidable dame told her ominously and Louisa wondered if her ex-virgin status was written across her forehead for all to see, then told herself it was just a guilty conscience that made her blush and do as she was bid.

'You are in deep disgrace with our domestic tyrant,' Hugh told her unhelpfully.

'Not as deep as you must have been when she first set eyes on the state you got her precious house in while she was gone. She must have wanted to skin you alive then, even after my efforts to improve matters a little.'

'It's not her house, but your brother's.'

'Believe that if you must,' she muttered as her brother followed them into the room and all chance for a satisfying private argument about nothing in particular was lost for the time being as they ate their meal in uneasy silence.

'A word with you both, if you please,' Kit said shortly, once Hugh had thrown down his napkin and Louisa gave up even pretending to eat more than a few bites of her breakfast.

Since she thought Hugh as intent on avoiding those words and drifting on with everything unresolved as she was, she categorised both him and herself cowards and strolled towards Kit's book-room without an argument. The disadvantages of having fallen among gentlemen occurred to her as they bowed her ahead of them and she could almost feel Hugh whatever-he-was-calling-himself-today eyeing the sway of her hips and wolfishly appreciating any glimpses of her slender legs afforded by her soft muslin skirts brushing against her body as she walked. She let herself marvel at such an unlikely fashion pertaining in modern Britain, when it was far more suited to somewhere much hotter and more leisurely, to distract herself from the thought that it felt powerful to know she held Hugh's attention so completely it was almost something she could reach out and touch.

'What is it now, Kit?' she asked impatiently when they reached his comfortable study and she lost the advantage.

'You two,' he said abruptly and she raised her eyebrows. 'You will stay in this room together until I have a decision one way or the other out of you about your marriage. Hugh—you will forget your late wife for a moment and consider what you and my sister can have instead and whether you truly want to live without it. Louisa—you will stand and listen to what he has to say like a grown woman and not a little savage just dragged in off the streets against her will, then you will answer him only after some of that mature consideration you keep telling me you're capable of, at least if you wish me to ever take a single word you say seriously ever again.'

'Oh, I will, will I?' she flamed, but it was wasted because he hadn't waited for an argument and shut the door on them with a decided snap instead.

She strode over to the window and plumped down on the seat cushions to stare moodily out over the small garden beyond and waited to hear what Hugh had to say with a sinking heart.

'He's right, you know,' Hugh told her moodily.

'I know,' she said with a sigh, 'but don't expect me to like him very much for it just at the moment.'

'Which will make a change from disliking me, I suppose.'

'I don't dislike you.'

'That's a start, then, so perhaps we can proceed to the business in hand without the accompaniment of raised voices or fisticuffs?'

'No, I don't wish to be an item on a business agenda.'

He sighed. She remembered Kit ordering her to be reasonable and sighed herself, before meeting his unreadable gaze as serenely as she could make herself. Not her best move so far, since she only had to look into his eyes for the intimacy of last night's dark loving to ambush her with all sorts of possible futures. Having little experience of deep emotion between a man and a woman, she couldn't tell if it was only lust that burned under the acute intelligence in Hugh Darke's silvered gaze.

'No, I don't suppose you do,' he conceded, 'but we must decide what to do anyway.'

'At this exact minute?' she asked, not sure why she wanted to procrastinate when the very thought of him ever marrying anyone else was unendurable.

'Yes, and a great deal hinges on your reply to my proposal, Louisa.'

'Hugh Darke for one,' she said, feeling oddly cast down by the idea of losing a man who never was. 'If I don't agree to marry you, then he will have to disappear, will he not?'

'His days are numbered, whatever you decide,' Hugh said, with a rather bitter twist to his supposedly careless smile at the idea of losing his alter-ego.

'Because of your association with me?'

'No, because of the choices I must make, Eloise or no.'

'Please don't try and comfort me with clever words, Captain. If not for what happened last night, you would be able to sail under Kit's colours for as long as you chose to do so, would you not?'

'Maybe I would, but how honest would that have been of me, I wonder?'

'Oddly enough, honesty and honour don't figure high on

my list of priorities, Captain. I'd choose survival and as small a lie as necessary over them any day.'

'Witness your blatant inability to walk away from a friend in trouble, or not lay down everything you are for any stranger who happened to be in trouble? Don't make yourself out to be someone you're not to me, Louisa. At least grant us that much honesty with each other, even if there's to be nothing more.'

She paused and watched him cautiously, alert for any hint of mockery or doubt in his suddenly very austere countenance; she could see nothing but sincerity there, so she let herself ask the question at the heart of all this.

'We really shouldn't marry though, should we, Hugh?' she said very softly at last. 'Not people like us,' she added with real regret.

'People like me, you mean? What have you ever done wrong, Louisa?'

'I've always been difficult and intransigent and I don't suffer fools gladly or fake laughter when I only feel boredom, and that's just to start with,' she confessed.

'Sounds like heaven to me,' he quipped and suddenly she felt a deep shaft of pain open up at the idea that their marriage could indeed have been wonderful.

'No, because if you were to marry me, it would make re-establishing yourself in society twice as hard as it would be with a better wife,' she warned.

'Now you're being ridiculous, and mawkish with it,' he condemned roughly, as if he truly believed it.

'Then I'm astonished you want to marry me, but I was forgetting, wasn't I? You really don't want to marry me at all. We got carried away by propinquity and now you feel honour bound to wed me, despite the fact that I deliberately misled you about my virgin status.'

'I might have restrained myself a little more if I'd known,' he told her in that dark-velvet voice that sent hot shivers racing down her spine like little splurges of lightning, 'but not to the extent of letting you find an excuse to leave me, not once I knew this damnable wanting was mutual.'

'Does it have to be damnable?' she whispered, achingly aware that this incessant need of each other felt very far from it to her.

'What do you think?' he murmured back as they stared into each other's eyes as if their very lives depended on reading the right answer to that question.

'I have to hope that it doesn't,' she managed, refusing to drop her eyelids and shelter her thoughts and dreams from his gaze. 'It doesn't have to be paradise, I won't beg for love or even offer it until I know if that's what I feel for you, but it can be more than hellish between us, don't you think, Hugh? It's certainly more than I ever imagined feeling for any man already.'

'Oh, you sweet idiot,' he said with a twisted smile she could feel as much as see from such close quarters.

'Because I have hopes?' she asked, rather hurt that she'd come so far from her resolution never to marry to meet him with those hopes for something more, only to have them thrown back in her face.

'Because of who I am,' he said starkly, pain in his eyes now and such sharp distaste for himself in his deep voice that it somehow made her want to cry.

She blinked very hard, knowing he would see it as pity when it was a far more complex emotion than sympathy for a wronged man. 'It's only because of who you are that I'm even considering marrying you, Hugo Kenton,' she said, putting enough distance between them to look him fully in the face while she admitted it.

'When who I am should send you screaming to your brother for any alternative he can come up with to save your good name?' he replied, as if he'd like to be cold and almost amused enough to put her off him, but somehow couldn't quite bring the lie on to his tongue or into his eyes.

'No, because who you are is an honourable man who cares about others and would die protecting someone he loves if he had to. If I am ever to be a mother, and it's a great surprise for me to find out how very much I want that status after all now you've put the idea in my head, then I want that man as father of my children, Hugh,' she countered as strongly as she could.

She stood back and saw him battle between hope and dread and opened her eyes a little wider to stem the heat of tears that really threatened this time and would probably ruin everything. No doubt he'd seen enough tears to flood the Nile from his unfaithful wife and she refused to use such a weapon to win even the shallowest argument between them, because of that wretched woman's counterfeit sorrow and an innate sense of fair play.

For the same reason, she told herself, she kept a tender smile off her mouth by biting her lips, because no doubt he'd seen enough of those to distrust even the gentlest of curves on a female mouth. At this rate she would end up pretending to be emotionless and suddenly she knew that fighting not to be like Ariadne Kenton would ruin their marriage, if they made one, as surely as floods of tears and a constant parade of lovers. If Hugh married her, he would get Louisa Alstone: stubborn, difficult and as disobliging as the *ton* and almost everyone else seemed to find her. Giving a sharp nod to confirm her determination never to lie about her emotions, either way, she met his eyes with a challenge in her own.

'We began this argument last night, while you still had the scorch of how we were together biting at your conscience. Now we are arguing backwards and I'm sick of it, Mr Kenton. So, do you want to marry me or don't you?'

'If I were any other man but the one I am, then, yes, I do.'

She clicked her tongue with impatience at such a leaden declaration. 'Doesn't sound like it to me,' she informed him shortly.

'Then will you marry me, Miss Louisa Alstone?'

'What about all your ifs and buts, Captain?'

'To the devil with them, as long as you know I may never be exonerated from the scandal hanging over me and can accept it?'

'I can,' she said, knowing he had the might of Kit and Ben's stubborn wills behind his case as well as her own whether he liked it or not now, and that, whether they ended up married or not, that backing would continue.

'Then will you wed me, woman?'

'Yes,' she agreed on a sigh even she didn't understand.

'Good, then perhaps we should inform your brother of our decision, so it may be got on with as soon as possible,' he agreed and she felt as if she was back to being that item on his agenda of things to do today.

'Perhaps we should,' she agreed rather listlessly.

'I promise not to be a drunkard with you, Louisa,' he said stiffly, when she'd thought the topic of their marriage closed off and done with for now.

'I asked you for no promises,' she replied as her memory dragged up all the abject ones her father had made her mother, then broken as easily as if they'd never been spoken as soon as he went out of the front door.

'Forget your father. I will never take more than three glasses of anything in any one day again, for my own sake if you don't want it to be for yours, Eloise. It's high time I stopped hiding in a brandy bottle; it had got vastly tedious, even when I wasn't getting myself into trouble with outrageously behaved female pirates.'

'Rake,' she accused obligingly.

'Not any more,' he argued with a would-be saintly smile.

'Eloise would be highly disappointed to hear that,' she murmured in a throaty purr as she brushed against him with a provocative, stray-cat rub that she hoped left him as instantly aroused as she was herself.

'Then perhaps we could make an exception for Mademoiselle La Rochelle?'

'And Captain Darke?'

'He can play, too, if you think we can find room enough in our marriage bed for both the rogues.'

'Somehow we'll find it, Captain,' she assured him with a mock-innocent smile and felt reassured by the wicked glint in his eyes at that intriguing idea.

'Are you intending to be happy then, little sister?' Kit asked when they eventually ran him down in the stables, checking on his restless team as well as the swift riding horses he kept for both necessity and pleasure.

'Yes, we think so, don't we, Hugh?' Louisa smiled, turning to look into silver-shot blue eyes.

'I'm going to be, so I dare say your brother and his best friend will take it in turns to beat me to a pulp if I fail to make you so too, my lovely,' he said and she was so glad he didn't quite call her 'love' that she smiled and did her best to look as dazzled and sweetly happy as any newly made fiancée.

'St Margaret's in three days,' Kit told them implacably and that was that.

Chapter Eleven

'So besides arranging my wedding for me, what else have you been about?' Hugh asked his employer as soon as Louisa had been dragged off to discuss wedding finery by a surprisingly enthusiastic Mrs Calhoun and he'd run Kit to earth in his book-room.

'Business,' Kit said uninformatively.

'Personal business?'

'Very,' Kit told him with a bland look that would put most men at a distance.

'So whose personal business have you been engaged on?' Hugh persisted.

'Yours, since you're about to become part of my family.'

'Damn it, Kit, don't you think I can deal with it myself then?' Hugh said, knowing very well what business it was and how he wished the whole dirty affair was dead and done with, along with his old life.

'You have had three years to do so and now it's become urgent.'

'Why? By some miracle your sister believes me innocent, you and Ben would never have given me one of your precious ships if you thought I was going to murder the first man who crossed me, so why the sudden haste?'

'Because your father is dying,' Kit told him sombrely and Hugh had to turn away and pace over to the window to stare bleakly out and hide his feelings.

'I wouldn't have thought I'd care after he ordered me to go to the devil alone, but oddly enough I seem to all the same.'

'We all have that conundrum to deal with, my friend,' Kit said gently.

Hugh turned to meet his steady gaze, recalling what Louisa had told him of her father's death. 'I was luckier than you. He was a good parent to all three of us, once upon a time.'

'Yet at least I knew what to expect of my sire.'

'Nothing?'

'Precisely, but we digress, Hugh. My demons are for me to fight, as and when I choose to do so; yours won't wait any longer.'

'The lawyers will certainly scratch their heads over the succession, given the estrangement that had existed between us for so long, but surely nothing has changed? I still didn't murder my wife, or my brother, and nobody can prove that I did, any more than I can shake off these rumours that I'm guilty.'

'It might stir them up and make the magistrates take notice, whether they want to or not. There are whispers about calling in the Runners to ask you and your friend the innkeeper sharper questions than you faced at the time.'

'Who puts them about, Kit? Who the devil is doing this? My second cousin, Arthur Kenton, is the only other heir and he's eighty if he's a day. Unless he's wed his housekeeper in the last three years and produced a legitimate brat in his old age, he can't have any real interest in the Gracemont estate or the title.'

'No, he's perfectly happy for you to succeed, so long as you don't wed another empty-headed demi-rep.'

Hugh gave a gruff bark of surprised laughter as he could imagine old Arthur saying those very words. 'You've seen him, then?'

'Him and most of your other living relatives,' Kit admitted and when Hugh considered his mother had been the youngest daughter of a family of eight, it suddenly seemed no wonder his employer had been away for so long. 'Including your father, of course—you will find him very much changed, I suspect.'

'I might, if I had the slightest intention of going anywhere near Gracemont Priory while he's still inhabiting it. He ordered me never to "befoul any of my roofs with your presence while I still have breath in my body" the last time I saw him and I fully intend to obey him, in that if in nothing else.'

'I never met a man more sorry for what he did in the heat of his grief for your brother, if that's any consolation to you?' Kit said.

Hugh stared bleakly back at him as he struggled with the full horror of the moment when his father had made it clear he thought his younger son guilty of murdering his elder one, even if the rest of the world had been forced to absolve him and must now rely on rumours to damn him with.

'Maybe I didn't do it, Kit, but I still married Ariadne Lockstone and brought her into his house, so that her latest lover could strangle her, then shoot my brother in the back one dark night.'

'And you did that deliberately, did you? Wed a gently-bred

whore, just so you could destroy your brother and your father's peace into the bargain?'

'No, of course not. I wed her because I was a big-headed, besotted fool who thought he'd captured the sweet-natured little beauty all the other men in the *ton* wanted. I had no idea half the rakes on the town had already been in her bed and the other half would very shortly follow in their footsteps. No wonder she latched on to the only fool with money and a convenient career overseas who was still fool enough to beg her to marry him.'

'Not your father's fault either, Hugh. Maybe he should have thrown her out of his house when he found out the woman took lovers like most women change their clothing, but perhaps he'd decided to wait until you applied for a legal separation through the proper channels.'

'He was the one who forbade me to do so. That would have been far too public an admission of failure and Marcus would provide him with legitimate heirs, so any by-blows my wife chose to inflict on the family must be tolerated rather than leave his precious name tarnished by such a scandal,' Hugh said bitterly.

'You can never know if he would have decided to endure that humiliation or not now, for all he was wrong to try to dictate your life. All he cares about now is having you home again, if only so you can care for your sister and the people on his estates when he quits this world.'

'That sounds like him, too. You've been very busy on my behalf.'

'He sent for me,' his friend explained dispassionately.

'He sent for you? No word to his own son, but he must send for my friend and employer? Was it to tell you what an unsatisfactory heir he has to put up with and how heavily it presses on his soul and his conscience to leave all he's ever cared for in such unworthy hands?'

'No, he spoke to me of his bitter regret at being so lost in grief and shame that he pushed you away and let you think he believed you guilty of a crime it just isn't in your nature to commit.'

'That would be because he did believe it—my father told me to get out of his house and never come back, my friend. Don't make me doubt my ears and eyes as well as everything else. To hell with him and Gracemont—if it tumbles down tomorrow I won't give a tinker's damn,' Hugh lied.

'Soon it will be yours; you can demolish it if you hate it so much.'

'To hell with that! I'll not see my sister homeless and our people left to starve,' Hugh raged in a fine passion, until he realised what he'd just said and plumped down in one of the comfortable armchairs by the fireplace and glared at the makings of a fire laid there as if it held all the answers he wished he had.

'Here, drink this,' Kit demanded, setting a glass of fine brandy at his elbow, then ghosting out of the room.

'Hugh?' Louisa asked softly as she met his frowning eyes with puzzlement in her own, so at least Kit hadn't told him what an idiot he was before sending her to soothe his savage brow, now his so-called friend had forced him to face his true feelings for his old home and the inheritance it sounded as if he'd be receiving all too soon.

'A promise no sooner given than broken,' he told her bitterly, raising the brandy glass at her in a mock toast before downing the contents in one swallow.

'Only if you intend to consume the rest of Kit's decanter as well, and I told you I didn't want that promise.'

'Nor any of the other ones I have to give,' he said gloomily.

'No, I want them, Hugh, but first it would be good if you could learn to mean them before you make them.'

'Why not?' he said recklessly. 'No doubt I'll argue black's white soon after, as your confounded brother tricked me into doing before he sent you to calm the beast.'

'He's my confounded brother and it's my privilege to mis-name him, not yours. Anyway, Kit can only manipulate you into saying whatever it was you didn't want to say if you allow him to. You should know by now how sly and slippery he can be when he's intent on doing good to those who don't want to be done good to,' she said unsympathetically.

'How can I agree with the second part of that without breaching your prohibition from the first?' he asked with a fleeting smile that acknowledged how difficult and stubborn he was probably being. 'My father is dying, Louisa,' he told her in a rush, saw pity in her deep-cobalt gaze and rose impatiently to his feet so he could pace restlessly and not meet them again until it had gone.

'Ah, Hugh?' she asked softly, as if she wanted to find a way of comforting him, but didn't know how, and something seemed to break inside him as he fought back what he considered unmanly tears at the loss of a man who'd once looked him coldly in the eyes and sworn his second son was as dead to him as his first.

'He ordered me out of his house, told me he was ashamed to own me as his son and ordered me never to try to contact him or my little sister again, and now he's dying, Louisa.'

'And you love him, despite all he's said and done?'

'Yes,' he managed between gritted teeth as he strode up

and down Kit's fine Turkey carpet, fighting the full effects of that admission with the only action available to him.

'Which makes you a better man than he ever was,' she said gently, halting his restless pacing by simply standing in his path.

'I don't think it's a competition,' he said on a shaken laugh and walked straight into her arms and felt them close about him as if it was exactly where he'd needed to be since the moment Kit told him Sir Horace Kenton had finally hit an obstacle he couldn't wilfully ignore or order out of his way.

'It's not, of course, but did you and your brother never have a friendly one between you? I know that we all did for our mother's approval,' she said gently and he smiled, grateful for the reminder of how much he and his brother and sister had loved each another, once upon a time.

'Now you mention it, I believe we did. It was scattered to the four winds as soon as I entered the Navy, of course. Hard to keep up a rivalry about who had the most sugar plums and the least number of stern lectures on our heathen ways with a few thousand leagues of ocean parting us.'

'And you loved him dearly as well, didn't you?'

'Yes, but I could still have harmed him, Louisa. You know all too well how savagely a drunkard can lash out in his cups and I was very drunk the night my wife and brother died, and remembered very little about it the next morning.'

'From my experience you're not a violent drunk, Hugh,' she said softly, raising a hand to gently frame the side of his face. 'A man's true character comes out when he's in his cups and you were certainly in yours the night I encountered Captain Darke for the second time.'

Merely feeling her slender fingers against his skin sent a shiver of awareness through him and reminded him exactly how he'd felt when she appeared out of the night. 'You were lucky I didn't fall on you like a savage right there and then, given the ridiculous state I was in about you. I'd dreamt about you every night, cursed you every day when I woke up rampant and unsatisfied and wanting you like some sort of satyr. I'd only got myself so inebriated in the first place in order to forget you for an hour or two, and there you were, standing there like the answer to my wildest fantasies and making me forget I was at least raised a gentleman.'

'Did you really dream about me?' she asked, as if the idea trumped everything else and was almost wonderful to her.

He groaned and managed a rueful smile even as he put some very necessary distance between them to keep himself from showing her exactly what he'd dreamt about her all over again. 'You really don't have any idea how enchanting you actually are to the opposite sex, do you, Miss Alstone? Which is almost unbelievable, given that you've been the toast of St James's since you made your début in society.'

'Oh, I don't give a fig for all that,' she said dismissively, as if she didn't even like to be reminded of it, and Hugh decided he'd never met a woman with less natural vanity. 'All it takes to please those gentlemen is for a female to have a moderate fortune and all the usual appendages in the right place, plus a set of features that might look well on their daughters, should the lady breed such inconvenient creatures in the quest for an heir. It's all about bloodstock and very little to do with hopes and dreams, Hugh.'

'True, but what about those hopes and dreams, Louisa?' he said seriously; his appalling lack of self-control meant she had little choice but to marry him now, and he should at least have known about them before he spoilt them.

'I didn't know I had any until yesterday,' she said.

Fighting the feeling that it would be both wondrous and awesome to be the source and solution of Louisa Alstone's dreams, he raised an eyebrow in a silent question he couldn't bring himself to ask out loud.

'Then I found out that I wanted your fire and passion and consideration as well as your strength and integrity, Hugh, and that I'd been fooling myself all those years in thinking that I couldn't make a family with a man who could offer me all that.'

'Along with a name almost as black as Lucifer's to go with it?' he made himself ask bleakly.

'If the world is stupid enough to give you one, then, yes,' she assured him steadily, meeting his eyes as if she believed in his innocence absolutely. It was heady and flattering and he fought down an unworthy sense of triumph that this astonishing, brave and truly beautiful woman believed in him, despite all the horror and spite talked about him.

'The world has a way of intruding on life, Louisa, and I'm a guilty man in the eyes of most of it,' he warned.

'Then we'll have to make them see you as you really are.'

'Don't work me up me into some sort of damaged hero, Louisa. I'm not the stuff martyrs are made of, or heroes for that matter.'

'Of course you're not, but nor are you capable of murdering your wife or your brother, and I don't care what the rest of the world says. I don't even care if you doubt yourself, Hugh, because I know you didn't do it.'

'I was so furious, so hurt and ashamed that I couldn't satisfy my own wife, Louisa,' he whispered at last. 'Ariadne needed men, not just one man; she had to have their attention as much as food and water and air to breathe. I hated what she made herself, hated what she'd done to me, but most of all I hated the way my brother watched her with contempt and a hint of lust while she preened and flirted with them all. After months at sea, brooding over the idea that my brother might be tupping my wife in my absence, I was already half-mad with jealousy and grief even before I got home and my father accused me of being a cruel husband, who drove his innocent wife into the arms of other men with his harsh temper and unnatural coldness.'

'More fool him, then,' she told him with a rather wicked smile that said he was certainly not cold or harsh with her. 'And, as you were proven to be laid out insensible a few miles away at the time of their deaths, how can you be so stupid and arrogant as to believe you hurt them in the face of the evidence? You would sooner have shot yourself in the back than your brother, whatever disgraceful state you were in at the time,' she told him as he gave up on distance and held her more tightly than he probably realised.

Louisa felt him struggle with his emotions and wished he'd just let go of them and trust her. Some instinct told her that he was too damaged by what had happened that awful night and afterwards, to fully confide in a woman he was marrying only because the world would consider he'd ruined her if he didn't. This was no time to worry about her own abraded emotions, though; he needed comfort and she needed to offer it to him.

'I couldn't fight my father's accusations,' he admitted tersely. 'The idea I could have killed Marcus while out of my senses on brandy and fury seemed to blast my very soul black and deprive me of speech. My wife didn't love me, but that was nothing compared to remembering how jealous I'd been of her and my own brother. I let her infidelities make me a drunken fool lost in a brandy bottle and if only I'd been stronger, Louisa, if only I had bothered to insist on a legal separation, both of them would probably still be alive today. I couldn't admit so finally that I'd failed my wife and my family and look what happened to them because I was a coward.'

'She was the one who failed, you stubborn idiot of a man. If Kit and I have to catch the murderer behind your brother's death to make you realise none of it is your fault, then we'll do it just to prove ourselves right, you know? It's a family failing.'

'I have noticed,' he admitted with a faint smile.

Louisa hated the venal coward who'd let this good man suffer for his own crimes, but she had to be infuriated with him as well, in case she broke down and cried for him instead. 'You think you should have guarded your wife and brother from harm instead of getting drunk, don't you? You're not omnipotent, Captain Kenton, and I wouldn't want you for my husband if you were,' she told him sternly.

She felt him chuckle against her skin and some of the terrible tension seep out of his powerful body, felt the breath in her lungs freeze, then gasp out as the feel of him breathing so close to her made her knees weaken. He seemed to note the intimacy at the same moment and pressed a heated kiss to the accelerated pulse in the hollow at the base of her throat. Fire shot through her in a white-hot flash and she felt him harden in instant response. How totally he wanted her, she thought wonderingly, then he groaned and drew in a deep breath, before exerting his iron will over his need and hers, so he could hold her at arm's length and eye her reproachfully, as if she was Eloise again, a blatant seductress who was wilfully over-eager to be ravished by his passionate attentions.

'I can and will keep my hands off you for two more days, Louisa Alstone,' he informed her sternly, as if she was the one who'd recklessly turned comfort into passion and not him. 'It might nigh kill me, but I swear I'll do it,' he told her and met the challenge in her eyes with a laugh in his own. 'At least I will if you'll only help me by resisting this fever between us, rather than conspiring with my dratted body to make me a liar.'

'If we are really going to marry, then we share it all, Hugh,' she said seriously.

'We certainly share that,' he responded, his eyes not quite meeting hers.

'Not just the nights, but the days as well,' she informed him calmly, although her accelerated heartbeat told her how important it was that he understand her, even when he didn't want to.

'Are you planning to shadow my every move in future, then? It will certainly make for an unusual marriage; if not necessarily one I like the sound of.'

'I plan to share your problems, as you will mine,' she made herself say calmly, knowing he was trying to use her temper against her.

'You'll probably cause most of them.'

'Don't push me away, Hugh,' she pleaded, although pride urged her to do exactly what he wanted and walk away from him and their marriage even now.

'I have to try, don't you see? A murderer's possessions are forfeit, woman.'

'But you're not a murderer, Hugh.'

'If that fragile alibi fails, then I'll be tried as one and, guilty or not, I'll probably hang as one.'

Chapter Twelve

Louisa shrugged, trying not to let Hugh see that the very idea of losing him made her feel as if she was suddenly made of ice after all, and might shatter into a million icicles if he so much as breathed on her the wrong way.

'Would you have me walk away from you, then?' she asked painfully.

'Yes,' he said, face set like a stone mask as his eyes didn't quite meet hers again and she knew he was lying.

A small splinter of warmth thawed the absolute chill afflicting her and threatened to thaw her into a supplicant, begging for something she didn't quite understand wanting in the first place. Whatever it was, she couldn't let it slip away.

'Liar,' she whispered softly.

His eyes turned from hers completely as he glared across the room as if he wanted to go back to his pacing in peace and fool them both he was better left to deal with this alone. Suddenly his strong mouth twisted as if in agony and his silver-shot blue eyes were full on hers as he stopped shielding himself from her at last.

'Guilty,' he ground out. 'I'm a liar and a thief. I fly under false colours and take what they value most from those I love. Pray not to love me; fight not to marry me, Louisa Alstone. Go to the ends of the earth to avoid me, but for God's sake don't let me destroy you as everyone else in my life has been destroyed.'

'Do I look like some silly little martyr looking for a cause, Hugh Kenton?' she demanded furiously. 'No, I damned well don't and if I'd grown up sighing over heroes in storybooks, or longing to be rescued by the knight out of a fairy tale it might be fair enough of you to try to warn me off like this. If you don't realise how well I know my own mind by now, then perhaps time will teach you better, but I won't walk away from you that easily. I refuse to deprive our child of a father who'd fight the devil himself for its safety and well-being, even if you can't seem to stomach the idea of me as its mother.'

'It's certainly not that, but there may not be a child,' he said as if driven to point out all the drawbacks of becoming his wife to her once again.

'And if there is, I'm certainly not running after you in a few months' time when it's obvious I'm your discarded lover. It's now or never if you intend to wed me.'

'Do you think I don't want to marry you, woman?' he growled as if she was doing her best to torture him.

'All the signs seem to point that way.'

'Then they're wrong. I want you as I never wanted another woman in my life before, Louisa Alstone. I think about you when I should be busy with so many other things that I marvel Kit's empire didn't collapse in his absence for want of attention. I wake up in the morning wanting you and go to bed at night racked with longing for you in my bed and at my board.'

'You've only known me for two days.'

'Two minutes were enough for me, and it's all of three weeks since I first set eyes on you, you impossible, stubborn, naggy-tempered witch,' he told her with such disgust that she felt obscurely pleased he considered her so irresistible he'd longed for her since that day in Kit's office as well.

'Me, too,' she admitted.

'You too what?' he said, running an impatient hand through his already wildly disordered dark hair.

'I wanted you from the first moment I set eyes on you,' she told him boldly.

'Ah, Louisa, how the devil am I going to get through the next two days without going completely insane with needing you?' he asked as if he thought it a very real possibility.

'You don't have to,' she offered shamelessly, refusing to drop her eyes and pretend to be a shrinking maiden when she was neither.

'You don't know your brother as well as you think if you're not aware that he'll tear me apart if I lay a hand on you again before I wed you.'

'This isn't the only roof in London.'

'It is for the next two days—now stop tempting me, woman. I need to marshal my senses, not have them scattered to the four winds.'

'Well, if we're not allowed to do that, we might as well put our energies into catching your enemy while we still have them,' she said with a steady look she hoped told him she wasn't going to be sitting at home embroidering wedding garters for the next two days.

'I suppose there is no point in me forbidding you to set foot outside this house on anything less frivolous than a trip to the dressmaker?'

'Absolutely none,' she confirmed smugly.

'I don't think you were a neglected child at all, Louisa Alstone,' he accused her crossly. 'You were obviously so spoilt that none of your unfortunate family dared to cross you in any way. I'd have been beaten and locked in my room for a quarter of the exploits you seem to have got away with without so much as a blink from those who should have stopped you.'

'They'd have had to tie me to my bed, but never mind,' she consoled him unrepentantly. 'Think how useful it will be when we have children,' she said virtuously. 'Between your sins and mine, they'll never be able to hoodwink either of us that they're all sweetness and light, while behaving like little demons as soon as our backs are turned.'

'Alluring though the prospect might be, I think it's time to talk about something else,' he said huskily and Louisa had to believe he found the idea of those little dark-haired devils of theirs as seductive and downright wonderful as she did.

'Very well, then, it's probably high time we called Kit back in to pool our knowledge and considered what to do next.'

He groaned as if he didn't like that alternative much either, but tucked her hand within the crook of his elbow all the same and they went to find her brother.

'Stubborn, ungovernable woman,' he said as they strolled towards Kit's sitting room.

'Arrogant, intractable man,' she replied placidly.

'Still minded to wed each other, despite all the quarrelling, then?' Kit asked absently, as they invaded his privacy once again.

'Yes, planning to drive each other demented for the next fifty years or so,' Hugh said with such smugness that Louisa's heart warmed and her smile softened.

'On the understanding it would be a shame to inflict such glaring defects of character elsewhere when we can nag each other to death instead,' she countered with a challenging look for her brother and her husband-to-be.

'I can hardly wait for you to begin a lifetime of annoying each other and leave me in peace, then,' Kit said with a relieved and surprisingly boyish grin as he rang for the finest burgundy in his cellar to celebrate.

They drank a toast to their astonishing new future and sipped the fine vintage as the full significance of it all began to sink in. One day, probably all too soon, Louisa realised, she was going to be a lady after all—a real one, with a title she couldn't ignore if she tried. It was enough to make her have second thoughts, until she looked at Hugh and realised he needed someone brassy and unconventional and badly behaved to stand beside him.

None of the sweet little maids he must have grown up with would outstare and outmanoeuvre those intent on throwing Hugh's past sins and other dark deeds at his head. It occurred to her that if he'd been the heroic gentleman of breeding and repute he must once have been, she would probably have refused him, however compromised she might be. He was the only gentleman she could marry; out of all those deluded enough to ask her, he was the only one she could risk being her true self with, she realised, as she watched him stare into the subtle depths of the fine wine in his glass as if it might be able to tell him how all this came about.

'We have to get Lord Rarebridge alone,' she announced to distract him.

'We?' Kit said mildly enough.

'I'm as deep in this as either of you,' she said, knowing the only way to fight her brother's protective instincts was to remind him how little she needed protecting, then perhaps he could convince Hugh.

'I know you'll stick your nose in and ruin everything if we don't include you, little sister, but I won't admit this is any of your business even so,' Kit argued.

'If the end result is what I want, I don't much care, and his lordship will rush to help a lady in distress, whatever her reputation,' she said to think up an alternative scheme before they crept off without her to catch Lord Rarebridge at his club or some other harebrained scheme that would result in one of them being hurt.

'Dearest Uncle William and the insect-worm have been silent on that subject; they went to ground as soon as your escape was discovered and are no doubt cowering in fear of my fury,' Kit said so impassively Louisa knew they were right to be terrified.

'I believe husbands take precedence over brothers,' Hugh growled unhelpfully and Louisa was tempted to throw something at one of them or stamp her feet.

'So what about Lord Rarebridge?' she asked stonily.

'First the lord and then the lackeys,' Hugh drawled in quite the grand manner and she only just managed not to scream with frustration and count to ten, because she had got her way, hadn't she?

'You say the lady is injured?' Viscount Rarebridge asked the bewigged and liveried footman who had just rushed down the quiet path he'd taken to haunting in Hyde Park, whenever his father's town house seemed too full of his elder sister's enormous brood of children. Now this dratted manservant was bothering him instead, he wished he'd stayed home and endured the racket, but he reluctantly agreed to help the man assist a lady to a more populous area and summon help.

'She'll likely be dead by the time we gets there,' the fellow muttered with the sort of insolence he'd expect of a servant hired for the Season.

'And why should I believe there is a lady at all, my man?' he asked in a supercilious tone that made Kit Alstone itch to plant him a facer.

'Since she were wailing about her poor ankle fit to make a statue cry, I certainly ain't imagined her, mister,' he said, tempted to be done with all this play-acting and just scurry the popinjay along in his wake.

'There's something devilish familiar about you. Have I seen you before?'

'Not like this you ain't,' the footman assured him gruffly, 'and young Miss needs 'elp some time this week, my lord.'

'You're an impudent knave, and I've half a mind not to take another step with you,' Lord Rarebridge blustered.

Luckily Louisa let out a very convincing wail of distress from where she was no doubt sprawled impatiently on the ground as if she dared not get up, and Kit thrust the viscount in front of him and into the quiet corner of Hyde Park where his sister had insisted they would not be disturbed. Glad his friend would soon be responsible for his sister's wilder starts, and very sure Hugh would protect her far more fiercely than he could when he was busy on the other side of the world far too often, he nevertheless had to admire his sister's acting abilities as she allowed his lordship to assist her to get to her good foot and hop to a nearby seat, where she subsided in convincing agony to rub her perfectly sound ankle.

His lordship just hovered in front of her, looking acutely uncomfortable, and Kit's estimate of the man's intelligence went even lower when Hugh appeared at his side and the idiot just gaped at him as if he'd seen some sort of ghostly apparition.

'Good Gad, Kenton?' he gasped.

'As you say,' Hugh drawled.

'Don't blame me, Rarebridge, I was quite ready to call you out first and ask questions later,' Kit assured the reedy little peacock menacingly, when he'd removed the wig and tucked it into his pocket before running his hand through his hair and wondering aloud how any man put up with such an abomination for long.

'We mean you no harm, your lordship,' Louisa said as she rose from her seat on two perfectly sound ankles and Lord Rarebridge looked more hunted than ever.

'Then why contrive such a scandalous meeting, ma'am?' he asked sharply.

'Because you have been plotting against mine, if not against me,' she said softly and suddenly his lordship found himself wondering if females were as weak and in need of protection as he had always considered them to be.

'I think she means me, Rory,' Hugh informed him laconically.

'Never thought I'd hear you admit to being any woman's lapdog,' his lordship did his best to sneer, but seemed to know it was a poor attempt and Hugh merely stared at his erstwhile friend as if he didn't quite know who he was any more.

'But this lady isn't just any woman, as I'm sure you will agree,' Hugh argued very softly and the very mildness of his manner made Lord Rarebridge shudder.

'My apologies, Miss Alstone,' he said with a coldly correct bow in Louisa's direction as he finally recalled who she was, and that she had once turned down his half-hearted offer of marriage.

'Accepted, my lord, so long as you tell me exactly why you had my affianced husband followed halfway across London yesterday.'

'Good heavens, ma'am, how could you possibly know about that?' he asked without stopping to think how incriminating his words were.

'I tracked you and your very dangerous tools down myself, my lord,' she replied as coolly as if admitting she was due to attend Almack's tonight to endure dry bread and butter and lemonade with this year's crop of débutantes.

'Don't be ridiculous,' he ordered impatiently.

'I'm not, but you certainly are,' she assured him, then felt as much as saw Hugh move to dominate his lordship's bemused attention without having to do anything so crass as push her aside or talk over her.

'Never mind the how, Rory, I want the why,' he said bluntly.

'I don't see why I shouldn't tell you,' he said rather spitefully. 'The wider world thinks of you as a murderer, even if they can't seem to get on and prove it.'

'So you set yourself the task of doing it for them?'

'I decided to discover the truth,' he said so virtuously that Louisa itched to be a man for a minute or two so she could vent her rising temper on this prancing fool without Hugh and her brother being able to stop her.

'I doubt you'll find it by looking in places like that, but if you're so convinced of my guilt a simple denial won't stop you,' Hugh said as if discussing the weather.

'It might. You refused to defend yourself when we all expected you to face up to whatever you had done when poor little Ariadne died, so your word as a gentleman that you didn't kill your wife and brother might go a long way with your friends,' the coward offered, as if he thought for one moment the rest of the world would accept Hugh's say so that he didn't do it, when a solid alibi apparently held no weight.

'And you intend to prove yourself a friend by using some of the worst rogues in London to track my movements? With friends like you, I'll soon be able to retire all my enemies, Rarebridge.'

'Damn it, man, have you any idea what you've done to your unfortunate sister? Poor little creature doesn't deserve the snubs and sneers she has to endure while she lives with the scandal you won't stand and face.'

'I've never thought of my sister as a poor little creature and I'll be very surprised if she thinks of herself as such, and where was I to face down the gossip, Rory, the dock or the gutter?' Hugh asked implacably and Louisa nearly cheered aloud to hear him fight for himself at long last.

'I don't know, but you shouldn't have disappeared like a fugitive,' Lord Rarebridge argued sulkily, as if his bluster was draining away and leaving him wondering what it was all about himself.

'I was too busy surviving to worry about how things looked to the rest of the world,' Hugh said bleakly and Louisa willed him to admit why he'd left his home so finally that his sister was doubly bereft.

'Where were you then, Hugo?' his lordship asked more moderately.

'At sea, in more ways than one,' Hugh admitted with a shrug and a rueful smile for Louisa that made her step a little closer to offer her support. 'I drank, gamed and fought my way round the less reputable taverns of London until I landed in that gutter. It took two strong men to carry me home and dry me out, then Mr Alstone and his good friend and business partner decided to put my seamanship to good use, instead of turning me back out to go to the devil as my so-called friends would have done. I have worked as a ship's master ever since, Rory, and I hardly think you and your kind would wish to associate with such men, nor we with you.'

'Why didn't you write to your sister, then?' his lordship asked, leaving Hugh's implied contempt for the likes of him unchallenged.

'Because my father forbade it and I could hardly ask her to go behind his back—all that would have got her was more ranting and raving about undutiful daughters than she already had to endure.'

'The devil,' his lordship said and sank down on the marble bench. 'It was all a lie, then,' he muttered mysteriously and seemed utterly deflated.

'What was a lie, my lord?' Louisa asked as patiently as she could, for she scented the stamp of the real villain behind all this at last, instead of this idle and foolish young man, so bored with his life he was looking for trouble to fall into.

'I received some letters,' Lord Rarebridge admitted reluctantly.

'From whom did these missives come then?' Hugh demanded impatiently.

'I don't know,' the viscount mumbled, evidently ashamed of himself for paying heed to such spiteful stuff now they'd shown up what a shabby thing his wonderful crusade really was.

'So you pursued an innocent man on the say so of a person who lacked the courage to own his name?' she asked incredulously.

'At first I tore them up or threw them in the fire,' he said defensively.

'But then…?' she encouraged him.

'Then he offered more detail that I couldn't help but take notice of, told me things only a witness to what happened that night could ever know.'

'Or perhaps the perpetrator of it all himself?' she snapped furiously.

'Good Gad, d'you really think so?' he asked as he shot to his feet as if stung, which he would be if there was any justice, Louisa decided vengefully, by a very virulent and persistent gadfly, that lived for a very long time and loved the taste of stupid young aristocrat so much it kept biting and biting.

'Hugo Kenton would never shoot a man in the back, let alone his own brother, so who else is there? If there were any true witnesses to those terrible crimes, they would have come forwards before now and I'm quite sure Sir Horace Kenton offered a large reward to encourage them to do so at the time.'

'You know, I do believe you're right.'

'How amazing,' she said acerbically and was even more astonished by him when he nodded solemnly, as if he'd just witnessed a rare phenomenon.

'So where are the letters now, Rory?' Hugh asked more gently, as if resigned to the dimness of this particular viscount and preparing to stand between him and his fiery fiancée for his protection.

'Letters?' he said, as if being asked where he'd left somebody's pet elephant.

'Yes, the unsigned letters that set you on my tail,' Hugh explained patiently.

'Oh, them,' his lordship said glumly. 'I lost them.'

Louisa locked her hands together in lieu of wrapping them

round the noble idiot's neck and squeezing hard and even Hugh seemed to hold back with an effort from seizing him and shaking some sense out of him.

'Can you recall their content, Rory?' he asked calmly enough.

'Probably, if you give me enough time to think.'

Louisa felt Hugh squeeze her tense fingers in warning and stood back to let him deal with this oddly naïve young man. It made her wonder how old they both were, these former friends, and marvel at the differences between the pampered heir of an earldom and the battle-hardened second son of a baronet. Even without the trauma of the last few years, her Hugh would be twice the man his lordship could ever become and she wondered if Hugh's sister felt anything but contempt for such a straw man. The viscount clearly admired Miss Kenton, and probably had half an eye on the fact that she would inherit everything if her brother was arraigned, then hung for murder, but she doubted he had the brains to actively pursue Hugo without some more deadly hand pulling his strings.

'Come and see if you can put any of them down on paper for us then, Rory. It's very important that we have every shred of evidence we can find if this man is ever to be apprehended. Will you do that for me, old friend?'

'Course I will, Hugo, do anything for you, you know that.'

'I do, Rory, I know exactly what you'd do for me now,' Hugh told his one-time playmate and shrugged at Kit and Louisa as he silently acknowledged how true that remark was.

Chapter Thirteen

'Viscount Rarebridge and his ilk make you wonder how the aristocracy manage to keep such a determined grasp on both government and country,' Kit said ruefully as they waited for Hugh to finish writing his lordship's scattered memories in his pocket book and rejoin them.

'Do you think that idiot will remember anything much of what was actually in those letters?' Louisa asked anxiously.

'Aye, he's not got an awful lot in his head to distract him. It's probably my duty to inform his father what he's been up to so he'll drag him off to the country out of harm's way, so at least I'll be his new worst enemy then instead of Hugh.'

'Perhaps, but how do we get our hands on the true villain behind all this?'

'*We* don't, Lou, and don't waste that wide-eyed innocent look on me.'

'I'm involved; you can't pretend it doesn't matter to me and that I should stay at home and knit socks.'

'Heaven forbid, I've seen your knitting.'

'Don't laugh at me, Kit,' she demanded, knowing that if she let them, he and Hugh would cut her out of this whole business and she simply couldn't sit about waiting to hear if they had been hurt or arrested.

'I'm not, but do you really think it's going to help Hugh's sense of himself if you constantly fight his battles for him, little sister? Only an idiot would hide his past from his wife, but he must slay his own dragons, love.'

Louisa fumed in silence for a while, listening to the birds sing blithely and the distant sounds of children playing in the afternoon sun. The noises of the city were muted in this quiet corner of Mayfair and she reflected that only days ago she had been one of the chattering crowd in Rotten Row at the fashionable hour. How glad she was to be done with all that, although as Mrs Hugo Kenton, in town for a few weeks to enjoy the diversions of fashionable life, she might enjoy herself far more than being scurried from one ball to another by her aunt.

She certainly hadn't come across one man it would cost her a pang to leave behind when she wed Hugh. Some of her suitors had been handsome or fabulously rich or even both, and one or two were witty and keenly intelligent, but none of them had instantly held her attention as Hugh the pirate, or Hugh the poet, or whoever he truly was, could just by being in the same room. Marriage to Hugh could be an endless adventure if they got it right, so she supposed she would have to adapt her life to his if he was willing to reciprocate.

'I suppose you're right,' she finally admitted.

'That's more of an admission than his lordship's that a mere female might have come upon a fact by accident,' he teased her and she chuckled reluctantly.

'Am I a managing woman, Kit?' she asked, heard the wistfulness in her own voice and wondered what on earth Hugh

Darke had done to her. No, Hugo Kenton, she reminded herself, and wondered even more.

'You might be, if you wed the wrong man.'

'I wasn't intending to wed one at all,' she admitted.

'Which is exactly why Hugo Kenton is the right man for you, little sister; he's certainly the only one who's ever caused you to swerve an inch from a course you'd set your mind on taking.'

'You make me sound so formidable,' she protested.

'No. How could I be so crass?' he teased her and she gave him an urchin grin and went back to listening to quiet sounds around them, not letting herself admit even in her head that she was listening for Hugh's near-silent approach until she finally saw him pace lithely down the path to meet them.

'Did you get anything more out of him?' Kit asked once they were back in his neat town carriage and on their way home.

'All he could recall, I'll show you once we're back in Chelsea,' Hugh said tersely and they lapsed into silence.

'Were we followed, Grimme?' Hugh asked the new groom at journey's end.

'Twice over, sir, first cove very obvious, second as quiet as you like,' Grimme answered and waited as if expecting an order to go after one or other.

'Not tonight,' Hugh finally decided. 'I know who sent one and we'll pick our ground before we take the other one on.'

'Aye, sir,' Grimme said and went off to attend to the horses.

'Are you ever going to tell us, then?' Louisa demanded the instant Hugh shut the door of Kit's study behind him.

'There's not much to tell,' he answered, gratefully accepting a brandy glass from his brother-in-law-to-be and raising it in a silent toast as he mouthed 'three' at Louisa to tell her he hadn't forgotten that promise after all.

'I should like some tea,' she informed him majestically and he didn't dare even think what he really wanted, not for another two days at any rate.

Kit confounded him by going off to order the tea tray from his housekeeper and Hugh eyed his own particular termagant with hungry patience.

'He trusts us,' he said at last.

'I suspect he trusts you rather more than me, knowing how your gentlemanly instincts trump my ladylike ones,' she said with a smile that admitted more than he'd dared hope for when she agreed to marry him for the sake of a maybe-child, but not quite as much as he'd dreamt of in those heady dreams of her sweet and hot and in thrall to him in every way a woman can be to a man.

'Stop trying to convince me and everyone else you're not a lady, my dear,' he advised her rather wearily and sat back in his chair to contemplate the fine cognac in his glass rather than the much more tempting sight of Miss Louisa Alstone, elegantly dressed and almost back to her Ice-Diamond perfection.

'Do I grow tedious, Mr Kenton?'

'No, only infuriating. Disappointed?'

'Not really, just a little bit scared,' she admitted and he resisted the temptation to snatch her out of her seat by the empty fire and into his arms, so he could offer comfort and chase the shadows from her eyes.

'You? I thought nothing frightened, Louisa Alstone.'

'Your family does, because I never planned to marry a gentleman; never bothered to study household economy so I could take over a great house one day, or learnt to love country life. I can't even ride properly, Hugh,' she ended, as if that was the greatest sin of all.

'No need to sound so mournful about it, my Eloise. You'll learn whatever you need to and ignore what you don't and if we end up at Gracemont Priory there will be a housekeeper and butler to manage the house and bailiffs and a land steward for each of the estates, so neither of us need take on too much to begin with. I'm not trained to it either, Louisa,' he reassured her, kneeling on the hearthrug in front of her to take her chilled hands in his and warm them. 'I'm the second son, remember? Nobody taught me to judge yields or breed livestock or price timber. I can ride well enough, but Marcus was the real horseman, and I'm more accustomed to a quarterdeck than an estate office. We'll learn it all together, Louisa, and do well enough, I dare say; I don't think there's much you couldn't do if you set your mind to it.'

'Then I *am* a managing female,' she said tragically, recalling her previous conversation with her brother.

'So long as you don't try managing me, you can exert your organising skills on my father's houses and estates with my blessing,' he told her, pulling her forwards so their gazes were level and she could see all the feeling he dared show in his eyes.

'Houses? Estates?' she questioned as he fought not to lose himself in the blue depths of her eyes. 'You mean there's more than one?' she added as if he'd confessed to some sort of family mania or ancient curse.

'One or more, what difference does it make?'

'I'm becoming more of a misalliance by the second for you, Hugh—whatever will your family say?'

'My sister will love you, my ancient second cousin and heir will apparently approve of any woman I marry who isn't a noble whore like the last one, and my father has no say in the matter if he wants me home playing the dutiful heir for the remainder of his life.'

'Oh, that's all right then,' she said forlornly and he couldn't stop himself from leaning forwards that extra inch to kiss her on her temptation of a mouth in order to stop her uncharacteristic attack of self-doubt.

'Idiot,' he chided as he ran a line of kisses along the lovely, giveaway fullness of her lower lip, then back to explore her upper one with just as much care and fascination. 'This gives so much away,' he told her on a groan and pulled back to fight the powerful urge to lay her down on Kit's hearth rug and take her again in broad daylight.

For one thing, her brother would surely kill him for it this time, and for another she deserved more respect, even if she didn't seem to want it. Instead of giving in to the urge to ravish and pleasure and enjoy her as fast and urgently as his body and most of his instincts demanded, he ran his forefinger along the sensuous curve of her lips where his mouth had just travelled and let his need and frustration and tenderness for this wonder of a female show in his heavy-lidded gaze as he watched her react to his touch.

'Gives what away?' she muttered as if only half-interested in his answer, much more concerned with the feel of him exploring the very words on her lips.

'The real Louisa,' he murmured as he outlined her mouth again. The feel of it under the sensitive pad of his finger end was almost as seductive as the marvel of it softening into eagerness and passion under his kisses. 'You're not what you pretend, or even entirely what you think yourself to be, but no wonder you had to defend the vulnerability of this, the passion of it, the fierceness of your feelings,' he told her as he

ranged that fingertip along her fine creamy skin and up over
her high cheekbones to drift it over her half-closed eyelids,
her smooth, narrow brow and down along her jaw-line and
back to that so-fascinating mouth again.

'Kiss me, Hugh,' she demanded shakily against the finger
she tried to catch in her mouth, even as he danced it away
again and her eyes burned every bit as passionately, looked
as vulnerable and fiercely wanting as they had in those wild
dreams of his.

'I dare not,' he whispered, giving in to the temptation to
stroke that one slight point of contact he did dare between
them by exploring along one of her finely made earlobes and
learning the intriguing curls and curves of it to so tenderly
he felt her shiver with desire. 'Once I started to, I couldn't
stop,' he confessed and sat back on his heels to meet her gaze,
waiting for her fierce accusations and the bite of her temper
for half-seducing her, then drawing back, leaving her unsatisfied, restless and needy with the passion that ran between
them like some untapped force of nature.

'The day after tomorrow, we won't have to stop,' she whispered, looking him straight in the eye and letting him see that
wait would be hard for her too.

'Seems more like years, doesn't it?' he murmured ruefully, something greater than all his scruples and self-doubts
threatening the isolation he'd forced on his old self in order
to survive, something that might have been his heart, if he
still had one. He ached with the hugeness and threat of what
promised between them and sprang to his feet in cowardly
relief when Kit made a purposely noisy entrance to his own
book-room, carrying the tea tray Louisa had demanded.

'I assume you waited for me before looking for clues to

your enemy's identity?' he asked as if he thought they'd been yards apart ever since he left.

'What considerate folk we are,' Hugh said blandly.

'So what does it say that we don't know already?' his friend asked and laid the tea-tray on the table at Louisa's side, leaving her to pour a cup with a look that said she probably needed it.

Hugh read through the sparsely covered page once more and stared into space for a moment, thinking about Rory and other one-time friends and neighbours and how they might fit into those terrible days he'd done his best to forget.

'There's something I can't quite understand what happened. It's there at the back of my mind, but not quite there, if you see what I mean?' he finally said, waving the paper as if it might incite the elusive memory into life.

'Then why not let us read it while you try?' Louisa demanded, forgetting all about those resolutions to be a little less forthright in her eagerness.

'So what did I once see or hear or maybe even imagine?' he mused, but absent-mindedly handed over his notebook for her to examine while he tried to pin down that annoying wisp of something not quite right.

Scanning through Lord Rarebridge's sometimes random memories of the letter that had set him off, Louisa felt acutely disappointed and more than a little shocked by the terse malice of it, so she passed the book to Kit and drank her tea.

'No more than a line or two at a time,' Kit said. 'The man's cunning enough not to risk getting carried away and being identified.'

'Which argues he has a talent for intrigue, or that Rory might know his normal handwriting,' Hugh replied.

'Did his lordship remember how the original letters arrived?' Louisa asked, still marvelling that the man could take such vitriol as gospel, then set out to damn an old friend on their say so. 'He knew his victim, didn't he?' she suddenly realised. 'He knew Lord Rarebridge was a credulous, bored fool with a *tendresse* for your sister and your father's acres.'

'Which argues that he's one of the *ton*, don't you think? A man who knows Rory and used those letters to produce the result he wanted.'

'But why would he want you found and followed by one of the most ruthless gangs in London, Hugh?' Kit asked, frowning at the pocketbook in his hand as if it would reform its letters and tell him the answer if he stared at it long enough.

'Maybe their real orders didn't come from Rarebridge, but the man himself. You know as well as I do that if you find the right gang master and pay him enough gold, he'll arrange a murder and even give up one of his less-valued gang members to take the drop for it.'

'And Rarebridge obviously thought he was giving the orders, but he's not exactly a deep thinker, is he? If they had been paid to kill you, rather than merely track you down as that spineless lordling of yours thought, then your dim friend would have taken the blame for your murder when those hired bullies were caught,' Kit replied grimly.

'It could have been part of his scheme to rid himself of two obstacles at once,' Louisa said, shuddering at the horrific idea of Hugh lying dead on a murderer's say so. 'But why put such a plan into action in the first place, after three years of sitting on his hands and doing no worse than stir up the odd rumour against you?'

'Because my father is so ill and I'm the only heir he's got to the Priory and estates, as my sister doesn't seem to want them,' Hugh answered.

'There's probably more to it than that, Hugh, but the very idea of your presence in the area seems to have our murderer in a panic. He obviously prefers you in London or halfway across the world and safely estranged from your family, and beyond the pale of local society,' Kit said thoughtfully.

'So he probably lives near your precious Gracemont?' Louisa asked.

'Either that or he visits regularly enough not to easily stop doing so if I was living there once more.'

'We need a list of the local families and their friends and relations, so we can eliminate them from the list of suspects, then visit the ones that are left,' Louisa said brightly.

'Over my dead body,' Kit rapped out harshly and Hugh just glared as if she'd suggested going about the neighbourhood with no clothes on.

'We need to do more than that, even if I was prepared to let you make such a target of yourself,' Hugh eventually said gruffly. 'It will be obvious enough to this rogue, whoever he might be, what we're up to if we turn up at every house in the area as soon as I get home with my new bride.'

'Precisely, bride visits,' Louisa said smugly and sat back in her chair to wait for them to realise what a perfect scheme it was.

'Most of the households in the area will turn me away from their doors, new bride or not,' Hugh replied with a bitter smile she recognised as armour.

'They'll be sorry when the real villain is unmasked,' she said hotly.

'Maybe,' he replied with a shrug of would-be indifference.

'And he's intent on not letting Hugh go home in the first place,' Kit pointed out.

'So we have tonight and tomorrow to track him down and stop him.'

'Of course we have,' Hugh agreed sarcastically.

'Let's get on with it, then,' she said, all those resolutions to become more tractable and sweetly feminine flying out of the window.

'It'll take a while to write that list you're demanding,' Hugh protested, but sat down at the library table and drew the blotter towards him even so. 'An inventory of my wife's local lovers is probably the best place to start,' he said impassively.

'You knew who they were?' she asked, shocked that the woman could openly humiliate him like that.

'The whole neighbourhood knew,' he said as if it didn't matter.

'I suppose servants will gossip,' she said, half to herself.

'No more than their so-called betters and, for some self-torturing reason I can't currently understand, I made it my business to know who they all were.'

Hugh had to mend his pen before the list was done. As it went down one column and then another, Louisa felt naïve and astonished and quietly furious that so many men could treat a gentleman like him, and a serving officer in Nelson's navy who risked his life time and again for their protection, with so little respect. Apparently even her early experiences of life on the streets hadn't quite prepared her for the politer betrayals of the *ton*.

'Finished?' Kit asked with a wry look that probably went a lot further towards softening this ordeal for Hugh than all the temper and tears she was fighting on his behalf and she silently acknowledged there were times when men understood other men very much better than women could.

'No,' Hugh said as he stared down at the list as if he didn't quite know where it had come from, 'there's one name that still eludes me.'

'Let's see how your list compares with mine, then?' Kit said calmly and unlocked his desk to take out another closely written sheet. 'I made it up from the information your father had been able to discover and that very instructive visit to your second cousin, who appears to know all the gossip in the West Country.'

'The old rogue,' Hugh said with apparent fondness, as he studied both lists then added one or two names to each one that had been overlooked. He looked mildly surprised as he read over them and still he hesitated to hand over the lists for their consideration. 'One of her lovers used to come to Ariadne's room after dark, masked and dressed from head to toe in black, at least according to Dickon and his friends in the taproom. They had hours of raucous amusement speculating over the young nodcock's identity, once they thought I was too drunk to care what they talked about any more.'

'Dressed in black?' Louisa echoed hollowly, unable to believe what her ears were telling her, although it was vital to their search. 'Oh, surely not?' she said aloud so they stared at her as if wondering about her sanity. 'Don't you recall how I was dressed the night I came back into your life, Captain Darke?' she asked Hugh when she'd finally decided she wasn't running mad.

'You were all in black, and it might be best if I didn't recall the exact details. Are you suggesting *you* might have murdered my wife and my brother, my dear? Highly unlikely, considering you were still in the schoolroom at the time and are obviously not that way inclined,' he reminded her with a wolfish grin that reminded her how very masculine she preferred her lover to be.

'Louisa *is* my sister, Kenton,' Kit protested with a fierce frown, but she was too busy fitting two and two together to worry about his ruffled sensibilities.

'And where do you think I got it from?' she asked, overly patient at their uncharacteristic slow-wittedness.

'It wasn't a problem at the forefront of my mind at the time,' Hugh drawled and she spared a warm shiver of delighted awareness for the heat and memories in his heavy-lidded eyes.

'I did notice,' she said drily, 'but I stole the shirt and breeches and lost an equally black coat along the way. I balked at the mask in case anyone saw me, thought I was intent on stealing their silver and raised a hue and cry.'

'Where did you steal them from, then?' he asked, suddenly as sharply interested in that question as she could wish.

'Charlton Hawberry,' she said, still hardly able to believe what her mind was telling her. 'He had them locked in a very fine cedar chest in his dressing room.'

Chapter Fourteen

Recalling her boredom upon being shut in that poky little room with a narrow truckle bed and nothing to do but poke around in his ridiculous wardrobe for most of the day, Louisa decided Charlton Hawberry would receive no less than his due if she'd stumbled on his darkest secrets while she was in there. It was probably best not to remember just now how she'd later been forced to take part in a seedy masquerade when her uncle was brought up to see her with her own clothes half-ripped off and ensconced in the vulgar splendour of Charlton's bedchamber as if she'd been there all day, and night.

'It seemed the ideal dress for a night-time escape, so I just stole it and didn't give much thought to why it was hidden away so ridiculously. I did wonder if he'd set up some sort of latter-day Hell Fire Club with what he thought fittingly satanic regalia, but I was more interested in getting away than examining his motives for possessing such an outfit in the first place. Keeping it in such a fine box, with a lock that gave me some trouble to pick, was a mistake as far as I was concerned, since I was so bored in his horrible dressing room that I whiled away the tedious hours, once I'd done my best to escape by conventional methods, with learning how to open it.'

'I should have tracked him down and killed him just for that,' Hugh said with a grim smile that made him look more wolfish than ever.

'And I should have done a lot more than kicking him in the… Well, I'll leave you to work out where I kicked him.'

That surprised a bark of genuine laughter out of him and broke the heavy tension in the room for a moment, but the implications of what she'd found in that locked box were too stark to ignore, given the story they were finally putting together.

'He must know that you picked the lock and stole his disguise by now,' Hugh said, as if that was the most significant fact of all.

'Whatever he knows, or doesn't know, it was proof of what he'd done and I took it away,' she reproached herself bleakly.

'If you hadn't opened it, we would have taken a great deal longer to work out what he is, even if I'm very sure I never met a man called Charlton Hawberry at any of my neighbours' houses, and I would remember a name like that, even if I was as drunk as a lord at the time.'

'It has to be an alias,' Kit confirmed tersely. 'I was a fool not to realise he was flying under false colours when he disappeared so completely after Louisa's escape that it was almost as if he'd never been.'

'Which of course he hadn't, not that he was worth knowing in any guise,' she added disgustedly.

'So who on earth can he be?' Hugh asked, as if she ought to know.

'How do I know?' she said impatiently. 'I heard and saw

nothing that would give us a clue to his real identity, either before or after he abducted me.'

'But you did see him and, however he tried to disguise himself, he couldn't alter his basic physique or the colour of his eyes,' Kit pointed out, looking to her for a description of her erstwhile suitor she was struggling to put together.

'He's just nondescript,' she said with a shrug. 'The first time he attended one of Aunt Poole's At Homes, I couldn't recall a single thing about him afterwards, for all Uncle William kept talking about him as if the Prince of Wales himself had chosen to honour his drawing room with his presence.'

'Having been handsomely paid to do so, no doubt,' Hugh observed.

'No doubt at all, but if Charlton is the murderer, it makes his motives far more sinister, don't you think?' she pointed out. 'I am your employer's sister, which put me at the very heart of the Stone & Shaw business. If he'd managed to wed me, he no doubt believed he'd be able to get you dismissed and further disgraced, so you would never dare return home.'

'Not so,' Kit said grimly. 'Marrying my sister by force would not endear him to me and Hugh's no mere employee, he's a shareholder and a friend.'

'Does Charlton know that, do you think? His main strength seems to be his ability to fade away from a place as if he'd never been there, but he's weak in every other way and I don't think he's very subtle either, or he would never have committed murder in the first place,' Louisa said.

'No, he's clearly a reactor and not a planner, since his schemes are never particularly good, but that makes him very dangerous indeed,' Kit warned.

'And his plan has gone very wrong, since Hugh's about to

marry into the Alstone family and not him. So who knows about the marriage so far?' Louisa asked her brother.

'The vicar of St Margaret's, most of the clerics at Lambeth Palace, and the lawyers, of course,' he replied grimly.

'An open secret, then?' she said and met Hugh's eyes with a rueful smile.

'More or less,' he agreed with a distracted frown. 'And what a fine way to kill all his birds with one stone if there should be a tragic accident on the way home from the church, don't you think?'

'An accident where all three of us were killed—surely that would be almost impossible to engineer?'

'Perhaps,' Hugh agreed distractedly, 'but he'll make some sort of move. He'll have to, since he knows he'll hang anyway if he's caught. What's the man got to lose by attacking us when he's committed two murders already?'

'Everything, I should imagine,' Louisa said as she realised anew just how desperate and dangerous this so-called Charlton Hawberry must be.

'Yes, and why wear that mask in the first place, I wonder?' Hugh mused. 'The rest of the county seemed happy enough to take the garden stairs up to Ariadne's chamber once the rest of my father's household were asleep; indeed, I heard it was nicknamed the Backstairs to Heaven by some of the local wags.'

'Perhaps he's married?' she suggested, trying not to pity Hugh for that appalling betrayal when he didn't want her sympathy or anyone else's.

'As are half the worst rakes of the *ton*, but they don't go about their carousing and seducing dressed in such a theatrical fashion,' Kit pointed out.

'You would know far more about that subject than I,' Louisa replied sternly, 'but perhaps Hawberry has more to hide than most men.'

'Or more to lose, perhaps?' Hugh said as he tapped the list on the edge of the desk and looked very thoughtful indeed.

'So he's a man who likes illicit pleasures, but lacks the sort of natural arrogance to find the risk of being caught out and identified part of the fun. Somehow he had to care about his reputation, even when visiting a lady of...' Louisa let her voice trail off because she realised what she had been about to say of Hugh's dead wife and, even if she'd sickened him with her lovers and her lies, he must have loved her once upon a time, or why marry her in the first place when he could have had his pick of the débutantes?

'Dubious morals and tarnished reputation?' he finished for her. 'No need to wrap it up in clean linen, my dear, I've had three years to come to terms with what my wife was. Indeed, by the side of her horrible death and my brother's murder, her chosen way of life hardly seems very important any more.'

'Maybe not to you,' Kit said thoughtfully, 'but it obviously mattered very much to our mysterious Mr Hawberry.'

'So why should it mean so much for him to be seen, when it would have been a minor setback to any other man?' Louisa asked, shaking her head over the puzzle of who, or what, Charlton Hawberry really was.

'Because he would lose more than them if he was found out,' Hugh said slowly. 'He must be in a position of moral authority to dread discovery so.'

'Either a law lord or a politician of some sort then, or perhaps even a cleric?' she offered eagerly.

'Which fits him best then, Lou?' her brother asked. 'You have actually met the man, you've been in his home and, even if it was only a temporary one where he had to be careful not to reveal his true self, everyone gives a little away through their possessions and the way they insist their household is conducted. How would you best describe your insect-worm?'

'Secretive, fussy, nondescript,' she managed as she racked her brains to something to say about the man, apart from the fact that even the thought of being in the same room with him made her flesh creep. 'He's very cold, with fishy eyes that make you feel as if there's nobody much behind them, but really I got the impression he's very intelligent, but not very clever with it, if you know what I mean?'

'I do, which is a conundrum in itself,' Hugh said, as if he was trying to fit such a man against any he might know.

'It's almost as if he doesn't feel in the way that other people feel. As if he has no idea other people have emotions and needs, because his own are so important that they blot out anyone and everyone in his way.'

'And there stands any cold-blooded murderer,' Kit said frustratedly and she sighed, impatient with herself for not being able to describe the man who must be the ruthless killer trying to get Hugh hung for his own crimes.

'Such a man would speed rapidly along his chosen path to glory for a while, but probably only get so far along it before he hit obstacles,' Hugh said as if thinking out loud. 'Chilly ruthlessness will get a man so far and no further, but to rise to the top requires a touch of greatness, which it sounds as if this Charlton Hawberry lacks.'

'That's him exactly,' Louisa agreed, finally allowing herself to hope they could do this, track the monster down and overcome him before he managed to hurt Hugh even more than he already had.

'So who is he?' he said, obviously running all his former neighbours through his head in an attempt to weed one out.

'All we know is he's ruthless and ambitious with an unprepossessing exterior and a purely physical need of beautiful women.'

'He didn't seem to need me very much, thank goodness,' she said and saw Kit exchange a wry look with Hugh over her head. 'I suppose you're silently informing each other that he prefers whores to ladies?'

'Well, virtuous ladies at any rate—he doesn't seem to have objected to making my wife the object of his desire,' Hugh observed cynically.

'And I do know some men like to hurt women for their own filthy gratification,' she said before they could sidestep that issue as well. 'I grew up in the stews, you know, and I'm not blind or entirely stupid.'

'Louisa's right, Hugh, even if I wish she didn't know anything of such dark dealings. What if the perverted fool went too far that night, your wife tried to fight him off, then your brother heard her fight for life?'

'But why kill them both if he was masked and disguised like that?'

'Because a man could hardly keep himself masked and pristine when a young and desperate woman was tearing at his hands and face in terror for her very life,' Kit said, preoccupied with reconstructing the past as dispassionately as he could since Hugh would probably never manage to, being so close to the victims of that terrible night. 'Your brother must have seen enough to recognise her attacker before he went to raise the alarm. He was probably intent on making sure everyone knew exactly what he'd seen, rather than wasting time stopping to fight with the louse when I suspect your wife was already dead. Maybe he was even looking for his brother—if he could sober you up long enough to listen—but the bastard shot to kill, so Marcus Kenton never told anyone what he'd seen.'

There was silence in the cosy room as they took in the full horror of what had probably happened that night. Louisa found herself pitying Hugh's late wife's terrible end, even if the woman had inflicted such pain and damage on the man she loved as Ariadne Kenton could never have loved him, and done what she had.

Oh, no. She *loved* Hugh Kenton!

What an idiot to think she was safe from that huge and frightening emotion, just because her mother had loved a man who wasn't fit to tie her shoelaces. The idea that she had chosen far better than her mother, even if she hadn't known until now that she was choosing her true love, struck her, but she was too busy coping with this latest disaster to fully appreciate it just now.

'Are you going to faint, Louisa?' Kit asked her so sharply her shock must be a bit too obvious on her face.

'Of course not—when did I ever do that?'

'Never, but there's always a first time, I suppose.'

'Not for me. Now, how are we going to track this killer down? It's all very well knowing what he's done; what we need now is proof of his identity.'

Hugh looked very thoughtful as he considered ways and means. 'We must force him into the open somehow, so I wonder how contrite Rarebridge is.'

'Extremely, I should imagine,' Kit agreed and Louisa wondered how men held whole conversations with barely a word of sense between them.

'An elegant evening reception for an old friend and neighbour he feels he has wronged in the past and his new wife should serve,' she said before they could come up with some scheme to exclude her and put themselves in acute danger.

'I doubt if he'll spring for that; his father keeps him very short and his house is full with his sister's vast tribe of children descending on him. Apparently she refused to leave them at home, but insisted on bringing them up for the only Season when she's not been either with child or giving birth since her marriage. Even I almost felt sorry for Rory, surrounded as he is with four young children and attendant nannies as well as that unfortunate husband of his sister's,' Hugh said.

'Why is he so unfortunate?' she asked.

'I don't really know, he just is,' Hugh replied with an inarticulate shrug. 'No way of describing him other than that, really.'

'If you don't think he will co-operate, I'll visit our cousin Lord Carnwood and prod his conscience instead,' Louisa said calmly, although the notion of bearding the family dragon in his den made her quail.

'No, Louisa, I received news today that our cousin's grandson and heir has died, so I expect the Earl is only in town at all to find out if he can disinherit me, since I am his heir presumptive now,' Kit said with a wry grimace that told them how little he actually wanted to inherit the earldom and all its attendant responsibilities.

'I'm very sorry for him then, despite the fact he should have helped Mama out when we were young, even if Papa was a hopeless case. His heir must have been little more than a boy.'

'Sixteen,' Kit agreed and she could see how hard the news had hit him.

'His poor parents,' she said with a shake of her head for the appalling grief they must be suffering.

'They were killed in an accident eight or nine years ago,'

Hugh volunteered. 'I believe the boy has sisters, but they can't inherit an earldom and as the eldest of them ran off with some unsuitable rogue a twelvemonth ago it's probably as well.'

'Aye,' Kit agreed abstractedly and went back to staring at nothing in particular while he brooded on the unexpected turn his life had taken.

'Then I shall have to work on Lord Rarebridge's uneasy conscience instead,' Louisa announced and could have sworn she heard a silent moan of dread.

It had been an unexpectedly magical day, Louisa decided as she ascended the steps of Kinsham House just as the sun was setting and the birds in the trees in the gardens around the square were singing themselves to sleep, if the *ton* allowed them peace enough to do so. She let the whispering silk skirts of her wedding gown fall to skim her slender ankles and embroidered satin slippers, then turned to smile at her new husband. Despite their enemy still being at large, Hugh seemed as happy and relaxed as he had been all day and she had just married the man she loved, so even with the vague unease she would always feel until Charlton Hawberry was apprehended, she still felt like dancing for joy.

'You look like the perfect model for a newlywed gentleman,' she teased her husband of half a day, and who would have thought Louisa Alstone, as was, would ever lay claim to one of those?

'And I daren't even look at you, madam wife, in case I ruin my gentlemanly façade by falling on you like a ravening beast,' he muttered in her ear before turning to smile benignly as Lord Kinsham's butler wished them both very happy on behalf of his lordship's London staff.

Hugh thanked him sincerely, but his smile for Viscount

Rarebridge, standing behind his father's butler to receive them inside the generous marble hall, held much less warmth. Louisa soon saw that Lord Kinsham's elegant saloon was crammed with curious guests, despite the scant notice they'd received, and blessed the curiosity of Hugh's former friends and neighbours as she reminded herself she wasn't here to rehabilitate him in their eyes; that would have to come later.

'Am I allowed to kiss the bride?' Rory asked jovially, then backed hastily away when he saw the warning in Hugh's suddenly feral gaze. 'Only asking, old fellow,' he excused himself mildly and Louisa sensed her husband putting the beast very carefully back in his cage and shivered with delighted anticipation of later tonight, when this charade was over and their wedding night could begin in earnest.

'My dear Mrs Kenton,' Lady Calliope Hibiscombe gushed as she stepped forwards to fill the silence her brother's question left. 'You are both very welcome, and may I congratulate you on your marriage?' Lord Rarebridge's sister asked and turned to raise her eyebrows at the butler in her role as hostess for the evening, so he could usher in the champagne the world was not supposed to know Kit had sent round earlier for his lordship and his guests to toast the bride and groom.

'Thank you, Lady Calliope, I am very happy to be married to such a wonderful husband and it is indeed kind of you and your brother to throw a lavish party for us at such very short notice,' Louisa managed in return and they smiled at each other, while Hugh's one-time friends and neighbours looked on as if at a play.

'I believe you know my brother, Mr Christopher Alstone?' she asked as she motioned Kit forwards to take his share of the attention.

'Indeed I do,' Lady Calliope said much more warmly as

she welcomed the Earl of Carnwood's new heir and Louisa suspected she was calculating how to marry him off to her best advantage.

Deciding that, of the two, she preferred Lord Rarebridge's amiable vacuity to his sister's calculated insincerity, Louisa gave a sparkling smile to the assembled company and clung to Hugh's arm as if she never intended letting go.

She was introduced to a succession of guests and had to fight hard not to glare at each one and ask why they'd been such false friends to Hugh when he stood so much in need of them. He kept up a blandly smiling appearance at her side and seemed charmed to be reacquainted with them all and, if he could act so superbly in the face of their hypocrisy, she could stand at his side and pretend to be as naïve as the majority of the guests clearly thought she must be to have wed him in the first place.

'Such a shame that Sir Horace and Miss Kenton could not be here to share your joy, is it not?' one of the more openly curious ladies asked her once most of Hugh's attention had been engaged by her downtrodden husband.

'Indeed, when you consider how ill the poor gentleman is, no doubt you understand why we wed with such haste? I simply had to be at my husband's side over the next difficult months to provide as much comfort and support as can be had in such circumstances,' she said with modestly lowered eyes.

'It does you credit, my child, but what a shame you lack the guiding hand of a steady parent at such a time, for his situation could become very difficult indeed,' the lady said spitefully and if this was the sort of unspoken malice Hugh had to contend with, Louisa decided it really was no wonder he'd preferred the gutter, then the sea.

'You have observed my brother, I believe, ma'am?' Louisa asked sweetly.

'Oh, yes, of course,' the woman replied with a sidelong glance at Kit that said she had observed and relished the sight of him, as a still-handsome married woman who felt free to attract such dangerous gentlemen must, once her husband had his heir and a spare as hers apparently did.

'If I need guidance through shark-infested waters, I shall be able to call on him for any help I need. Although I doubt I'll require it, considering my husband is such an expert on sharks.'

'Quite,' the lady said sourly and went off to inform her fellow scandalmongers that the bride was a harridan in the making, and probably deserved to marry a man with the shadow of murder lurking so persistently over his head that no true lady would agree to have him.

'Fighting dragons for me again, Louisa mine?' Hugh asked softly as he clinked his champagne glass against hers and smiled down at her in an intimate toast that momentarily excluded everyone else.

'I can't help it, Hugh,' she murmured in reply, 'they are so very brazen.'

'Which is why they became dragons in the first place,' he said gently and she was tempted to forget all about rooting out their villain to lure her new husband out of this room and find one a lot more private.

'Has anything jogged your memory?' she whispered as if exchanging sweet nothings with her bridegroom.

'Not until now,' he told her distractedly and she tried to shift round to see who he was looking at so intently, but he confounded her by moving to block her view.

'Now who's the dragon slayer?' she muttered crossly.

'I am,' he said unrepentantly and she could tell he'd just sent her brother some sort of signal because Kit suddenly materialised at their side. 'Did you see?' he asked brusquely.

'Before he slipped upstairs and no doubt developed a sick headache? I certainly did, but we can't scotch that particular snake tonight unless he slithers back into view, given his position in the household.'

'No, indeed, the height of bad manners,' Hugh agreed with a satirical look at the assembled company that said he had a very poor opinion of the polite world just at the moment.

'And deeply unfair on the man's unlucky family,' Kit confirmed and Louisa stamped her foot and glared at both of them.

'Talking about bad manners, neither of yours would stand up to scrutiny tonight,' she said haughtily.

'Will you accept what I say and carry on with this charade as if all we have on our minds tonight is rehabilitating my reputation, love?' Hugh asked and Louisa felt her anger subside far too easily.

'Very well,' she agreed with a heavy sigh. 'Don't expect me to become a pattern card of wifely obedience though, will you?'

'Perish the thought,' he said with a smile that did strange things to her insides.

'I think we could all dance, don't you?' Lady Calliope was cleverly appealing to the older matrons who might disapprove. 'I know dear Hugh and his bride begged us not to throw an impromptu ball to celebrate their nuptials, but I see no harm in a few elegant measures between old friends.'

'Excellent notion, Cal,' Viscount Rarebridge agreed and a pair of superannuated ladies agreed to provide the music, so the butler supervised the rolling back of the fine Aubusson carpet and one of the ladies struck up a merry tune, then pronounced herself satisfied with both music and instrument.

'The bride and groom must begin the first dance,' Lady Calliope announced as Hugh and Louisa walked on to the floor hand in hand and a ripple of applause and nervous laughter ran round the room.

Chapter Fifteen

'They really don't know what to make of us, do they?' Louisa asked as she and Hugh went through the formalities and waited for the other couples to take the floor in their wake.

'Not fish, nor flesh, nor good red herring are we, my Eloise?' he asked with a wry look that made her want to walk into his strong arms and stop there.

'I'm not, but you were their neighbour and playmate once upon a time. No doubt you set daughters' and sisters' hearts aflutter when you came home from the sea a hero of Trafalgar and all those other dreadful battles you were engaged in. They must have known you as a fine and honourable young gentleman, sure to go far on your chosen path to glory, but now they pretend they barely know you.'

'Not everyone is courageous as you,' he told her philosophically. 'We arranged this farce for our own purposes, so we can hardly complain if they're here to satisfy their rampant curiosity, rather than be reconciled with a rogue like me.'

'You're not a rogue,' she defended him against his own strictures as they began the measure and passed down the line of waiting ladies and gentlemen.

'Oh, come now, my dear, you know perfectly well that I am,' he said wickedly and gave her a blazing look before he solemnly bowed to the next lady in line and whisked her off to perform the figure with elegant aplomb.

'You're right,' she whispered as they passed each other in the dance.

'I know,' he murmured back and was off again with another fascinated lady.

'Just as well I'm an adventuress, then,' she told him at the next opportunity and gave her partner a fascinating smile before flitting off down the line with him.

'He just told me I'm a lucky dog,' Hugh muttered dourly next time they met.

'Well, you are,' she replied and smiled even more enchantingly at the next gentleman in line.

'All right, you can stop now. I'm more than jealous enough to punch the next man you smile at in the mouth, in the midst of the dance or not,' he informed her more than half-seriously as they settled back into their pairing for the weave to be taken over by the next pair.

'Well, that really would provide fodder for the gossips,' she said demurely and settled back into the blissful state of only seeing her new husband for the rest of the dance, then happily consented to move among the spectators at his side during the next one.

'Feeling better now?' she whispered as they drifted from one middle-aged couple to another.

'What do you think?' he demanded with a message in his silver-shot blue eyes that made her shiver with sensuous anticipation.

'How much longer do we have to stay, do you think?' she

asked as they halted between acquaintances to look only at each other.

'It is our party,' he demurred.

'Then surely we should be able to leave it whenever we choose?'

'With your vengeful purposes still unsatisfied, my Louisa, are you sure you're feeling quite well?'

'I might not be,' she trailed suggestively. 'I could be overwrought and even a little bit overawed by the solemnity of the occasion, if you would like me to be.'

'Not when you're glowing like the happy dawn, my love. Have I told you that you look breathtakingly beautiful in that gown, with your hair so perfectly right for you and that sapphire set Kit gave you the same glorious shade as your eyes? I wish I'd thought of buying you something half as lovely, but I suspect I wouldn't have found anything to equal them in London.'

'He said they came from a very shady gem merchant he met on his travels, and he wouldn't tell me exactly where he acquired them. I can't help wondering if they were really intended for me when he bought them though, Hugh, for there was such a faraway look in his eyes when he gave them to me it was almost as if he was saying farewell to a dream.'

'Whereas I've got my dream here in my arms,' he told her so unexpectedly she really was almost overcome, if more by a surge of lust and love and anticipation of tonight than by the occasion.

'You say such lovely things to me,' she murmured, not caring that his father's neighbours and most of his former acquaintance was watching them, either openly or under cover of making conversation with each other.

'And you don't believe a word of them, do you?' he said

as if her lack of faith in him jarred on his newfound contentment.

'I can't accustom myself to being anyone's dream, Hugh,' she said seriously.

'And no doubt I'm more like your nightmare than *your* dream,' he parried bitterly, as if he had to defend the sensitive man she now knew he was, behind all that to-the-devil-with-you air of his, from being trampled on once more.

'You are so much more than a dream to me, my love,' she finally declared, because she wouldn't see him hurt ever again if she could prevent it, even if she was the one doing the hurting. 'You're my hope, where I only had loneliness and isolation before I met you, and my warmth and laughter, when I expected to go alone to my grave. I want you rather urgently as well, which surprises me even if it doesn't seem to shock you. After all, I was perfectly content to be called the Ice Diamond before I encountered Captain Darke one fine day and began to melt on the spot. So you *are* the dream I never dared even dream before I met you, Hugh, and I still don't quite know what I did to deserve you, or that I ever did, in fact, and now I've got you I can't wait to be your wife in every sense of the word.'

'Oh Louisa mine, I love you so dearly I swear that I never even knew the meaning of the word until now,' he said on a long sigh of relief and acceptance that made her heart sing, 'but please let's go home and put it all into practice as soon as we can get out of here without insulting someone irretrievably, as they're probably going to be our neighbours all too soon,' he added and she looked up at him with love and laughter and complicity in her eyes and agreed without another word.

* * *

'I'll have my maid find your cloak and anything else your woman left here ready for your homeward journey, my dear,' Lady Calliope assured Louisa as she shepherded her into the ladies' withdrawing room and did her best to pretend she believed her glowing guest of honour was truly overcome by the heat and the strain of marrying a rake earlier today, in the teeth of all the evidence.

'Thank you, Lady Calliope,' she said meekly and subsided onto a conveniently placed chair to wait and dream of her own particular rogue in peace.

'Are you sure you wouldn't like another of the maids to attend you, as you seem to lack one of your own at the moment?'

'Quite sure, I thank you, it has been a lovely evening, your ladyship, but I should like a little quiet to recover my senses before we leave,' she said truthfully enough, for she wanted to sit and treasure the incredible fact that in a few minutes she would be going home with the man she loved and he loved her in return.

Lady Calliope nodded as if quite content to let the lie Louisa was in the least bit overcome stand, so she could get back to gossiping about her with her friends. Louisa hardly noticed her hostess go as she hugged such a wonderful revelation to her heart. It was such an unexpected delight that she'd somehow discovered her one real love, and he her, that she begrudged sharing it with a group of people who had failed to appreciate his wonderful qualities so appallingly in the past.

'At last, my dear, I thought I should never find the chance to get you to myself once more,' a voice that truly came out of her worst nightmares told her silkily, before she'd hardly even got started on dreaming about her husband and lover and deliciously anticipating the night to come.

She gasped and sprang to her feet at the sight of the man she knew as Charlton Hawberry, standing just inside the door opposite the one she and Lady Calliope had used, looking as if he'd had all his dreams come true as well tonight, and certain that she wouldn't like any of them.

'Nothing to say, oh-so-intrepid Miss Alstone?' he sneered.

'Mrs Kenton,' she corrected before she could stop the words on her tongue.

'Ah, yes, how satisfying it will be to take his second wife as well as his first one from him. I dare say the loss of the famous Ice Diamond in his marriage bed will break him and this time he really won't care if he lives or dies. What a good joke that the first Mrs Kenton took lovers with a little less thought than she changed her gowns and the second is as frigid as an icicle. I'm probably doing the man a favour by depriving him of a fine case of frostbite when he tries to bed you.'

This time she refused to rise to his sneers or his revolting words and just stared at him for a moment, then looked away as if from something repulsive. All the time she was trying to find a way to escape him. If she could just keep him boasting about his cleverness for long enough the maid would come in with her splendid new evening cloak, and surely she'd scream for help when she saw the lady she came to help being held at the point of this vile little man's pistol.

'You wouldn't dare shoot me here,' she challenged as she mentally searched the room for a weapon to defend herself with, because she'd never wanted to die less than she did tonight.

'I was thinking of something more subtle,' he said as he

removed a white-silk stocking from his pocket that looked very similar to the ones she'd donned earlier, with a rush of joyous anticipation at the thought of Hugh taking them off again, very slowly and sensuously. 'Courtesy of my wife, you understand,' he informed her as if she would want to know whose stocking he wanted to strangle her with.

'You're Mr Hibiscombe?' she asked and suddenly knew she was right. No wonder he'd known exactly how to play on his brother-in-law's weaknesses, no great surprise that he'd hidden his guilt for so long with such powerful connections and a seat in the House of Commons to help him do so either.

'Yes,' he said flatly. 'I am *Mr* Hibiscombe and very shortly even your undeserving husband will be a baronet. My wife has a title, her idiot brother has a better one and my very noble father-in-law had to be blackmailed and bought to accept me as his son-in-law, but *I* do not have a title, madam, and I intend to get one very soon, although unfortunately you won't live to see it.'

'Why on earth would you want one?' she couldn't help but ask, picturing Kit's grim face when he told them he'd become heir to an earldom.

'You are a very stupid woman—of course I want to distinguish myself from my inferiors and take up my seat in the House of Lords at long last. Do you think being a mere Member of Parliament is enough for a man like me? Staying a mere mister will not do for any gentleman with ambition and drive and I've had enough of being no more than tolerated by my aristocratic relatives by marriage.'

'And you'll never receive a peerage of any sort if you're in Newgate awaiting hanging. No, I quite see your dilemma now,' she said as blandly as she could.

She could see with hindsight why he could afford to attend

her uncle and aunt's At Homes because they had no political bent and moved in very different circles to the ones he clearly aspired to. The vanity of the creature astonished her; perhaps if she encouraged him to trumpet his cleverness over the rest of the world, she might stand a chance of getting away from him unscathed after all.

'Why on earth did you kidnap me if you were already married?' she asked casually, as if his answer hardly mattered.

'I suppose there's no harm telling you,' he mused as if unable to resist the chance to preen at his own superiority. 'I had no interest in marrying the Ice Diamond—what could you bring me, especially once I learnt a little more about your colourful past? No, your disappearance was merely to ensure your oh-so-clever brother was occupied while I rid myself of the problem caused by Hugo Kenton's inconvenient reappearance.' With his back to the door he'd come in by, he hadn't seen it open a mere crack as the maid heard voices within and decided to find out if it was safe to enter without breaking up some unimaginable tête-à-tête.

'How extraordinary of you, Mr Hibiscombe, but I don't understand how the first Mrs Kenton fitted into your grand scheme of things?' She trailed the question in the hope the maid was quick on the uptake and would realise her mistress's husband was a murderer, so she could fetch help before he did it again.

'My wife is boring,' he said coldly and she wondered how Lady Calliope tolerated him on even a day-to-day basis, let alone taking him to her bed often enough to give rise to the brood of children Lord Rarebridge complained about at every opportunity. 'She would never have agreed to wed me if she wasn't,' he added with a shrug. 'The late Mrs Kenton was exciting and forbidden and I enjoyed cuckolding that idiot you just married without anyone knowing I was doing it. All the others were as lacking in subtlety as the woman herself and, eventually, I found out that she was quite incapable of discretion. She laughed at me and then she threatened me,' he added, astonishment in his reedy voice as if he was almost talking to himself and marvelling at the temerity of Ariadne Kenton for daring to mock him.

There was silence from outside the room and Louisa could only hope that the maid had either gone to get help, or was listening to the vain little peacock damn himself further. She had no intention of dying to oblige this cardboard monster, but it would be such a relief if she didn't have to fight him for her life, tonight of all nights.

'What did she threaten you with?' she managed to ask.

'Exposure,' he said with a prim shudder. 'She said she would go to my father-in-law the Earl and tell him what sort of man his precious daughter had married and then she would confront Calliope and make sure she knew as well, so nobody could keep it from her for the sake of her peace of mind.'

'I can see your problem,' she lied.

'It was very vexing; obviously government ministers have mistresses and expect their juniors to have them too, but such women should know their place and at least keep a still tongue in their heads. That strumpet Kenton married went about in the same circles as I, as if she was fit company for gentlemen; she even suggested she was quite happy to let him sue me for criminal conversation with her. She actually wanted to be divorced by the blundering idiot, she told me so.'

'Why?' she asked unoriginally, but she didn't think he would be marking her for varied conversation when all he cared about were his own words.

'Apparently she felt guilty about marrying him, but not

about me or any of the unsuspecting fools she took as lovers afterwards. She told me she should never have wed him, which was quite true, of course; she should have sought employment in the nearest brothel, since she had such a natural talent for whoring.'

'It sounds more like a sickness to me,' she said, at last feeling compassion for the obviously very damaged woman Hugh had wed.

Hearing what had horrified this self-serving monster the most, she almost forgave Ariadne for the terrible damage she had inflicted on Hugh. Under all her vanity and frenetic flirting and that parade of lovers, the poor soul had obviously possessed something her murderer so signally lacked: a conscience.

'It was stupidity. I would never have had to kill her if she'd agreed to keep quiet as she promised to do before I agreed to bed her.'

'You'd never have had to kill her at all if you had resisted the urge to betray your wife in the first place,' she pointed out rather rashly, but having recalled how this man was leading a campaign to cleanse the Haymarket of prostitutes and banish them to prison or houses of correction, she simply couldn't keep a still tongue in her head in the face of his hypocrisy.

'Why not seek pleasure in her bed when I had precious little in my own?'

'I suppose you dared not beat or half-strangle the daughter of such a powerful man for your own sick gratification?' she scorned and realised her mistake when an insane gleam of excitement lit his water-colour eyes.

'I see you truly are a child of the streets for all that much vaunted coldness, my dear,' he said with dawning excitement in his fishy gaze and Louisa fought the urge to retch at the very thought of all he wanted to do to her, before he inflicted the same grim death as he had on her predecessor to silence her and torture Hugh.

Fighting her fear and revulsion at what he'd done, and what he wanted to do, she backed a little further away and closed her hand on a pretty little French clock on one of the pier tables behind her.

'What about Hugh's brother?' she made herself ask, in case the maid was still listening and this revolting little man actually did put a bullet in her, because that was what he'd have to do if he wanted to kill her. She wouldn't let herself be violated and cowed at the point of a gun.

'He always was an idiot—it's a family trait, you know? Service to your country and honour and duty and a lot of other nonsense. Apparently he wanted his precious brother to divorce that woman, too, so he'd been keeping a list of all her lovers to be used in court whenever he finally managed to persuade his father the woman was a blot on that precious honour of theirs and must be got rid of.'

'So you snuffed out two far-better people than you could ever be that night,' she told him recklessly.

'How dare you? How can you compare *me* to a whore and a fool?'

'Discreditably,' she told him fiercely and hefted the clock at him, but then had to hunch her shoulders in an instinctive move to protect herself from flying debris, as the little clock shattered in midair when he shot it to save his gun hand, and proved a far better shot as well as even more instinctively cunning than she'd credited.

'Did you think I only had the one?' he asked with a sneer, as he took the second of the pair from his coat pocket and sited it at her heart.

'I thought I could damage your gun hand so badly that it wouldn't matter,' she said just as coolly, but there wasn't the slightest chance it would work twice.

He waved the stocking at her as he moved towards her. 'You forget, my dear, it's important that Kenton's second wife go the same way as the first so there can be no doubt left in anyone's mind to his guilt.'

At last she saw the door behind him open wider and a huddle of shocked faces behind Hugh's agonised one as he focused on the deadly weapon so steadily targeted at her heart. Remembering their last conversation, she did her best to blank all expression from her face as she met Hibiscombe's dead eyes to keep his gaze solely focus on her—better to die herself than watch him kill Hugh, then have to live without him.

'Do you think these rooms are altogether soundproof?' she asked to try to keep his attention solely on her.

'Who cares? They're making enough noise at your nuptial dance to drown out cannon fire,' he said with a dismissive shrug. 'It will be your wake as well.'

'I think not, Fulton,' Lady Calliope declared as she opened the main door into the room and stepped into his line of fire before he could even react to her presence. 'And I care that you risk our children's future; I care that I made those poor children with a monster; and I care far more that they will have to live with the knowledge of what you've done for the rest of their lives.'

'Why?' he said blankly. 'I've got it all under control now, so nobody will ever find out. If you will just stand out of the way for a few seconds, my dear, I'll kill her and all will be well again. When it's done we can go back to the ballroom and announce that the bride has been killed and let everyone reach the obvious conclusion that her husband has killed again.'

'No, you won't. Even if I were as mad as you clearly are and agreed to your ridiculous scheme, do you think they're all going to keep quiet and go away, just because you tell them to?' Lady Calliope demanded as she waved rather theatrically at the group of spectators behind him.

By now there was such a gleam of insanity in the man's once-blank eyes that Louisa wondered if he might even shoot his wife and be done with it. Instead, he twisted round very suddenly and aimed at Hugh instead. He was actually in the act of pulling the trigger when Louisa's next weapon hit him on the shoulder.

In the shocked silence that followed Hugh inspected the tear on the sleeve of his once-immaculate wedding coat of darkest blue superfine and raised one eyebrow at his bride. 'Just as well there was nothing in it,' he said blandly as he eyed the shards of demure white pottery now scattered on the carpet.

'Well, there was nothing else handy that might have done the trick,' she explained coolly, as she eyed the broken remnants of the impromptu weapon she'd found in the pot cupboard nearby.

Complicity and laughter and such warm relief that neither of them dared explore it at present shone in his eyes as they met hers over the top of their enemy's head.

'Catch hold of him for me, will you, Rory, before he weasels out of here?' Hugh asked the Viscount, who was standing inside the door by which his sister had entered the room with his mouth open.

'He was going to shoot my sister,' Lord Rarebridge said as if they might not have noticed.

'And murder mine,' Kit said grimly as he seized one of Hibiscombe's arms very roughly and the Viscount grasped the other.

'Since he actually murdered my brother and Ariadne, I hope you're not planning to provide him with a purse full of guineas and a swift passage to the Americas so he can disappear?' Hugh warned before they bustled the loudly protesting Hibiscombe out of the room and into the Earl's library where they could hold him more easily, and privately, while they decided what was really to be done with him.

Chapter Sixteen

'You have my very sincere sympathy, Lady Calliope,' Hugh observed as he made a coolly composed bow to the visibly shaking woman, 'and my profound admiration for your courage,' he added and kissed her hand.

'I've been a fool,' she said with a sad shake of her head as she squeezed his hand and took a moment of comfort from a very old friend before she let it go.

Looking round for someone to support such a brave woman in her hour of need, Louisa shot the assembled spectators a look of contempt and tentatively offered Lady Calliope her own arm, since no other was forthcoming.

'I don't think so,' she argued. 'Nobody suspected what he truly was. Not one single person here tonight can put their hand on their heart and honestly declare they had even the shadow of a doubt about Mr Hibiscombe's actions or indeed his sanity until tonight,' she lied, because she had a very shrewd notion Hugh and her brother had begun to suspect both.

'He is a very plausible villain and I certainly never suspected him of anything more than being a sanctimonious young upstart,' one of the piano-playing ladies observed and stepped forwards to take Lady Calliope's other arm and her sister came out of the crowd to guard her flank.

'And whatever happens, you will always have the support of your family, my dear,' a gentleman Louisa vaguely recalled being introduced as a cousin of the Earl's stepped up to say as if he really meant it.

'Yes, indeed, it is quite obvious you knew nothing of what he was up to, now or in the past,' his wife said rather less sincerely, but she gave Louisa a nod that said, *This is my job*, as she ousted her from Lady Calliope's side, ready to escort her from the room and offer that support privately as well as in public.

'Will you see that all our guests go home safely?' Lady Calliope asked rather helplessly, before leaving the room with her attendants.

So Louisa and Hugh went back into the saloon and offered vague explanations about a sudden family crisis and Mr Hibiscombe being taken 'really rather ill' that nobody truly believed, but found it impossible to argue with. At last even the most persistent gossip of them all gave up and ordered her carriage before she could find out what had really gone on tonight, and they listened to the wheels of her ancient town chariot rumble away across the square and exchanged a look of profound relief with the much-tried butler. Wrapping her thickly lined velvet cloak more closely round herself against the chill that was probably more in her head than on the surprisingly soft April breeze, Louisa turned to look up at her new husband, and reassure herself again that he was nearly as unhurt as she was by Hibiscombe's best efforts to kill them.

'We will find out what your brother and Rarebridge are planning to do with the rat and then go home, shall we, love? I don't know about you, but I think I've had more than enough excitement for one day,' Hugh said with a rueful smile.

'I thought he'd killed you,' she confessed shakily and he ignored the presence of Lord Kinsham's staff to pull her into his arms and lead her inside, snuggled against the reassuring warmth of his side like the cherished new bride she was, rather than at the proscribed distance for a politely allied pair of aristocrats.

'And if not for that brave woman, he would have done his evil best to kill you in front of us all,' he said and tugged her into a quiet ante-room so they could embrace and soothe and marvel over each other in relative privacy for a few moments. 'Poor little Callie, and to think we all laughed when she wed that vermin and told ourselves he must possess hidden depths only she could see.'

'Yet they must have been happy enough to have produced the tribe of children your friend is always complaining about,' Louisa said as she marvelled at how little Lady Calliope could have known her repellent spouse to have embraced motherhood so enthusiastically.

'Looking back, I can see now that she only wed him in order to produce children and love them. She was brought up to think herself unlovable because she was the first-born and happened to be a girl child, instead of the heir everyone wanted. Isn't it astonishing how much harm we do our children with our expectations and faulty priorities?'

'Since all we were ever expected to do was stay alive at little cost to our father, I have no idea how you aristocrats bring up your progeny.'

'There you are, you see? You thought you were underprivileged, but how we poor downtrodden second sons and irrelevant daughters would have envied you such astonishing freedom from expectation,' he said with an expression of saintly resignation and hint at hardships borne so patiently that she hit the battered shoulder of his wedding coat and saw him wince.

'He did hurt you,' she said desperately, trying to rip the already-damaged cloth off his shoulders so she could examine him for damage, her heart racing and breath threatening to step up into panic as it seemed to her he was gallantly hiding some terrible injury he hadn't wanted to reveal in front of the curious.

'It's nothing, Louisa, just a graze and a slight bruise. I doubt there's even any blood on me for you to fuss over; if you undress me here and now to make sure, there will be no preventing me from doing the same to you. We don't need to get ourselves caught out in a scandalous liaison to add to the other eventful happenings this evening, love,' he protested and tugged the once-beautiful tailored garment back on to his shoulder as he gave her an exasperated look. 'And I really thought you Alstones were made of sterner stuff than this.'

'I'm not an Alstone any more though, am I? So how should I know how you Kenton/Darkes go on? I'm new made, Hugh. Mrs Hugo Kenton apparently to be of Gracemont Priory has a lot of self-discovery to endure over the next few weeks and I think I would far rather have been Mrs Darke of the high seas.'

'You'll cope, Mrs Kenton, with everything else you've survived up to now; a surly father-in-law, a few hundred tenants and a crumbling old barn of a house in the middle of Somerset should pose you few enough problems.'

'Thank you, I feel so much better now,' she said ruefully.

'I would have found it far more demanding to be Captain Darke, who had to endure the terror of knowing his wife was aboard every time he saw an enemy sail on the horizon. You have no idea how terrified that would have made me for your safety, my darling, and what my father has inadvertently spared me by deciding to want his errant son home after all.'

'Shall you miss the life though, Hugh?' she said seriously, knowing that she would hate it if he was forever longing for a freedom that was now over.

'Not really, life at sea is nine-parts tedium to one-part frantic action much of the time and you really have no concept of how terrified I was every time we cleared for action and waited for the enemy to fight.'

'But you haven't been in the Navy these last three years,' she pointed out, still doubtful he wouldn't grow bored with her and rural contentment.

'And the occupation your brother and his best friend offered me was exactly what I needed at the time, but we're agreed that becoming a full partner in their enterprise will keep me out of mischief once I've got the Gracemont estates under control. Any longing I ever had for adventures on the high seas has long faded away, Louisa, and I would far rather be ashore with my beautiful bride and a growing band of nigh-ungovernable brats in our image.'

'Good, then perhaps it's high time we went home and got on with making them, husband,' she reminded him demurely.

'No perhaps about it,' he assured her huskily, 'but first we must tie up one or two loose ends,' he added more soberly and her thoughts turned to the unfortunate woman upstairs and the hard life she must now face as sole parent to her own tribe of children.

'They can't gossip and snigger and pillory Lady Calliope as they did you, can they, Hugh? Like you, the worst she's guilty of is misjudgement about the person she married and she's paid heavily enough for that already. I don't think she's been at all happy with him, do you?'

'No, I think she made a mistake and lived with it as well as she knew how, but her family will stand by her now you've shamed them into it. There will still be gossip though, love— it's in the nature of dragons to gather and broadcast that as eagerly as they possibly can.'

'It must be very noisy as well as deeply unpleasant in their lairs, then.'

'Oh, deeply,' he said and ushered her out of their temporary sanctuary and along the wide corridor to knock on the library door without even trying to leave her behind, so at least he'd already begun to include his wife in his life, or decided there was no point in trying to exclude her.

'I'm so glad you've finally realised I'm not a die-away miss to be sheltered from the uncomfortable realities of life,' she said with a provocative sideways glance at him as they heard Kit's invitation to enter and opened the door.

'I may be an idiot, but even I know when I'm flogging a dead horse, and don't forget you're not a miss of any sort any more.'

'I know,' she said with great self-satisfaction and made him grin boyishly at the idea that she eagerly embraced marriage to him.

The reminder of all that was to come for them as man and wife was the antidote he probably needed for the sight of the repellent Hibiscombe, hunched over the Earl's desk, frantically scribbling. The Viscount was standing over him like the sternest of schoolmasters, looking as if he was about to correct his spelling and handwriting in no uncertain terms if he strayed from the straight and narrow lines he'd drawn up for him.

'We offered him a choice between a convenient shooting accident while he was cleaning those guns of his and writing a signed confession, then submitting to the madhouse, and d'you know what?' Rory asked incredulously. 'The little rat's plumped for the madhouse.'

'Dear, dear,' Louisa observed sympathetically, suddenly fighting what must be hysterical laughter at the flummoxed expression on his lordship's face. 'Some people really are totally outside the pale, are they not?' she added for good measure and felt Kit's glare at her facetiousness from across the room.

'You may trust us to deal with him from now on,' her brother informed her and Hugh sternly and directed the little rat in question to keep writing and not leave anything out.

'Yes,' his lordship replied simply to her question, with a fearsome frown that told them exactly what he thought of his brother-in-law. 'Alstone and I have sent for one of the magistrates from Bow Street, whom he assures me is discreet and not liable to broadcast the tale when we explain about my sister and the children. Then my man will go and fetch whichever lunatic doctor he recommends, so that we can have this vermin officially declared insane and remove him from poor Cal's life for ever. Sorry about such a hole-in-corner end to this miserable business, Kenton, but there's my sister and her brats to think of now, and a trial wouldn't have brought anyone back, would it?'

With those rare words of wisdom from his lordship echoing in her mind, Louisa meekly allowed her new husband to guide her out of the house and into the waiting carriage and even managed not to mind very much when the release of so many years of tension meant that all they did that night was sleep in each other's arms, even though it was their official wedding night.

Chapter Seventeen

'That's it, then, we're properly married and alone again at long last,' Hugo Kenton said to his bride the following evening as they finally ran up the steps of the elegant Palladian-style villa a few miles outside Brighton that he'd hired for the next week or two. 'And hopefully there's nobody else who will have the gall to try to keep me from my new wife and my clear marital duty to seduce her until she can't recall her own name, let alone those of our enemies and anyone else who might feel they have the right to interrupt our honeymoon.'

'I was beginning to wonder if I'd have to climb out of a window again to get you to myself,' Louisa replied.

'Perish the thought,' he said sternly.

'You don't have much faith in my abilities, do you?'

'I'm sure you could give the most furtive cracksman lessons, but I don't think my nerves would stand it.'

'Faint heart, but I promise not to climb anything more dangerous than those stairs yonder, so long as it isn't a dire emergency, and you wouldn't want me to sit about dithering if it was one of those, now would you?'

'Well, that's something, I suppose; all I have to do now is

keep you away from burning buildings and marooned kittens and my hair might not have to go white overnight after all.'

'I think you'd look very distinguished, and you have to admit that if I hadn't done it in the first place we would never have met again.'

'That's something else I must learn to be thankful for then, I suppose,' he said with a lugubrious sigh and such warmth in his silver-blue eyes she wondered how she'd ever thought them cold, but she couldn't let the topic go, despite the temptation to just let that warmth wash over her and waft them both up stairs and into a dreamy night of kissing and caressing and an awful lot more.

'But the way we met for the second time, the way I behaved that night and the next, meant that we had to get married, Hugh,' she said seriously, for it still rankled that in rescuing herself she'd trapped him.

'And are you regretting that already?' he asked gruffly.

'Of course not, but you must have mixed feelings about taking another wife.'

'You make me sound like a pasha who has far more than just the one wife about the place and just thought he might casually add another to his stock of them.'

'Don't get any ideas and don't change the subject. You know very well what I mean and you haven't exactly won yourself a prize in me.'

'By the time another day dawns, you won't have a single doubt left in your stubborn head as to how much I want you as my one-and-only wife, Louisa,' he threatened deliciously and she went breathless with anticipation as he took her light cloak and draped it carefully over a gilt chair, before pulling out another from the laden dining table and seating her with one or two apparently accidental touches that threatened to melt her from the inside out.

'Ooh, I shall look forward to that, then.'

'Not too much I hope, considering we have our delayed wedding night to plough through somehow or another first,' he said and she laughed and felt the shocks and upsets of yesterday recede at last, leaving behind them the delicious tension of anticipating the longed-for night to come.

'I expect you'll find a way to get us through it,' she told him blandly.

'Plainly I'll have to, since bold and beautiful Eloise La Rochelle was only a figment of our heated imaginations.' He slanted her an untrustworthy smile and she pencilled 'ruthless pirate' back on to her internal picture of him and shivered with delighted anticipation.

'You could teach me how to become more like her,' she suggested.

'And have half the West Country beating a path to our door to try and wrest you from me? Not in a million years.'

'I meant in private,' she protested. 'And Eloise and her pirate captain never really got to know each other properly, did they?' she added wickedly. Seeing how his gaze went blank, then lit with fire at the idea, she filed it for later and allowed all her love and wanting back into her own gaze. 'I will never look at another man, Hugh,' she promised him solemnly at last. 'Why should I when I have you?'

He took her hand and played with her beautiful rings as if to remind himself of all the promise and promises between them, then he met her gaze and deliberately let his guard fall until she could see something of the hopeful young man he'd once been, before he raised those barriers to protect himself from a loss and grief and fury that must have felt nigh intolerable to him.

'If everything hadn't happened just as it did, I wouldn't have met you one dark and fateful night, Eloise-Louisa, and just think how boring my life would have been. Now I really hope you've finished eating, because I'm fast discovering love is a very poor preventive of amorous intent and other husbandly lapses of consideration.'

'I never wanted to fall in love,' she said with a reminiscent shrug for her once-guarded self.

'Do you think I ran round London dancing with glee when I found out why I couldn't get you out of my head day or night? You're one of the most beautiful creatures I ever laid eyes on, and I only have to feel you enter a room to want you mercilessly.'

'When I first met you I thought you were dark and dangerous and there was something in your eyes that promised me you could make me feel things I have never wanted to. No wonder I dreaded ever setting eyes on you again.'

'Aye, well, at least I can understand that much, having felt something very similar myself.'

'Then understand this, Hugh Darke, or Hugo Kenton or whoever you happen to be calling yourself just at the moment. I meant to seduce you that first night at Kit's house, when I found you so castaway and gruff and bearlike and completely, unimaginably desirable that I wanted you so badly that it hurt to draw back.'

Louisa saw him doing his best not to let his eyes cross at the very thought of her so rampantly predatory and filed away that idea for future reference as well.

'Why did you, then?' he asked hoarsely.

'What would you have done then if you woke up next morning to find me in your bed and remembered you'd just taken my virginity?'

'I'd have railed at you for giving it away so lightly, I expect.'

'You railed at me anyway,' she pointed out with a half-smile, half-frown for the drunken antics of unregenerate rakes.

'It was obligatory after the weeks I'd endured longing for you with almost every waking and sleeping thought. But since you want to know, if I'd woken to find you in my bed like that, I would have dragged you off to my lair and had my wicked way with you again and again for our very mutual pleasure, until Kit came back and found out what I'd done to his precious little sister and killed me. After that, I wouldn't have been able to do anything much.'

'Good point.'

'I like it, although I wouldn't have done if it had actually happened.'

'Now I'm confused, but to get back to that night, even though I was so tempted to be an ex-virgin and escape Uncle William and Charlton forever, I nobly resisted your stubbly kisses and sweaty embrace.'

'I remember that bit,' he grumbled.

'Are you sure?' she sniped, then reminded herself they were having a very serious conversation here and frowned at him severely.

'Even if I was dead I would remember that bit,' he confirmed as if it was engraved on his heart.

'I wish you'd stop harping on death. I want you alive, Hugo Kenton.'

'So you can have your wicked way with me?' he asked hopefully.

'So I can make you regret ever being born if you ever take up with the likes of Eloise La Rochelle again. But now we're on the subject of Eloise once again, I knew that I'd put myself in the most ridiculous situation with you by pretending to be her and I wanted you so badly it almost made my bones ache, yet I couldn't have you because if I did then you'd know I'd lied and wasn't Eloise at all. Then you were followed and I was so scared, Hugh. I was so terrified, so utterly afraid they'd succeed in capturing and killing you and that I'd lose you, that I didn't care about such a little thing as whether or not I was a virgin anymore, I just wanted to be as close to you as I could get.'

'So you cared about me a little bit, even then?'

'I cared about you so much it felt like a betrayal of every promise I had ever made myself not to follow in my mother's footsteps, not to love blindly and never to need a man so much I'd put up with anything he did or said to just so I could have the privilege of carrying on loving him.'

To her furious amazement, Hugh laughed at this agonised confession and tugged her out of her chair with an impatient glance at the cold collation under their uninterested noses.

'You're no more capable of blind adoration than I am of wanting it in the first place, my own particular virago,' he informed her firmly. 'Do you imagine any fault I rejoice in will ever go unrecorded and ruthlessly reformed by my wife, because I can assure you that I don't,' he said as he towed her back into the hall and stopped in front of the fine pier table and the large gilt-framed mirror above it. 'Look at yourself, Louisa,' he urged, gently turning her face from his towards their reflected selves so she could examine her own face, or she could have if she hadn't been so busy devouring his with hungry eyes. 'No, really look at yourself; you have my full permission not to take your eyes off me once we've got this last ridiculous folly of yours out of the way, but concentrate for now.'

Reluctantly she obeyed him and stared at her own reflection, surprised at how different she looked under the spell of passion, but otherwise unimpressed. 'What am I supposed to be looking at?'

'Not what, but whom: this woman is Louisa Kenton, she is recklessly brave, ridiculously determined not to divulge to anyone how afraid she sometimes is of climbing out of windows and playing the female buccaneer, and she would throw herself to the lions if they showed signs of wanting to devour someone she loved instead of her. Her besotted husband knows her to be the most enchantingly lovely lady he ever laid eyes on, and he very shortly intends to lay more than his eyes on a whole lot more of her, by the way. He adores her quick wits and her bold tongue and even finds her short temper and pithy turns of phrase amusing most of the time.

'No doubt, in time and after a lot of brimstone-and-bluster temper tantrums of his own, he'll learn to control his fury at her unruly habit of running herself straight into any danger that happens along, hopefully before he's ground his teeth to stubs and bitten his nails to the quick. One thing he will never do, though, is expect her to follow any of his commands without at least an hour's debate about it, or encourage her to believe he'd like her better if she was a passive doormat of a woman he could swagger off and forget about while he was busy drinking or gambling or carousing himself into an early grave.'

He raised his hands to caress her shoulders and the woman in the mirror now looked as if she'd been presented with the moon and stars as his gaze softened with what she knew was true love.

'I don't doubt your mother was a good woman, Louisa,' he carried on more gently. 'Or that she suffered a very great deal for indulging her youthful passion for a man who clearly didn't deserve her, but you are not your mother.'

'No, I'm not, am I?' she agreed as she finally believed it.

'And before you start another avenue of self-flagellation, you're nothing like your father either. Somehow they gave life to four remarkable people in you and your brothers and sister, so their ill-starred marriage clearly wasn't in vain. I would have out-waited and out-snarled and out-stamped your brother, even after he'd beaten me to a pulp for taking your maidenhead, if he'd opposed our marriage, Louisa. I'd even have taken the battering I undoubtedly deserved from your gigantic friend Ben Shaw's mighty fists when he came home, if that was what it took to marry you. In fact, I think I would have done anything to gain you as my wife, so look what a lionheart you've gained in me?'

'More of a chicken-heart that first night I'd have said at the time, if you'd only asked me,' she teased and stroked the side of his face, feeling a slight suggestion of beard under her appreciative fingers and bringing back sensual memories of that first night and a very stubbly Hugh Darke, and the wild woman who'd descended on him out of the night and would have fallen into his arms like the wanton she'd claimed to be, given even a smidgen more encouragement.

'Shrew,' he whispered as he shivered with desire and anticipation from that one exploring caress.

'Not a mouse, then?' she asked as his mouth seemed to come satisfyingly close, then disappointingly firm and evade hers as he seemed to despair of ever getting her upstairs under her own steam.

'Never a mouse, my love, more of a tigress,' he informed her just before he hefted her over his shoulder as easily as if she were a sack of feathers rather than a healthy young woman and started up the stairs while she was still startled about seeing the world from upside down.

'I'll certainly scratch your eyes out for you if you don't hurry up and put me down, you toad,' she protested furiously, but he carried on doggedly getting her where he wanted her by the fastest method possible. 'Insufferable, intolerable weasel that you are,' she raved at him, secretly wondering which of them would be the more breathless and lightheaded by the time he reached his destination, then he did and she found out.

'Isn't it lucky that some considerate person left the door to the master suite wide open for us, my dear?' he asked her as if they were taking a leisurely stroll about their luxurious temporary home. 'Otherwise I might have had to dump you into the nearest chair whilst I wrestled with the door and that would have quite ruined the mood, don't you think?'

'Dump me…' she spluttered before recovering a few of her wits. 'You uncouth beast.' She hit what part of him she could reach with her fist as he turned round with her still writhing about on his shoulder to survey their extravagantly furnished bedchamber with such leisurely appreciation she knew he was enjoying himself a little too much at her expense.

'Run out of creatures vile enough to compare me to, my sweet?' he asked smoothly and shifted her so her body draped itself very closely about his as he let her slide back on to her feet even though her skirts were rucked up against his breeches and she knew just how aroused he was after her explicitly informative journey back to solid ground.

'I'll think of something,' she assured him breathlessly, but he didn't give her the time.

Instead he took her mouth in a fiercely desperate kiss that told her volumes about his state of mind and body and any doubts she'd ever had that he wanted her to the edge of madness evaporated under the heat of that kiss. Every bit as eager, she opened her mouth wantonly under his. His tongue tangled with hers and she closed her eyes and just revelled in real, substantial Hugh under her exploring hands, where she'd had to make do with the most shocking dreams and frustrating memories for far too long.

Engulfed in her Hugo's warmth and strength and feeling as if she was surrounded by urgent, so very much-needed man, she ignored the vague discomfort of an elegant bedpost at her back as she used it to stretch further up against him than she could of her own accord as he backed her blindly towards whatever surface stopped them first. Oh, this was wonderful, so all engrossing that Aunt Poole and half the strictest hostesses of the *ton* might have been watching on a set of very odd chaperon's benches for all she knew or cared. She let out a very necessary breath and gasped in another while she had the chance and felt so many of her inhibitions and insecurities leave the room along with those imaginary dragons.

'I love you, Hugo,' she informed him, using the name she was only now adjusting to, as he realised just where he'd placed her and turned her about so his back was to the smoothly turned mahogany instead while he busied himself exploring her back through the ivory silk of her gown; then, while he happened to be round there, he undid each satin-covered button until he could get down to just exploring uncovered Louisa instead. 'I really and truly love you,' she added and all the surprise she felt about the startling reality of their love must have been obvious in her voice, because it made him laugh and she felt as well as heard it since they stood so close his voice echoed through her own narrower ribcage and had a delightful effect on her already hard-peaked nipples and very aroused breasts.

'Good,' he spared breath to tell her before he silenced them both by shucking her undone gown off her shoulders and setting his mouth to one of those begging nipples before he could disentangle her arms from the puffy little apologies for sleeves a spring bride could afford to have on her going-away gown.

Trapped in a fine web of loving and absolute desire, Louisa felt her head go back as she arched to encourage her husband's possession and she gasped out something incomprehensible to both of them as words faded from her understanding of the world. Then she was lying dazed and not quite sure how she'd got there on the bed, with her gown a pool of neglected dusky-rose silk on the floor and she was vaguely conscious that Hugo was busy ripping off his own finery with eager abandon. Somehow she managed to force her suddenly heavy-lidded eyelids open so that she could appreciate the view; maybe the sight of them—all darkest of midnight blue, and dilated at actually being able to see the splendour of his golden-skinned torso, heavy with muscle and taut with wanting her—properly for the first time made him even more urgent. Lying like some wickedly sensual empress eyeing her lover, she let her kiss-swollen mouth open on an 'Oh?' of curiosity and just the slightest touch of awed apprehension as he tore off his boots, then struggled out of his breeches and finely clocked stockings in one fluid move and stood for a moment in all his naked glory.

It really surprised her that he was such a glorious sight, despite that magical interval in Kit and Ben's deeply shadowed warehouse. Thanks to him she knew exactly how a man made love to a woman, but he was so beautiful in his obviously extreme need of her. Not a word he'd appreciate if she said it out loud, of course, but he was all finely honed muscle and long, lean limbs, but her gaze centred on his manhood with eager fascination. A girl—and she realised she had been a girl until he made her his woman too many days ago now to recall—could speculate and wonder about what gentlemen were like under their clothes and even peer curiously at classical statues of apparently perfect young gods without their togas, but nothing could ever equal the fact of a naked man's raw desire for a woman he very clearly wanted very badly indeed. Or at least it couldn't equal her naked man's desire for her, as she had no interest whatsoever in seeing any others.

'You're obviously a very proud man in every sense of the world,' she managed to recover enough language to tell him huskily.

'Very proud of you, love,' he rumbled back, 'very desperate for you.'

'Then you'd best come closer,' she whispered, 'very much closer would be my best guess, as well as my pleasure.'

'So close we'll be one,' he half-promised and half-warned her as he smoothly surged on to the bed and the heated fact of his skin against hers sharpened every sense she had with anticipation.

'We already are,' she murmured and wondered at his rumble of male amusement, until he moved so he was resting half across her splayed body while still holding most of his weight on his impressively muscled arms.

'Just wait and see, or rather wait and feel, how very much better it can be with a decent bed under us and the whole night ahead of us,' he promised, then sank his head and a little of his weight towards her, so he could kiss her with what felt like all of him as well as just his wickedly knowing mouth.

Silenced for once, she loved the weight and strength of him and wriggled her legs against his to urge him closer, faster into this, their first sanctioned, married loving and she wondered that it could feel so wonderful and novel and right. Frustratingly he just used his superior strength to lift himself off her again for a while to gently, almost soothingly brush kisses across her brow, then her eyelids, then her cheekbones as her eyes opened again almost of their own accord when he worked his way down those cheekbones to slip kisses along the line of her jaw and back up to her mouth. There he lingered, eyes open and full of all he felt for her as they stared wonderingly at each other. His gaze was molten silver, shot with blue, his breath quick and shallow and she could feel herself quivering with excitement and scorching desire. Maybe even Hugo thought she was ready for more, because he hiked up the gossamer chemise that was all the boning and lining of her gown had needed beneath it and set himself to learn the burning heated place at the centre of her again as she parted her thighs eagerly to welcome his touch. Their mesmerised gazes still held as he tantalised and roused her, teaching her how much he loved the dark, springy curls at her secret centre, how he loved the soft wet folds of her outer sex even more and how he absolutely adored her molten inner core.

Her hands were almost as busy, even if she was still too shy to boldly set her hand to his rampantly aroused member. Yet she learnt how sleek and sensitive the corded muscles supporting his spine were as they flexed under her fascinated touch. He delved one of those wickedly exploring fingers of his further into her and she moaned a demand as that pulse of pure need tightened, then subsided around it only to burn again even more strongly. She gasped an incoherent protest and tried her best to pull him closer to her, kneading his tightly muscled buttocks with demanding fingers as she knew she had to have him inside her and love him in every sense of the word. Had to appease the hot, almost painful need to be full of the rigid, straining manhood he was denying them both until she was nearly weeping with frustration.

'Hugh,' she demanded reverting to the name of the man she had first fallen for, 'you in me. Must have you in me', and if he didn't spread her legs and take her soon she'd have to scissor her legs together and try to appease this grinding, magical need without him.

'Aye, it's high time we had each other again, my love,' he affirmed and raised her knees, then eased his emphatically aroused shaft into her at last and she sighed with blissful relief, so stretched and full of this wonder of a man, and her wide-eyed gaze sought his for confirmation that this was them, husband and wife, together on the road to somewhere wonderful at last. 'Let me come right into you again, my darling love,' he demanded and she relaxed her inner muscles, took the fact of him into herself in more than just the physical and trusted him absolutely.

She felt the freedom of this time, after he had gentled himself so much to take the fact of her virginity last time they'd loved, and that never-to-be-forgotten first time gave way to this equally important next time, now they truly loved and openly acknowledged it. Then he raised her knee a little higher, rocked back until he could angle her more receptively for one long, desperate thrust and she was his lover in every way there was once more. It didn't hurt this time and she gasped as he slid home into the very depths of her and burning need took over as Hugo withdrew from her so far that she let out a long moan of frustrated desire, then he thrust home again and sweet heat bloomed inside her like wildfire. The rhythm of his thrust and withdrawal taught her an even deeper delight in each other than she'd dared imagine before now and she eagerly moved to learn it.

His body set a glorious rhythm and his mouth enforced it first on one tightly aroused breast, then the other until she was thrashing her head from side to side in desperate pleading as that great and relentless force they experienced before beat at them in unison and beckoned that sensual edge to all this blissful closeness she remembered falling over last time they loved so completely, even if neither of them had fully known at the time how powerful that love truly was. He increased their already-wild rhythm, plunged into her even more deeply as he gasped out a plea of his own, then took her mouth in a long, desperate kiss, his eyes wide open on hers this time as his tongue plunged in time with his mighty body and something so exquisite bloomed between them that she felt tears glaze her open eyes, as she gazed into his wildly silvered blue eyes and finally let go.

They span into ecstasy as she felt her body spasm with heat and light and fulfilment, pulse after pulse of absolute pleasure ripping through both of them as he convulsed in driven fulfilment inside her and she felt the hot surge of his seed release within her, even as the last ripples of her own unimaginable pleasure smoothed her into satiated bliss and complete freedom and lovely little pulses of their ecstasy occasionally rocked her as she drifted at least halfway back to earth.

'Love you,' she said as soon as she had enough breath.

'You certainly did,' he murmured huskily as he withdrew from her and rolled them over far enough so he could pull the covers over them and cocoon their cooling bodies in the warmth of their marriage bed.

'I'm so glad I love you, Hugo, my own Hugh,' she confided.

'Then I'm very glad that you do to,' he teased.

'Monster,' she told him with a sleepy, contented chuckle that couldn't be bothered with *faux* outrage just at the moment.

'And very happy to report that I still love you, even after having my wicked way with you once more.'

'It really was lovely and wicked as well, wasn't it?' she asked, still a little insecure about her own attractions, even though he'd just proved how irresistible he found her in the most unarguable fashion imaginable.

'Just as you are, my lovely, wicked wife,' he told her with a long, sweet kiss of confirmation and heat stirred and snapped deep inside her belly all over again for a moment, before subsiding to a contented thrum of satisfaction.

'How many times a night do husbands and wives get to do that, husband?' she asked sleepily as she nestled her wildly tangled, dark-chestnut curls against his naked shoulder and sighed with contentment.

'Wasn't that enough wonderment for one wedding night?'

'This is certainly a very memorable wedding, but does it matter to you that we didn't wait for tonight to love each other, Hugo?'

'No, I shall look back on that stack of coffee sacks and a musty old warehouse with fondness for the rest of my life, love. But I shall now have to buy this place after all, exactly as its current owner wants me to and probably at some ridiculous price, because he'll know how much it means to me as soon as I open my mouth to agree. Then at least we can come back here every year and remind ourselves how exquisitely we made love on our actual wedding night, then do it all over again,' he told her with a quick kiss to the top of those rebellious curls of hers.

'We have so much in front of us, Hugo,' she said a little too seriously for a woman who'd just made spectacular love in her husband's arms, and he secretly marvelled at his own self-restraint in not hammering into her with wild need as soon as his unruly body had rubbed against hers once more and longed to do so from that first desperately sweet kiss to the last.

'We have each other, love. Nobody else stands a chance against Captain Hugo Kenton and his warrior wife now we're finally united.'

'Least of all Captain Hugo Kenton,' she told him with a great yawn and settled into his arms with a sigh of utter happiness.

'He was a lost cause the instant you set eyes on him.'

'So how many weeks do you think we'll spend at Gracemont Priory before you have enough and we can go to sea together instead, Captain?'

'Not that again,' he said in disgust. 'I think I've created a monster,' he added as he recalled how it was his own fault if his wife now believed in herself enough to fight for the right to carry out every hare-brained scheme that came into her lovely head.

'No, just a wife,' she argued and butted her head against his shoulder in a gesture of affection he found more touching than any poem or sophisticated phrase his first wife and one or two other lovers had deployed to try to capture his until-now elusive heart.

'And I challenge any man in England to produce a more ruthless, scheming, intractable one than I've won myself, my Mrs Louisa-Eloise Alstone-Kenton.'

'But you love me anyway?' she asked eagerly.

'Oh, yes, until the day I die and beyond, my love,' he promised and luckily he was a man of his word.

* * * * *

The Rake of
Hollowhurst Castle

ELIZABETH BEACON

Chapter One

Roxanne Courland stood in the bay of delicately leaded windows that lit the drawing room of Hollowhurst Castle and watched darkness overtake the gloriously unimproved gardens. Soon the quaint old topiary would become a series of unearthly shapes and the holly grove the blackest of shadows. Rumours about the grove being planted by witches, whose terrible curses would fall on anyone unwary enough to visit it after dark, were rife in the surrounding villages. Roxanne thought such tall tales had been invented to frighten the maids away from temptation, though, and wondered if such cunning tactics still worked in the year of Our Lord eighteen hundred and eighteen. Not that it would make an ideal trysting place, of course, but once upon a time she'd have waited all night long for a lover among its spiky darkness, if he'd only asked her to.

Silly, impressionable Rosie Courland and her elder sisters had hidden in its shelter to catch their first glimpse

of the guests their brother had invited for Christmas ten
years ago, because it was close on midnight and even
her elder sister Joanna should have been in bed hours
before. How different that joyful season had been at the
giddy age of fourteen, she thought now, her heart sore
at the likelihood of spending another festive season in
splendid isolation. Then she'd been so excited she could
barely stop herself squeaking with anticipation as she
shifted from one foot to the other in the snow, her boots
gradually getting wetter and her feet colder, despite her
restlessness.

'For pity's sake keep still, Rosie,' seventeen-year-old
Joanna had hissed furiously at her. But keeping still was
something elderly people like her sisters did, along with
not running and never arguing with one's elders, even
if they were wrong and needed to know it.

'It's prickly and dark in here, as well as freezing
cold. Why can't we hide in the oaks by the Solar Tower,
or up the Tower for that matter?' she complained half-
heartedly.

'Because you can't see the drive, of course, and
there's no leaves on the oak trees to hide us from anyone
who heard a squeak from you and swung their lantern
in our direction, you silly, infuriating child,' Maria told
her scornfully, ever ready to trumpet her two years'
superiority in age over her annoying little sister.

'Silly child yourself, maybe you can't see much from
the ground over there, but we could have climbed the
oaks, or even looked out from the roof with Grandpapa's
telescope. Nobody would see us up there in the dark at
any rate and we'd be a lot more comfortable.'

'Someone would have caught us sneaking up the stairs
the way you rattle on, even if we could see anything up

there in the dark with one telescope between three of us. Anyway, I'm not climbing trees in the pitch darkness and Uncle Granger threatened to send you to school the last time you borrowed his spyglass and broke it, so have some sense, do. Either go inside and wait quietly in the warm like a good little girl, or stay here and stop moaning,' Joanna had whispered impatiently, then gone back to staring fixedly at the avenue as if her life depended on seeing any sign of movement.

'You're both so stuffy since you started putting your hair up, I'm surprised you don't petrify like that silly statue of Virtue in the library. All either of you ever do nowadays is talk about clothes and novels that make no sense at all and you strike the most ridiculous attitudes so the boys will admire you, when they'd like you a whole lot more if you stopped being so stupid.'

'She's just a little girl who's scared of the witches, Joanna, ignore her,' Maria had urged.

It would have felt better if she'd bothered to whisper a few witchy cackles and invented a bloodcurdling curse or two to frighten her away, but instead Maria had turned her back and taken Joanna's arm, as if their annoying little sister was irrelevant. Roxanne had felt hurt and bewildered when her previously intrepid eldest sister became ever more remote and grown-up, then Joanna even began to agree with Maria's constant criticisms rather than taking Roxanne's part. If that was what growing up and falling in love did for you, she'd sworn to herself as she stood shivering in the shadows fighting off tears, she'd never commit such arrant folly.

Coming back to the here and now, she recalled that resolution with a wry smile. It must have been the worst-kept vow in the long and eventful history of the

Courlands of Hollowhurst, for just then Maria's unusually sharp ears had detected the faintest jingle of a harness, and Roxanne had frozen into stillness as she heard how the sound of approaching voices carried uncannily across the deep snow. Not daring to move a muscle lest they be discovered and excluded from the Christmas feasts for standing in a snowdrift at twelve o'clock at night, all three sisters had stood like enchanted beings from some hoary legend and strained every sense toward the travellers.

Their brother David, riding his prized grey gelding, had shown up first through the darkness and they had strained their eyes to see who was with him. Roxanne had heard her eldest sister's involuntary gasp of pleasure and relief as she glimpsed Tom Varleigh's chestnut hunter when the lodge-keeper Fulton's lamp swung towards him; then Fulton turned back to guiding the young gentlemen up the drive, and Rosie had felt her heart thud in fear for the changes some instinct warned her were surely coming. Telling herself she was exasperated because Joanna had made far more noise than she, Rosie nudged her sister sharply to remind her where they were and what they were risking, and peered through the darkness to see if Davy had brought anyone else back from Cambridge with him. Then she forgot her apprehension, trying to make out the third rider when it became obvious not even two young gentlemen could make such a merry outcry on sighting journey's end.

Suddenly there was a blaze of light as the household within finally heard the sounds of horses' hooves, and the ringing calls of young men at the end of a long and gruelling ride were carrying on the still air. Then a huge horse, as fell and powerful as the darkness itself, reared up at the unexpected bloom of lights and Rosie held her breath, expecting to see his rider plunge heavily into the nearest snowdrift. Instead, that remarkable young man controlled the great brute with an ease the fiery animal must have found near to insulting and only laughed at his antics.

'Get down with you, Brutus, you confounded commoner,' a voice as dark and distinctive as his mount rang out joyfully, as if his rider had enjoyed the tussle for supremacy that Brutus already seemed to know he'd lost from the half-hearted nature of his last trial of strength with his conqueror—until the next time.

Rosie had watched with spellbound awe as the stranger mastered the curvetting horse with ease, then leapt out of the saddle as soon as the fiery beast was quiet and produced a carrot from the depths of his greatcoat pocket, which he bestowed on the huge black stallion with an affectionate pat.

'He's certainly not changed for the better since I was last in England,' the young man had shouted cheerfully at Tom Varleigh, who was watching the show with an appreciative grin on his face.

'Why d'you think I chose the chestnut when my father offered us the pick of his stable?' Tom replied.

'Because you have an unfriendly wish to see me summarily unshipped into the snow, dear cousin?' the stranger said as part of his identity became clear to the girls, who strained to see and hear all.

A cousin of well-connected Tom Varleigh, and he'd been overseas, probably with the military if the cut of that greatcoat was anything to go by. Rosie could practically hear Maria calculating his eligibility or otherwise to become her husband as soon as she could arrange it, and she had felt a primitive scream of denial rise just in time to hold it back and briefly wonder at herself, before her attention was once more fixed on the young man in front of them.

'I've a far stronger one not to take a tumble myself,' Tom had admitted.

The tall stranger responded by laughing and picking up a handful of snow to throw at Tom. They had a fine snowball battle going and all three young men looked as if they really had fallen off their horses into the heavy drifts after all when Sir Granger Courland appeared in the wide doorway and laughed even more loudly than his youthful visitors at their boisterous antics.

A smile lifted Roxanne's wistfully curved lips now at that poignant memory of her great-uncle, enjoying his duties as master and host of Hollowhurst Castle to the full, even as she blinked back a tear that he was no longer here to do so. Uncle Granger had been born to welcome guests and throw open his generous hall to them, she decided, picturing his still tall figure that had grown a little stout over the years. Sir Granger's hair had still been dark at sixty-five, even if his side-whiskers were grey, and his great voice could often be heard from one end of the hunting field to the other. He'd seemed so undimmed by the march of time while she was growing up that she'd made the mistake of thinking him indestructible.

'Welcome, one and all, and the compliments of the season to you,' he'd bellowed at the suddenly still group, she remembered, finding the past more attractive than the present again. 'Whoever have you brought me, Davy? It's not that Varleigh fellow we kept falling over at every turn last summer, is it?'

David had laughed and pulled Tom into the light, where he smiled sheepishly and earnestly said he hoped he hadn't worn out his welcome.

'Never, you'll always find one by my fireside, lad—but who else do we have here? A circus rider, perhaps, or some damn-your-eyes cavalry officer?'

'Neither, sir, I'm Tom Varleigh's cousin, and only a humble sailor. Your grand-nephew invited me here for the season out of the goodness of his heart.'

'Goodness of his heart? He hasn't got any,' Uncle Granger teased his heir, who was nearly as soft-hearted and hospitable as he was himself. 'If he had, he'd have managed to get himself sent down weeks ago, for we all miss him sorely. Come on in, boy,' he bellowed and the stranger obeyed, laughing at some unheard comment from his cousin Tom as he went.

Once in front of the great doorway and almost within sight of a warm fire and a good meal after his long day, the stranger had taken off his sailor's bi-corn and the flaring light lovingly picked up the brightness of his curly blond hair that reflected gold back at them. From her hiding place, Roxanne had strained to see every detail of his lithe figure; a totally novel admiration she didn't truly understand making her drink in this splendid young man, from the wide grin on his tanned face to his travel-stained boots. He bowed elegantly to his host and presented himself to be duly inspected. The lamplight twinkled on the highly polished brass buttons and the single epaulette on his dark blue coat that indicated he was a lieutenant in his Majesty's Navy, once he'd stripped off his wet greatcoat and presented it to the waiting footman.

'Lieutenant Charles Afforde of the *Trojan* at your

service, Sir Granger,' he had said in that deep husky-toned voice that sent shivers down Rosie's spine as she peered out of the darkness, as enthralled as if she truly was under the spell of some ancient sorceress.

Little Rosie Courland had stood in her chilly hiding place and forgotten the cold and the spiny darkness, awed by every detail of this young demi-god as she fell youthfully and completely in love after all. She'd felt the deep, unknown thrill of it shiver right through her at the very thought of actually meeting such a splendid specimen of manhood instead of worshipping from afar. Miss Roxanne Courland recalled with a cynical grimace how underwhelmed he'd been by that meeting when it came and tried not to squirm for her youthful, deluded self, even as her memory insisted on drawing her back to that snowy night so long ago, as if intent on reminding her what folly extreme youth was capable of.

'Didn't know Samphire had a boy in the navy,' her uncle had roared on, oblivious to the fact that his youngest great-niece had just had her world rebuilt by one careless smile into the snow-laden night from his unexpected guest.

Roxanne remembered wondering how her great-uncle could be oblivious to such a momentous moment and smiled wryly at her childish self-importance. It had certainly *felt* unforgettable to the silly schoolroom miss who had stood and watched Lieutenant Charles Afforde hungrily that night, as if recalling every detail of his handsome face might one day save her life or change the orbit of the spheres.

'He doesn't, sir,' the blond Adonis had admitted cheerfully. 'The last earl was my grandfather and took me in as a scrubby brat, but I'm just a mere nephew to the new earl.'

'Well, any relative of old Pickle is welcome under my roof.'

'Thank you, sir, although my grandfather didn't care to be reminded of that nickname in his latter years.'

'Grown too full of his own importance, had he?' Sir Granger had roared gleefully. 'I must tell you how richly he deserved it when you're not frozen and tired half to death.'

'And I warrant that's a tale that'll make good listening,' Charles Afforde had remarked laughingly.

'That it will, m'boy,' Uncle Granger had replied, 'but come on inside, all three of you, so we can shut the doors. I prefer what warmth there is from the fires we light to try and keep this great barn warm kept inside instead of taking the chill off the park, my lads.'

With a quick glance of concern for his mount, Lieutenant Afforde had obviously decided he was as well, and as bad tempered, as ever, and left the animal to his host's head groom so that he could enter the welcoming portals of Hollowhurst Castle with a light heart. For one moment he'd paused on the threshold and it seemed to Rosie Courland in her cold and prickly hiding place as if he had somehow seen all three of them, bunched together spellbound in the darkness as they watched the new arrivals play like boys, then be welcomed as men.

That younger Roxanne had held her breath as if he might hear such a soft sound over the yards that separated them and decided that, one day, she was going to marry Charles Afforde, when she was properly grown up and beautiful and he'd become a great admiral, easily as famous as the great, much-mourned, Viscount Nelson. For that minute at least, she'd known that he had seen her and acknowledged their meeting was deeply significant to both of them. Even when he largely ignored her during that Christmas season in favour of Joanna, Maria and the vicar's Junoesque eighteen-year-old daughter, she'd still been convinced he was amusing himself while he waited for her to be ready for marriage. She would wait for him, she'd decided with all the fervent passion of her headlong nature, but instead she'd grown up and discovered fairytales were just that.

Roxanne's lips twisted into a grimace of distaste and impatience at her young and over-romantic self. Sir Charles Afforde was indeed a lion nowadays; successful, courageous and independently wealthy from prize money and the family trust he'd finally taken control of, according to David's sporadic letters. Then there was that baronetcy he'd won by his own efforts, bestowed on him by a grateful country for gallant service in the late wars. His elevated naval rank of commodore might revert to a mere captaincy when he was on land and no longer in command of his squadron, but no doubt at all he'd have been made admiral if he had stayed in the navy when Bonaparte was finally defeated, even if the Admiralty had had to promote a dozen senior officers to flag rank ashore on half-pay to give such a capable and proven captain his admiral's flag.

On the other hand, Miss Roxanne Courland had fulfilled her early promise by growing up to be as dark as the fashion was fair, and far too decided a character for the ridiculous mode that demanded a lady should pretend extreme sensibility and embrace idleness. Little wonder few gentlemen had the nerve to so much as dance with her, let alone lay their hands and hearts at her impatiently tapping feet.

Just as well she'd long ago given up her secret dream of capturing Charles Afforde's fickle heart then, for no doubt he'd choose a sophisticated beauty when he finally took a wife and not a countrified beanpole of four and twenty but, considering she doubted he possessed a heart to lose, wasn't that just as well?

She was happy enough as Aunt Roxanne now Joanna and her Tom Varleigh had made her so three times over; and she was just good old Rosie to her brother, the spinster sister who held the reins of Hollowhurst in her capable hands while he travelled to the furthest corners of the earth. So the real question was what on earth could that dashing hero Sir Charles Afforde want with her humble self? His letter lay on the delicate rose-wood desk that she used for her correspondence and she cautiously considered it through the gathering darkness, as if to get closer might somehow conjure him up out of the dusky shadows.

The wretched thing had done nothing but disturb her since it arrived two days ago, its terse content worrying away at her customary serenity until she was tempted to throw it in the fire and have done with him, even if she couldn't bring herself to actually do it. Maybe something remained from the old days, then—not the illusion that she could tame the wild rover under all that rakish charm, but a dream dead and done with that was reminding her a much younger, ridiculously romantic Roxanne would probably hate the person she'd become.

Chapter Two

With an impatient sigh, Roxanne decided to put Sir Charles Afforde out of her mind until he called and told her what he actually wanted with her after so many years. There was plenty to divert her, after all, for times were hard since the end of the war and it was proving a struggle to keep Hollowhurst untouched by it all, and then there was Davy's latest letter. She shivered, sensing something new and worrying behind her brother's evasive reception of her ingenious solution to some vexing estate business.

Instead of carelessly agreeing to anything she proposed as usual, Sir David Courland wrote instead of the many charms offered by his latest landfall. Despite the late war between Great Britain and the American States, he seemed very welcome in New England and wrote enthusiastically of its many beauties, particularly those of a certain Miss Philomena Harbury, whose virtues apparently knew no bounds. Her brother was obviously fathoms deep in love, and Roxanne hoped her family would not stand in their way.

David might be a baronet and wealthy landowner, but his constant racketing about the world would make him a challenging husband, even without the fact of him owning Hollowhurst to ensure they would be parted from her kin by a vast ocean sooner or later, if he and his Philomena married. Given that the girl would have to give up so much to marry him, how could Roxanne expect the new Lady Courland to share her strange new home with a sister-in-law accustomed to ruling it unopposed?

She'd learn to love Mulberry House, Roxanne reassured herself, picturing the neat and airy dwelling in Hollowhurst village that her uncle had purchased lest his nieces were unwed and now left to her because she was going to need it. The mistress of such a fine house would command respect in the area, as long as she learned to behave more like a lady and less like the lord of the manor. Yet she watched the quaint old gardens fade into darkness and sighed as she tried to visualise herself occupied with planning rosebeds, visiting her neighbours and good works. She'd have time to stay with her favourite aunts in Bath at last and at Varleigh with the ever-expanding Varleigh family, maybe even a duty visit at Balsover Granta with Maria, now Countess of Balsover, followed perhaps by the heady delights of London for the Season. Roxanne shook her head and wondered how she'd endure a life of idle uselessness.

'You're very lucky, my girl,' she chided herself out loud. 'You should be counting your blessings.'

'Should you indeed, Miss Courland?' a deep voice spoke out of the darkness and nearly made her jump out of her skin. 'I always considered that a sadly futile exercise when ordered to do so by my tutors.'

'Who the deuce are you?' she snapped back, although she would have known his deep voice anywhere.

'What a very good question,' he replied, the devil-may-care grin she remembered so well becoming visible as well as audible when he stepped out of the shadows and into the dying light from the bay windows. 'I remember you very well, ma'am, but no doubt I've faded into the mists of your memory by now. Charles Afforde, very much at your service, Miss Courland.'

'Sir Charles,' she acknowledged absently, still struggling to settle the errant heartbeat the mere sound of his voice provoked.

'Perhaps you remember me, after all, considering you take such a flattering interest in my humble career, Miss Courland?'

'My brother writes of you in his letters, and reports of your daring deeds reach us even in a backwater like Hollowhurst, Commodore Afforde.'

'The navy and I have parted company, so I don't use my rank, and I was only ever a commodore when in command of my squadron, you know.'

'Do you miss it?' she asked absently, then told herself crossly not to ask such personal questions on the strength of the merest acquaintance. 'I beg your pardon, that was impertinent of me.'

'Not at all, our families have been friendly since before the Flood and your eldest sister is my cousin's wife, so I think we may presume on both connections and friendship, don't you? And the answer is, yes, I miss the limitless possibilities of the sea, but a battle is as grim a business at sea as on land and I'd been fighting them for far too long. They do say a true sailor only retires when he's safely underground, or underwater, so life on shore might pall one day, I suppose.'

'So you're giving shore life a try out, then?' she replied sharply, for his easy assumption that he could spring up out of the shadows in her own home and be offered a warm welcome was annoying now the shock had abated.

'You think me presumptuous perhaps, Miss Courland?' he asked, apparently unmoved by her sarcasm.

'I think you're likely to be bored and disillusioned when the novelty wears off, Sir Charles.'

'You have become very frank in your opinions,' he replied solemnly, but she could see enough of his expression through the gloom to know he was laughing at her. 'And what a paltry fellow you do think me.'

'How could I when your deeds are trumpeted throughout the land? That would be presumptuous and ungracious, Captain.'

'Then why do I think you don't care if I consider you a perfect lady or a hoyden, Miss Courland?'

'I really don't know, why do you think so, sir? Could it be that you just walked into my home unannounced and strolled about as if you owned it? It would never do for me to be so lost to the claims of simple hospitality as to point out such a vast presumption on your part, now would it?'

'No, particularly now that I can't stay here, as I planned, with you living alone in this scrambling fashion,' he replied, the humour fading from his deep voice as he looked surprisingly stern in the shadowed light.

'My mode of life is none of your concern.'

'Ah, but it is, Miss Courland. It's of very material

concern to me, since it currently stands between me and my new life.'

'Don't be ridiculous. Nothing I do has an effect on the way you live your life, Sir Charles, and I think you're fit for Bedlam if you believe it does.'

'Again, you are very frank,' he said, such genial amusement in his deep voice that she wished she could forget she was a lady long enough to slap him.

Then he sobered again and she saw he was eyeing her shadowy figure in the fading light. Her dark gown must be adding to the gathering gloom and her face probably appeared almost ghostly in the twilight, but that was no reason for him to stare at her as if trying to resolve a vexing riddle.

'You haven't heard from your brother lately, I take it?' he asked softly at last and there was something in his voice that sounded almost like pity. She shivered in sudden fear as she tried to reassure herself all was well.

'Not for several weeks,' she finally admitted as if the words had been racked out of her.

He was silent for a while as if pondering his next move and she refused to fill it with idle chatter when she hadn't even invited him to walk into her brother's drawing room and make himself at home. Anyway, she hated discussing her family with a man who was now a stranger, and the fact that she'd once heaped so many ridiculous hopes on his broad shoulders just made it worse. He was standing closer now and she'd be a fool not to notice he was more ridiculously handsome than ever. The careless glow of youth had left his face, along with any lingering innocence, and his features had hardened in maturity until he looked like a formidable

Greek god—powerful Zeus instead of careless Apollo, perhaps.

Yet he seemed almost impatient of his looks, although he probably made little enough effort to fight off the women who flirted with him whenever he ventured into society or the *demi-monde,* if rumour was true. No doubt the idiotic females lined up to be seduced by the smiling devil he was now, and they were welcome to him. Roxanne infinitely preferred the younger, less jaded Charles Afforde of a decade ago to this cynical rake.

Colours were beginning to fade from the world along with the daylight, so she couldn't tell if his eyes were as breathtakingly blue as ever, but they were certainly sharper and more disillusioned as he looked down at her as if trying to read her thoughts, which was one more good reason to keep him at arm's length. The last thing she wanted was to become an open book to him, so he could amuse himself with a list of her peculiarities whenever he had an idle hour to spare.

'I think you'll find Davy's life has changed more than usual during that time,' he said carefully at last, as if he was weighing every word, then tempering them to avoid a hysterical feminine reaction.

Luckily she'd given up the vapours at a very early age, as Maria was far too good at them to stand competition. 'Tell me,' she demanded flatly, suddenly knowing this was going to be one of those painful revelations no words could soften.

'He's wed, Miss Courland. In fact, I was his groomsman, so there can be no doubting the truth of it, and a very fine wife he's won himself, as well.'

'I'm not in the least surprised,' she returned calmly

enough, for hadn't she been thinking of that eventuality ever since that last letter from her brother was so full of his lovely Philomena? Even if she did feel shocked by the stark fact of David marrying without taking trouble to inform his family of it himself.

'He also assured me he has no intention of returning to England for more than a visit. I'm sorry to break such news to you so abruptly, but either Davy couldn't put his soul on paper, after all, or his letter has gone astray.'

Sir Charles Afforde looked distinctly uncomfortable about being the one to tell her. She could imagine him as sternly self-composed when having to go in front of his admiral with ill news, although Davy's happiness wasn't bad news, of course, yet she was torn between joy for him and terrible anxiety for all she held dear here.

'Not coming back?' she said at last and couldn't hold back the most important question, 'But what about Hollowhurst?'

Roxanne had no idea why she asked him the fate of her home with an absentee master committed to another country. Maybe her reign would continue, but apprehension set flocks of butterflies aflutter in her stomach and confirmed it was unlikely. At least she hoped it was apprehension, for Charles Afforde was very close now, and she was human, even if she was also a superannuated old maid.

'That's where I come in, I fear,' he admitted gruffly.

'You fear? When did you ever do that, Sir Charles?' she asked stiffly, wondering just why he hadn't said all this in a letter.

'You'd probably be surprised, but my flawed personality isn't pertinent to the facts. The truth with no frills and furbelows on it, Miss Courland, is that your brother has sold me the castle and estate so he can invest in his wife's estates and other ventures in the country he's adopted as his own.'

Roxanne gasped and let herself feel the momentous weight of change on her slim shoulders for a long, terrible moment. Then she braced them and forced her chaotic feelings to the back of her mind as she met his eyes steadily. The appalling reality of Davy's betrayal could wait until she was alone; she refused to let her shock and grief show in front of Charles.

'But what of legal formalities and viewing the farm accounts?' she heard herself protest, feeling as if she was listening to a stranger producing caveats as to why the truth couldn't be true.

'No need of that between us, he named a fair price and I paid it. Your brother was ever an honest man.'

'You call him so, but took advantage of his honesty, I dare say. He's newly in love and that's never time to take a hard look at the future,' she shot at him, fury surging through her in an invigorating tide as she looked for someone to blame and found him very handy indeed.

'You know better, Miss Courland. I always took you for the most intelligent of your family, so you must know your brother found his inheritance a burden rather than a joy. Davy has no love of the land and takes little pleasure in being lord of the manor. It's my belief that America will suit him very well, and he already insists on being known as plain Mr Courland and is impatient with the old order for holding back the new.'

'You don't share his Jacobin notions, Sir Charles?' she snapped scornfully, as lashing out at him staved off the painful thought that Charles Afforde knew her brother better than she did herself.

'No, I'm quite content to command, but I was raised to it, Miss Courland, and learned early that it was my duty as an officer to lead. The life that never suited Davy will do me very well.'

Roxanne shivered again and hugged her arms about her body as if hoping to ward off the chill of the autumnal evening and this appalling news. She was having her childish dreams come true in the most twisted and cheerless fashion imaginable. Once she'd yearned for this man, striven to become a correct young lady in order to deserve him, until she finally realised he wasn't worth it. She'd wasted the painful intensity of the very young on a handsome face and now felt betrayed again. Except he meant nothing to her, so retiring to Mulberry House sooner than she'd dreaded wasn't the catastrophe it currently felt. What a relief to be spared the sight of him striding along in Uncle Granger's shoes and lording it over her beloved home.

'My brother was raised to take command here one day,' she heard herself protest weakly and wondered why she bothered.

'Of course he always knew he'd inherit,' Sir Charles Afforde told her carefully and Roxanne wondered if shock made his voice echo in her ears like the voice of doom.

He'd be horrified if she gave in to the painful thudding of her heartbeat in her ears and fainted, but at least the mere sound of his voice no longer made her tingle down to her toes and at too many points in between.

'You must know he never really took to the life, though, Miss Courland,' he continued. 'Indeed, Davy always claimed you were more suited to the role of landowner than he, but Hollowhurst would be too great a burden for a woman to bear alone, given the nature of the society we live in.'

'Thank you for knowing my capabilities better than I do myself, Sir Charles, and on such a short acquaintance, as well.'

'Ten years is no trifling term, ma'am.'

'It *is* when we barely knew each other even then and have not seen each other to speak to since my eldest sister's wedding to your cousin nine years ago.'

'Then we can look forward to improving our friendship, can we not? Especially as we're to be such close neighbours.'

'I hope you don't expect me to be overcome with delight at the prospect,' she muttered just loudly enough for him to hear her, then fixed a false, social smile and hoped he knew how much she'd love to slap him. 'So we are,' she said aloud with a forced lightness he'd be a fool to mistake for cordiality. 'Pray, how long do I have to remove myself from here, sir, or do you wish me to decamp tonight?'

'I would never be so hardhearted, Miss Courland, despite the fact you obviously think me capable of any crime short of murder.' He gazed at her through the increasing gloom and she saw his eyebrows rise in apparent amusement, the infuriating devil! 'Ah,' he went on, the laughter she'd once listened for so eagerly running through his deep voice in a warm invitation to share his amusement, 'so you don't set even that limit on my villainy.'

'Of course I do,' she spluttered as the good manners everyone had tried so hard to drum into her made a weak attempt to control her temper and, she had to admit it to herself, her pain. 'I can tell you're not a monster.'

'Can you, my dear Miss Courland? I doubt it, but take as long as you like to gather your new household about you, and take what you want with you, so long as you leave me some furniture and a bed to sleep in.'

'I'll take no more than is mine,' she informed him haughtily, seething at his apparent belief that she'd strip the house to its bare bones in some vulgar attempt at revenge.

'And have the neighbourhood accuse me of turning you out with not much more than the clothes on your back? That really wouldn't do my credit any good in the district, now would it? I claim the privilege of changing my mind and will return tomorrow to make sure you don't distort my good intentions into infamy, Miss Courland, and leave with little more than the clothes you stand up in. I'd be a scandal and a hissing in the area if I turned you out with such apparent cruelty.'

'I doubt it,' she said impatiently, imagining the effect his looks and wealth would have on the local ladies. 'Do as you please, sir, and, as this is your house, I certainly can't stop you coming and going as you please.'

'You can so long as you persist in not employing a chaperone.'

'Whatever follies I choose to commit are mine, Sir Charles, and have nothing to do with you.'

'They do when you make yourself extraordinary by them. You're the sister of one of my oldest and dearest friends, Miss Courland, and while you might have run rings round him however early he got up in the morning, I'm no easygoing David Courland in search of a quiet life.'

'That's self-evident,' she told him darkly, those good manners she'd congratulated herself on threatening to slip away if she yielded to temptation and punched him on his patrician nose as she longed to do.

'Good, then, as we've established I'm certainly not your brother, hadn't we better consider how we're to remedy your chaperone-less state?'

'No, *we* had not. If I'm to be saddled with one, I'll select her myself. Indeed, it would be highly improper for a man like you to select a duenna for a single lady.'

'True,' he said without noticeable shame, 'but I do have the odd female relative, you know. And one or two respectable friends who've yet to cast me off, who have ladies to lend their aid if I explain your situation.'

'You do surprise me, sir.'

'I always endeavour to confound expectations, ma'am, especially when they're so very low.'

'I'm quite sure you do, but pray don't put yourself to the trouble of disproving mine. I look forward to us seeing very little of one another once I've packed up and left Hollowhurst for good. You'll be far too busy managing such a large estate to worry about socialising with your neighbours for a while, and I intend to travel, so I dare say we'll hardly ever meet. My brother isn't the only member of our family possessed of itchy feet,' she lied.

Chapter Three

In fact, Roxanne would have been content to continue at Hollowhurst for the rest of her life if fate had only allowed it, but she needed an excuse to avoid the new owner of her beloved home in the months to come. Travelling would do as well as any other plan, and was far better than staying and risking being charmed out of her fury by the very man who'd just deprived her of useful occupation.

'But I hope you don't plan to set out just yet, and certainly not alone?'

'That, sir, is my business.'

'In so far as you are of age I suppose that's true, but David asked me to look to your welfare and happiness in his absence and I warn you that I fully intend to do so. I suspect we're both about to discover that there's no stricter mentor for a lady of quality than a reformed rake, Miss Courland.'

'Then you're reformed, are you, Sir Charles? I can't claim to have seen any indication of it so far.'

'You may not think so, ma'am, but you've enjoyed the fruits of my good intention ever since I walked in and found you communing with the twilight.'

'I have? How fortunate for me.'

'Fortunate indeed,' he returned blandly and even through the gloom she'd be an idiot to mistake the wolf-ish glint in his eyes for anything but what it was and feel unease, despite her determination not to let him fluster or intimidate her.

'Then perhaps you'd take yourself back to wherever you came from for the night, Sir Charles, since it would be such a shame to spoil it all now.'

'Yet something tells me you're truly wild at heart. Do you secretly prefer recklessly courting danger to pretending respectability, Miss Courland?'

'Don't presume to know me,' she snapped back, much tried and confused by her own reactions to the veiled threat in his husky voice.

She'd got over the idea that Charles Afforde was put on this earth to be her destined mate many years ago. He was a dangerous rake and, despite his undoubted heroism in battle, she doubted he made a single move on land without calculating its effect. Why, then, was her silly heart racing with excitement like some mad moth sighting a brilliant light and speeding towards it, eager for its own destruction? She was woman enough to know he'd just introduced his sensual appetites and experience into this shadowy encounter, but she was old and wise enough not to call his bluff now, wasn't she?

'Then discovering your secrets will add spice to the

game, my dear,' he mused, almost as if he was talking to himself; suddenly he was very close.

It was so dark now she could only gauge his intentions by the tension in his silence and a hint of something new and unsettling in the outline of his powerful body. Then he lowered his head and captured her lips with his and only that contact sparked between them like lightning, but such a contact that she felt half-scorched and half-terrified. She was free, she told herself with little effect; she could disengage from the searing touch of mouth on mouth and be in sight of sanity in a mere breath. Yet the clamour of emotions and curiosity that took over her reeling senses wouldn't let her move.

His mouth was surprisingly soft on hers; deliberately unthreatening, a cynical voice informed her sternly, but she blocked her inner ear to it. The sensual reality of Charles Afforde's kiss on her eager lips at last overcame her defences with no effort at all and she felt him deepen the pressure of his kiss with such a warm welcome, she bitterly decided when she reviewed events later, that she might as well have offered him everything he hadn't already taken from her and let joy be totally unconfined. Not that joy made much of an effort to restrict itself as her mouth opened under his in a wanton response to his more insistent caress. She felt such a lift of her silly heart that he might be excused for thinking her an experienced flirt, if not a full-blown sensualist.

But wouldn't he know the feel of one of those abandoned women when he met one, for it would only be the sort of welcome he was used to? That hated, warning voice was at it again, even as the sound of his breath hitched just a second or two quicker than usual. She struggled between the heady notion that he wasn't used to such fire flaring between him and his lovers and the cold voice of common sense. Then he opened his sinfully tempting mouth on hers and silently asked for something even more intimate. Gasping in breath they could only share, so close as they were, she succumbed to heat and pleasure and curiosity and opened for him as he silently demanded.

Now she was done for, even at the moment when he'd proved himself a rake, after all. His tongue first probed the swollen wetness of lips that finally knew what they'd been made for, then delved within, as if exploring the most exquisitely delicious sensation he'd ever encountered. He gave an unconscious hum of satisfaction in his throat that woke her sensual self from its silly daydreams and showed her just how potent a kiss could be. A flush of heat threatened to melt her as he openly revelled in the chaos he'd wrought, the feel of him seducing and plundering with her absolute consent warming her primly covered bosom and suddenly rosy cheeks in a sharp flush of need that warned what untold, forbidden pleasures he still had left to teach her.

Breathing fast and shallow, she forced herself to jump back from him as if he'd scalded her. He might well have done just that, she decided, and she wouldn't know the full extent of the damage until she had privacy and calm enough to assess it. Yet her mouth felt bereft as his kiss cooled on the chill evening air, and suddenly she felt the cold of the October night and noted the diamond wink of stars emerging in an almost frosty sky.

'Oh, what have you done now?' she heard herself gasp out, as if protesting something crucially important, but also impossible.

'I hardly know,' he replied and his deep voice was

hoarse with something that sounded like bemusement and regret, as if he had felt the wonder and novelty of that kiss as deeply as she. Which was a self-deceiving lie, of course; he'd kissed so many women he probably couldn't provide a full list of them even under torture!

'Liar,' she accused softly and stepped back again so that the scent and heat and reality of him couldn't trip her senses again.

With distance came the full slap of sanity, and she was tempted to sink on to the cushioned window seat and cradle her silly head in her hands and weep. What had she done, for goodness' sake? Only actively encouraged a rake to believe her a great deal more willing to be seduced than she was and rekindled all those silly girlish fantasies of being kissed by her pirate prince. No, she wouldn't permit them to haunt her, and she resolved to avoid his company whenever possible, as they'd be living too close until she went on her travels.

'I think you should leave now, Captain,' she heard herself say in a stiff voice that should tell him what a proper and starchy spinster she really was.

'I believe you're right, Miss Courland,' he replied softly and the thread of something she couldn't quite read in his deep voice tantalised her with ifs and maybe's, but she stalwartly shrugged them aside.

'The Feathers does an excellent ordinary,' she went on blithely, as if she had no idea he could make her forget her own name with an idle kiss.

'My thanks, but I have good friends living not ten miles away.' For some reason he sounded as if he didn't relish being dismissed as a lightweight who'd forget what had just happened on the promise of a hot meal and a soft bed for the night.

'Indeed?' she replied with a haughty look that was probably wasted in the gloom. 'Then I'll call for a groom to light you to your destination.'

'No need, it's a fine starlit night and I have my private servant and a groom with me. It's more than time we were on the road if we're to reach my friends' house before they retire for the night, so I'll wish you a good night, Miss Courland,' he replied, and she could just discern his quick bow of farewell before she could ring for a lantern to guide his way. 'Rushmore will have acquired a light by now,' he assured her shortly.

'Goodbye then, Sir Charles,' she said, wishing there was the slightest hope he wouldn't return to haunt her.

'Until tomorrow,' he confirmed, and she listened to his assured steps as he found his way down the hall and into the early darkness, seemingly without the slightest hesitation.

She waited until she heard three sets of hoofbeats retreat down the drive before she rang the bell for candles and all the help she could muster. There was a great deal to do before she could sleep tonight if she was to be all but gone when Sir Charles arrived in the morning. Another encounter like that and she might do something even more ridiculous, and suddenly there were worse things than being evicted from her beloved home, after all.

While Hollowhurst Castle was jolted out of its accustomed calm by a mistress who'd become a whirlwind of frenetic energy, a dozen or so miles away Westmeade Manor was serenely comfortable. Charles tried not to envy his old friend Rob Besford, the younger son of the Earl of Foxwell, his contented domesticity with his lovely wife and smiled as he contemplated what Miss Courland would think of such a disgrace to the rakehell fraternity as he was proving to be. Not a great deal, he suspected, and absently contemplated the intriguing task of changing her mind.

'So will you do it, Charles?' Caroline Besford asked him.

Charles wondered cautiously what he was being asked to do, but luckily Rob took pity on him and explained.

'My wife is asking you to be godparent to our next offspring in her own unique manner, Charles. On the principle that you've already committed most of the follies he or she will need to steer clear of if they're to grow into an honest and sober citizen, I suppose,' Rob Besford told him, looking lazily content as he lounged beside his very pregnant wife.

'Couldn't you ask Will Wrovillton instead? After all, you plan to give this one his name,' Charles argued half-heartedly.

'Only if it turns out to be a boy,' Caro said with a wicked sparkle in her eyes as she encouraged him to imagine the fate of a girl called William. 'If it does, we want to name him after Rob's brother and James insists it must be a second name as it would cause too much confusion if there were two James Besfords, even though James is Viscount Littleworth as well, and I can't see it myself. We thought Charles James unkind, since Charles James Fox has only been dead for a decade or so. So we couldn't name this one after you *and* Rob's brother, Charles. Maybe next time,' she ended with a teasing look at Rob that he carefully ignored.

'With Fox having been so fiery a Whig and notoriously profligate with it, it'd be a backhanded turn to serve any brat to name him so, I suppose, but did Will turn down your offer to make him the child's godfather after landing him with William James as a name instead?' Charles asked suspiciously.

'He couldn't turn us down because we can't find him. No doubt he's knee-deep in some daft venture,' Rob replied with exasperated resignation.

'With his wife at his side,' Charles agreed with a reminiscent smile, for if ever he'd come across a fine pair of madcaps they were Lord Wrovillton and his highly unconventional lady.

'That's a certainty, I should say,' Caro confirmed.

'She's as bad as he is,' Charles pointed out.

'Worse,' she agreed placidly, considering Alice, Lady Wrovillton, was her best friend, 'and it's my belief you never forgave Alice for marrying Will instead of you, Charles.'

'No, it's Rob I'm furious with for wedding the one woman I'd gladly sacrifice my single status for,' he argued solemnly and for a moment Caroline looked horrified, until she noticed the wicked glint in his brilliantly blue eyes and threw a cushion at him.

'Boy or girl, your coming child has no more chance of growing up a sober citizen with you two as parents than its big sister has, and she has my sympathy, by the way,' Charles informed her with mock severity. 'It's clearly my duty to set a better example to your children and, as little Sophia is halfway to being as big a minx as her mama, I might as well start earlier with the next one.'

'More than halfway, if you ask me—so you'll do it, Charles?' Rob asked, as if the answer really mattered to him, despite Charles's rakehell reputation and apparent unsuitability as a spiritual guide.

'Gladly,' Charles agreed at last, touched to be asked, watching the besotted look on Rob's face as he smiled at his wife and feeling the lure of seeing a wife of his own great with his child.

First of all he'd need to marry one, of course, and that might prove more of a challenge than he'd expected. Rosie Courland with her ardent dark eyes and wild midnight curls had become a strong woman with guarded dark eyes and tightly restrained midnight curls, so what of his promise to win and wed her that he'd made Davy Courland now? An idea born of guilty conscience on Davy's side and convenience on his, perhaps, but he needed a capable wife to help him run his new house and estates, even if tonight it had all felt much less convenient and more urgent. Memory of their kiss in the twilight threatened to spin him into a world of his own again, so he forced himself to concentrate on the matter in hand.

'If she's a girl, you might run off with her yourself one day, of course, so we'd best find you a wife to save Rob killing you,' Caro teased roguishly.

'You, my girl, haven't improved at all with marriage and motherhood,' he replied sternly, hoping pregnancy would stop Caro from introducing him to half the neighbourhood when he'd just met the woman he was going to marry.

'Never mind that,' Rob told his wife impatiently, obviously sharing Charles's fears. 'Here's your maid come to cluck over you and quite right for once. It's high time you were in bed, Caro.'

'Only if you'll take me there,' she said with a wicked

smile and a shameless lack of hospitality Charles could only applaud.

To watch them now, who'd think the Besfords' marriage had got off to an appalling start? Charles suppressed a shudder at the memory of that stiff and chilly ceremony, with bride and groom as loving towards each other as the Regent and his unfortunate princess must have been at theirs. Luckily they came to a better understanding once Caro had grown bored with being Rob's despised and neglected wife and pretended to be Cleo Tournier, courtesan to one very particular, stubborn aristocrat, who looked as if he loved being stuck fast in his devious wife's toils nowadays.

'I'd like nothing better, my Cleo.' Rob answered her brazen encouragement to take her to bed forthwith with a scorching look that made Caro blush like a peony, Charles was amused to see.

All the same, he felt a sneaking envy of their delight in one another. He'd never love Miss Courland as Rob undoubtedly loved his Caroline and she loved him, yet he'd seen enough of the closeness and fire between them to wonder what such absolute intimacy would be like. He'd always taken life more lightly than Rob he mused as he accepted his candle and obligingly took himself off to his comfortable bed. A marriage of convenience would suit him, especially when it promised passionate nights of mutual satisfaction. He couldn't embrace the married state with the enthusiasm Rob demonstrated, but he'd be an attentive and faithful husband to Miss Roxanne Courland until death did them part, whether she liked it or not!

Roxanne had gone to bed very late after packing the first of her belongings and got up early to begin the task of despatching them to Mulberry House and starting on the rest. She supposed she should be grateful to Sir Charles for provoking her into moving house so quickly, for if she'd been left to linger over each old letter and beloved childhood book it might have taken weeks, if not months. As it was, she'd set herself a mere day of frantic activity to remove all she held most dear, and already the farm dray was setting off, laden with a quantity of trunks and boxes of books that astonished her. Her lips tightened as she contemplated what the arrogant baronet would say about the half-empty shelves in Uncle Granger's personal library, but she wasn't having a stranger selling or disregarding what it had taken him a lifetime to collect.

Having seen the lord-of-the-feast side of her great-uncle, she wondered if Charles Afforde knew about Uncle Granger's quieter interests: his love of fine music and his patronage of poets and artists once thought obscure and outlandish. She must make sure someone packed the fine collection of watercolours from her own room as she shuddered at the thought of coming back to beg for anything left behind. Among them was an exquisite painting of Hollowhurst Castle by Mr Turner that she'd no intention of leaving for the Castle's new owner. Considering he was rich enough to buy Davy's heritage, he'd just have to commission one for himself if he wanted one.

Like an automaton that had wound down in mid-dance, she suddenly sank into a chair and let the truth sink in. Hollowhurst and all it meant to her had a new owner, and what had once seemed set in stone was now as fugitive as a house of cards. How could Davy do such a thing? she raged silently. Surely he trusted her to run the estate and keep the castle in good order? And one day his son might feel very different about the impressive heritage he should have had. She felt angry tears threaten the rigid composure she'd imposed on herself since she realised just why Charles Afforde had returned and barely managed to fight them back.

'It was never meant to be like this, you know.' Charles Afforde's deep voice interrupted from the doorway, and she was so startled she looked up with fury and grief naked in her dark gaze.

'I can't see how you expected me to feel otherwise,' she said and tried to freeze her sorrow until later, when he wasn't by to watch.

'I expected Davy to prepare you for this, if nothing else,' he said rather cryptically, and she wondered what on earth he meant.

What other disaster could there be, given her home was now his and her whole world was rocking on its axis? She shivered at the very thought of more unwelcome revelations and dismissed the idea; nothing could be worse than the bombshell he'd already dropped, after all.

'Well, he didn't,' she replied flatly.

Surely the end result was the same? Possession, she decided furiously and once more wished futilely that she'd been born a man. Not that it would have done her any good since Davy was older and the heir, but he might have reconsidered if he'd a brother devoted to the estate he found a burden. Yet a mere woman must stand by and watch the lords of the earth dispossess her of all she held dear, she railed silently.

'Obviously not, and I suppose the mail boats between here and America are unreliable at this time of year,' he replied with a hint of impatience at her truism, 'but I never intended driving you from your home at a moment's notice, Miss Courland. Take as long as you like over the business, I have time since I left the sea and can spare as long as you need and more.'

'I'll be ready today; I always knew I'd have to leave when Davy married. I can't see how two women could rule the same roost and stay friends.'

'Such is the unfairness of English law, is it not? The eldest male heir gets the best plums and the others scrabble for what's left.'

Chapter Four

Roxanne wondered fleetingly if Sir Charles resented not being Lord Samphire's heir, then dismissed it as a silly idea. If ever she'd met a man capable of forging his own destiny, it was Sir Charles Afforde. No doubt he'd been able to buy Hollowhurst by his own efforts after such a successful career, even without that very substantial trust fund from his mother that Davy had told her of long ago, when she was still eager for every snippet of information she could garner about this stranger.

Naval captains with a reputation like his must have been turning crew away instead of having to press-gang them, eager as they'd be for a share of his prizes. None of which meant she had to like him, she reassured herself stalwartly and managed to recover her barely suppressed fury at him. If she didn't, she'd break down in front of him, and such weakness was intolerable.

'I've no need to "scrabble", sir,' she assured him stiffly. 'My uncle left me a fine house in Hollowhurst village and his personal property. Didn't my brother inform you of the terms of his will when he sold you Hollowhurst?'

'He said there was a fine line to tread between his great-uncle's personal property and the goods and chattels that came with the castle. One you must have expected to walk if he brought a bride home.'

'I might feel more generous towards my brother,' she snapped, because she saw pity in his blue eyes and she'd prefer anything to that, even a cold fury she sensed would freeze her to the marrow if he ever unleashed it.

'Yet I've no intention of arguing about a few court cupboards and worm-eaten refectory tables, Miss Courland, so pray take what you like,' he countered coolly.

'And *I* won't ransack the place in search of my inheritance, Sir Charles. My house is already furnished and all I require will fit on the farm dray when it returns. You'll find your bookshelves a little empty and one or two walls bare, but I'm no magpie to be going about the place gathering everything I can.'

'I suspect you'd rather leave much of what's yours behind out of sheer pride, lest you be thought grasping. I give you fair warning I'll send it after you if you're foolish enough to do that.'

'Then I'll send it back. I already told you I've no room.'

'Perhaps we should place the excess in a field halfway between our houses and fight a duel for it one morning?' he said as if their argument was mildly amusing, but in danger of becoming tedious.

Well, it didn't amuse her; she set her teeth and wondered why she'd got into this unproductive dispute in the first place. Of course she'd intended to be gone before he arrived, but he'd outmanoeuvred her and she suddenly knew how all those French captains felt when the famous, or infamous, *Condottiere's* sails appeared on the horizon.

'Do you intend to fill the castle with daybeds in the Egyptian style and chairs and tables with alligator feet, then?' she asked sweetly.

'No,' he replied shortly. 'I prefer comfort to fashion.'

'Then you'll just have to accept that most of the furniture was built to fit a castle and would look ridiculous in a house less than fifty years old.'

'And you'll have to accept I'm here to stay and have no intention of being cut by half the neighbourhood for throwing you out of your home at half a day's notice with little more than your clothes and a few trifles.'

'Even if you have,' she replied with glee, feeling almost happy she was leaving for the first time since he announced his purchase last night.

'Not a bit of it; I've just told your local vicar that I'm away to stay with my family for at least a sennight in order to give you time to find a suitable chaperone and remove from the Castle. He and his wife thought it a noble act of consideration on my part.'

'But they occupy a living bestowed at your discretion, do they not? And know you not at all, Sir Charles.'

'Only by repute,' he said with a significant look she interpreted as a reproach to her for judging him on that basis herself. He'd no idea how bitterly he'd disappointed her young girl's dreams in making that rakehell reputation, and it was up to her to make sure he never found out.

'Then I'm sure you have nothing to worry about,' she said stiffly. 'A returning hero takes precedence over a wronged woman any day of the week. Witness Odysseus's triumphant return from ten years of chasing about the Aegean after assorted goddesses and nymphs, in contrast to poor Penelope's slaughtered maids and all that interminable weaving she had to do as well as fighting off her importunate suitors.'

'Oh, I hardly think you fall into that category, Miss Courland. Indeed, I doubt any man would be brave enough to try to make you do anything you didn't wish to. Anyway, I can hardly throw you out into the snow with nothing but the clothes on your back when you're known to be a considerable heiress, and one who's very fastidious indeed about *her* suitors.'

She hadn't thought local society took much notice of her or her potential marriage, except to criticise her for acting as her uncle's steward and refusing to employ a duenna to look down her nose at such a poor example of a lady. She had much to learn about her new occupation of doing very little in a suitably ladylike fashion.

'You'll be much sought after now that you're free to be entertained by your neighbours,' he went on as if attempting to reassure her. Roxanne could tell from the glint in his apparently guileless blue eyes that he was secretly enjoying the notion of her struggling to adapt to her new role, and tried not to give him the satisfaction of glowering furiously back. 'You'll have time on your hands enough to visit all of them now, Miss Courland,' he went on smoothly, as if he was trying to be gallant and not utterly infuriating, 'and they certainly wish to visit you if the vicar, his wife and their promising son just down from Oxford are anything to do by.'

'I'm glad my uncle taught me to discern a false friend from a true one then,' she replied stalwartly, trying not to let a shiver of apprehension slide down her spine at the very thought of such an existence. 'I've no desire whatsoever to be wed for my money.'

'Nor I—perhaps we should wed one another to avert such a travesty,' he joked, and she felt a dart of the old pain, more intense if anything, and cursed that old infatuation for haunting her still.

'Since that's about as likely as black becoming white, I suggest you look elsewhere for a bride, Sir Charles,' she said scornfully.

'I'll settle into my new life before looking about me for a lady brave enough to take me on,' he parried lightly.

Roxanne tried not to be disappointed as he reverted to type and took on the shallow social manners common among the *haut ton,* at least if her memory of her one uncomfortable Season was anything to go by. She'd felt out of place and bored for most of her three months in the capital, and as glad to come home again as Uncle Granger was to see her. Her sister Maria had delighted in that milieu and had worked her way up the social ladder from noble young matron to society hostess, but Roxanne hadn't felt the slightest urge to join her, let alone rival her in any way.

'Indeed?' she replied repressively.

'I'll need to feel my way among local society after usurping a long-established family,' he replied with apparent sincerity, then looked spuriously anxious as he watched her struggle to remain distantly polite. 'But first I insist you find a congenial companion, Miss Courland. No lady of your years and birth can live alone without being taken advantage of or bringing scandal on herself and her family. If you don't look about you for a chaperone, I'll do it for you. The local matrons will consider a respectable duenna essential now I've come amongst you, and no lone damsel can be considered beyond my villainy, and I've my own reputation to think about, after all.'

'You don't have one, at least not one any lady dares discuss and be received in polite society. As for employing a duenna for me, I have already told you it would be highly improper. I'd be ostracised if I took one of *your* choosing,' she said haughtily, her gaze clashing with his.

'I promised your brother I'd look after you in his stead,' he told her with a glint in his eyes that looked very unbrotherly indeed.

'Exactly how old do you think I am, sir?' she asked defensively.

'Hardly out of the schoolroom,' he replied, with a wolfish smile that gave his words the lie.

'I'm four and twenty and on the shelf. I dare say I could take up residence at Mulberry House without any chaperone but my maid and nobody would raise an eyebrow except you.'

'There you're very much mistaken, my dear, but if you choose not to be visited or invited out, I dare say you'll grow used to the life of a recluse,' he replied ruthlessly, but at least she'd wiped that annoying, indulgent-of-female-folly grin off his face.

Impatient of the petty rules of society she might be, reclusive she wasn't, and hated to admit he was right. She *could* live so, but it'd be a very limited existence and she was too young to embark on a hermit's career.

'I'm not your dear, Sir Charles, and will thank you to address me in proper form.'

'You have no idea what you are just yet, Miss Courland, and I suggest you take a few weeks to find out before you launch yourself into local society as their most scandalous exhibit,' he retorted brusquely.

'You could be right, but this subject is becoming tedious, or do you want me to put that admission in writing and have it published?'

'No, I want you to behave yourself,' he informed her as sternly as if she was fourteen again and he her legal and moral guardian, not the biggest rogue to break a score of susceptible hearts every time he came ashore.

'Really? And I just want you to go away so that I can start my new life,' she snapped back, smarting at the idea of all those unfortunate, abandoned females and how nearly she'd become one of them.

'Then want must be your master,' he said laconically and lounged against the intricately carved fireplace, since she'd omitted to invite him to sit.

She was about to spark back at him, regardless of the fact she must get on with her neighbours in future and he'd be the most important of them, but a rustle of silk petticoats announced a new arrival and stopped her.

'Good morning. I believe you must be Miss Courland?' a lady very obviously with child greeted her from the open doorway.

Roxanne sprang to her feet and offered the stranger a seat, trying to feel as overjoyed at so timely an interruption as she ought to be.

'I couldn't make anyone hear so I'm afraid I invited myself in,' her visitor told her with an engaging smile.

Roxanne could see no resemblance whatsoever to

Sir Charles Afforde about the lady's warm golden eyes and heart-shaped face and searched her mind for any possible clues as to her identity. She doubted the lady was related to him and was obviously far too respectable to be a left-handed connection. Not that he'd sink so low as to install his pregnant mistress at the Castle before Roxanne had quit it, she decided with weary resignation.

'Pray forgive me, Miss Courland, I'm Mrs Robert Besford of Westmeade Manor, but please call me Caro. My husband and Sir Charles have been friends since they were unappealing brats in short coats, so I barged in, since I couldn't wait any longer to make your acquaintance.'

Roxanne could see no reason why a boyhood friendship between this lady's husband and Charles Afforde should make her and Mrs Besford friends, too, but found it impossible to snub the vivacious young woman or refuse the warm understanding in Caro's golden-brown gaze.

'I'm very pleased to meet you, Mrs Besford,' she said, holding out her hand in greeting and having it firmly shaken by one that looked too small and slender to contain such strength and resolution.

'Caro,' her new friend insisted and Roxanne smiled back.

'Then I must be Roxanne, Caro, for I gave up being Rosie when my brother insisted on calling me Rosie-Posie long after I grew up.'

'Gentlemen can be so effortlessly maddening, can't they?' Caro replied.

'My apologies, Caro,' Sir Charles said, looking uncomfortable, 'I'd no idea you'd arrive so close on my heels. I'll make sure my groom has seen to your horses, as Miss Courland's men are busy, if you'll excuse me?'

'Gladly. Pray go and soothe Rob's anxiety about me by discussing where you're going to acquire the blood-stock you intend on breeding,' Mrs Besford said with an airy wave and, to Roxanne's surprise, he meekly did as he was bid.

'He thinks he has to humour me,' Caroline told her with a conspiratorial smile. 'Especially since he woke my household last night by shouting something incomprehensible at the top of his voice in his sleep. According to my husband, many men have nightmares after taking part in battles or skirmishes, but goodness knows what set Charles off in the midst of the Kent countryside in peacetime. His manservant managed to calm him down without waking him and the rest of us went back to sleep, but Charles is mortified this morning and I'm taking shameless advantage. I'll soon be kept busy at home with this new baby and my little daughter, so I exploited his guilty conscience when he tried to leave me behind this morning. I think Rob's still fighting off the vapours after dreading every bump and bend we travelled over on my behalf,' Caro confided. 'I dare say he almost wishes himself back at Waterloo, the poor man, but I'm bored with being treated like spun glass and thought you might welcome some support, even if I'm of precious little use.'

'I was beginning to wonder if I'd get out of here without turning into a watering pot, or throwing something fragile and irreplaceable at Sir Charles, so you're very welcome, I assure you.'

'You seem too strong to give way to your emotions

like that, Roxanne, but I know how hard it is to stay serene in such trying circumstances,' Caro said, and Roxanne saw a fleeting shadow of some remembered sadness cloud her guest's unusual eyes.

It was scouted the instant Robert Besford appeared, a worried look on his handsome face. Roxanne thought Caro was blooming, but since he evidently cared a great deal for his wife, Mr Besford's anxiety was rather touching.

'Good morning,' he said with a graceful bow, while his startlingly green eyes ran over his wife as if taking an inventory.

Caro rolled her eyes and tried to look stern, before laughing and shaking her head at him, 'This is Miss Courland, Rob,' she admonished.

'I know. We've met before, haven't we, Miss Courland?' he replied with a rueful smile of apology for his distracted state.

'Good morning, Colonel Besford,' she replied with a smile, for who could resist the Besfords' evident delight in each other?

'I'm colonel no longer, not even in my brevet rank as staff officer, now I've sold out,' he told her cheerfully enough.

'Or so he says,' Caro added darkly and Roxanne laughed at the look the Honourable Robert turned on his wife.

'And no order of mine was ever knowingly obeyed by my wife,' he told Roxanne ruefully and ducked dextrously as a cushion flew past his left ear and thudded harmlessly against the oak panelling.

'Oh, I'm so sorry,' Caro said, hand over her mouth and her eyes dancing. 'It's become a habit,' she admitted, and Roxanne decided she'd enjoy local society if it offered such lively company, after all.

'I'll make sure I take a suit of armour with me to Mulberry House,' she replied solemnly, and they were all laughing when Charles entered the room.

He was enchanted by this light-hearted and laughing Roxanne Courland. He'd turned her world upside down and behaved like a bad-tempered bear this morning, so no wonder he'd not seen her so until now, but suddenly he knew she'd break his heart if he let her and felt the breath stall in his chest as he saw her as she ought to be, if her family had cherished and adored her, instead of leaving her alone to brave the world. He acquitted Sir Granger of deliberate cruelty, but to raise her as mistress here, when she could only be second-in-command at her brother's whim, was unthinkingly callous.

Roxanne must at least taste the life of a single young woman of birth and fortune before he wed her, but it'd have to be a mere bite, as this need dragging at him insistently wouldn't be ignored for long. He imagined her beautifully gowned and coiffured and decided he was about to let himself in for the most tortuous few weeks of his life. Stepping forwards, he watched the mischief leave her darkest brown eyes and her merry smile die. There was time to alter that state of affairs, he reassured himself. Perhaps she'd look favourably on his suit if he made her mistress here again. Highly unlikely she'd wed ever him for himself, now, and wasn't that just as well?

'I asked for refreshments to be served here, if you don't object, Miss Courland?' he said.

'I've no right to object, Sir Charles,' she replied.

'A lady always has rights,' he argued. She had rights, and obligations—common politeness being one of them.

'How nice for us,' she replied stubbornly.

'It must be,' he replied, and she glared at him before embarking on a discussion about babies with Caro designed to exclude sane gentlemen, except that his friend Rob seemed to find it as fascinating as they did.

He'd never be that much of a fool about his wife and children, Charles assured himself. He'd be an interested and even a fond father, especially as his own sire had consigned him to his formidable grandmother's care without a backward look at an early age. Charles's lips twisted in a sardonic smile as he recalled a day when the father he had yearned for came home at last. Louis Afforde had fainted at the sight of him, coming round to murmur artistically, 'The boy is too like her—my one, my only, my dear departed love. He offends my eyes and grieves my suffering heart.'

Louis, an aspiring poet, promptly went straight back to London and his current 'only' love and left his son with an aversion to romantic love and a gap in his young life where his remaining parent should have been. Packed off to live with his grandparents at the age of six, Charles swore he'd never fall in love, whatever love might be. Eyeing Rob now doting over the wife he'd once professed to hate, he decided he still didn't know what it was and was quite content with his ignorance. He'd respect and admire his wife—if he desired her as well that was a handsome bonus—but he'd never love her.

Nor would he make a cake of himself over being a

husband and father as Rob appeared happy to. His children would have fond but sensible parents, which was just as well considering his grandmother was too old to take on a pack of brats now. He thought the Dowager Countess of Samphire would like Miss Courland as a granddaughter-in-law and he doubted Roxanne would quail at meeting such a brusque and ruthless old lady, and then caught himself out in a dreamy smile with horrified shock.

Roxanne would make a good wife and mother and he'd be faithful and respect her, but he'd not live in her pocket. Something told him it wouldn't be that simple, but he ignored it because he'd promised her brother he'd marry her if she'd have him, and he wanted her. Having his child would settle her into her new role as his wife, and the thought of it made him march to the window and gaze out at the view while he got himself back under control. The idea of seeing Roxanne sensually awake and fully aware of herself as a woman for the first time sent him into such a stew of urgency that he was unfit for company. It boded ill for his detachment, he admitted to himself as he fought primitive passions, but very well for begetting his brats!

'Fascinating view, is it?' Rob asked with a satirical smile as he came to stand by his old friend, too much understanding of Charles's response to Roxanne Courland in his steady green gaze for comfort.

'All the more so for being mine,' he replied softly.

'Possessiveness, it's the curse of our sex,' Rob taunted, and Charles wondered if he wasn't yet truly forgiven for trying to win Rob's lady off him, although he'd been as blithely ignorant of who she really was as her husband had been at the time.

He had admired Caro's refusal to sit back and meekly accept that their arranged marriage was an abomination to her husband, and her ingenious campaign to win him to her bed by foul means when fair ones must fail, since Rob had vowed never to share any room with his wife after their wedding. Rob had danced to the seductive and scandalous new courtesan Cleo Tournier's tune without a clue that she was his unwanted and despised wife, and Charles decided vengefully that he was glad he'd helped her tame the one-time rake now watching him as if he was a specimen on a pin.

'You could be right,' he replied calmly enough.

'Be careful what you're at,' Rob warned him silkily. 'Miss Courland isn't up to the games you play and she's far from unprotected.'

'She needs no protection from me,' Charles replied shortly.

'Have you undergone a sea change then, Charles?'

'A permanent one,' he replied, gaze steady on Rob's challenging one.

'Good God, I think you really mean it.'

'I do.'

'It'll provide me with an interesting diversion to watch you try to achieve that aim then,' Rob said with a grin that almost made Charles wish them both twenty years younger, so he could treat him to the appropriate punch on the nose. 'I don't think Miss Courland will be easily persuaded you're not a wild sea-rover any more,' he warned with unholy delight.

'I'm beginning to agree with you,' Charles muttered darkly and stared broodingly at the quirky old garden he'd acquired with his new property.

'Sometimes the chase is all the more worth winning

when it seems nigh impossible,' Rob said, softening his challenge as he sent a significant glance at his lady, who'd led him a fine dance before letting her husband catch her just as she'd planned all along.

'I'm planning a change of lifestyle, not abject surrender,' Charles protested uneasily.

'And sometimes there's victory in defeat, although that's not a concept I expect a grizzled old sea dog to understand.'

'Since you talk in riddles, no wonder I can't make head or tail of them.'

'You'll see,' Rob said with an irritatingly superior smile and turned back to the fascinating spectacle of his wife like a compass to the north.

Chapter Five

Taking tea and cake in a lady's sitting room like some tame *cicisbeo,* Charles fought an unaccustomed urge to snap and snarl at all and sundry and reminded himself he had a reputation as a dangerous charmer to uphold. He didn't feel very charming when Roxanne Courland refused to look at him and made certain their fingers didn't touch when she passed him his teacup. If his one-time crew could see him now, they'd laugh themselves into a collective apoplexy and save the hangman a job, he reflected bitterly.

Instead of dwelling on his current woes, he decided to set about solving one or two of them. First he must find a suitable lady to chaperone his prospective bride. Not easy when only he and Davy Courland knew he was to wed. He sipped his tea with a creditable attempt at looking as if he enjoyed it and took a mental inventory. His formidable grandmother would put in an appearance when Caro's whelp was due since she doted on her, so he must have someone in place before she decided to take the role herself.

There was Great-Aunt Laetetia Varleigh, his grandmother's spinster sister. Yet Aunt Letty lacked the inner core of loving softness Lady Samphire hid behind a formidable manner. No, she wouldn't do, even if she'd leave Varleigh village to lapse into the hotbed of scandal it might become without her constant vigilance. He was reluctantly contemplating advertising when his latest conversation with Tom Varleigh slotted into his mind and made the solution seem so obvious he felt a fool for missing it.

'Stella refuses to come and live with myself and Joanna now poor Marcus Lavender's dead,' Tom had told him. 'She claims Joanna doesn't need another female cluttering up Varleigh Manor, so she's living at the Dower House with Mama and Great-Aunt Letty. She's stubborn and headstrong, but even my big sister doesn't deserve that, Charles. Before six months are up, she'll murder one of them or be fit for Bedlam herself.'

It would be ideal, he told himself, wondering fleetingly if he was as interfering and arrogant as Miss Courland believed him to be. Cousin Stella was in her early thirties and the respectable widow of a fine man who'd died at the ill-starred Battle of Toulouse when, if only they'd known it, the Great War was over and a peace treaty already signed. Stella would be glad of an alternative to living at Varleigh Dower House even if she was too stubborn to admit it, and her chaperonage would be more theory than fact if he knew Stella. Yes, that would suit all three of them very well. Now all he need do was get Stella here without Roxanne realising it was his doing.

A carefully worded plea to Roxanne's sister to send her word of any suitable duennas might serve, as long as Roxanne never discovered he'd sent it. Eyeing Caro speculatively, he wondered if she numbered the sociable younger Varleighs among her recent acquaintance. He shuddered at the thought of her entrée to the *demi-monde,* even if it was gained in pursuit of her renegade husband, and hoped it never became common knowledge.

Such a scandal would certainly not enhance the standing of his bride-to-be, if her chaperone had come recommended by even a pretend courtesan and, unlike Rob Besford, he intended to make sure his wife never had the slightest excuse to cause a scandal in pursuit of his closest sensual attention. He reassured himself it was perfectly natural to want to watch his Roxanne blossom in her proper sphere and that he was in no danger of falling in love with her. His wife must be a socially assured and adept hostess and serenely self-possessed under pressure, and if she became his passionate lover in the bargain, that would just be a wonderful bonus.

Yet did he want her to change? She was rather magnificent as she was, and he admired her stubborn determination to go her own way—except it would ultimately prove disastrous. If he let her, she'd dwindle into a maiden aunt, neither happy nor unhappy and criminally wasted. Or she'd marry some weak-kneed idiot who'd let her govern both their lives. The very idea of her chancing instead upon some tyrant who'd try to break her glorious spirit made him shudder and drink his tea after all, only realising he'd drained his cup when he looked into it with offended disdain.

'It's all right, Charles, some of us drink it all the time and so far have come to no harm at all,' Caro teased.

'But you don't know what it might do to me if I drink enough of it.'

'I admit I'm not a man and have absolutely no desire to be one, but it's a risk I'm quite prepared to take as a mere female, even if you're too much of a coward to take it on,' she parried effortlessly, and he saw Roxanne shoot her a doubtful look, as if Caro might not know she was supping with the devil and therefore needed a very long spoon.

He smiled into his surprisingly empty teacup and wondered if he ought to inform her that his friend's wife was perfectly safe from any wiles he had stored up for the unwary. Best not, perhaps, it might be useful to keep her in ignorance of the fact that, unlike Caro, she was very unsafe indeed.

'You mustn't do that, Miss Roxanne, it's no job for a lady,' Cobbins, formerly head gardener of Hollowhurst Castle, informed Roxanne a week after she moved into Mulberry House. Even Sir Charles hadn't been able to protest her managing for the time being with the chaperonage of her personal maid, the Castle housekeeper and far too many members of her former household to fit comfortably into Mulberry House.

'Why not?' she challenged grumpily, since every time she found a promising occupation to while away the tedious hours, somebody would raise their head from doing nothing in particular and tell her it wasn't ladylike.

''Cause you'll get scratched,' he explained with the patience of a responsible adult addressing a child who'd stolen her mama's best scissors to deadhead the few late-blooming roses Mulberry House rejoiced in. 'You could even get muddy,' he added with every sign of horror.

As if he hadn't seen her muddy and exhausted many a time after a long day spent in the saddle going about Uncle Granger's business, Roxanne thought with disgust. 'Right, that's it!' she informed him sharply, reaching the end of a tether she'd clung to with exemplary patience. 'I've had enough of this ridiculous situation. In a quarter of an hour I expect you and your many underlings to assemble in the kitchen, where Cook will undoubtedly curse you all for getting in her way, but I plan to address my household and it's the only place you can all fit without being tight packed as sprats in a barrel. Pray inform Whistler that I expect the stablemen to attend as well, and woe betide them if their boots aren't clean.'

'But why, Miss Roxanne?' Cobbins protested with the familiarity of a man who'd known her since she was born.

'Do as I say and you'll find out soon enough,' she informed him smartly and swept back into the house to issue an edict to the indoor staff.

'Whatever's going on, Miss Rosie?' asked Tabby, her personal maid and suddenly the strictest chaperone the most finicky duchess could require for her precious offspring, whether Roxanne wanted her to be or not, which she definitely didn't, she decided rebelliously.

'In ten minutes you'll find out along with everyone else, and you might as well occupy five of them by setting my hair to rights and give us both something to do.'

Tabby sniffed regally. 'Some of us can work and talk at the same time, ma'am,' she claimed but took down the rough chignon Roxanne had scrabbled together when she managed to rise, dress and steal out of the house without encountering any of her entourage for once, only because she did so before anyone but the boot boy and the scullery maid were stirring. Never mind *their* aghast expressions on discovering the lady of the house was stealing through the side door even before the sun reluctantly rose on a misty autumn morning, she'd managed her wild ride over the autumn landscape at last, and it'd been worth every exhilarating moment.

'But we undoubtedly work faster in silence,' Roxanne told her newly dragonlike maid in a tone she hoped was commanding enough to brook no argument and refused to elaborate, even in the face of extreme provocation. Despite her impatience with such finicky and ladylike occupations as fine grooming and pernickety dressing, Roxanne felt better once her hair was neat and she was dressed in a slightly more fashionable gown, so maybe Tabby was right about ordering some new ones next time she went to Rye.

Such frippery notions went clean out of her head when she reached the kitchens and met the eyes of her assembled staff. Just as she'd predicted, Cook looked as if she'd like to beat the stable-boys with her formidable-looking ladle, and the gardeners' feet were shuffling as if they had a mind of their own and might carry them back to their proper domain of their own accord if something wasn't done or said very soon.

'What's afoot, Miss Rosie?' Cook asked her with a terrifying frown that would reduce most ladies to a heap of fine clothes and incoherence.

Luckily Roxanne knew a heart of gold beat under

that formidable exterior, and it only needed the long line of giggling maids who lined up to be abused by the paper tiger as soon as they were old enough to work to confirm that Cook inspired love and loyalty in all those who served her, which brought Roxanne neatly back to her sheep.

'I asked you all to assemble here this morning in order that I might tell you how deeply I'm honoured and moved by your steadfast loyalty to dear Uncle Granger and myself and to thank you for following me to Mulberry House in such large numbers. Which brings me neatly to the other reason I wanted to speak to you: by now I think we all realise this house is too small to accommodate a household large enough to run a castle, and I suggest…no,' Roxanne corrected herself as she saw the stubborn set to Cook's, Cobbins's, Whistler's and the butler's collective mouths, 'I *insist* that most of you return to Hollowhurst and take up your accustomed roles.'

An incoming wave of muttered protests threatened to become a tidal roar, but she held up her hand and it subsided to a few harrumphs of disagreement from the ringleaders.

'I want you to consider how you all intend to occupy yourselves serving a mistress who doesn't entertain or visit much and has no need of the exceptional skills required to run a castle or to progress in your chosen spheres.'

The maids and gardeners, grooms and stable boys eyed each other doubtfully, and Roxanne tried to tailor her speech to make the tougher part of her audience return to their proper domains and quit hers.

'Sir Charles needs skilled staff to guide him in his

new life. Command at sea must be very different to life as a country gentleman with a huge old house and a large estate to administer. I was wrong to encourage any of you to leave, but you know my hasty temper and no real damage has been done yet. Stay here much longer and Sir Charles will hire a pack of strangers to run Hollowhurst, and I doubt that's what any of us want.'

'Maybe you're correct, Miss Courland,' Mereson, the stately butler, acknowledged with a bland look that led the assembled audience to doubt it, 'but Sir Granger's first concern was always for your welfare, so Cook, Cobbins, Whistler and myself will remain in your service.' He eyed the other three sternly, but received only fervent nods and ayes and managed to look pleased with himself without spoiling the impassive façade of a superior butler, trained from birth to run Hollowhurst below-stairs as Sir Granger had been raised to rule above them.

'I thank you, but my uncle would be the first to tell you not to be an awkward pack of idiots and get back to where you're needed.' Mulish expressions turned to doubtful frowns as they silently admitted she was right. Sensing victory, Roxanne pressed ruthlessly on. 'You trained your deputies, so how can you doubt they're capable of bothering me with unsolicited advice at all turns while running my house, stables and gardens almost as efficiently as you would? Meanwhile, you can help Sir Charles in his new life as the master of Hollowhurst Castle, knowing that I'm in safe hands.'

'Bravo, Miss Courland, I couldn't have put it better myself, and I must add a personal plea for as many of you as Miss Courland can spare to take pity on me and come and help me run the castle before I'm properly in the basket for lack of your skills.'

Sir Charles Afforde then strolled further into the overcrowded room to stand by her side, and Roxanne wasn't sure if she was more furious with him for looking as if they'd hatched this argument between them or with her staff for silently ghosting out of his way as if he'd every right to barge into her house and interfere without the least encouragement. Holding on to her temper while trying to look as if she concurred with his every word, although she'd like to kick him sharply in the shins, took every ounce of self-control Roxanne possessed.

'Good morning, Sir Charles,' she managed to greet him civilly.

'Good morning, Miss Courland, and good morning to you all,' he responded cheerfully, as if he was calling on her in her drawing room and not lounging about the commodious kitchen as if he owned that as well.

A general murmur greeted him, ranging from stately politeness to a flutter of delight from the flightier maids, and again Roxanne had to choke back fury. Just because he was ridiculously handsome and a hero of the late wars, everyone forgot he was also a rake and a rogue. Wishing she hadn't encouraged any of the female staff to return to the castle, she frowned repressively at them and won nervous, excited giggles for her pains. Hoping he was too gentlemanly to take advantage, Roxanne scowled fiercely at him, but he seemed unimpressed and just gave one of his piratical grins.

'I suggest you take the rest of the day to consider what I've said,' she suggested to her assembled staff, having little hope of the female section of it hearing her, as their attention was centred on Sir Charles lounging beside her as if he was as welcome as the flowers in spring.

'Indeed we will, Miss Courland,' Mereson intoned on behalf of all his minions. After giving the chief among them a few significant looks, he made sure they dispersed to their supposed places in her household, and Roxanne wondered, not for the first time, how on earth they managed to fit into it without constant collisions.

At last only the kitchen staff were left, and the last giggling housemaid had been towed away by more sensible friends. Roxanne looked on Sir Charles with even less favour as he refused to notice she wanted him gone.

'There's scones and fresh blackberry jelly if you'd like me to send them through to the drawing room, Miss Rosie,' Cook prompted, and Roxanne decided her light-as-air touch with such pastries was no compensation for an interfering nature, and Sir Charles was welcome to her.

'Then will you join me, Sir Charles?' she managed to say graciously enough. 'Such a treat is not to be lightly missed, I can assure you.'

'My thanks, Miss Courland, but it defeats me how you managed to find room for so many in this rather compact house and still omitted to engage a companion to make my visit respectable,' he carped as she led the way to her not-yet-formal drawing room.

'If my companion and my reputation were any concern of yours, Sir Charles, I might explain myself. As they're not, I feel no need to do so.'

'They soon will be if you get yourself ruined in the eyes of the world because you're too stubborn to engage a duenna. I feel compelled to see you set right, Miss

Courland, as I'm the most likely cause of our neighbours whispering scandal about you living alone so close to the Castle if you don't see sense and employ a duenna.'

When she would have burst out into an indignant denial that he had any rights or obligations toward her, he held up his hand and Roxanne could see just how this supposedly light-hearted rogue had commanded his own ship and several others with ease.

'It's not because I possess a managing nature that I plague you about this, although I admit that's part of it, but I promised your brother I'd make sure you were well settled and happy. Setting the gossips tattling about you before you've hardly got your boxes unpacked and your furniture arranged doesn't augur well, Miss Courland. But if you cherish some bizarre plan to get yourself ostracised by polite society so you may become a recluse and ignore all your neighbours, then tell me now and I'll leave you to get on with it.'

Oh, how she'd like to snap some smart retort back at him, to claim her position in local society was too secure to need his approval or interference. Inwardly seething, she managed to give him a sickly smile in recognition that he was a guest under her roof, and her uncle had taught her that obliged her to at least try to be hospitable. Somehow she managed to contain the flood of protest longing for release into what she hoped were a few pithy sentences he wouldn't be able to argue with.

'You're not my brother and I'm not obliged to explain myself to you, Sir Charles. I absolve you from any promise you made him and beg you won't give me another thought. I have many plans for the future, but none of them are any concern of yours. You'll have most of your staff back by nightfall, so I suggest you put your own house in order and leave me to manage mine.'

'You're the sister of a good friend as well as my cousin Tom Varleigh's sister-in-law, so do you honestly think I'll stand by and watch you ruin yourself in the eyes of your own kind when I've any power to stop you, ma'am?'

She'd been wavering until he added that 'ma'am'—such a world of impatience and frustration as it contained, and such an awful promise of what she might become: a mere ma'am, a superannuated spinster with too much money and too little sense to find herself a husband. Now she was no longer the mistress of Hollowhurst, would she be seen by local society as another annoying female with no male to guide and centre her, a dangerous woman contained by their disapproval and then, when the years passed and she'd become a quiz, maybe their laughter? Roxanne shuddered and did her best to hide her misgivings from the abominable man.

'I'm very pleased to say you possess no power over me, Sir Charles,' she informed him haughtily and enjoyed the frustration in his eyes.

'Mrs Lavender has arrived, Miss Roxanne,' Mereson intoned from the doorway, which called an abrupt halt to their argument and made it annoyingly plain she'd already listened to him and found herself a chaperone.

'Stella!' Roxanne gasped and ran out into the hall to welcome her visitor, genuinely pleased to see her, but also glad Stella's arrival gave her the excuse to ignore the wretched man for a few precious moments. Her letter asking Tom Varleigh's sister to lend her countenance, if she could tolerate the task, had met with a very ready response, considering it must have got to Varleigh only hours before Stella set out.

'Oh, Roxanne, how lovely to see you again, and if you're quite sure I won't be in the way, I'd really love to stay,' Mrs Stella Lavender greeted her.

'I think you're the only female I could endure having here to lend me countenance, if you're prepared to take on such an onerous task.'

'It'll be my pleasure, especially since this rogue's nearby to make sure you need a chaperone rather badly,' Stella replied, with a delighted chuckle as she sighted Sir Charles lounging in the drawing-room doorway. 'How d'you do, Don Carlos?' she greeted her cousin and hugged him as impulsively and affectionately as she just had Roxanne.

Standing back to watch them exchange cousinly and not particularly respectful greetings, Roxanne wondered about this new Charles Afforde. With his cousin he was affable and charming; there was none of that knife-edge of rakish impudence or insufferable superiority she disliked so much marring his manner with this woman he evidently loved and respected.

This Sir Charles seemed infinitely more dangerous than the one who'd been inciting her to fury so very recently, and she wondered wistfully what it would be like to be at the heart of his family rather than reluctantly hovering on the edge of it, doing her best not to long for a loving friendship between them. Well, perhaps a little bit more than friendship, if the truth be known—a dash of danger, perhaps a spark of the fire he'd lit in her with that incendiary kiss the first day he came back to Hollowhurst?

Transformed by such caring, his potent caress of

mouth on startled mouth in that romantic autumn twi-light might easily have seduced her into falling in love with him all over again, at the very moment he'd taken her once-safe world and blown it apart as efficiently as if he'd landed a broadside on it from his old flagship. It was just as well that he showed no sign of either loving or respecting her as he plainly did Stella then, wasn't it? If her heart was to stay safe and well armoured against him, she could do with all the help she could get from his arrogant determination to get his own way and the memory of just what disillusion awaited any female stupid enough to dream impossible dreams about Captain Charles Afforde, R.N., of course.

'And you, Mrs Star?' he asked his cousin now, with a frown of gentle concern as he saw and probably felt the loss of weight from an already slender frame and pushed Stella a little further away to note her shadowed eyes. 'You're not as well as you'd like us all to think, are you, my dear one?' he quizzed her gently, and Roxanne blinked back a tear in sympathy with the one Stella sur-reptitiously wiped away, then did her best to turn into a smile.

'I shall be now I'm away from Mama's attempts to marry me off to every unattached gentleman she knows under the age of seventy and Great-Aunt Letty's per-petual gossip,' she said with heartfelt relief.

Chapter Six

$\sim\!\!\infty\!\!\sim$

At last Roxanne felt the promise of easing into her new life and her new home, as seeing how much Stella wanted to be useful made her feel better about needing her help. Used to coping alone, Roxanne finally admitted to herself that she needed Stella's lively company and good advice on making her new place in the world. Perhaps being needed would help Stella adjust to life as a widow of limited means if she felt she had a place and a purpose.

She'd dreaded engaging a duenna until Joanna's last letter told her how unhappy her sister-in-law seemed. If Stella agreed to join her, much about her current situation that seemed out of kilter would be tolerable after all, she'd decided, as she made the invitation to join her at Mulberry House. She might even enjoy socialising with her neighbours and attending assemblies in the local towns with such lively company. She took a second look at Stella's fine-drawn features and too-slender frame and decided even such mild dissipation must wait until they were both a little better prepared to enjoy it.

'I hardly dared hope you'd come so soon,' she informed her new chaperone as she ushered her into the drawing room and urged her closer to the fire.

'Wild horses wouldn't have kept me away, but I really ought to change,' Stella demurred, with a doubtful glance at immaculate black skirts.

'Don't be ridiculous, Cousin,' Sir Charles argued impatiently as he strolled into the room in her wake, for all the world as if he owned Mulberry House as well as Hollowhurst Castle, Roxanne thought rebelliously. 'If you want to catch a chill, I doubt if Miss Courland wants to nurse you through it.'

'I'd happily do so if necessary, but I'd prefer you to stay hale and hearty for your own sake, Stella, dear,' Roxanne assured her friend and wished he'd go away. Instead he gave her that annoying, bland smile and sat in a gilded and brocaded chair she immediately disliked for not collapsing under him as he crossed one long, elegantly booted leg over the other.

'How reassuring,' Stella joked rather lamely and began to look better as the warmth from the fire reached her chilled limbs and pinched-looking fingers.

'And here are the promised scones and jam at long last,' Sir Charles murmured; if Roxanne hadn't been so relieved to see the tea tray on Stella's behalf, she might have risked a hostile glare and violated all the Courland traditions of hospitality.

'Ah, this is wonderful,' Stella informed them with a sigh of satisfaction as she sipped fragrant China tea and stretched her sensibly shod feet towards the warmth.

'And I thank you for encouraging Cook to return to

the Castle if this is an example of her handiwork, Miss Courland. It was an act of supreme self-sacrifice,' Sir Charles said as he took another scone and added jam and cream as eagerly as a hungry boy.

Roxanne had to fight against the appeal of so masculine and powerful a man allowing boyish delight to eclipse his usual rakish persona. He's an unscrupulous rogue, she reminded herself sternly. The occasional glimpse of the younger, less cynical Charles Afforde she remembered only proved what a hardened rascal he was now. Forced into the role of gracious hostess, Roxanne rang for more scones and innocently informed Mereson that Sir Charles was so partial to Mulberry House tea he'd surely need another cup, so he should send in a pot especially for him.

'Vixen,' she heard Sir Charles murmur with a sleepy suggestion of intimacy that made Roxanne shiver with a feeling she assured herself was just a goose walking over her grave.

'The master of Hollowhurst must learn to appreciate the finer things in life,' she assured him solemnly, only to see a gleam of devilment light his azure eyes.

'I assure you, Miss Courland, that I enjoy them already,' he informed her even more softly, and she was intensely annoyed to feel herself flush as she avoided the open challenge in his brilliant, taunting gaze.

Only just restraining a flounce of disdain even she'd only half-believe in, Roxanne was puzzled at catching a distinct glow of satisfaction in Stella's warm brown eyes over their ludicrous exchange. What was there to be pleased about in his empty attempts at flirtation, and what could Stella be thinking of? Surely she didn't imagine there was anything more between her and Charles Afforde than exasperation on both sides?

Nothing could be less likely to re-ignite the sweet schoolgirl fantasies she'd once woven about Lieutenant Charles Afforde than current reality, and she was glad to have made such a recovery from those silly daydreams. Somehow or another, Roxanne resolved, she'd make her companion realise she was immune to his charm. He was Stella's cousin when all was said and done, so she supposed she must go about the task gently and not come straight out and tell her she found Sir Charles Afforde the most annoying gentleman she'd ever met.

'Now that my presence here is as respectable as a bishop's,' he went on now, certain he was right in his own eyes at least, 'at least I'll be able to call and pay my respects to you both without sneaking in through the kitchen door to avoid the curiosity and censure of our neighbours, Miss Courland.'

'You'll certainly arouse it now if they see you leave by the front door when it must be obvious you sneaked in the back,' she replied disdainfully.

'We'll have to hope they're not in the habit of watching the comings and goings at Mulberry House very closely then, or risk my leaving by the back door and causing wild speculation if anyone sees me,' he countered effortlessly, and she found herself hating him all over again.

'I dislike dishonest dealings above anything, Sir Charles. Of course you must leave openly, with no excuses needed to call and see how your cousin did after her journey, even if you had no idea she was coming.'

For a moment Roxanne thought she caught a hint of chagrin in Sir Charles's cerulean gaze, but told herself she was mistaken. She thought he'd probably bend the truth so someone he loved could hear a lesser version, but at heart he wasn't a liar and she wondered how she knew that so surely.

'Of course you do,' he responded lightly, so she decided she must have been mistaken in thinking he'd something to hide, 'and what a useful addition to Miss Courland's household you're proving already, Stella, love.'

'Yes, it quite gives me a glow of virtuous self-satisfaction,' Mrs Lavender told her cousin lightly, and Roxanne was glad to see the ghost of her friend's mischievous smile light her pale face, reminding them she'd once been a very happily married woman and not the shadow of herself grief and the blundering attempts of her mama and great-aunt to 'take Stella out of herself' had made her.

If Stella could find another man who'd love and appreciate her as her major had done, she'd be so much happier creating a comfortable home for her own family than enduring her mother and great-aunt's company, or hiring herself out as companion or chaperone to ageing maidens such as herself. Roxanne resolved to go against all her previous resolutions to avoid local society as often as she could, now Sir Charles must be a part of it, and accept as many invitations as Stella's currently precarious health allowed. The thought that where a cousin he cared for went, Sir Charles Afforde would almost certainly follow, Roxanne dismissed as something to be endured in the cause of friendship and fell to plotting how to get Stella out of mourning and into something more cheerful.

'Ah, here's your tea, Sir Charles,' she rewarded

herself by gloating as Mereson led the usual procession into the room.

'No, no, ladies, I'd hate to deprive you of a drink you all seem to love so well,' he protested lamely, and Roxanne almost let her heart soften.

'But there's plenty for all of us,' Stella put in with a sly wink in her direction that made Roxanne realise she liked her new companion even more than she remembered, especially as she seemed to have even fewer illusions about this handsome rogue than she did herself.

'True, but alas I can't linger here enjoying myself all day. It's high time I returned to my echoing hall and readied it for the return of those who know how to make it a bit more homely,' Sir Charles said with what sounded like a weary sigh, and Roxanne wondered if she was supposed to feel sorry for him. She didn't, of course, she reassured herself fiercely; if he didn't like being master of a huge and ancient pile he shouldn't have bought it in the first place.

'I hope the staff I'm doing my best to send back will be welcome, Sir Charles?' she asked loftily as she rose to bid him adieu.

'With wide-open arms, Miss Courland,' he replied with a bland look and a careless bow that settled one of her internal arguments about him.

She definitely didn't pity such an arrogantly devilish gentleman his lone state. There'd be besotted young ladies lining up to do that as soon as they could decently persuade their parents to call on him, and she'd just made that more possible by restoring his senior servants to their accustomed place and making sure his household ran almost as smoothly as if he possessed a chatelaine to keep a sharp eye on it all. Good, she told herself with approval, as pitying the wretch in any way would stretch her compassion to its limits.

'Hurry up, Roxanne, we'll be dreadfully late!' Stella called from outside the door and Roxanne fidgeted on the dressing stool once again.

'No, you don't, Miss Rosie,' Tabby countermanded and took the irons from their stand by the fire and applied them to Roxanne's glossy ebony locks with fierce concentration.

'Don't you hear Mrs Lavender, Tabby? She says we'll be late and the last thing my hair needs is more curls,' she protested weakly, wondering where the self-confident chatelaine of Hollowhurst had gone.

'Who cares if you're late? When you get there, at least you'll be worth looking at—and I'm not adding curls, I'm putting the ones you've already got into some sort of order for once. You're going to be the belle of the ball if I have anything to do with it, Miss Roxanne, like it or not.'

'You and half the tradesmen in Kent,' Roxanne muttered like a rebellious child and thought vengefully of all the mercers, dressmakers, milliners, glovers and shoemakers Stella had dragged her to over the course of the last week. No doubt the whole lot were dining out on the vast amounts of money they'd made out of her for the first time in years.

'And it's high time you sent some trade their way,' her maid scolded back, 'they've made little enough out of you these last few years, and I've had no chance to practise my skills as a proper lady's maid, either. So hold still, Miss Rosie, or else I might burn your ear.'

'Had I known you longed to work for a fashion plate,

I'd have given you a reference so you could do so, you know,' Roxanne said half-seriously and surprised a look of horror on her maid's face that was swiftly hidden.

'You're well enough when you remember to act like a lady, Miss Roxanne,' Tabby informed her sternly and then stood back to examine her handiwork critically. 'And you certainly look like one tonight, so we're half-way there,' she ventured, a smile softening her tight-lipped expression.

'Yes,' Roxanne agreed without vanity, 'I do look very neat and well groomed, don't I?'

'Neat and well groomed?' Tabby echoed incredulously, raising her eyes to the heavens as if seeking divine inspiration. 'You look lovely, Miss Rosie, and there's a good many gentlemen bound to agree with me tonight.'

'They won't pay me any extraordinary attention; most of them have known me since I was a babe and are quite used to me.'

'Oh, but I think they will, and even if some don't, not all of them are blind or daft,' Tabby replied with an infuriating, I-know-better-than-you smile.

'We'll see,' Roxanne said, rising to her feet and enjoying the unaccustomed luxury of dusky rose silk flowing about her as her skirts settled and whispered with her every movement.

In truth, she was rather in awe of the immaculate lady of fashion looking back at her from her pier-glass tonight. For so long she'd taken little note of her hair, except to see that it was neatly confined to a net or the severe chignon she adopted when the management of Hollowhurst began to devolve on to her shoulders and she had little time for anything more elaborate. Then there was her figure, which she now realised hadn't been so obvious to all and sundry since she came out and was much less womanly. She'd battled with Stella and the dressmaker about the low neckline of her fashionable gown when it was being made, and only the lure Stella finally offered of putting off her blacks if she did as they said had persuaded her to do as they wanted and not order a fichu or another half an ell of fabric inserted into this ridiculously low neckline.

Yet, as she smoothed the already immaculate silk over her flat belly and softly curved hips, Roxanne felt a secret lick of pleasure at the radical transformation in her appearance since Stella and Tabby decided it was high time they took her in hand. Nobody could call her a quiz tonight, or overlook her as she gossiped with the older ladies who were inclined to annex her and tell her how they'd all been desperately in love with her great-uncle once upon a time and tried all the tricks under the sun to attract his attention to no avail. One of them had hinted that Uncle Granger had been in love with her grandmother and, once she arrived at Hollowhurst wed to his brother, had never looked at another woman. That comment had sent her home feeling so sad that it was days before he'd been convinced she wasn't sickening for something and they could enjoy their usual easy banter. All that was lost to her now, she remembered and had to blink back a tear he would have scolded her for.

'Sir Granger would be so proud of you tonight,' Tabby murmured, showing her mind was running on similar lines, but luckily Stella finally lost patience and bustled into the room just then and ended what was in danger of becoming a welter of sentiment.

'Oh, just look at you, Roxanne!' Stella said with a

very satisfied smile as she took in the new gown, the stylish hairstyle and the soft sheen of a fine set of pearls about Roxanne's slender neck. 'You look lovely, just as you always should have done.' Roxanne must have looked puzzled, for Stella went on, 'Don't try to tell me Maria Balsover didn't choose all those limp and totally unflattering gowns you wore when you made your come out under her and her mama-in-law's supposed wing, for I won't believe you, Roxanne. She was determined you'd not outshine her—how shocking to her pride if you had made a marriage equal in status to her own.'

Stella sounded as if she'd been bottling up her feelings on the matter for a very long time and could no longer contain them and Roxanne could hardly take umbrage on her sister's behalf when it was probably true. She'd been too young and then too indifferent during that long-ago and disastrous Season to see what Maria was about. At first she'd fooled herself that she was waiting for a certain dashing naval officer to come home from the sea and to realise she was the only wife he could ever dream of taking. Then she had realised what a rake and a rogue he'd become and didn't care what she looked like because she knew she'd never marry.

Little fool, she chided herself now, yes, he was too busy stealing other men's wives to look at her twice when she was seventeen, but there were better men she could have wed. Yet she couldn't regret coming back to Hollowhurst and spending those precious years with her uncle, even if all she'd learnt about managing the estate and the castle was wasted now she was a mere country gentlewoman.

'Mrs Lavender's right, Miss Rosie,' Tabby seconded

with a wise nod. 'Miss Maria refused to listen to a word I said about what suited you.'

Roxanne shrugged, for she hadn't met any man in London she'd the least qualm about leaving behind, so it didn't matter now. 'Well, tonight Maria isn't here and we are, and you, Mrs Lavender, are looking particularly splendid in that pretty silvery lilac, especially considering I very nearly had to knock you unconscious and have you carried into the dressmaker's with it, you were so wedded to that interminable black.'

Stella's mouth set in a stubborn line for a moment, then she caught a glimpse of herself in the pier-glass and couldn't hold to her resolution never to be happy again once she lost her dashing major.

'I do like it,' she admitted, looking so shocked that Roxanne and Tabby laughed, and it set the evening off on a light-hearted note that lasted all the way to the mellow old hall the Longboroughs had lived in as far back as anyone could recall.

'By Jove, you look so very fine tonight I hardly dare speak to either of you,' Squire Longborough assured them in his gruff voice. 'You'll have our local bucks falling over themselves to dance with you as soon as you show your faces, so just see you save me a dance each, eh? Got to do the pretty until Lavinia says I've poured enough oil on all comers to choke a duchess, but save me a good old country dance apiece, there's good girls.'

Seeing Stella half-confounded and half-delighted to be called a girl and gruffly ordered to dance with their host when she fully expected to get away with her usual excuse that widows didn't dance, Roxanne was about to twit her about it when she turned a little too far and met the intense, intent blue gaze of Sir Charles Afforde instead. Arrested in mid-laugh, she felt as if someone had just launched a hot spear straight at her most intimate core and altered everything. Everyone else faded into a murmur of faintly heard babble, a bright veil of dream figures no more real than ghosts. Suddenly she was a girl again, as sure that he must love her as strongly as she knew one day she would be mature enough, deep enough, to love him.

Missing a step, she felt her breath stall, her heartbeat race and her skin flush with some unknown, unthought-of heat she certainly shouldn't be feeling for someone who tormented and infuriated her as severely as Sir Charles Afforde did. Held still and bound to him for a long moment by his bright, compelling gaze, she stood on the edge of something even she never quite anticipated in her wildest dreams. Her lips were a little apart, her breath a little hurried and her eyes a touch feverish as they darkened to pure velvet black in the candlelight.

'Ah, Miss Courland,' the son of the house interrupted their discovery of each other.

Young Joe Longborough shot a glare at the man he obviously regarded as an interloper and gave Roxanne a reproachful look she didn't care for at all. She didn't relish being so violently awakened from her daydream, she decided with an exasperated glare for both gentlemen that should have put them firmly in their places.

'Ah, Mr Longborough,' she parodied crossly.

'I came to claim a waltz,' he informed her pompously.

'Then I suggest you go away again,' Roxanne told him crossly, 'and don't come back until you've learnt some lessons in gentlemanly conduct from your papa, Joseph Longborough,' she ordered and turned back to Stella with a condemning glare for both gentlemen.

Joseph's ears reddened visibly and his rather heavy features contorted with temper. He shot out a hand to pull her back and force his mastery on a mere woman who dared find his manners boorish and his personality lacking in charm, but he felt his arm locked in a grip of honed steel instead.

'You won't lay so much as a finger on Miss Courland without her express permission,' Charles told him in a low, menacing murmur even sharp-eared Roxanne failed to pick out of the general hubbub in the splendid old room. 'Try it,' he warned his host's son with a look intended to freeze the dolt to his very bones, 'and I'll break your arm and make you wail like a baby in front of everyone here tonight.'

'How dare you threaten me in my own home? I'll see you thrown out on your misbegotten ear,' Joseph blustered, but he wasn't fool enough to raise his voice above a whisper and let their dispute become public property.

Sensing extreme masculine tension, although she hadn't heard any of their actual words, Stella intervened. 'Have you met my famous cousin, Mr Longborough? Commodore Sir Charles Afforde, lately of the Mediterranean Fleet and now of Hollowhurst Castle. And, Charles, this is Mr Longborough, elder son of the Squire and his charming lady,' she said genially, even if her eyes warned Charles that he must contain the temper, which only his close friends and those unfortunate enough to rouse it were aware he possessed, while under his hospitable neighbours' roof. Joseph gulped and backed swiftly away, just as she'd intended.

'Longborough,' Charles responded with a perfunctory bow.

'An honour, Sir Charles,' Joseph managed almost convincingly. Apparently even he didn't want to carry on behaving like a boor in front of a hero of the late wars, a seasoned warrior who could outdo him on every field of arms he could think of. 'I must greet my father's other guests,' he mumbled and stumped off to do what he'd vowed not to when his mother had asked for his support.

Chapter Seven

'Well, Charles?' Stella asked ironically.

'Not nearly as well as yourself and Miss Courland, that's very plain to see,' he replied as smoothly as if he hadn't just offered both an outright and an implicit challenge to his host's son.

'Why, thank you, how flattering,' she returned and shifted her attention to Roxanne, who was strangely silent at her side.

'How do you do, Sir Charles?' finally Roxanne managed in a distant voice, still reeling from that odd moment of recognition between them, the eerie feeling of being isolated with him outside reality. Something she didn't quite catch or understand had just passed between him and Joe as well, and normally she didn't like not knowing everything that was going on about her.

'Better now,' he told her with a smile that mocked himself for once instead of her and threatened to rock her back into the strange world they'd almost stepped into just now.

'Good, but it's a little warm in here tonight, is it not?' she asked him, in the face of Stella's incredulous expression that told her that, while it was a noble and impressive venue for a country ball, Squire Longborough's ancestral hall was definitely *not* warm, despite the fires burning at each end.

'I dare say it will be as soon as the dancing begins,' he replied with a look suspiciously like that a man might give when overlooking an eccentricity in a woman he respected or maybe even loved.

What a mistake it would be to sink into his subtle enchantment and believe he'd ever passionately love her. Better to remember that foolish illusion had once lit up her life with a false, glittering promise only ever alive in her imagination. He hadn't lifted a finger to draw such a silly little idiot in as she'd been then; perhaps she deserved the pain her infatuation had caused her all those years ago. Nothing was to be trusted about tonight then, least of all her senses, and Roxanne wished she'd worn her old brown velvet evening gown and not ventured into the dangerous world of fashion.

'So may I have your dance cards, ladies?' he enquired, as if they'd been deliberately withholding them.

'You can have Roxanne's, but I don't intend to dance,' Stella said.

'Then I shall not, either,' Roxanne declared, deciding that would suit her very well.

'Shall I declare my resolution to do likewise and stand out every measure with you both, like a third wallflower?' Sir Charles teased his cousin, but if Stella didn't know he was determined to see her dance despite herself, Roxanne rather thought she didn't know him, after all.

'You can if you like, I still don't dance,' Stella countered mulishly, and Roxanne realised she'd underestimated her. Her companion knew her cousin very well, and was determined to go her own way despite him. Admiring such stern resolution, she lifted her chin in silent support.

'I will if you will,' he taunted softly, and Roxanne was certain something more than just the surface banter, half-serious and half in jest, was at issue between them.

'But I've already loved and lost,' Stella argued, confirming Roxanne's conclusion that she didn't fully understand what they were arguing about.

'Which makes you a very lucky woman. So are we three going to dance tonight or not?' he asked, with a sly, almost beseeching sidelong glance at Roxanne that seemed to hold more meaning for him and his cousin than it did for her. She held her breath while the silent debate went on, feeling excluded, wondering if she would ever know either well enough to make out what they were arguing about.

'If you really must,' Stella finally conceded, sighing long-sufferingly as she handed over her dance card and watched him initial it.

'Miss Courland?' he asked expectantly, once he'd handed Stella's card back to her and held out his hand expectantly for hers.

Feeling as if she was committing herself to something far more than a mere dance, she finally gave it to him, feeling disconcertingly as if a spark had leapt from his fingertips to hers as they touched fleetingly during the transfer.

'Two waltzes?' she protested as she received her card back so cautiously she only touched it at the opposite side to him and even then with the very tips of her fingers.

'More would render us conspicuous,' he told her flippantly, and suddenly her palm itched for a very different reason, since she'd very much like to box his ears with it.

'I barely know you, Sir Charles.'

'Something two waltzes might fairly be expected to remedy, don't you agree, Miss Courland?'

'Not in the least. I intend to save my breath for my dancing and shall use my eyes to guide my steps, this being the first time I've danced a waltz in company. It was considered scandalous hereabouts until recently, you know.'

'And yet you still know how to dance it? How very shocking of you, Miss Courland, to have acquired such a *risqué* skill in secret.'

Wretched, wretched man, Roxanne decided, clenching her teeth determinedly to stop herself telling him exactly what she thought of him with almost half the county within earshot.

'There is little anyone could call secret about being taught the steps by my sister's husband Tom Varleigh and their eldest daughter while my sister played for us all, especially considering my niece is but eight years of age, or have you quite forgotten her, Sir Charles?'

'Nobody could forget little Julia Varleigh, and I certainly shouldn't dare to,' he asserted with a reminiscent smile at the thought of the Varleighs' precocious eldest daughter; Roxanne saw it with a sinking heart.

If only he'd carried on being careless and even a little callous, distaste for such a flinty-hearted man might have built up some sort of armour about her much-tried senses. Instead, he looked like a doting uncle when he spoke of her adored niece, and she began to see that he was as capable of feeling strong affection and maybe even love as the next man—indeed, probably *more* capable than a good many careless gentlemen. How very unfair of him, she decided huffily and frowned at the monster for his failure to be one.

'No,' Stella intervened with a significant glance at one of the local gossips who was straining every nerve to overhear as much as she could of the new owner of Hollowhurst and its dispossessed chatelaine's conversation. 'Nobody would dare overlook my niece, and nor should they, but she's not here and you are. So are you both intent on setting the tabbies in a flutter by arguing over Roxanne's dance-card all night, or can the rest of us please get on with enjoying ourselves?'

'Very well, but why do I have to waltz twice with Captain Afforde when there are perfectly good sets of country dances planned?' Roxanne protested querulously, much as eight-year-old Miss Julia Varleigh might at being sent off to bed on such a night and not allowed to join in, so a part of her wasn't at all surprised when the cousins exchanged rueful glances over her head.

'Because Captain Afforde doesn't enjoy seeing his partner flirt with her host for the night in the middle of what was supposed to be their dance,' Charles informed her with a heat in his gaze that told Roxanne he was only half-joking about her easy, joking flirtation with their host for tonight.

'Mr Longborough was a boyhood friend of my uncle's. Indeed, he's more of an honorary uncle to me than what you vulgarly classify as a "flirt", and his wife knows it and thinks it's as funny as the rest of us do. To imply otherwise is just stupid and crass, Sir Charles,' she accused, trying to tell herself he'd no right to unnerve her with heated looks that promised more than that swift, disturbing, overheating kiss he'd pressed on her lips the first night they met again, even if it would only be to maze her senses into getting her to do whatever he wanted.

The too-brief caress of his firm mouth on her surprised one had caused her more than enough trouble over the last few weeks, thank you very much, without adding more sleepless nights and silly daydreams to it and make her wonder even more if she'd really changed from the deluded girl who'd once thought herself so in love with him. It had all been an illusion, after all, and she had to remember that in the face of any temptation he could offer.

'Then consider me stupid,' he replied with a wry twist of his intriguing mouth as he admitted to what she could only interpret as jealousy—but surely to be jealous he'd need to care about her in the first place? 'Now here's your partner for the first dance come to claim you, Miss Courland, so pray recall how much you hate to be conspicuous and go and dance with the poor man, will you?' he teased.

Roxanne wondered if she'd ever understand the infuriating, intriguing man, even as she guiltily realised she didn't want to leave his side to dance with another.

'Gladly,' she said and went to do so with a decided flounce of the whispering old-rose skirts that had given her such satisfaction when she put them on tonight. She wouldn't let his rakish tendencies spoil a special night, and she smiled and danced to such effect that Sir Charles had to fight his way through a crowd of her admirers before he could claim her for the first of those waltzes.

'Young puppies,' he muttered under his breath when she finally tore herself away from her court, with a dazzling smile of farewell for a boy she'd known since he was in his cradle.

'I beg your pardon?' she replied innocently enough.

'You heard, and be very careful whom you encourage to chase after you to prove to me that I'm one of many.'

'One of many what?'

'You know very well, but in case you feel the need to flirt with any more schoolboys or roués to prove your point, I'll gratify your vanity by admitting to be a member of your court tonight, Miss Courland. Satisfied?'

As if she ever could be, Roxanne silently despaired, wondering if he'd known where she was during every instant they were apart as acutely as she'd been aware of *his* every move. Nothing she could find to berate herself with about feeble-minded females, who'd yearned after the impossible once and should never do so again, could cure her of being acutely conscious of Sir Charles Afforde and all that he said and did—always and, she suspected, for ever. However, she *could* conceal her besotted state from him until he grew bored with his games and amused himself elsewhere.

'Was I doing that?' she asked innocently, even as she felt his strength envelop her with warmth and power as he swept her on to the dance floor, and couldn't quite suppress a gasp as her body threatened to betray her.

'Oh, yes, you definitely were,' he murmured and went some way to chilling the wildfire that threatened to eat her up as he controlled their physical reaction to each other and led her smoothly into the dance.

'How silly of me,' she muttered darkly and risked an upward glance at his face as their bodies managed the waltz without much input from her. He looked blandly charmed by her company, on the surface. So why did she think he was less than charmed by this whole business than he pretended?

'I don't think you silly at all,' he told her rather absently. 'Life might be very much simpler if only I could,' he ended, as if he couldn't help himself, and then watched her with guarded, even sombre eyes.

'Then pray feel free to do so,' she invited in a rather hollow attempt to pretend there was nothing very significant between them. 'I'm all for simplicity, Sir Charles.'

'Hah! If only that were true, Miss Courland, how easy this whole business would be for us to conclude.'

For some reason a shiver chilled its way down her spine, despite the warmth generated by their movements and the shockingly real feeling of his guiding hand upon her waist, his body next to hers. Such a wild mix of excitement, turmoil and apprehension he sparked in her that Roxanne almost longed to be dancing with someone less disturbing, less masculine, less in every way than Captain, lately Commodore, Sir Charles Afforde.

'What business?' she finally recalled her wandering wits enough to ask.

Was that a conscious, almost guilty expression that flitted so fast across his handsome face she wondered if she'd imagined it? It must be, for the next moment he assumed his familiar, cynical mask of the genial and not-often-denied rake, and she seemed a fool to herself for ever imagining he was other than as he seemed.

'Becoming lord and master of so much history and tradition, of course, Miss Courland—your great-uncle left very large boots for a man to try to fill.'

'That he did,' she agreed loyally, wondering if that was why Davy never seemed to feel much joy at the prospect of inheriting them.

'And of course you have your own dubious reputation to live up to,' she half-teased and half-taunted him, then regretted wanting to do either as a flicker of what might be pain lit his suddenly expressive face, as he left himself unguarded long enough to let her see something of his innermost thoughts.

'Of course,' he echoed with all his defences firmly back in place while he obligingly leered at her to prove it.

'Pray try not to be any more annoying than you can help, Sir Charles.'

'Why not? You expect so little it seems a shame to disappoint you.'

'I could respect you,' she offered, half-seriously.

'Don't do that, never do that,' he said so fervently that she stared full into his extraordinary eyes; she saw there such turmoil and slumbering passion that she'd have faltered to a halt if not for his strong, steady arm guiding her so ruthlessly efficient in figures he could obviously dance in his sleep.

'Ah…' Momentarily silenced by something glimpsed and then just as swiftly hidden again, she gathered her wits and reminded herself he was right.

By profession, he was a defender of his country, a fearless warrior with the wits and training as well as the strength to beat a cunning and determined enemy time after time. By reputation, he was a seducer of beautiful women, a cuckolder of careless husbands and a cynical manipulator of society's skewed rules that dictated a single gentleman could sow wild oats with delighted abandon, whilst single ladies must keep themselves chaste and pure and ignorant of what their potential husbands were up to. A small voice in the back of her head told her that a man about to put his life at risk so often during a distinguished but lonely command was entitled to seek comfort in a willing woman's arms, but she suppressed it ruthlessly.

'Very well, I promise to please us both in future by regarding you with unyielding contempt, and I think our dance is at an end, Sir Charles, so you may now let me go.'

'Always happy to oblige a lady,' he drawled and carelessly renounced all the warmth and intimacy her body had been cunningly enjoying while her mind was busy elsewhere, at least most of the time.

Roxanne shivered as he bowed as elegantly to her as if she were a duchess. She gave a disdainful, too-deep curtsy in return, then rose from it lithely before he could offer his hand to help her rise.

'So I have heard, Sir Charles, so I have heard,' she

drawled back and maintained an aloof silence as he followed her back to Stella's side as if, Roxanne thought sadly, they were a married couple who'd wed for all the wrong reasons and didn't particularly like each other anymore.

'Scoundrel,' she muttered crossly under her breath as she watched him walk away, then she cursed her unwary tongue when Stella slewed in her seat to stare up at her incredulously.

'Charles? What on earth has he said to you to lead you to name him so? I swear he's usually so meticulously polite to single ladies of fortune or expectations that I'd given up all hope for him, but if he's been living up to that ridiculously overblown reputation of his with you, then perhaps there's hope for him, after all,' she said with a familiar glint of mischief in her eyes that almost led Roxanne to shudder, except that would really give her away.

'Banish the very thought from your mind,' she cautioned sternly.

'Why? It would make such an excellent solution for two stubborn conundrums—he'd gain a lively and knowledgeable wife, and you'd get a fine husband with all the qualities he does his very best to disguise or deny.'

'I haven't the least desire to marry Sir Charles,' Roxanne defended herself far too fervently and felt Stella's scrutiny while she pretended to watch her fellow guests as if the idea wasn't worth a moment's consideration.

'Then you must be blind or light in your attic, my dear. Not one woman in a hundred could look at my disreputable cousin and *not* want to be wedded and bedded by him, or at least one of the two if that wasn't possible.'

'A very strange chaperone you're proving to be, encouraging your charge to fall for a rogue who seems to have no intention of marrying anyone, even if he's perfectly happy to bed as many beautiful women as are foolish enough to throw themselves at him without benefit of clergy.'

'Now there I think you're wrong—would you care to lay me odds?'

'Really, Stella, that's going a little far in such polite company,' she reproached her friend mock-seriously, deeply relieved when her next partner presented himself and the whole uncomfortable topic was dropped.

Could Stella possibly be right, though? The very thought of Sir Charles marrying anyone else sat uncomfortably with Roxanne, despite her long-held conviction that, if she let him, he'd break her heart along with all the others already in his vast collection. Lingering infatuation, she dismissed uneasily and smiled incautiously at Joe Longborough before regretting her stupidity for the rest of the evening when he took it for more encouragement than most gentlemen would an open and shameless attempt at seduction.

'Is that cub bothering you?' Sir Charles asked her gruffly as soon as they were fairly launched on the supper waltz, and at least it distracted Roxanne from the inevitable and deeply annoying reaction of her body against his powerful one for a few moments.

'Joe is a mere boy,' she told him, incredulity in her voice that he could doubt it. After all, Joe had proved his immaturity from the moment he had shambled into his parents' hall and set about offending their guests.

'He's more than powerful enough to force his silly wants on a woman, even one who thinks herself invulnerable,' he said stiffly.

'Now why do I seem to sense I'm the deluded female you refer to?' she asked with a weary irony she'd probably learnt from him.

'I haven't seen him paw and growl over any other female here tonight. Whatever can you be thinking of to encourage him, Miss Courland? If it's intended to make me furious with you both, I have to say it's working and you might regret the fact before we're much older.'

'What a very fine opinion of yourself you do have, Captain,' Roxanne informed him coldly, trying her best to hold herself aloof and rigid in his arms when the music relentlessly beat on and bound them closer to each other than any unengaged couple could hope, or fear, to be and keep their reputations. 'I don't share it, and you have no right to interfere in my affairs.'

'You intend to marry the young idiot, then?'

'Of course not. I'd rather marry you, and that's not saying very much for poor Joe's ridiculous pretensions,' she said lightly enough, but she lied and acknowledged it to herself with a sinking heart.

'Be careful, Miss Courland, it's only considered safe to goad a wolf from a much greater distance than the one currently between us,' he informed her rather harshly, then lessened that space imperceptibly to prove how honed and prone to pouncing he was, she assumed crossly.

She did her best to tell herself the racing of her heart was a by-product of the dance and nothing to do with his muttered threat and implied possession of her fullest attention. He might impose his will on hers, if she wasn't a well-connected lady of independent means. So it was quite wrong to wish herself otherwise for one heady night—yes, of course it was!

Roxanne held herself a little more stiffly in his arms and forced herself to remember their respectability and all the watching, calculating eyes following their progress about the room. Nothing could be more wrong than to carelessly grab what she wanted, when he'd be bound to offer his hand to her come the grey light of dawn—if he was fool enough to take her to his bed in the first place. The idea of entering a forced marriage to a reluctant husband should have been enough to kill any feral longing stone dead, so it was utterly wanton to still feel such heat, such a delightful sense of promise and the delicious mysteries tantalisingly close to being solved with that nightmare ringing about her mind.

'You goad yourself, sir. This is all imagination,' she told him scornfully.

'Idiot woman!' he gritted, sounding like a much-tried wolf now, and she should be glad when the heated possession died out of his gaze so it became steely once more.

'Not so, and I can handle Joe's silly infatuation perfectly well, Sir Charles. I've been doing so since he left the schoolroom, after all.'

'Not very successfully since he seems to suffer the delusion he can force you to yield to his absurd wooing if he tries hard enough.'

'He's not usually as bad as this,' she finally admitted.

'I guessed that much, the silly young fool,' he replied, looking slightly self-satisfied that Joe Longborough sensed a potent rival in him.

'He'll grow up one day.'

'Maybe not soon enough,' he warned, and Roxanne shivered at the warning in his voice and wondered if he was right to be concerned.

Bridging that slight gap she'd set between them with such sterling effort, Sir Charles managed to engulf her in comfort and strength all at the same time. There's nothing to fear from me, he seemed to be suggesting as their bodies resumed an instinctive rhythm. I'm never less than controlled, never fool enough to force what I can't charm and seduce out of you of your free will. He was probably right, she decided sadly, and heard the musicians wind their brisk rhythm down to a dying whisper with what might be relief.

'Be wary, Miss Courland, that's all I ask,' he cautioned as he bowed to her in thanks for their dance.

'Oh, believe me, I shall be,' she promised and saw him smile with a lift of her silly heart as he acknowledged what a double-edged sword he'd just handed her.

Chapter Eight

Sir Charles made sure that when he took Roxanne into supper they formed part of a merry party with Stella and the Squire's eldest daughter and her bluff and uncomplicated husband. There was nothing intimate or threatening about the way he somehow guessed what she wanted to eat or drink before she hardly knew it herself. Then he handed her over to the Squire at the end of the supper interval and watched them dance an energetic measure as if he was an indulgent octogenarian rather than the biggest rake in Kent. She'd never understand men, Roxanne concluded wearily as Sir Charles finally handed her and Stella into the carriage he'd sent for them earlier, then sprang lightly on to his horse to follow it through a mere three miles of moonlit lanes.

Luckily Stella seemed as weary after her exertions on the dance floor as Roxanne felt at the conclusion of an oddly unsatisfactory evening, despite much merriment and the presence of so many good friends. She ran admiring fingers over her silk gown even if she couldn't see colours in the faint light of the moon. It suited her, she thought with a pleased smile not even aching feet could wipe away. Dressed so, she'd shed her insecurities and her inhibitions for a few heady hours and fooled herself she was seventeen again, but this time dressed to perfection and as close to being the belle of the ball one rather castaway gentleman had proclaimed her as she'd ever be.

Fortunately they were home before she'd had time to reach the end of any silly fantasies about Sir Charles finding her irresistible now her hair was almost tame and her dress as smart as any London Incomparable's. He wasn't the romantic hero she'd once dreamt of so single-mindedly. She was certainly no heroine and forced herself to watch carefully in the moonlight and the flare of a flaming torch that her new butler produced rather dramatically to light his ladies safely within Mulberry House for the night.

Unfair of that torchlight to pick up the rich gold of Sir Charles's wind-ruffled hair then, or of the moonlight to outline his powerful form all the more while it shadowed his expression as he helped her down and held her hand just a moment longer than he needed to, as if almost as conscious as she was that she was holding her breath, waiting for something wonderful or terrible to happen. If Stella hadn't been there, if Simkins wasn't standing waiting with his fiery brand flaring and fussing on the breeze, she thought Sir Charles might have kissed her. Instead, he turned until the light revealed his usual careless smile and bid them both a pleasant goodnight, gave Simkins a friendly wave, then got on his horse and rode away.

'Annoying man!' Stella announced as they turned and walked into the house. 'Always was, always will be.'

'I know, but I hadn't realised you did. I thought you were even quite fond of him,' Roxanne teased to hide her acute sense of anti-climax, as if the night had promised her the moon and the stars, but instead delivered nothing more glamorous than tired feet and a mild headache.

'I am, the great blundering fool,' his exasperated cousin confirmed as they made their weary way upstairs. 'Although I quite often ask myself why.'

'And the answer?' Roxanne couldn't stop herself asking.

'Because he's nothing like he pretends to be,' Stella responded after long moments of careful consideration, 'and because I know very well there's no more loving and selfless man on this earth when he truly gives himself in love or friendship.'

'And does he do that very often?' Oh dear, Roxanne, and where did that betraying, faux-casual question come from? she asked herself with a shake of her head that Stella probably saw, despite the late hour and her apparent tiredness.

'He's a very good friend,' Stella evaded, then seemed to realise that wasn't enough of an answer to a question that had taken on ridiculous importance for her listener. 'He loves some of his family and one or two close friends—Rob Besford and his wife, to name but two—and he was as sure and solid as a rock for me when Mark was killed. If you're asking me how he rates as a lover, I must pass. As his cousin I'd be the last person any of his flirts would confide in on that subject.'

'Have there been so very many of them, then?'

'Very many, as he's an excellent flirt, which you can see well enough for yourself. He's usually funny and gallant and light-hearted, and ladies fall over themselves to be flattered and flustered by him, but if we're talking about anything more serious then I suspect no, not nearly as many as his colourful reputation suggests.'

'Then why is he considered so notorious?'

'Because he chose to be, once upon a time. Initially his dubious reputation annoyed his father and stepmother and most of his stepsisters, mainly because they're a pack of mawkish idiots, which gave him a great deal of satisfaction. I've sensed that since the end of the wars and his retirement from the sea, he's found his bad name more of a millstone about his neck than something to preen himself over, though.'

'I often used to wonder why he seemed nothing like the rogue he's reputed to be,' Roxanne said dreamily, picturing the dashing young man she'd once thought she knew deliberately setting out to blacken his own name in order to annoy his absent family. They must have hurt him so badly to cause him to do that, and for some reason, the pain of that young man hurt her, too.

'It seems to me that you used to wonder about my wild young cousin a lot more than you ever let on, Roxanne Courland,' her friend accused lightly, and Roxanne shivered as she realised how close she'd come to revealing that past infatuation with Lieutenant Afforde.

'I was young and impressionable,' she managed to say lightly and shrug, as if she'd long ago put off any last wisp of that girlish crush.

'And now you're so very, very old,' Stella teased.

'I'm certainly extremely weary,' she countered with a wide yawn.

'Of course you are.'

'And pining for my bed, which will be cooling by the minute since I told Tabby not to wait up.'

'Then sweet dreams, Roxanne. I wonder what my cousin Charles will be dreaming of tonight as he tosses and turns in that ridiculous bed and echoing barrack of a chamber the master of Hollowhurst is supposed to sleep in of a night?' her so-called friend ended archly and whisked herself into her room with a pert goodnight before Roxanne could think of anything crushing to say in reply to such a ridiculous question.

Puzzled by her own dreams, when she had eventually managed to have them, and somehow out of sorts with her new life once again, the next morning Roxanne donned her most ancient riding habit and ordered a challenging mount brought round, then strode restlessly out to the stables because she couldn't bring herself to stand still and wait.

'He's full of devilment and oats, Miss Roxanne,' Jake, her newly promoted head groom, warned as he struggled to hold the fiery young colt.

'So am I,' she snapped back in a fit of unaccustomed temper she knew she'd be ashamed of later, and so restless that she paced the spotless yard until Jake led out the curvetting horse from the back of the sweetest and fleetest mare he could find. Despite the allure of Juno's presence, the colt was too eager to be off and running to follow even her like a meek farm horse.

'Down, Donnie lad,' Jake grumbled half-heartedly as the young horse reared, then danced with impatience.

'How's my boy?' Roxanne greeted him with obvious delight and Jake watched the young rogue sidle up to her as if he hadn't the faintest idea who'd been kicking the sides out of his stall just now. 'My handsome Adonis, my darling boy,' she murmured in his responsive ear as it twitched to catch every word she said as if he understood every one.

'He's a young devil,' Jake informed them both dourly.

'Nonsense,' she defended her favourite, 'he's just young and full of life and you spoil him even more than I do.'

'Perhaps,' Jake conceded, still looking glum as he contemplated the young chestnut. Sure enough, he watched the pair of them disappear over the horizon ten minutes later and wondered dourly when he might be privileged to see them again and if there was any point continuing. Shrugging as he set lively Juno into an easy canter, he decided even Miss Roxanne was beyond his ken and he wished she'd find a husband to control her starts. He contemplated another thirty or forty years of trying to save her neck and nearly marched up to the castle and asked for his old job back.

Even Roxanne didn't know what was stirring her into such a fidgety state today, but she was damned if she'd ride sedately and disappoint Adonis because a lady was never supposed to be out of sight of her groom or to gallop or allow her horse to take fences when a gate was there to be opened.

'They can all go straight to perdition, can't they, Donnie?' she murmured and his ears flicked back eagerly to catch every word. 'I'm not cut out to be a sedate and proper lady.' If he had been human, his snort might be interpreted as amused and even scornful agreement.

'That's right, they're welcome to their tatting and their delicately refined nerves, aren't they, boy?'

She sounded less certain than she liked, for without a great estate to manage, her dominion over a grand house and her assured place in the world, how could she maintain her rebellion against the role of fine lady and stay sane? There was so little to do when you were a lady of means and no real responsibility. So little that your mind fell to mulling over the alternatives unless you were very careful indeed. She'd been so careful not to do so that she'd hardly slept a wink for what had remained of the night and knew sooner or later her idiocy would catch up with her. Not yet though, for she was still young, still strong and still far too alive to give in to the notions of polite ladylike behaviour and turn about to go tamely home.

'Come on, Donnie, there's the sea!' she cried and let him quicken his pace as the lure of a long gallop across the flat beach caught them both.

Her heartbeat quickened to almost match Adonis's mad pace as they thundered across the sand, until they reached the sea and he amused himself and her by playing with the waves as they would have played with him. All the pins finally fell out of Roxanne's hair with their speed and her neat jockey cap fell away with them to let her midnight locks flare out behind them in a silky banner caught by the speed of their passage. To the devil with being a respectable gentlewoman for a few blessed hours, she decided, and with Sir Charles Afforde with his questions and conundrums. She gave herself up to the sheer exhilaration of feeling her long hair flow free with the speed of their passing, the fire and vigour of her mount and the youthful, singing blood coursing through her lithe body.

From his vantage point above the beach, Sir Charles Afforde checked his own fidgeting mount and watched her headlong progress, trying hard not to admire her reckless bravery. No, it wasn't even that, he concluded, half-exasperated and half-captivated by the sight of her flouting every convention she could with determined abandon. The female centaur down on the sands didn't even *think* of the dangers even a brilliant rider could encounter when she was so caught up in speed. How could she be brave in the face of a danger she didn't possess the sense to recognise? So he did it for her, and the potential terror was like a frozen fist around his heart.

How dare she? How could she, when she must know she was his to her very bones and they'd end up man and wife as sure as today would be followed by tomorrow and this week by the next? In that agile, supple, stubborn female frame there might well beat the heart of a lioness, but their future was at the mercy of her ill-timed, cross-grained struggle to evade him and her destiny. What if she let her concentration slip and took a tumble—would she survive to become his wife at such a reckless, ridiculous pace? Not in one piece and it was fury at her lack of consideration for anyone who cared for her that made his fingers clench on the reins until his own spirited mount began to dance in protest, nothing more painful.

Charles soothed the gelding; for once in his life, he had to watch and wait on the hand of fate rather than shape it himself. When had she become his fate, then? Was it when he made his old friend David Courland a promise neither of them had considered seriously enough at the time or when he saw her across that shadowed room and wanted her with a long, silent and merciless roar of possession? Who knew?

Then there was the shameful germ of need he'd carried with him for much longer, since he first set eyes on her when she was all of fourteen years old and already passionate, stubborn and vital, yet as wild and innocent as an unbroken filly. He'd made himself turn aside from that painfully young Roxanne, reproached by her innocence; he was already the other side of a vast ocean of experience compared to her total lack of it. She'd been completely ignorant of what she was encouraging when she eyed him with unfledged encouragement during that memorable Christmas season so long ago, but would she eye him with half that much enthusiasm now she was old enough for him to return it with compound interest?

Instead, all he got was constant provocation and her cheerful flouting of every rule society put in place to protect single, unprotected females with more daring than sense. He glared at her retreating back and decided he'd given her enough of a start to risk following. He nudged his horse into eager motion and let him run out a fraction of his rider's frustrations. Now Roxanne Courland was four and twenty, and every glimpse he had of her lithe figure as she pelted along the sands roused him to painful consciousness of how much he needed her, yet the contrary female was determined not to admit how profoundly *she* needed him.

She was his lady, his bed-mate, the woman he wanted to seduce until she was near to weeping with longing for his very thorough possession and the one who might one day match his hasty passion as he took her before they both fainted for the wanting of each other. One day, very soon, he promised himself as he rose in the stirrups to crouch on Thor's neck and to give him that small extra advantage he needed to catch up with their fleet-footed rival, as well as distracting his rider from the very physical discomfort that the bare idea of what he'd really like to do to Roxanne Courland inflicted on his disobedient body.

It wasn't until the eager young colt Roxanne was riding began to slow at last that he gained enough ground for her to hear him over the noise of her own passing, and she finally reined in to see who had the audacity to follow her. She might have known, she concluded as she recognised Sir Charles Afforde and a powerfully muscled gelding a couple of years older than her Adonis and therefore not at all easily outrun. Nothing to do but turn and greet the last man she wanted to see this morning with careless politeness, she decided. So why did her heartbeat insist on quickening instead of slowing, and why was a wild fantasy of him riding towards her as her lover, her other half and her strength, insisting on playing out in the feral part of her imagination that she dearly wished would give up and go away?

'Sir Charles,' she managed to greet him coolly enough, as she soothed Adonis who scented a challenge on the morning breeze that insisted on playing with her wildly tangled tresses and reminding her she probably couldn't pretend she was in her drawing room greeting an acquaintance.

'Roxanne,' he acknowledged shortly, looking as if he would prefer her to be brought before him aboard ship for suitable punishment.

'I can't recall making you free of my name,' she said recklessly, given the sharp fury and something even more feral and dangerous that she could see in his eyes now he was too close for comfort.

'Oh, you do that by your conduct this morning, Rox-an-ne,' he replied, drawing out the syllables as if preparing to carry them off to his lair, along with the rest of her, and ravish them away until she couldn't recall if they belonged to her or not.

She hadn't known how much she liked the glint of respect, and that suggestion of wild heat held in temporary abeyance, in his azure eyes whenever they rested on her, until it was banished by the wolfish boldness he turned on her now as he let that heat blaze without control. To punish her. Somehow she'd roused the devil in him by trying her best to exorcise it in herself and wasn't that an irony to conjure with when she had the leisure and safety to do so?

'A true gentleman adheres to his own standards, whatever the imagined provocation of others,' she told him coldly, as if images of their limbs tangled in some wanton, private dance were a million miles from her mind.

'How noble of him,' he informed her huskily, sin and desire informing every word as he leaned forwards and snatched a hard, hot kiss from her lips that told her he'd been restraining himself fiercely at their first truly adult encounter, after all.

Only Adonis's dancing, protesting furiously under her as he reacted like the wild spirit he was to the proximity of the gelding Charles rode, reminded her to be equally angry. Young as he was, Adonis was still a stallion. Maybe it wasn't the quieter beast under her tormentor he was objecting to, after all, she decided darkly, as she glared at the man who rode him. He was shameless and stared at her as if her clothes had blown away along with her hairpins and her cap. At least Adonis's restless reaction to a possible rival gave her the excuse to concentrate on something other than the man who seemed to think he'd bought a right to govern her along with Davy's inheritance.

'Go away!' she ordered hotly, nodding at Adonis as he bared his teeth at the infuriating gelding, who looked as if he'd whistle and cross his legs to prove how ridiculous he found all this, if he were only a human. Adonis roared a challenge and would have given his imagined rival a nip if she hadn't turned his head at the last moment. 'You're annoying my horse.'

'Only your horse? I must be slipping.'

As she controlled Adonis with her knees and her will, she bared her teeth at him in a mock snarl and met his blue gaze with a glare of her own. 'Oh, no, you're being every bit as annoying as even you can contrive today. Congratulations, Captain.'

'I haven't even started yet,' he slapped back, then unfairly took the wind out of her sails by suddenly seeming to find them sitting here trading insults irresistibly amusing.

'Unfair,' she reproached, wondering what a third party would have made of their half-spoken, half-taken-for-granted conversation.

'Don't do it again without me?' Suddenly his voice sounded less supremely arrogant and demanding than driven and even, heavens above, pleading.

'Can he keep up?' she heard herself ask, with a nod at the gelding she knew was unnecessary, but it gave her time to think about how that second kiss might change things between them if she let it.

'Easily,' he drawled, understanding of her evasive tactics easy to read in his eyes.

She would never be a woman of mystery while Sir Charles Afforde knew far too much about her sex for comfort. Roxanne shifted in the saddle as the sharp goad of something too close to pain bit into her at the thought of just how he'd gained all that annoying insight, whatever Stella's reservations about his reported legion of lovers. If he'd only had even one or two, which she doubted, it was one or two more than she'd had.

'A little too easily,' she muttered and pretended to believe they were talking about horses while she impatiently gathered up her streaming tresses and deftly tied them back with the length of narrow, corded ribbon Tabby always put in her pocket for just such an eventuality. A pity, then, that the possessiveness in his eyes was all too easily read as his gaze lingered on the shiny ebony mass of it and frustrated her attempts to turn their encounter into something more restrained, along with her hair.

'I find it extraordinarily beautiful, whatever you do to it, and so I won't beg you never to cut it lest you immediately decided to do so. Even cropped about your ears it would still be an enchantress's lure, so you can forget that notion a-borning, Miss Courland.'

'Black hair shows a woman's age more surely than any other colour,' she assured him repressively. 'In a few years time you'll see that clearly enough whenever we meet.'

'Rather more than a few, I think, my dear, but I can't

see the day ever dawning when I'll find it less than lovely, even if we're both white as snow.'

She felt a quick rush of that fierce heat she was growing so reluctantly accustomed to at the thought of him being there to see her grow old, then a flush of sweetness overlaid it at the idea he'd see beauty in her when youth had abandoned them both. Not that vigour would while they still had breath in their bodies, she decided wryly, as the notion of such a lifetime of intimacy felt even harder to beat than the one of letting him teach her the glories of love in his bed, then watch him walk away. No, that way madness lay!

Chapter Nine

'Flattery is just words when all's said and done, Sir Charles,' she informed him stiffly and tried not to read his opinion of her craven avoidance strategy in his mocking gaze.

'And words can sometimes mean exactly what they say, Roxanne, but you're obviously not ready to hear them today. We'll revisit the topic when you've gained a better grasp on truth and lies, along with your temper.'

'There's nothing wrong with my hold on reality, I assure you, sir,' she snapped, exasperated at his assumption he knew her better than she did herself. 'I'm a respectable lady who has no intention of becoming otherwise, and you're a rake. I won't let you play your games with my heart or my body.'

'Ah, but I'm not playing, Rosie, dear,' he informed her in a husky undertone that seemed to pick out some wicked air on the way to her ears and warm it. It trailed heat and shivers down her spine to earth at that feminine core of heat that she really was going to have to learn to control better in future.

'I don't answer to that absurd nickname any more, or to the presumption you follow it with, so I'll bid you good day, sir.' She would have wheeled Adonis and left Captain Afforde to enjoy a temporary victory, if only he'd let her. Instead he shot out a lean, strong hand and clasped her reins as easily and surely as if they restrained a fluffy puppy instead of seventeen hands of restive young stallion. 'Let go!'

'No, you just agreed not to gallop about like a reckless idiot. I didn't expect a Courland's word to mean so little that you discard it so easily no sooner than it's given,' he drawled, ice hardening his gaze as he held hers.

'I didn't promise anything, and I wouldn't need to go anywhere in a hurry if you'd only leave me in peace.'

'You gave me your consent to behave like the rational being you so hotly claim to be as surely as if it was written in blood. Now kindly act like a sensible adult if you wish to be treated like one.'

'Stop it! One moment you kiss me as if you're entitled to, then you claim the right to govern my actions, Sir Charles. I won't be treated like a thing, and I'm no man's possession, nor will I ever be so.'

'Yet you'll be mine, Roxanne,' he assured her implacably, arrogantly certain that because he said it would be so and then even the fates couldn't argue, let alone Miss Roxanne Courland. 'Just as surely as I'll be yours.'

'Mine and half the faster matrons' and *demi-monde*,' she scoffed, trying to convince herself that she hated his calm assumption she'd accept him as her lover, or even her husband, just because he wanted her to.

'No, yours alone,' he promised without the least hint of a smile or a crossing of his fingers behind his back.

'Well, I won't be yours,' she managed to inform him with gruff steeliness, so it was a shame she failed to hold his implacable blue gaze while she did so, wasn't it?

'Which shows how much you know, Miss Courland—you're mine as sure as the fact that the sun rises in the morning. All that stands between us and that truth is your inability to admit it.'

'Don't be ridiculous, there's nothing between us whatsoever. I don't intend to marry and I'll certainly never marry you, Sir Charles.'

'I should wait to be asked if I were you, Miss Courland,' he said, with a return to the infuriating flippancy she'd never expected to greet with such relief.

'I'd really rather not,' she told him stiffly and dug her heels into Adonis's side so that he sprang across the sands in an eager canter and then an all-out gallop that gave the lie to any hope Sir Charles might cherish that her magnificent colt was too tired to race anything.

Yet try as they might, neither she nor Adonis could completely shake off their unwanted companions. Any attempt to outpace or outfox them with Roxanne's superior knowledge of the area were easily outflanked, and the four of them arrived in Hollowhurst's stable-yard before Roxanne even noticed she'd gone there automatically instead of returning to her new home.

'Just look at the state of you, Miss Rosie,' Whistler chided and reminded her of one very good reason she'd sent him back to the castle.

None of Hollowhurst's older servants seemed to have

noticed she was four and twenty now and quite capable of running her own life, and, however much she loved them for their care of her, it still irked her that they wouldn't admit she was quite capable of taking care of herself.

'What of it, when you've seen me look so hundreds of times before?' she protested.

'Not in front of a fine gentleman like Sir Charles,' he grumbled and Roxanne was glad Charles was too busy checking his mount over to hear.

'No, but in front of a far greater one,' she told him impatiently and Whistler just shook his head.

'No disrespect meant to the old master, Miss Rosie, but this one's a good 'un, too. You shouldn't go about looking just any old how in front of him.'

'I'll go about dressed like a coalheaver's wife if I take it into my head to do so. Now stand aside and at least pretend to do as you are bid for once in your life, will you? I need to get home and see what's to do in my absence.'

'You haven't got the reins of such a compact household safely in your hands yet then, Miss Courland?' Charles asked her with another of those quizzical smiles he seemed to use to keep the world at bay.

Now where had that uncomfortable insight come from? Just as well not to think too deeply on that for now, she decided and refused to be diverted. 'No, shocking, isn't it?' she asked between her teeth and smiled just as insincerely back at him.

'Deeply,' he drawled and suddenly his humour and his smile became open and boyish and let her in. She decided dazedly that she really didn't wish to be in his deepest confidence, but her emotions insisted on ignoring her. 'While it would be as improper of you to visit my drawing room alone as it would be for me to ask you to, Miss Courland, do you care to take a stroll in the gardens while Whistler rubs your horse down for you and cools him down? It hardly seems fair to plunge even so eager a colt straight back to your normal breakneck speed of travel before he's had a rest.'

He was right, damn him! Never having been one to ignore the welfare of any creature because she was in a turmoil herself, Roxanne accepted Sir Charles's hands about her waist and very soon found herself lifted down from Adonis's sweating back and strolling beside her host towards the gardens she'd been looking out on such a short time ago before she met him again.

'Mereson, have a glass of my best burgundy sent out for both of us and we'll insult that fine statue of Jupiter in the Winter Garden by using him as a side table,' he told his hovering butler as they passed one of the many doors to his new home.

'Very well, Sir Charles,' Mereson agreed with a look that was probably meant to make them feel like errant schoolchildren and no doubt failed in his new employer's case even as Roxanne felt she'd run away from her lessons.

'He never did approve of Uncle Granger teaching me to judge a fine wine,' Roxanne recalled. 'I believe Mereson thinks proper ladies ought to restrict themselves to lemonade or ratafia when not drinking tea.'

'Not even for you, Miss Courland...' he said and she had to tell herself he didn't mean she was special to him at all; it was just a figure of speech.

'Since I can't stand either, you were quite right to

order wine for me, even if Stella might not approve of it, either.'

'She might not indeed, but, as she's not here and we are, I suggest we simply don't tell her.'

Now why did she almost hear a certain feral satisfaction behind that comment, as if getting her alone was just what he'd set out to achieve this morning? Best not to think about that just now, she decided, and concentrated on enjoying being back in her old haunts without the pressure of constantly wondering how much longer she could keep them up as they deserved.

'I suppose it was for the best,' she finally acknowledged absently, rather surprised to find she'd actually said it out loud, when only last week she'd rather have been horsewhipped than admit as much even to herself.

'What was that, Roxanne?' he asked, as if he knew perfectly well what she meant, but could hardly believe his ears.

'That you bought the estate when David never cared for it very much.'

'And you cared too much?'

'Maybe. When I was a child I certainly used to wish I'd been born the boy who could inherit it all one day, but I wasn't the first born whatever my sex and so would have missed out on it anyway.'

'I'm glad you were born a girl, even if you're not,' he told her and his smile was so reminiscent of the earlier, brilliantly hopeful Lieutenant Afforde she'd first met that she laughed delightedly. 'Do that again and I shall take full advantage of the fact that we're standing under a tree full of mistletoe, despite the fact that Mereson might come upon us at any moment,' he warned her, still with that joyful wolfishness in his brilliant gaze, as if he'd shed a decade of care all of a sudden and intended to enjoy whatever delights the day might bring with boyish recklessness.

'It would be a shame to waste it,' she amazed herself by replying and chuckled when he looked more startled, before taking her at her word and pulling her closer so he could kiss her very seriously indeed.

It was the kiss she'd dreamt of for so long, before she put aside such fantasies and got on with her life and he became the disillusioned man she sensed under his armour of rakish indifference to the world. His mouth was firm and teasing on hers and she felt every part of her soften towards him as she reached up and wrapped her hands around his strong neck to pull him even closer. Nobody could accuse him of taking advantage of her when she was very obviously enjoying his mouth on hers, his hard muscled body so close she could feel him breathe and loved the fact that his mighty chest rose and fell faster than usual against hers.

'Mmm,' he murmured against her shamelessly wanting mouth, as if the very taste of her was driving him distracted and his tongue flickered delight along their softened junction until she opened and welcomed him with a sigh they both understood better than words.

Shivers of unimaginable warmth shook her as he began a sensuous dance of exploration, and sensual curiosity begged her to discover more than she'd dreamt possible in her youthful fantasies. Raising herself further on tiptoe, she insinuated herself even closer to his mighty torso and stretched her curves against his angles, as if testing them for the best fit.

When he settled his hands on the small of her back

and it seemed as if he might use them to hold her away, she gave a protesting quiver and so he soothed them over her waist instead and then a little lower and something inside her flamed into wanting life as her old feelings for him burst into maturity without waiting for her mind to catch up. Her enthusiasm for this lovely intimacy must have tried him harder than he'd expected, for Roxanne felt as if some last restraint had snapped when he lifted her off her feet long enough to settle her on one of the exposed roots of the old tree and arrange her willing body against the hoary bark of its broad trunk so she didn't have to reach so high, and he had access to even more of her. She was in such a haze of warmth and need she hadn't even the wits left to spare to feel triumphant when he ceased exploring the sleek muscles of her slender back and busied himself with the tiny buttons of her riding jacket instead.

Frustrated by the fine lawn of her blouse and the even finer silk of the shift underneath, he did his best with what was for now and first encouraged her shamelessly peaked nipples by running a long, strong, questing finger to explore each one under the gossamer stuff. Throbbing fire bloomed at her centre and she gasped, lips damp and lush from kissing, so he spared his gaze from what his hands were learning and settled his mouth back against the sheer temptation of them instead. What hope was there of rational thought triumphing over such open masculine appreciation? she managed to ask herself distractedly, then went back to working on pure sensation when he tweaked those pebbled nipples he'd been appreciating so gratifyingly and revelled in the sweet, hot need that racked her.

How heady to feel the tremor of need that shook

through her so delightfully echoed by his reverential hands as he cupped her breasts and seemed to find them so perfect that he relinquished her mouth and settled his lips about her nipples to send her to yet another level of arousal as the soft silk between his mouth and her breast seemed to melt to nothing under his questing tongue. Damp and delightful on her sensitised skin, he then left one breast for the other, as if trying to decide where to feast most satisfyingly, and that clutch of heat and light at the joining of her legs flooded with a welcome she half-wanted to clench her thighs against, and half to open them and glory in whatever he could offer to relieve the heady pressure building there.

She whimpered with the unaccustomed drag and the sweet heaviness of that wanting and saw him raise his head and look down at her with a question in his eyes. Unable to deny how eager she was for his attention, and feeling like a reckless maiden risking all with her eager young lover, she just looked back, helpless with wanting, racked with a desire she didn't even fully understand and silently pleaded for more.

He gazed back at her as if trying to decide if he could let them go further. Impatient with his scruples, she bridged the gap between them and rubbed her sensitised breasts against his heavily muscled torso and thought she heard him gasp with an arousal that shadowed her own, so she shyly reached out her hands to find out more. Rubbing her slender palm under his waistcoat, she felt the fine lawn of his shirt over warm, supple skin, muscle and man, then found her goal and allowed herself a tweak similar to the one he had given her prouder nipples. He caught his breath and moaned, so she did it again and daringly leaned up and placed her mouth over the one it could find under all that masculine camouflage.

His hands tightened on her, cupping her, testing her where the straining of her stretched-up legs met her neat buttocks and Roxanne was sure she'd melted. Her cheekbones flushed with a hot bar of colour and she changed her stance so her hands could explore his tightly clenched stomach muscles under his shirt, as that was as close as she could currently get to his skin, unless she explored his absorbed face with her tensed, tactile fingers. Puzzling over such a dilemma, she almost got distracted from what he was doing to her while she was caught between one sensual banquet for her senses and another.

Those firm, strong and yet so gentle fingers of his hand left off stroking sensuous circles on her bottom to ease a little back, as if he was afraid of crushing her between the tree's ancient bark and his own rigid desire. She was a country woman who'd spent so long helping run her uncle's estates that she knew what went on between a man and a woman in bed must be similar to the mating of the rest of nature, or at least she did in theory. Suddenly theory united with practice and the hot need inside her demanded more than this wickedly torturous spiral of urgency and wanting from him. She shifted against the familiar old tree and Charles's completely aroused body, the evidence of his passion for her as blatant as she knew her own would be if he felt the wet heat at the heart of her beckon him to something she understood on one level and now longed to feel and feel and feel for herself.

'No, hush, love,' he whispered into one pink-tipped ear as she keened her wanting impatience.

Feeling him fighting both of them, she squirmed her slender curves against his rigidly aroused body, all the temptations Eve was capable of knowing by pure instinct riding her headlong urgency to complete what they'd started here and now, and to the devil with his scruples.

'I ache,' she told him reproachfully, 'I ache so much that I don't know if I'll ever be right again if you don't do whatever it is you're hesitating over.'

'I like that you ache for me, my wild lover, but we can't go any further than this here and now. I might get you with child for one thing, as I'm in no state to restrain myself sufficiently to avert one once I'm inside you.'

'It took even Joanna and Tom two years to beget their first one, and I can't think the delay was from lack of application on their part, can you?' she amazed herself by asking, with a look that should tell him just what she thought of such a timid lover, when his reputation argued the contrary.

'And the Besfords not even a week, if what he told me when he was reproaching himself for putting his wife in such danger while Sophia was busy getting herself born was true, and I doubt he was in a state to lie just then.'

Did that make them lucky or unlucky? Roxanne wondered as she surprised herself by indulging in that exploration of his handsome features with her fingers, after all. It made her think about them properly, without the overlay of cynicism with which he usually faced her and the world. His mouth was too sensitive to belong to a jaded rake, she concluded hazily as he shot her straight back into searing desire again by opening it and nibbling her finger, as if it was so delightful to have her in this state that he couldn't help himself. Heavy-eyed, she looked back at him hopefully, but could tell he was exerting his mighty will over his aroused body and trying to force a little space between them, so his manhood might stop demanding he listen to her with quite so much enthusiasm. She should be blushing and refusing to meet his fathomless blue eyes instead of boldly challenging him to ruin her as fast and as furiously as humanly possible.

'I thought you were supposed to be a rake,' she reproached him crossly, even as her wilful fingers explored his lean cheek and firm jaw, then ran over the surprisingly vulnerable line of his neck and round to enjoy the spot where his curling golden locks were cropped at his nape. She felt his response in a long slow shudder that racked his mighty body and raised those fine hairs under her fingers in an instinctive response to her touch that was echoed by her own at touching him so very intimately.

'Anyone who saw us thus would surely agree, as I very much doubt you make a habit of sporting so dangerously with riff-raff like myself, or I'd surely have heard of it by now and been forced to call someone out for even suggesting the possibility,' he joked, but Roxanne felt a deep, primitive shudder of fear—this time at the very thought of him risking this intriguing, magnificent body of his to a duellist's bullet.

'Don't even think of such a thing,' she reproached him, and she felt like shaking him for being such a damnably honourable rake, after all.

'Ah, there you are, boy!' a loud female voice boomed cheerfully from not much less than ten feet away.

Even as Roxanne wished she could disappear into

the friendly bark of the huge tree behind her back rather than be seen by anyone else while thus occupied, she marvelled at their complete absorption in each other. Both of them were too guarded to drop headlong into such oblivion to the wider world that they completely forgot about it in their fascination with each other, or so she'd thought until today. Today, she decided fervently, had taught her a great deal more about herself and Sir Charles Afforde than she was altogether sure she'd wanted to know.

'Grandmama,' he muttered with a sigh that might be a warning or even a welcome and, newly awake to his vulnerability to emotions she'd never credited him with until today, Roxanne detected love in his exasperated gaze, even as it iced to a warning the elderly lady deflected with a look of bland innocence none of them believed for a moment.

'Charles,' she acknowledged him with a brusque nod, then looked questioningly at Roxanne, who was furtively trying to right her appearance as best she could in the hope they were fully occupied with greeting each other. Which was far too sanguine as it happened, Roxanne, she chided herself, and flushed like a schoolgirl when caught tying her hair into that ridiculous pony's tail for the second time today.

'Miss Roxanne Courland,' he introduced her stiffly once she looked passably respectable at last, thanks to her furtive efforts, and he stepped far enough away from her side to allow Roxanne to make a shaky curtsy. 'And this is my grandmother, the Dowager Countess of Samphire, Roxanne.'

'Your ladyship,' Roxanne managed huskily, and if the old lady had any doubt what they'd been up to, that hoarse-voiced acknowledgement must have given the game away.

'I knew your great-uncle,' the lady responded, as breezily as if they'd met in Hyde Park. 'He was a fine man, even if he did have some totty-headed notions about bringing up his nieces.'

'He was the finest guardian any girl could wish for,' Roxanne defended him hotly and almost allowed herself to groan at her impulsive tongue, but that would only have made it worse.

Lady Samphire looked as if she'd like nothing better than a good sparring match with a worthy opponent, but Roxanne knew very well she wasn't up to it just now, might never be up to it again if Sir Charles didn't step a little further away from her and let her wits settle into some sort of order.

'He'd not be pleased with you today, then,' the lady replied, looking remarkably cheerful at the notion, 'unless there's something you wish to tell me, my boy?'

'Didn't I say?' Charles drawled carelessly, recovering his usual guarded persona again, much to Roxanne's bitter disappointment. 'Miss Courland has just agreed to become my wife.' He took her hand and squeezed it, as if frightened she'd brusquely deny every syllable and flounce away.

'Doubt it, m'boy,' Lady Samphire argued.

'Why?' he challenged sharply, apparently still too finely strung with tension to recall just who he was talking to, which might even persuade Roxanne the man she'd begun to want beyond all reason was buried under all that outraged ice and his usual armour of indifference, after all.

'Doubt if you got round to asking her anything that rational, if what I just saw of how you are together is aught to go by. I've waited a long time to see you thrown so far off your rake's podium by a girl that you'd fall flat on your handsome face at her feet, my lad, so I'd be lying if I pretended I was looking the other way while you did it.'

'Such rare honesty, Grandmama,' he said tightly, but didn't argue with that fanciful summary of his ardour, much to Roxanne's surprise.

Did he feel this tender novelty, then—this sense of barely comprehended possibilities opening up in front of him as uneasily and incredibly as she did? Could he possibly be as wound up with hope and fear and this raging need she was still trying to extinguish, despite such a sobering intrusion? He certainly seemed to be struggling to put his usual cynical composure in place, but what a heady idea, what a dangerously seductive hope.

'With the honour of Miss Courland's hand openly in mine, how could I do anything but renounce any other?' he said with a gallant bow she liked less than his former shaken honesty.

'You haven't really asked me to marry you and I certainly haven't said yes,' she informed him implacably.

'That's it, girl, you tell him,' his unnatural grandmother urged.

'And however much I love you, I'll ask you to keep your long nose out of business that doesn't concern you.' Charles rounded on his grandmother as if rapidly approaching the end of his tether.

'And I certainly won't wed a man who addresses his grandmama so rudely,' Roxanne stated, with what she thought magnificent scorn, considering she'd very recently been more or less begging him to complete her seduction—wouldn't that have made this scene utterly impossible to endure, rather than just excruciatingly embarrassing?

'It'd be better if you enquire into a man's relationship with his family before rather than after you let him seduce you next time then, m'girl,' her ladyship informed her blandly, and Roxanne gave an involuntary chuckle.

She heard Charles groan and recalled what he'd said about that just before she was swept into uncharted waters and for a moment let her fingers tighten on his as it all became possible again. No, she reminded herself sternly, under the chilly sunlight of a November day, it was impossible to marry just because her reputation was tarnished by her lack of self-control around a certain handsome rake. She loosed her hand from his and brazenly faced the surprisingly unworried Dowager Countess of Samphire, even as she felt surprisingly cold and lonely without the warm haven of his gentle, masculine fingers on hers to secretly revel in.

Chapter Ten

'I can assure you that matters didn't progress that far between us, your ladyship,' Roxanne reassured the Dowager Countess with as much dignity as she could summon in the circumstances, 'and therefore I feel no obligation to wed your grandson, even if you did just witness something happen between us that I'd rather you hadn't seen.'

'I'd deem it a favour if you'd have him all the same, though, for you seem to have a lot more about you than the usual wet gooses he saddles himself with, mainly because he's too tender hearted to make them go back to their husbands and actually work at something for once in their silly lives.'

Roxanne couldn't help herself, she snorted sceptically and wondered if the old lady really thought she was daft enough to swallow such a farrago of nonsense, but Lady Samphire's surprisingly clear blue eyes were steady, and instead Roxanne let herself wonder if Charles was such an easy touch for a bored lady, restive within the arranged marriage she'd probably fought so hard to attain and now found hollow and unsatisfying. She couldn't acquit him of all his sins, for hadn't she witnessed him flirting shamelessly, then leaving a ball with a married woman the one time she actually laid eyes on him during her miserable London Season?

He certainly hadn't looked in the least reluctant to be leaving with the loveliest female present that night and had had no attention to spare then for the gawky débutante who had been watching him so intensely she was surprised it hadn't bored a hole in his immaculately cut evening coat at the time. Then she'd felt as if his perfidy had blown the very foundations of her world apart. By living up, or down, to his reputation, he'd shattered the silly bubble of dreams she'd cocooned herself in for the three years since she had first laid eyes on him so terribly painfully that her seventeen-year-old self had been unable to cope with such bitter disillusionment and had had to be taken home, crying inconsolably, much to her newly-wed sister Maria's open disgust. She'd do well to remember that appalling feeling of betrayal and utter desolation and make sure she never gave him a chance to do it again.

'I feel like a bone caught between two very polite dogs,' he said now, trying to deflate the whole wretched business with his usual easy humour, but even Roxanne could see the attempt was off-key and wasn't surprised when Lady Samphire virtually ignored him.

'You could do a lot worse for yourself, Miss Courland,' she coaxed like a farmer's wife at market, trying to sell off a last dubious-looking cheese so that she could go home and put her feet up with a well-deserved cup of tea.

'No, thank you. If I were foolish enough to agree to such a proposal, I should never know if it was made out of concern for the reputation I've just risked of my own free will or for my own fair sake,' she ended, trying for that wry humour Charles so often hit more perfectly and sounding rather pedantic and silly instead.

It was true, though; she wouldn't wed him under such circumstances, even if half-a-dozen dowagers watched her being even more thoroughly seduced than Sir Charles Afforde had allowed her to be today.

'Your wine, Sir Charles,' Mereson chipped in, as he finally stepped forwards and offered a tray rejoicing in three glasses of glowing burgundy.

'Is anyone else joining us?' Roxanne queried almost hysterically, looking about her as if to discover who else had witnessed her being ridiculously careless of her good name in public with an acknowledged rake.

'Miss Roxanne?' Mereson said blankly with a look of reproach that would do justice to an offended duke.

'I take it nobody else will be joining this slightly odd bacchanal?'

'No, miss,' he replied repressively.

'Good, then pray direct them out here if any more of Sir Charles's friends or relatives decide to visit him unexpectedly,' she ordered a little too brightly. 'Oh, no, I'm not mistress here any more, am I? Then Sir Charles may do as he pleases with any further callers he intends entertaining today, because I'm going home.'

'Very good, Miss Roxanne, I will inform the stables you need your horse brought round,' Mereson said with superb composure and returned to the castle to do so.

'As far as I'm concerned, you *are* home, Roxanne,' Charles gently interrupted, stopping any more brittle words she could come up with, and Roxanne felt tears gather at the very idea, the first she'd allowed since the day of her uncle's funeral. It was as close to a declaration as she was going to get today, and even that limited invitation to share his life made her feel ridiculously off balance, especially when it was so far from announcing his undying devotion.

'Not any more,' she managed with a wobbly attempt at rationality, before he gave an exasperated sigh and pulled her back into the haven of his strong embrace. Self-restraint broke down at last, and she let herself cry out her bewilderment and grief against his broad chest.

'Bring her over here,' his grandmother ordered with a rather satisfied smile, for which he frowned at her, as if not quite knowing what to do with the welter of emotions he'd finally unleashed in Roxanne now she was crying out so many pent-up woes in his arms.

Lifting a gentle hand to stroke the ebony curls nestled so recklessly against his torso, Charles did his best to pretend the warm, contrary, sobbing female in his arms meant no more to him than any other. Meeting Lady Samphire's sceptical gaze with a mixture of defiance and sheepishness, he knew very well she saw far too much of his true feelings, as she always did, and concentrated on finding his large and manly handkerchief before Roxanne reduced his shirt to a sopping wet rag instead. 'Here you are, love,' he murmured into the lovely mass of her ebony hair as the ribbon gave up its work and came undone yet again, cloaking them both in the vibrant, fascinating veil of curls.

How any man could look on her thus and *not* want to run the silken weight of them over his hands as she rested naked and confiding in his arms after being well and truly loved was beyond him. The hand not engaged in soothing her tightened into a fist; he doubted whether one single nuance of the wildly heightened emotions between himself and Roxanne had escaped his eagle-eyed grandmother.

'Why were you proposing to take your wine with Miss Courland in the garden in November in the first place, Charles?' she asked curiously as she sat down on a nearby bench and sipped her glass with a connoisseur's appreciation.

'Propriety,' he replied shortly and felt a hard burn of colour flash across his cheeks under her sceptical gaze. 'A misplaced hope, as it happens,' he conceded.

'Still rather a touching idea, so perhaps there's hope for you after all, m'boy. All you have to do now is persuade the girl you really do want to marry her, and we can get you both up the aisle as soon as possible, after all.'

'I can get myself there, thank you very much, and you're only making my task harder,' he condemned rather harshly, for he'd felt Roxanne's resistance to the very idea and was surprised to find he didn't want her to leave his arms, even if she was only crying out all the tension and misery he'd caused her by buying the estate and then displacing her into a world far too little for her talents. Loving his wife would prove no hard task in one sense, but falling *in* love with her—now that would be another matter entirely.

'I'm not going to marry anyone just to save my reputation,' she muttered gruffly into his damp shoulder.

Why did it cost him such a pang to turn his back on the notion of just gathering her up in his arms and carrying her off to his bedchamber to seduce her ruthlessly until she changed her mind?

'I heard you the first time, Miss Propriety,' he assured her and felt almost godlike as she managed a feeble chuckle and finally pulled away from him to look up at him with reddened eyes that he somehow still found utterly irresistible.

'Even I'm not brazen enough to claim such a title after today, Sir Charles,' she assured him and he wondered why the faint hiccup of a fading sob as she tried to laugh at herself touched him far more than all the tears and tragedies any of his former lovers had acted out.

'Then drink your wine, my dear, and when you're feeling fully restored you can ride home and rest until you're your old self again and fit and eager to fight with me again another day.'

'I'm not your dear,' she informed him with a watery and not even very convincing defiance, and Charles fought not to tell her how very wrong she might well be.

'Whatever you say, ma'am,' he managed to say evenly, when all he really wanted was to carry out that very tempting scenario of whisking her off and slaking this merciless need of her that he should never have put into his own head when he was in such a painful state of rampantly unsated desire. 'If Miss Courland will kindly consent to go home and reassemble her usual fearsome armour, I'll engage to try to rob her of it even more thoroughly tomorrow. Is that better?'

'You know very well it isn't, you devil,' she accused, seeming to forget that she was doing her best to pretend to be a pattern card of propriety, whilst still wrapped securely in his embrace and resting against his broad chest as if she belonged there while she absently shredded his fine lawn handkerchief.

Turning away from the temptation to stare down at her until her eyes were velvet dark and full of that heady, driven passion for him once again, he met his grandmother's shrewd, speculative gaze in the act of inspecting them both and wondered once again exactly why he loved her so much.

'I have a very poor memory these days,' she assured them both virtuously and Charles felt Roxanne stiffen in his arms as she recalled exactly where, and with whom, she was.

'Congratulations, ma'am,' he said ironically. 'I never heard you voluntarily admit to feeling any of the trials of your age before today, so perhaps this will usher in a whole new phase to all our lives.'

'And it could be the end of me behaving like an old fool towards you, you undutiful rogue,' she snapped back with undiminished fervour, and Charles watched her appreciatively down the rest of her glass of one of his finest burgundies with resigned fondness. 'You have a fine palate, my boy,' she told him regally, 'although you should have, I suppose, since I taught you to appreciate a good wine when you ought to have been sitting at your stepmother's knee, learning to be as boring as the rest of my tribe of grandchildren.'

'Thank you for saving me from that fate at least,' he said ruefully and reluctantly let Roxanne go.

'I'm sorry for behaving like a ninny,' his lady said with such a gallant attempt at dignity that he felt like snatching her back into his arms and carrying her off to his highest tower room and locking them both in until the world went away, after all.

'I never met anyone less likely to add to that breed than yourself, Miss Courland,' he assured her and for once hated his own smooth patter as she took his very real admiration for mockery and flamed a furious glare at him. 'Truly you belong in a class of your own,' he went on, but saw he'd made bad worse as her ridiculous lack of self-confidence bumped up against his wretched reputation and made her certain he was taunting her.

'As do you, Sir Charles,' she informed him icily and turned regally away to offer Lady Samphire a stately curtsy and a sincere-enough-sounding adieu, before marching away with a swish of her gathered skirts and a toss of those midnight curls that should have informed him, if he needed confirmation, that it was beneath her dignity to even bid him farewell.

'Always told you that glib tongue of yours would lead you to disaster one day, m'boy,' his grandmother informed him gleefully.

'And just whose side are you on?' he rasped back, preoccupied with the sight of Roxanne's neatly rounded rear view as she stormed off towards the stable-yard.

'That of the angels,' she informed him piously, and even as half of his mind and most of his body was enjoying the view, the other half was not that credulous.

'Yes? Which lot of angels would that be then, sooty or sweet?' he asked as Roxanne finally rounded the corner and ruined a fine landscape for him by no longer completing it in his eyes.

'Know very well I can't abide sweetmeats, but that ain't to say I think heaven's anything like those fools of parsons would have us think; nobody with any sense would want to go there if it was.'

'You must be sure to let me know,' he said with a direct look that made her chuckle rather than take offence.

'To be sure, I will, for if anyone deserves to be haunted by a curmudgeonly ghost it's you, Charles, and at least nowadays I can feel a bit more confident of getting there before you do.'

'I thought I was bound for the nether regions,' he reminded her, nevertheless touched by the genuine emotion behind her flippant words and very conscious that he'd put her through years of constant anxiety during his naval service, for all she'd deny it with her last breath.

'You are, of course, unless you manage to find redemption,' she told him—was there a hint of seriousness behind her determined banter?

Charles thought perhaps there was and recalled his own unease with his life before he finally made the decision to leave the sea and purchase the Hollowhurst estates, where he rapidly discovered life could be full of surprises after all. But to call Roxanne his redemption—surely that was going a little too far? Especially considering the very compromising position she'd found them in just now. Most grandparents would be marching them before a priest at this very moment and demanding grovelling apologies all the while. Lady Samphire was a remarkable woman, he conceded with a wry smile, and it paid to watch her even more closely than the proverbial cartload of monkeys.

'The only thing I intend to find today is my land steward and the new housekeeper to inform her of your arrival, but not necessarily in that order,' he informed her lightly and was relieved when she accepted he didn't relish discussing the state of his soul or his frustrated body right now.

'Just as well, for I want to meet the latter and have no interest whatsoever in your land, considering it's in excellent heart. That girl should take more interest in her household and presenting a ladylike appearance to the world and less in things that don't concern her.'

'And how, pray, would the rest be paid for if she'd sat at her embroidery and let the estates go to rack and ruin when her uncle became ill? Davy Courland never had any more interest in the place than he would in a book of ladies' fashion plates,' he defended Roxanne rather hotly, realising his error in flying to his grandmother's lure when she forgot a countess's dignity and actually smirked.

'I suppose you think you're devilishly clever?' was all he could manage to come up with in his own defence, and heard himself sound like a fractious schoolboy with a groan.

'I don't just think it, I know it,' she informed him, superbly unworried that she sounded vain about it, and he did his best not to laugh and encourage her.

With Stella on the inside plotting and now his grandmother using every advantage she wouldn't scruple to employ, he and Roxanne stood little chance of remaining unwed long. Which, of course, suited him very well, it just didn't please him so much that they seemed to think it a love match.

Instead it would be a marriage of passionate friendship and good sense, he assured himself doggedly. He and Roxanne suited each other so neatly it would be foolish to ignore their underlying compatibility, and he wasn't a fool. Luckily he didn't believe her to be one, either, and soon she'd see for herself they could amount to more together than they ever would apart. All it would take was a few more of those incendiary kisses and she'd be as eager for the marriage bed as he was. Or almost as eager, he reminded himself ruefully, as frustrated need ground painfully as he reacted like an idiot to the idea of Roxanne and bed of any sort just at the moment, something he was perfectly certain hadn't escaped his grandmother's eagle-eyed gaze.

'I think she'll do,' Lady Samphire told him majestically, 'if you ever manage to persuade her you'll make her a good husband, of course.'

Feeling the sting of her sharp tongue rather more sharply than she probably intended for once, Charles looked back on his rakish past and regretted at least some of it for making Roxanne so very wary of him. After months at sea it had seemed normal for a healthy young male to find relief from frustration and loneliness in a skilled courtesan's arms. He doubted if anyone who hadn't experienced the highs, lows and the occasional becalmed boredom of a long sea voyage would understand the life a naval captain on duty, constantly aware of every detail of the day-to-day running of his ship to keep it at sea and in a fit state to offer battle when the need arose. Charles recalled the tension of detached command, when he'd borne responsibility for searching out the enemy and doing his best to outwit and defeat them. A successful frigate captain must be sharp enough, skilled enough, to bring the unwary to battle or outrun the unexpected day and night. And then he had to avoid being overfamiliar with his officers and crew, without being deemed indifferent to their well-being and aspirations. In many ways, it had suited him to be nigh as powerful as a king in his own country while at sea, waiting for the latest fat French merchantman to sail into his well-placed trap. However, the isolation of it could eat up a man's soul if he didn't take good care to keep himself sane.

'Roxanne, I'm awed by your stamina, but don't you feel worn out after dancing half the night away and then spending a whole morning in the saddle?' Stella asked mildly as Roxanne failed to reach her bedchamber without being seen. She sincerely hoped her face didn't betray her turmoil and did her best not to flush like a schoolgirl under her friend's speculative gaze.

'It seems ridiculous now, but I quite lost track of time and need to set myself to rights before anyone calls and sees me looking like this,' she replied, with an airy wave at her own person that she hoped would excuse her hurrying off without further ado.

'Indeed you do,' Stella agreed with a smile that robbed her agreement of any sting, but Roxanne shifted uncomfortably under her shrewd gaze all the same.

'Yes, well, the sooner I let Tabby make me fit to be seen again the better, for I'm certainly not presentable at the moment. Whatever would your mama say if she could see me now?'

'Heaven forefend,' Stella replied with heartfelt fervour, and Roxanne only had to think of the furore if Mrs Varleigh Senior had seen her brazenly kissing Sir Charles Afforde to blanch at the very idea.

'I really must change,' she excused herself before she gave herself away completely and dashed into her bedchamber to set the bell ringing frantically for Tabby.

Wincing at the very thought, she nevertheless forced herself to look in the mirror and was horrified by the damage that a wild ride and an even wilder kiss from a rake had wrought on her appearance. A stranger coming across her by chance might be forgiven for thinking her a tramping woman dressed in the cast-offs of some charitably inclined lady.

'Lord, I look a terrible fright,' she muttered at herself, but couldn't tear her gaze away from the wild woman in the mirror.

Fanciful though it sounded, she looked as if she'd had a flame lit inside her, almost as if her normally workaday dark brown eyes had felt the warmth of some star-drenched southern night and now couldn't quite forget it. Or perhaps, her more prosaic self informed her sternly, she just looked as if she'd come close to being seduced by one of the worst rakes known to the *ton*. He was a danger to her reputation, of course, but not her heart—which was perfectly intact this time and only racing because she'd come so close to being forced to wed that rake and regret it for the rest of her days.

'But would you *really* have regretted it so much, Roxanne?' she demanded brusquely of the houri in the mirror and saw the wretch smirk and then wriggle with delight, like an excited schoolgirl promised a heady treat. 'No, I rather thought not,' she condemned herself roundly, then wondered what anyone hearing her would think of her sanity. That she didn't actually have any, of course, but any lady who let herself be kissed and caressed and almost seduced by Sir Charles Afforde, and who then sneakily yearned for him to do it all over again as soon as possible, couldn't be considered totally rational.

'Just look at the state of you, Miss Roxanne!' Tabby burst out as she hurried into the room to find out why her mistress had sounded her bell as if she thought the house might be afire.

'Yes, I just was,' she replied ungrammatically and once again fought an annoying, self-conscious blush as her maid took in her full disarray.

Curse it—she should have done her best to put Miss Courland, spinster lady of means and very much mistress of herself and no one else, back together without any help. Except she'd considered the task beyond her.

'Well, you'll never do to receive visitors as you are, so you'd best hold still for once while I do the best I can and hope Mrs Lavender manages to keep them busy.'

'Who's called, then?' Roxanne asked with would-be carelessness, wondering with a silly leap of the heart if Sir Charles had already followed her back here to continue the forbidden, and yet so mutually pleasurable, task of completing her seduction.

'Mr Joseph Longborough and that Huntley boy, to name but two,' Tabby replied pertly as she seized Roxanne's hairbrush and began a ruthless attack on her wildly curling mane.

'Ouch!' she protested, the sinking of her heart at the very idea of facing those two callow youths after her encounter with the far deadlier, more handsome and much more wickedly tempting Sir Charles almost diverting her from the pain in her scalp.

'If you will go galloping about the countryside like some wild schoolboy, you can just learn to take the consequences, Miss Rosie,' her maid informed her grimly, but Roxanne knew from that familiar form of address that she was almost forgiven. 'And since you've come home without that ribbon I put in your pocket for the very purpose of preventing this mess, I dare say that handsome buck from the Castle had something to do with it,' she muttered darkly, but Roxanne pretended to be deaf—it was either that or protest too much, and she wasn't prepared to risk doing that with someone who knew her too well.

'Finished?' she enquired sweetly instead.

Tabby snorted disgustedly. 'As if anyone could put this disaster in a fit state to be seen that quickly,' she snapped and resorted to the fine silver comb Roxanne dreaded to tease out a stubborn tangle. 'I don't know why I never thought to ask your sister for a reference. I dare say a lady's maid of my experience and patience could command whatever sum she cared to ask from a lady with the least pretension to caring what she looked like if she had a reference from a respectable countess at her back,' she chided, and Roxanne would have nodded sagely to encourage such a scheme, if only she wasn't firmly anchored by a thick hank of hair.

'You're welcome to try it, of course, but I don't know how long such a lady would put up with being nagged and abused by her own maid.'

Tabby sniffed and, finally satisfied that Roxanne's hair was as smooth as she could make it in the time available, began to pin it into a style she'd obviously spent the morning learning from Stella's maid. Watching it take shape in the mirror, Roxanne thought the softer style became her very well. So well that she couldn't bring herself to order Tabby to dismantle it and put her old, plain coiffeur back together to discourage Joe's callow attentions. This told her two things: one, that his clumsy attempts to annex her and her dowry no longer felt significant, and, two, that looking well in case another, more potent, gentleman called was almost too critical to her sense of well-being for comfort.

'Now sit still while I find a gown that's fit for you to be seen in, Miss Rosie,' her irascible maid chided her, as if she was fourteen again instead of ten years older and wiser.

'It's only a couple of youths who've seen me looking far worse while I was busy round the estate about my uncle's business,' Roxanne protested feebly, but Tabby was too caught up in Stella's campaign to turn Roxanne into a fashion plate to take much notice, particularly when Roxanne was half in thrall to the idea herself.

Chapter Eleven

Ten minutes later, just as Stella was doing her best to come up with yet another polite question to stretch Joe Longborough's banal remarks into a conversation, Roxanne joined her in the drawing room and knew she'd made another mistake. The gown Tabby had chosen, and that she'd half-heartedly protested was too smart for afternoon visits from her neighbours, had looked the height of demure respectability until she put it on. Crimson velvet of so dark a hue that it looked almost black, until the soft stuff caught the light and turned to rich burgundy, was not the sort of colour to allow its wearer to fade into the background. Another error of judgement on her part, Roxanne decided, as a shaft of autumn sunlight slanted into the room and made her a little too noticeable in the rich golden light.

'Miss Courland,' Joe observed with what he probably thought of as dangerous slowness while his greedy eyes did their best to gobble her whole.

'Mr Longborough,' she said shortly and dodged him to nod just as abruptly to his friend and skirt around them both to join Stella on the sofa where neither gentleman, fortunately, possessed the scandalous ill manners to try to join them.

'Tea, Roxanne dear?' Stella asked her, eyebrows raised and the faintest, most unforgivable, hint of a laugh in her voice.

'Of course, that would be most refreshing.'

'After your busy morning.'

Roxanne just nodded, wondering what on earth her friend was up to.

'And here comes my cousin to join our merry band,' Stella remarked with the blandest, most deceiving of smiles. 'I must ring for another cup.'

'Indeed you must,' Roxanne managed, the dizzying prospect of meeting the wretched man so soon after he'd kissed her almost senseless, rejected her demands to be completely seduced by him with insulting ease, then had the bad taste to be discovered doing so by his grandmother before he'd made her cry so spinelessly in his arms nearly made her bolt for her room, whatever anyone thought of such hysterical cowardice. 'We all know just how partial Sir Charles is to an excellent cup of tea.'

'Miss Courland, Stella my loved one,' Sir Charles greeted them with a bow of such elegance that Roxanne could see Joe trying to store it away for future imitation, despite the fact he obviously hated his rival.

'Curse the whole damned lot of them!' Roxanne muttered vengefully under her breath, but saved her best glare for the newcomer. After all, Joe might be a self-opinionated lout, but he hadn't failed to seduce her today, then turned up on her doorstep not an hour later as if it was no more significant than a casual wave across a crowded room between friends.

'Longborough, Huntley,' he added, with a nod that should have made both her other visitors conscious he was the dominant male of the party.

'Afforde,' Joe drawled recklessly and Roxanne expected him to be blistered by a challenging stare from Charles's impenetrably blue eyes any second—and just when had she begun to think of him as Charles and not Sir Charles or even Captain Afforde?

Of course, being ignored in favour of Simkins would make Joe squirm far more effectively, especially as her butler chose that moment to produce that extra cup on a silver salver, along with a glass of rich burgundy, which he handed to Charles as if he were already master of the house.

'Neatly done, Simkins,' Charles observed with a smile of complicity and encouragement for her newly promoted butler, and Roxanne wasn't sure whether to agree with him or march out of the room with her nose in the air.

'Have you acquired tickets for the subscription ball at Tunbridge next week, gentlemen?' Stella asked the two younger gentlemen before war could be openly declared.

'Indeed we have,' Mr Huntley agreed eagerly, looking as if he'd like to tow his friend out of the room before he rashly challenged a man who could outwit and outgun him on any field of battle. 'Looking forward to it. Came to beg the privilege of the first dance, didn't we, Joe?'

'How charming of you, Mr Longborough,' Stella twittered as if she believed every word she was saying.

'I'll be delighted to grant it to you, of course—so flattering to be asked at my age.'

Despite her ire, Roxanne almost ruined everything by laughing out loud as Joe's expression gave his thoughts away. 'Honoured,' he finally managed through gritted teeth, while looking as if he'd prefer strangling Stella to dancing with her.

'Then I hope I can claim the honour of *your* hand, Miss Courland?' Mr Huntley asked with a sheepish look at his friend as he took advantage of his confusion.

'Of course you can, Mr Huntley,' she had to reply, and indeed she'd far rather be stumped about the room by over-enthusiastic Mr Huntley than informed how greatly she'd benefit by marrying a man who'd inherit his father's acres and position in due course by Joe.

She thought it was that information that made her dislike Joe Longborough so heartily nowadays, for she was very fond of the squire, and the spectacle of his uncouth son longing for him to quit his shoes so he could step into them the sooner made her feel distinctly sick.

'I fear I have business in town next week and therefore cannot beg for any dances from either of you,' Sir Charles put in smoothly, and Roxanne wondered why the whole idea of attending the local subscription ball suddenly seemed such a poor one if he wasn't to be there.

'Such a shame,' she muttered darkly and received a mocking smile in return as she marvelled at the sharpness of his hearing.

'But I have every intention of returning in time for the evening party my grandmother has decided I'm to throw in her honour, Miss Courland,' he added with a long, intimate look she very much hoped was camouflaged by Stella and Mr Huntley's gallant attempts at cheerful conversation. 'And as my grandmother is to remain at Hollowhurst while I'm in town, she's instructed me to call, Miss Courland, and ask you to visit and be introduced before I leave, in order that she might "have some civilised company whilst you're gallivanting about the country, boy", I think were her exact words.'

'That sounds like my Great-Aunt Augusta,' Stella said with a sage nod, and Joe just looked as if he'd like to strangle every one of them, including the Dowager, very slowly.

'Until next week then, ladies,' he said by way of farewell, along with one of those ungainly nods of dismissal he'd wasted on Charles up until then.

'I think I'd have had to develop a cold by next week, if not for that rather nice young man he brought with him,' Stella said reflectively once the two younger gentlemen had left.

'I'm fairly certain I'd have joined you, except Joseph Longborough would never let poor Mr Huntley forget I'd cried off from that dance on the flimsiest of pretexts,' Roxanne agreed with a brief grimace for Joe's appalling manners.

'So we'll go then, even if we're to be deprived of your company, Cousin Charles,' Stella informed him with that ironic smile that often made her true thoughts impenetrable to Roxanne.

There was obviously a very strong affection between the cousins, but did that necessarily mean Stella was matchmaking? Probably, Roxanne decided with a sigh and sipped her tea as if she'd nothing to contribute to the conversation Stella and Sir Charles kept up with little apparent effort.

Quite when the perfidious baronet gestured his cousin from the room, Roxanne couldn't have said, since she'd been woolgathering for several minutes when he must have done so, but she roused herself from her reverie to see Stella's lilac skirts belling out behind her with the speed of her going and looked up and met his eyes with a haughty question in her own.

'You didn't think I came here this afternoon for the sole purpose of exchanging veiled insults with your would-be cavalier, I hope? Especially since he's not a very appealing cavalier to waste our time on,' he asked with one eyebrow raised in a world-weary look she imagined Joe probably spent useless hours in front of his dressing mirror trying to imitate.

'No, you also came to tell your cousin that you'll be leaving Hollowhurst for a while and that next week you'll be hosting an evening party with your grandma-ma, did you not? So you see, Sir Charles, I was listening to the salient points of your conversation, after all.'

'You are becoming quite the social adept, Miss Cour-land,' he informed her loftily and then chuckled as her right hand fisted without her even thinking about it. 'That's better; if I ever feel the need to converse with female automata I can rely on most of my stepsisters to oblige me. Pray don't ever aspire to such vapid cor-rectness, will you, Miss Courland? It would be a crime against nature.'

'I didn't know you had any stepsisters,' she said and despaired of herself for falling into the trap of being curious about his relatives when she should be concen-trating on being furious with him for intruding on her life in far too many ways.

'Apparently complete oblivion to my continuing

existence is socially unacceptable to my immediate, if not my close, family, so occasionally I'm summoned to spend a few days being bored to distraction at my father's expense. Since he married their mother and I didn't, I really can't imagine why we all put ourselves through the discomfort of finding out all over again that we have nothing in common.'

'How awful,' she was surprised into saying sincerely when she'd been so determined to keep him at a polite distance.

'I suppose it is really,' he agreed with a sigh, and Roxanne felt he was letting her see a side of himself he usually kept well hidden from the world. 'My mother died when I was born and my father acquired my stepmother and her tribe of daughters some years after I'd been virtually adopted by my grandparents, so it wouldn't be an exaggeration to say we're virtually strangers to each other.'

'You and your father aren't close, then?'

'Not by a country mile, Miss Courland.'

'Poor little boy,' Roxanne said with those treacherous tears heating her eyes again, much to her annoyance when she looked up and saw him watching her as if amazed he could engender such emotions. 'Not that you look as if you suffered unduly from his neglect,' she informed him hardily.

'Oh, I didn't, so pray don't waste your pity on me, Roxanne. My grandparents spoilt me within an inch of becoming unbearable.'

'Only within an inch?'

'Torment, but even if the navy didn't have a way of dealing summarily with toplofty boys with too-high an opinion of themselves, can you imagine my grandmother indulging anyone completely, let alone a scrubby brat?'

'She adores you,' Roxanne told him, remembering the softening of her ladyship's gaze as it dwelt on her handsome grandson when she didn't think he was looking.

'It's mutual, I assure you.'

'Good, but I dare say you didn't come here to discuss your family relations, Sir Charles,' she reminded him and herself.

'No, or only in a roundabout fashion,' he said with a thoughtful look at her that for some reason made her shiver with apprehension. 'I really came to ask you to marry me and *be* my family, Miss Courland.'

'Oh, that's all right, then,' she said faintly, as she felt the earth spin on its axis a little too realistically.

'Good, so you're not dead set against the idea, then?' he said clumsily, sounding as if he'd been knocked off his own superb balance for once.

'Of course I am,' she said crossly. 'I've never felt the least desire to make a marriage of convenience, Sir Charles, and you haven't done or said anything to convert me to the idea so far today, so of course I won't marry you. I already told you that and I might add that I find this scene embarrassing in the extreme and wish you'd spared both of us the trouble.'

'You'll just have to endure being embarrassed then, because I haven't finished,' he told her gruffly, as if she'd hurt him—but how could that be so?

To be hurt, he'd have to feel some deep emotion towards her and she doubted he'd let himself be that vulnerable. No, he didn't love her, and she wasn't sure what she felt for him, either, so that was fair enough. It was his serious contemplation of the idea of actually marrying her because she was well enough born, and not exactly repellent, that turned her stomach.

'I'm not obliged to stay here and listen to this any more than you're forced to waste your breath in such a foolish fashion,' she said regally, but he refused to accept her rebuff.

'Yes, I am. If anyone else saw us nearly make love on the lawn this afternoon then I feel every need to try to persuade you to see sense, before they can spread scandal and ruin your good name.'

'They didn't, and I've no intention of wedding you, Sir Charles, so I suggest you leave now before we risk saying something we'll regret.'

'Why not?'

'Why not what?'

'Why won't you marry me?' he asked as if genuinely puzzled.

'Because, contrary to your inflated opinion of yourself, Sir Charles, you're not irresistible,' she snapped contemptuously.

Again he quirked that annoying eyebrow at her and she felt herself blush hotly as she recalled her fiery response to his kisses and more intimate attentions earlier—wretched, wretched man!

'This morning I wasn't quite myself,' she mumbled, as if that explained everything.

'No, you were mine,' he insisted, a certain look in his eyes telling her he was recalling in too-vivid detail exactly how wanton she'd been in his arms.

'Never! Now if there's nothing else, I'm very tired, sir, and intend to rest before I must meet your cousin at the dinner table as if nothing untoward has occurred today, which it hasn't, of course.'

'Not through any fault of yours,' he told her dourly, looking as if he was torn between wanting to shake her or kiss her breathless all over again.

'I find your company tedious this afternoon, Sir Charles, and would prefer your room to your company, if you please,' she said, in an attempt to appeal to his innate good manners and make sure he did neither.

'I came to make a formal offer for your hand, Roxanne, and intend to do so whether you like it or not.'

'Well, I don't.'

'Nevertheless,' he replied through gritted teeth, 'I insist upon offering you the protection of my hand in marriage, Miss Courland, and beg you will think a little for once before you refuse me. I can offer you the role in life you were born to play as my wife. You will run my household, assist in managing my estates and stand at my side in every way as my equal. Can you put your hand on your heart, Roxanne, and say you're content living at Mulberry House as a lady of independent means with nothing much to do?'

Seeing that she opened her mouth to argue as soon as he gave her a chance, then shut it again as the lie wouldn't form, he shook his head to confirm what they both knew.

'Of course not, for you'd be perjuring yourself. Here you are, politely bored in my cousin's very good company, but you're still bored. At Hollowhurst, I can offer you everything that should have been yours by birthright and a husband who honours you, along with the promise of children of our own into the bargain.'

'No,' was all she could manage in reply and even she knew it was inadequate.

'Why, Roxanne, what else do you want of me, woman? What else could you want?'

'Love,' she finally admitted, acknowledging to herself that foolish young Rosie, who'd mourned his leaving that Christmas long ago as if her young heart had gone with him and she couldn't quite function without it, still couldn't face a marriage of pure sense and sensuality with this man.

That silly child, the one who'd languished and dreamt and been coldly disillusioned on her come out, wasn't dead, after all. No, the little idiot had just been sleeping, and here, at last, Roxanne held the answer to her questions as well as his. She'd never properly stopped loving him, and his arrival at Hollowhurst to usurp her had hurt so much because he'd not wanted to marry her for it first. Which didn't mean she had to accept the half-loaf he was offering, as if he couldn't understand why she wasn't snatching it out of his hand and thanking her lucky stars when she was four and twenty and obviously not destined to be offered such splendours again.

The silence in her once-comfortable drawing room grew until she'd filled it with all the answers to that one last, disastrous demand he might wish to agree to, but wouldn't be cruel enough to speak such a lie. Finally, feeling as if she really was at the end of her composure, she raised her hand in an inarticulate denial that she wanted an answer and turned to leave the room.

'Stop!' he demanded and she halted, but refused to turn, for what was the point when all she would see was horror at her words and perhaps even relief in his eyes that she knew it was impossible? 'If I *could* love anyone, it would be you,' he promised, and his voice was husky and his eyes, when she felt compelled to turn and meet them after all, were ardent with such sincerity she had to stay and listen, despite the fact that part of her was hurt almost unbearably.

'Truth to tell, I don't know if I have it in me to love. I remembered you so often, Rosie, the girl with the ardent eyes and the passionate mouth, despite her tender years and the fact that I already knew far more than you would ever dream of and didn't deserve you. That Christmas I told myself I'd found a girl worth waiting for, that you'd stay safe with your family until I could sweep you off your feet and take you with me the instant you were ready to marry me and sail the seven seas at my side.'

Since it was the dream she'd dreamt herself, she blinked determinedly and reminded herself it hadn't come true. He hadn't bothered to come back to Hollowhurst until the day he appeared out of the dusky gloom as if he was the ghost of all her stupid dreams made manifest, but too late to fulfil her childish fantasies, if not a full decade too late then by at least seven or eight years. 'Then why didn't you come back for me?' she demanded huskily.

'Because I saw too much, knew too much by then to besmirch your ardent young innocence,' he explained and ran his hand through his wildly disarrayed golden hair, as if struggling to find the words that usually sprang so glibly on to his tongue. 'I'm damaged goods, Roxanne. The moment I rode away from here that first time, I began to doubt I was good enough for you, but at the end of another few years at sea I knew very well that I wasn't. Did you think I didn't know you were there that night in London? I saw you and made sure that you had to watch me flirt and rake and gamble the night away and then leave that damned ball with a noble harlot on my arm.'

'Because you didn't care,' she said flatly, only to see him shake his head passionately, as if the emotions he denied being capable of wouldn't let her speak such blasphemy.

'No, because you'd grown up so hopeful, so rich with promise of the extraordinary woman you were about to become, and I couldn't let myself have you and spoil it all.'

'Well, I suppose I was a virgin, after all,' she informed him with such off-balance defensiveness she wasn't really surprised when the whip of her inferred meaning made him frown with disbelief, then look at her as if she was some new and not very pleasant species.

'Marriage or nothing, then and now,' he grated implacably.

'I can't recall being offered that choice when I was silly enough to accept eagerly, or we might have been miserably unhappy together for years by now,' she sniped back and groaned aloud as she realised she'd admitted that she would have accepted him eagerly then in her defensive fury.

'I knew it, I knew I couldn't want you like this unless you wanted me back,' he said clumsily and she wondered fleetingly if they were fated to flounder about trampling all over each other's finer feelings for the whole of this interminable day.

'I do feel something—a strong desire for you to go away and not trouble me with your feeble excuses and false promises ever again, Sir Charles.'

'No, you don't.'

'Allow me to know what I want better than you do, sir,'

'No, for you haven't the experience to know what you're feeling.' He held up his hand when she would have spoken, as if commanding his ship once more by force of will and the smallest gesture, and she shot him a dagger look. 'You ventured a little too deep into the sensual world of lovers for your own good today, Roxanne, but you're too much a lady to let yourself feel how deeply your body and mine worship each other now you're out of my arms. I swear that I never felt such a potent connection to any other woman before, so this is new ground even for me.'

'So apparently you desire me, but you don't love me. And, once upon a time, you would have offered for me if you only had had the courage to do so, but you didn't. Then you expect me to believe that now you've decided you can't live without me after all, and insist that a mere kiss that your grandmother kindly overlooked seeing must bind us together for ever?'

'Well, not quite for ever,' he was foolish enough to quip back.

'Not at all for ever, not even for a little bit of it, sir. I won't marry you, and, if you'd like me to do so, I'm quite prepared to have a notice inserted in the relevant papers to that effect.'

'Of course I wouldn't, don't be ridiculous.'

'Then oblige me by going away.'

'I might just as well, since you're going to argue that black's white any moment now, but I'll ask you again, Miss Roxanne Courland, and again and again until you see sense and say yes.'

'I already have, it's you who insists on being a bull-headed idiot.'

'A failing I've possessed since birth, or at least according to my grandmother,' he agreed, with a return to his usual light indifference that she somehow hated, although she'd been silently wishing he would stop being intense and so worryingly persistent for the last ten minutes.

'Good day, Sir Charles,' she replied repressively and stood back from his quickest path to the door in the hope he'd take it.

'On the whole I'd have to agree, it's been a *very* good one,' he informed her with silky menace as he obliged her by strolling toward the doorway as if he hadn't a care in the world, only to pause in front of her to inspect her with wolfish thoroughness. 'Indeed, the more memorable moments were truly exceptional, my Roxanne,' he added as his head lowered to hers, and the force of his gaze fascinated her, even as his mouth met hers with instant fire, complete desire flaming up between them as if they'd left off that long, sensuous embrace just seconds ago.

Her lips parted even as their eyes stayed open and aware, very aware. His were startlingly blue and wanting as he compelled her with his kiss, binding them into lovers as his mouth teased hers open under his and he plunged his tongue into the shameless welcome waiting for him. Before she could give herself away and let her hands reach up round his neck and pull him closer, even deeper into this undeniable need, he lifted his head and gave her a rather boyish smile that all but disarmed her.

'At least promise you'll remember this while I'm

away, Roxanne? I'm not sure I can live without you, and whatever I feel for you now, I promise you I never felt for another woman.'

Her turn to raise an eyebrow in sceptical cynicism, but he looked so pained by what he'd just told her she believed him and doubted she'd forget the thrill and heat while he was gone however much she wanted to.

'I'll remember,' she said carefully, unwilling to say anything he could misinterpret as agreeing to a marriage she couldn't endure on his terms.

'Until next week then, Miss Courland,' he said by way of farewell and made her an elegant bow before striding off with one last hungry look.

Listening to him joke with Simkins while he collected his hat and cane as if he hadn't a care in the world, Roxanne wondered if she'd dreamt the last minutes. At least it argued he suffered her own restless frustration for him to walk here in the first place, and a large part of her wished she was walking back to the Castle at his side, ready to share his life as his wife. Except he'd always keep part of himself back, and she couldn't bear such a marriage with him of all people.

For now it mightn't matter, could even add to her fascination with him and the delights he showed her when his wicked mouth, inventive hands and hard, very masculine body centred entirely on her pleasure for the breath-stealing moments when it didn't seem to matter if he loved her or even trusted her. One day, though, it would part them as surely as if he were still at sea and a thousand leagues away from her. It troubled her that she must find out his real reason for giving her such a disgust of him all those years ago in London before she dare trust him with her future, and she didn't think he'd ever willingly tell her.

No, it was her very self she must know was safe with him before she could be his wife, and love on one side couldn't sustain a good marriage without complete trust to bind them together. A bad marriage with Charles Afforde would be worse than staying at Mulberry House for the rest of her life. She'd long ago realised that fairy-tales were just that, but if he thought she'd settle for a lukewarm arranged marriage, he was mistaken. She touched her lips, exploring what he'd taught her, and felt tingles of heat shiver through her as she relived the memory of his passionate seduction. They were sensually compatible, but what use was that if he didn't want *her,* the real Roxanne?

Trying not to wonder how she'd endure the rest of her life without such delights, now she knew them and that more could follow, Roxanne left her drawing room with most of her flags flying and launched into a whirlwind inspection of her already immaculate house that set the servants' hall humming like a kettle about to let off a lot of steam.

Chapter Twelve

'You're very poor company tonight, Charles. I might as well have stayed in town, for all it's so deadly dull this time of year,' Lady Samphire told her grandson over dinner at Hollowhurst Castle that night.

'You couldn't bring yourself to stay away an instant longer,' he replied.

'Of course I could, but I admit I do have to amuse myself however I can at my age, especially now you've immured yourself in the country.'

'Admit it, you're a nosy old woman,' Charles said with a grin as he nodded dismissal to Mereson and the hovering footmen; he was never sure what his grandmother might say next and it seemed as well to limit the damage.

'I'm not nosy, I'm perceptive and wise,' she argued.

'And nosy.'

'If being concerned for your happiness makes me nosy then, yes, I'm guilty as charged. More dutiful grandsons would be grateful for the interest of their elders and betters and treat them with proper respect.'

'And you'd cut me out of your life for good if I ever showed the slightest signs of becoming such a spineless want-wit.'

'True, half an hour with that mealy-mouthed gaggle of females your father saddled himself with when he wed Euphemia Crawley always makes me wonder why I ain't been allowed to poison their soup as a service to humanity. Louis should've known better than to make up to a widow with five daughters. Bound to end in trouble,' Lady Samphire said brusquely.

Her notoriously crushing pronouncements were one reason why Mereson and his acolytes were probably listening at the door at this very moment, Charles decided ruefully, hoping they hadn't caught her gruff speech. He'd not been fully accepted as the master of Hollowhurst yet and didn't want them deciding the Afforde family were homicidal maniacs.

'I take it you're out of temper because I promised to attend my stepsister Charis's engagement party before you descended on me without warning?' he asked laconically.

'No fun if I'm expected,' she admitted and surprised him into a smile that reached his eyes for the first time that evening. 'That's better, no need to pretend you're a heartless rake and care for nobody with me, m'boy. You've done your best for that woman *and* those die-away girls while your father hides in his study writing second-rate poetry and drinking cherry brandy. Pretend to be hard-hearted as a stone statue with the rest of the world if you like, but I know you better, m'boy, I brought you up.'

'How could I forget, even if I wanted to?' he asked ruefully.

'Did your best to these last twenty years, you reprobate, but I'm glad you're settled at last, Charles. High time you found something to do with your life other than kill Frenchmen, and that girl suits you. She's got character.'

'That she has, too much to be easily persuaded to marry me.'

'Didn't seem to be fighting you off when I came across you both behaving disgracefully this morning,' she observed with a sidelong glance to see how he might react to such a reminder.

Luckily he'd known her a very long time and managed a bland smile, despite his urge to keep his relations with Roxanne fiercely private, even from his grandmother. 'And if only that were enough to convince her we'd suit,' he muttered, half to himself.

'If all you're worried about is her "suiting", no wonder she ain't convinced. You used to have a surer touch with women.'

'Roxanne Courland isn't just any woman,' he said shortly, unable to keep the words back, even as he knew she'd seize on them with glee.

'No, because she's *the* woman, isn't she?' she obliged happily.

'Certainly she's the woman I wish to make my wife,' he answered carefully, but obviously not carefully enough.

'And you think I'm fool enough to believe that's all there is to it? I wasn't born yesterday or even the day before that. You love her, boy, and it's high time you learnt it won't crack the world in two if you let her see who you really are under that rakehell reputation you've fostered so carefully.'

'I don't love her, I value her. Very highly indeed, but love is for boys.'

'And girls?'

'They wrap up their true need to feel friendship and trust towards the man they marry with soft words and rosy ideals. Luckily, Roxanne is a woman now and will soon realise that what we'll have if she weds me is better than a fleeting passion bound to fly out of the window at the first setback.'

'Had this argument about women and marriage with your friend Rob Besford lately, have you?' she said slyly.

'Hah! He's a traitor to the cause if ever I came across one. He made every error a husband could, before, during and after marrying Caro, and still ended up totally besotted with his wife and she with him.'

'My point exactly,' his grandmother said with satisfaction.

'I'm not about to follow his ridiculous example, so you can take that smug look off your face and set your mind to plotting how I can get Miss Courland to accept my suit some time before we're both old and grey. It's you who's always demanding I supply you with yet more great-grandchildren, after all, and at this rate we'll both be too decrepit to enjoy them.'

'I'm not decrepit,' she replied shortly, 'nor am I fool enough to persuade that girl to accept such a bad bargain as you'll make her if you don't feel more than lust and liking for her.'

'I'm not going to offer her a lie. I think too much of

her for that,' he said in a hard voice she rarely heard from him.

She sighed and said seriously, 'I love you, Charles, probably too much for my own good, but there are times when I could cheerfully push you into the nearest lake, you infuriate me so much. No, don't shrug me off, this is far too important for that,' she warned with a militant look. 'Just because your father made a figure of himself with his infatuations and his silly affairs when you were a boy, there's no need to think love's a figment of the imagination. Exact opposite, if you ask me, considering the idiot provides you with an excellent example of what love *isn't*. Must have dropped him on his head when he was a baby,' she ended, looking pained and deeply frustrated as she spoke of her third son.

'I dare say, or maybe he's a changeling,' he joked, hating to see her unhappy as she usually was when discussing his father.

'Then how come he looks so like your grandfather?'

'Speaking of whom, I don't see how you can insist I make a love match when you didn't yourself,' he pointed out cunningly, then instantly regretted it as her eyes clouded with memories and what he could have sworn was a haze of tears.

'That's exactly why. Samphire may not have made a love match, but I did. Not even for you could I sit by twiddling my thumbs while you put that girl through what I had to bear myself, Charles, it hurt too much for me to do that.'

'I'll be faithful to her until our respective dying days,' he protested half-heartedly.

He recalled the casual affection with which his

grandfather had treated his extraordinary wife, as if she were a particularly fine spaniel he'd taught a surprising variety of tricks, but still a favourite pet rather than an equal, and wondered anew at just how much pain his light-hearted grandfather had caused her over the years. She'd stayed at Verebourne Park, managing his house and estates and raising their five sons and then himself, while his grandfather lived more or less as he pleased.

Practical and down to earth as his own father had never been, the last Lord Samphire had been largely insensitive to his wife's feelings and needs and had lived an essentially separate life from her and his boys once he'd done his duty to the succession and sired them. He'd taken his seat in the Lords, done his duty and run his estates and then entertained his friends more like a single man than a husband and father. Although Charles had shared a fond relationship with the old reprobate, he'd often thought his grandmother as lonely within marriage as many spinsters were without one.

'I didn't mind his mistresses, I even rather liked that fierce Spanish opera singer he never quite dared leave in case she came after him with a dagger,' Lady Samphire told him with rare seriousness. 'It was the absence of so much of him when we *were* together that hurt so much. I can't find words to say how it felt to be unimportant to the man I loved, Charles; all I can tell you is I wouldn't put a female I liked as instantly as I did that girl of yours through a week, let alone a lifetime, of such a marriage if I could prevent it.'

'But she's not unimportant to me, and I'd never treat her as Grandfather did you, love. Do you think I learnt nothing from you all?'

For once his smile only won him a brooding look

and he shifted under it and decided he'd rather face the enemy again than see her unhappy.

'No, I think you learnt too much,' she argued sadly. 'Your father is a selfish lightweight who spent most of your boyhood falling in love with whatever bosomy blonde was his muse that week, while your grandfather found amusements outside marriage. You grew up watching me try not to be a fool over a man who set me on the same level as his favourite hunter, so it's little wonder you decided to hold aloof from such emotions.'

'It's not that,' he said impulsively, unable to bear the sight of her castigating herself for his own lack of romantic illusions.

'Then whatever is it?'

'Private,' he said sternly, for he refused to bare his soul even to her, but she'd given him a great deal to think about and at least a week spent with his father and stepfamily would give him plenty of time to do it in.

He was relieved when his grandmother shrugged, as if she'd done all she could to make him see reason, and put her formidable dowager mask back on before regally informing him she liked port and brandy and had no intention of being banished to the drawing room while he enjoyed his.

Yet had he let his father's and grandfather's poor examples colour his thinking? He frowned into his brandy glass and contemplated the idea of being so influenced with considerable dismay. He'd loved them both once upon a time, but nowadays Louis Afforde resented the son he'd rejected for being wealthy and successful when he was neither, and there was nothing he could do about that even if he wanted to.

He loved Lady Samphire, though; she'd filled the lonely places in his heart and given him the steadfast, but not uncritical, affection he'd needed to enjoy a care-free boyhood once he left his father's so-called care. So she was wrong in thinking he wouldn't love anyone. What he wouldn't do was fall for the myth of romantic love between a man and a woman. It was a comfortable enough illusion, he supposed, so long as said man and woman stayed away from high tragedy, of course. He'd never fancied himself a Romeo and the very thought made him smile sardonically into his fine cognac.

No, he'd an affection for Roxanne Courland that had already lasted far longer than any imaginary romance ever would, and he desired her with an unrelenting passion beyond anything he'd felt in the past for other women, but he refused to call it 'love' when love died and left the object of it alone and dissatisfied. His future with Roxanne was too important for that, and if they were to have a lifetime of affection and commitment with each other, he'd no intention of risking it all for the fancy façade of a gimcrack romance that might please everyone but him, until the gilt wore off.

'That colour suits you wonderfully well, Roxanne,' Stella told her as they let Mereson's acolytes take their warm cloaks and then spent a few moments brushing out the few creases the short journey from Mulberry House had put in their gowns.

'And I like midnight-blue velvet a good deal more than the black one you wanted, even if Lady Samphire will tell you she can't see much difference by candle-light, Stella,' Roxanne said as she controlled the slight shaking of her hand as she fussed with imaginary lint on her amber velvet skirts.

It was ten days since Sir Charles Afforde had proposed to her last and nothing short of wild horses would persuade her to admit that she'd missed him. Or that she felt ridiculously nervous of meeting him in public now he'd returned home and was probably still waiting for her to change her mind.

'Great-Aunt Augusta mourns the unwieldy panniers and acres of brocade I can just recall seeing her in when I was in my nursery, or at least when I should have been. Charles and I used to creep downstairs while our nurses gossiped by the fire in the day nursery to watch the grown-ups entertain.'

'I dare say you were an impossible pair,' Roxanne replied, as the very thought of Charles as a golden-haired scamp with a smile as deceptively innocent as a fair June morning threatened to melt her determination to resist his present, very adult appeal.

'According to her ladyship we were a pair of hell-born brats, but she still saw we got the finest titbits from her parties before summarily returning us to our beds whenever we got caught.'

Roxanne laughed and thought that sounded very like the formidable old lady who she'd soon discovered concealed a heart soft as butter under her gruff and cynical manner.

'I can tell you two haven't been pining for my company.' Sir Charles's deep voice broke into their conversation, and Roxanne thought he ought to be made to wear hobnailed boots at all times to stop him ghosting about the place, making her jump.

'Of course not,' she allowed herself to tell him with a smug smile.

'Whilst I, of course, have been desolate,' he told her soulfully.

'Mountebank,' she categorised him sternly.

'No, it's true,' he assured her, not seeming at all cast down by her unenthusiastic greeting. 'Anyone would be desolate to be marooned in the exclusive company of my closest family. I've just endured it for over a week and not even Miss Courland's finest swallowing-vinegar face, so often pulled at the very sight of me, I mourn to say, can dull the joy of making my escape without being forced to bring at least one of my female relatives home with me so she can make my life uncomfortable at her leisure.'

'You're planning to disown your grandmother, then?' she asked, carefully ignoring the warm glow in his eyes as they rested on her, giving his light-hearted flirtation the lie by silently conveying the message he had honourable intentions whether she liked them or not.

'No, although she says she'll disown me if I can't persuade you to marry me.'

'Oh, hush, Sir Charles!' she urged as she looked about to see who might be listening and would forever be eyeing her with eager speculation from now on. But had his comment been careless or cunning? She was inclined to believe the latter and glared at him militantly.

'I don't think anyone else heard him,' Stella declared, looking very interested while she pretended she wasn't really listening.

'You could always say "yes", and then we could announce it straight away,' he offered, as if it were a real possibility, though she had no intention of being stampeded into marriage by him or his grandmama.

'And I could also have the good sense to hope you're joking.'

'When I never was more serious in my life?' he quipped, but could that possibly be the faintest hint of hurt in his cerulean gaze? Most unlikely.

'I very much doubt it, sir, and this is neither the time nor the place for a serious discussion, even if you were.'

'No, indeed, but it's high time I put my name down for the supper dance, before your besotted swain tries to mill me down in his desperation to claim it.'

'Tries?' she asked with that useful, ironic raising of her eyebrows she'd learnt from him.

'Oh, yes, I'm not too gentlemanly to resist planting him a facer before either of us are very much older, Miss Courland, but I think we'd both prefer it if I didn't have to do so as his host.' She shuddered at the very thought and silently held out her dance card. 'Very wise,' he teased as he initialled away.

'Only two,' she warned.

'Do you think me a country clodpole as well, my dear?' he murmured as he handed her card back, making very sure their fingers met and she felt the spark of desire run through her at the contact, just as he did if the sudden heat in his eyes was anything to go by.

'I doubt you were that simple even when you were in short-coats,' she replied and tried not to feel pleased with herself when he laughed. The real laugh she loved, the one that lit his eyes with humour and lured her into a world of intimacy she'd not dreamt of in many long years, not since he ignored her at her come-out party, she reminded herself, and removed her hand from his as if he'd stung her.

'Until later, then?' he said, standing back and watching her cautiously, the lovely possibility that flashed between them so briefly suddenly gone.

'Later,' she echoed with a shiver that had nothing to do with the temperature in the blue saloon Lady Samphire had very sensibly decided to use for her party, rather than the loftier great hall that would take whole tree-trunks burning in each of its huge hearths to even take the chill off it now winter was so well on its way.

'And just what was all that about?' Stella demanded as soon as they were comfortably seated on an elegant *chaise longue* that certainly hadn't come with the castle furnishings.

'Nothing,' Roxanne said, fervently wishing it were true.

'Then that's the most interesting piece of nothing I've heard in a very long time,' her friend replied with a resolute look in her grey eyes that she'd probably be horrified to hear made her look very like her great-aunt. 'Ah, Mr Longborough, here we are, hardly sat down and you already want me to get up and dance with you. What a very energetic young gentleman you are, to be sure.'

For once Roxanne blessed Joe as she watched him reluctantly carry off his chattering partner to join the first set forming at the end of the room, where the carpets had been removed for safekeeping and safe dancing. She didn't want to dance, and she certainly didn't want anyone else to know about that disgraceful episode in the garden that she could now see outlined in the darkness by a bright blaze of candlelight and flambeaux. Sir

Charles surely couldn't have set them there for the very purpose of keeping it in the forefront of her mind?

It surprised her to find that what she really wanted at this moment was privacy. She imagined dancing by that golden light among the statues with Charles Afforde and him alone. Maybe just an orchestra shut away in the blue saloon where they couldn't see her and she couldn't see them. And Charles, of course—he could even wear a greatcoat in return for her best evening cloak if he didn't like the chill of the November night biting through that rather fine black evening coat and his immaculate evening breeches. She shivered, but again not from any feeling of coldness, and told herself not to be an idiot.

'Good evening, Mr Huntley,' she greeted her promised dance-partner with such a fine impression of delight that his eyes brightened and she gave an internal groan.

Now look what she'd done; soon she'd have three gentlemen proposing to her at every turn and not a one of them she could accept, unless Sir Charles underwent a complete about-face and decided he might be able to love her, after all.

'Miss Courland, you look so very beautiful tonight,' the young man said with such devastating enthusiasm she had to fight a fit of the giggles.

'Oh, no, I was never considered a beauty even in my younger days, and if you'd witnessed my come out all those years ago, sir, you'd certainly never classify me so,' she said in an effort to dampen his enthusiasm.

'Surely not so many years ago?' he asked archly.

'Seven,' she informed him flatly.

That made him pause, but the Huntleys were evidently made of stern stuff and he rallied. 'Then you must have been a very young débutante, Miss Courland,' he said gallantly, and she almost smiled at his ingenuity, but that would only encourage him and she truly didn't want to bruise his feelings, even if she doubted his heart was engaged.

'I was seventeen, sir, but that's no excuse. I made a spectacularly unsuccessful début and don't have the slightest desire to endure the London Season ever again,' she said, hoping her unsociable leanings would put him off angling for such an unsuitable, and ancient, bride.

Another mistake, it seemed, for he smiled with relief and looked at her as though she'd suddenly gone from acceptable to nigh perfect as a potential wife. 'Neither have I; in fact, I hate doing the pretty,' he assured her earnestly, then looked a little uncertain as he realised that might not be the most tactful thing to say to a woman he was attempting to court. 'Except when I mean it, of course,' he added, trying to rescue himself from a dangerous quagmire.

'Oh, of course. Now hadn't we better join your friend on the dance floor?' she admitted in a reasonable imitation of delighted anticipation.

'Not sure he's my friend any more,' he replied and Roxanne wondered how her life had become so complex, when until recently it'd been so simple.

'Young gentlemen have the habit of falling out, so I'm sure you'll very soon make it up with your friend, Mr Huntley,' she said encouragingly.

Once they both realised she had no intention of marrying either of them, any reason for continuing bitterness between them would fade as rapidly as it had appeared, wouldn't it?

'I don't mind telling you I've seen another side to Joe these last few weeks, Miss Courland,' he said uneasily, and Roxanne wondered exactly what had passed between them to turn this delightful young man from Joe's steadfast friend into such an uneasy rival.

'Well, here we are at the floor, sir, so let's forget our worries in the dance, shall we? I do like a merry country dance, don't you?'

'Of course, nothing can rival it,' he gallantly agreed, despite the fact that its measures ensured he spent very little time in conversation with his partner.

Roxanne spared him the occasional glance as he worked his way down the line of ladies, and her heart lightened to see him greet a good many with a far easier smile than he ever gave her. When he'd grown up a little, Mr Huntley would make some lucky girl a fine husband. What a shame he couldn't see how unsuitable a match they would make of it if she was fool enough to encourage him. Not only was she three years his senior, but she'd never make him a docile little wife, ready to adore him for the rest of their days and defer to his superior judgement. No, what he needed was a pretty girl who was ready, willing and able to fall in love with an uncomplicated gentleman with a kind heart. She'd gone past that before she even made her début, thanks to a certain gentleman she was doing her best to ignore as they wound down the measures of the same set.

'You know,' Sir Charles murmured in her ear as she tried to slip past him without any but the most casual contact, 'I'm not sure if I prefer dancing with you, Roxanne, or watching you move so enchantingly while some other idiot does so.'

'You categorise yourself as an idiot then, Sir Charles?

Surely you're being a little harsh on yourself?' she muttered back and whisked away before he could retaliate, but soon there would be that first waltz and doubtless he'd have his revenge.

Chapter Thirteen

'So *are* you going to marry my cousin, Roxanne?' Stella asked her relentlessly, as soon as she'd dispatched Mr Huntley and Joe Longborough to fetch lemonade, never mind that they didn't appear to be speaking to one another and neither she nor Roxanne was particularly thirsty.

'No,' she replied as softly as she could when her instinct was to shout it as loudly as possible, in the hope it would then become an irrefutable truth before she began to wonder at herself for turning him down as well.

'I can't imagine him ever meeting anyone who'd suit him better,' Stella replied mournfully. 'Won't you reconsider, Roxanne?'

'Certainly not.'

'Oh, very well then. I suppose he'll have to take his chance with some silly débutante who lacks the sense to ever be his equal.'

'Yes, he will.'

'Such a waste though, don't you think?' Stella said, using her fan to direct Roxanne's attention toward Sir Charles's superbly male figure by the door where he was gracefully waving aside a latecomer's self-reproaches.

He wasn't in the least overawed or out of place in this huge room, designed to trumpet its owner's wealth and position to all comers from royalty downwards. He'd stand out if he'd contented himself with living in a hovel, Roxanne decided despairingly, and little wonder her younger self had only had to set eyes on such a dominant, masculine warrior to decide he must be hers one day.

Now Roxanne watched him with every bit of the fascination Stella might wish for. He bowed to the gruff wife of a neighbouring squire and endured being slapped on the back by her husband with good-humoured patience, and she thought that, yes, he would make an excellent husband, as long as his wife wasn't in love with him. If she were, and Roxanne feared she might very well be, then he'd make her deeply unhappy, because he didn't seem at all willing to entertain the notion he might love her back. Yet wouldn't it also be agony to see him wed another? A question she'd done her best to avoid considering while he was away and might be meeting a paragon who wouldn't demand he loved her before she considered marriage.

'Not all débutantes are stupid,' she protested weakly, unable to tear her gaze from the tall figure of Charles Afforde, whose starkly elegant evening attire only added to his manly attractions, rather than having the grace to make him look just like any other man present tonight.

'But even the ones who are intelligent still have matchmaking mamas, who'll make very sure their daughters don't refuse a handsome baronet with a handsome property and an even more handsome fortune.'

'Rather a lot of handsomes there, don't you think?'

'No,' Stella insisted ruthlessly. 'Most females would tread on the faces of their friends in their eagerness if he danced with them twice, mamas or no, and you won't even consider marrying him when he begs you to.'

'He always dances with *me* twice,' she pointed out rather childishly.

'Yes, because he actually wants to marry you,' Stella pointed out with merciless patience. 'Charles was never one to raise false hopes.'

'But I've never harboured any,' Roxanne protested.

'What, never?'

Roxanne blushed and recalled the headlong, romantic girl she'd once been. Young though Lieutenant Afforde was at the time, he'd have been a fool *not* to notice her blatant adoration when they first met. She'd made sure he fell over her every time he turned round that Christmas when she'd confidently decided he must be her adult fate. Then she'd made her come out at a ridiculously young age, because he might not wait for her if she didn't badger Uncle Granger into arranging her début as soon as possible. Could any girl's hopes have been wilder or more unrealistic than young Rosie Courland's had proved all those years ago?

'Certainly not from the moment I realised at the tender age of seventeen that your cousin was a rake and hadn't the slightest intention of settling down with a wife, or at least not with one of his own.'

'How scandalous of you to have known such liaisons existed at so young an age.'

'Yes, wasn't it? Now can we talk of something else? I find myself growing weary of endlessly speculating about your cousin's wife.'

'As you just pointed out, dear Roxanne, he doesn't actually have one for us to speculate about.'

'No, and long may that situation last, for I pity the poor girl who takes him on when he does find one.'

'I think he already has,' Stella insisted stubbornly.

'Then you're wrong.'

'So does Great-Aunt Augusta, by the way; I can tell that by the way she keeps nodding and winking at me to hint I should leave you alone in order for my cousin to swoop down and claim you,' Stella said, attempting to rise to her feet as Lady Samphire was indeed indicating she should with almost comical contortions. Comical if they weren't aimed at Roxanne's public embarrassment.

'Then she's wrong, too, and don't you dare,' Roxanne said, holding on to Stella's midnight-blue skirts so that she had to pause halfway between sitting and standing, then plumped back down with a rueful shrug at her formidable aunt.

'So undignified,' she protested virtuously.

'Yes, isn't it?' Roxanne replied candidly, and Stella's eyes fell before the resolve in her own not to be manoeuvred into a *tête-à-tête* with Charles.

Dancing with him would be quite bad enough without being forced into his heady company for goodness knew how long while the company gossiped about them and Lady Samphire spread rumours with joyful abandon.

'I won't be trapped, tricked or persuaded into marriage with Sir Charles, Stella. Indeed, I'd choose scandal and opprobrium rather than let that happen.'

'I'm not trying to trick you, it's just that you're so right for each other,' Stella excused herself apologetically.

'Thank you, but excuse me if I disagree.'

'Why?'

'What do you mean, "why"? Of course it's a silly notion.'

'I don't see why it's such a ludicrous idea.'

'Because Sir Charles and myself are opposites in every way. He's just weary of raking and travelling the world, and I'm a novelty to him because I've never been anywhere much or even had a serious suitor. I also know his house and estates better than he does himself, and could run them for him while he's busy elsewhere, and there you have his reasons for marriage.'

'He's made a fine mess of that, then, hasn't he?' Stella said with what looked oddly like satisfaction from where Roxanne was sitting.

'He did his best to seduce me into it as well,' she admitted with a blush.

'How comforting to know some of his famous sang-froid hasn't deserted him, poor Charles.'

'Poor Charles?' Roxanne demanded. 'Family feeling must count for a lot, I know, but why should he be "poor Charles" when I'm the one being bombarded like some foreign citadel he's been ordered to conquer?'

'Because he'd do anything to avoid admitting to himself that he's head over heels in love with you, of course,' Stella explained, as if explaining the obvious to a very slow three-year-old.

Roxanne just sat there with her mouth open, staring at her companion with such astonishment that her ears buzzed with shock and hid the sound of approaching footsteps, if he had made any sound, of course.

'I believe this is our dance, Miss Courland,' the subject of it all observed urbanely, looking far more innocent than he'd any right to.

'Is it?' she asked him idiotically and blushed ridiculously as he met her eyes with an ironic question in his.

'Well, if you doubt me, I suppose we could always take a look at your dance-card,' he offered, but the prospect of having him come even close enough to do that made her wonder if she might lower herself to faking a fit of the vapours—how on earth was she going to endure a waltz in his arms?

'No, I recall it now,' she mumbled, fixing her eyes on the top button of his immaculate grey-silk waistcoat. Maybe if she refused to look at him, she'd be able to pretend to herself that she was dancing with just any gentleman.

'Whatever has my cousin been saying to you, Roxanne?' he asked as they joined the other couples on the dance floor and waited for the musicians to launch into the latest waltz tune from Vienna.

'Nothing very much,' she replied, just managing to avoid his acute gaze by focusing instead on his shoulder as he relentlessly adopted the position required, and her body reacted as if she'd been shocked by Signor Galvini's electrical machine.

'I thought we knew each other better than this, Roxanne,' he murmured, refusing to be the handsome marionette she would have preferred to dance with while she settled her nerves and examined Stella's outrageous assertion that he loved her for any grains of truth.

'Better than what?' she asked incautiously and cursed her body for twining itself as close to his as the dance and propriety would allow.

'Than avoiding my eyes as if you hate the very sight of me, or pretending we're polite acquaintances enduring a duty dance,' he insisted relentlessly. 'I'd rather you refused to take the floor in my company in the first place than this, Roxanne, for your behaviour informs me you regret our kiss and our intimacy, and that's like finding out the world's flat after all, and don't forget I'm a seaman, will you? That would hold serious implications for a man who might sail off the edge if he ever returned to his old occupation.'

Torn between finding him irresistible for his weak attempt at humour and hating the very idea of him sailing away from her, she flinched. Constant fear for his safety had been hard enough to live with when she was a silly girl infatuated with a handsome face, but now she was a grown woman and truly loved him, it would be close to hell.

'Don't,' she urged tensely.

'Don't what? Don't speak of such ridiculous things, or don't refuse to pretend all's well and it doesn't matter that you turn your eyes away from mine as if I might turn you to stone if you meet them? I'm sorry, but I can't oblige you, my dear; we've come too far for me to allow it.'

'Allow?' she asked haughtily, meeting his intense blue gaze with queenly dignity and nearly causing a collision by unconsciously halting to recruit all her energies to recover from the effort it had cost her.

'Come, you're clearly in no mood for all this flim-flam,' he informed her in a gruff voice and with a polite apology and a dazzling smile for the lady they'd just nearly caused to trip, he murmured something about the heat and swept her off the floor in the crook of a powerful arm.

'I suppose this must be your best commodore's manner?' she asked, as she obligingly wilted into his embrace to lend colour to his tale.

'Well, someone needs to take control,' he informed her angrily.

'I have an aversion to being controlled.'

'That much is self-evident, Miss Courland. You're so stubborn that you're in danger of cutting off both our noses to spite my face.'

'That doesn't even *sound* right,' she muttered darkly and surprised a bark of laughter out of him that nearly undid their whole story of her being overcome by anything but his presence.

'Slight cough,' he explained to Mrs Longborough in passing as he swept Roxanne towards the sofa where Stella was waiting.

'Lot of it about, young people today lack stamina,' she replied blandly.

'Not stamina, just good sense,' he replied with an openly condemning glance in Roxanne's direction.

'Must be catching,' the Squire's wife said with an abrupt nod at her own son that told them succinctly how few of his faults and foibles she'd missed.

'And therefore probably curable,' Charles said, a rueful smile at last eclipsing his unusually savage temper.

The very fact that she could infuriate him so easily made Roxanne pause and consider again Stella's startling declaration that he loved her. She certainly had it in her power to break through the cynically amused façade he used to fend off the world in general. Quite what that meant she hadn't yet worked out, but it meant something. Whatever that 'something' might be, she refused to embroider his story by drooping elegantly at Stella's side while he went to fetch yet more lemonade to revive her when she didn't need reviving.

'I should vastly prefer a cup of tea,' she informed him truthfully as she sat straight-backed in contravention of his fairy story.

'I'll inform Mereson; no doubt he'll produce it in the midst of an evening party with all the air of an archbishop asked to perform conjuring tricks, but he'll produce it all the same if I tell him it's for you.'

'He's always claimed to like a challenge,' Roxanne replied blandly.

'Don't we all?' he answered inexcusably, then strolled off to bother his butler with his impenetrable, ridiculous statements instead of her.

'Speaking of challenges, how *are* you intending to explain your exit from the dance when you now look as if you never had a day's illness in your entire life, Roxanne?' Stella asked curiously.

'Simple,' she explained grandly, 'I'll take a leaf out of Lady Samphire's book and refuse to justify my actions by pretending they didn't happen.'

'Oh, Lord, will you? The prospect of two of you marching about the neighbourhood manipulating all and sundry for their own good very nearly terrifies me enough to make me return to the Dower House and endure Mama and Great-Aunt Letty's endless moralising.'

'I only said a leaf, not the entire volume with appendix and addenda.'

'There are never any addenda to Great-Aunt Augusta's pronouncements for she simply *never* makes mistakes,' Stella declared solemnly, and Roxanne laughed. 'That's better, you look less likely to eat the next person who asks how you are now,' Stella added—how could she stay angry when her friend, companion and possible future relative was so witty, warm and caring?

Charles's family was not, perhaps, his closest blood kin but rather the family he loved and who loved him— Robert Besford and his unconventional wife; the absent and yet often-spoken-of Will, Lord Wrovillton, and his apparently even less conventional lady; then, closer to home, were Lady Samphire, Stella, and Tom Varleigh and, of course, her own sister Joanna. The people he'd just spent a weary week with should be his family, of course, but Roxanne didn't have to be told that Charles Afforde probably felt closer to his dogs or his horses.

'It's all your fault,' she felt compelled to tell Stella all the same.

'What is?'

'That I nearly tripped up Lady Trickley and caused even more widespread social catastrophe just now, as well as serious injury.'

'Oh, why?'

'You know perfectly well why.'

'I do, indeed—so, are you going to marry him?'

'Probably, but you, Stella Lavender, are even more of a devious schemer than your Aunt Samphire.'

'How appalling,' Stella said happily enough and she sat back to enjoy the spectacle as Charles re-entered the room with Mereson and an attendant footman bearing the tea-things on a series of silver salvers, as if present-ing treasure to royalty.

'And shall you be joining us for tea, Charles?' Stella asked innocently.

'I've drunk more of the stuff in the last couple of months than I ever did in the whole of the rest of my life as it is.'

'Confess, it's not as bad a beverage as you thought, now is it?'

'Cat lap,' he condemned as Mereson presented him with another of the glasses of fine burgundy he seemed to think Charles needed supplying with whenever tea was mentioned. 'So,' he murmured in Roxanne's ear as Stella tactfully allowed herself to be distracted by a neighbour, 'has this last week dragged on as tediously for you as it has done for me?'

'On the contrary, I was tolerably well amused,' she claimed.

'Maybe you had more conducive company then, for I certainly was not.'

'Stella and your grandmama would be furious if I said they were other than very good company, Sir Charles, and quite right, too.'

'I suppose so, but I badly missed yours,' he informed her, as if she owed him something for even so much as admitting he could do so.

'Very flattering,' she informed him with a satisfied nod she'd copied from Lady Samphire. If she was to accept him without a declaration of love, she'd no inten-tion of letting him be the only one with secrets.

'Flattering enough for you to accept me?' he asked lightly, but with a brooding intensity in his gaze that warned her not to take it at face value.

'That depends,' she prevaricated, feeling as if her younger self was standing behind her, jumping up and down with furious impatience as older and wiser Roxanne hovered between acceptance and refusal of the man of her dreams.

'On what?' he asked, as if he would dearly love to shake her, but was far too sophisticated a man of the world to be so reckless and unmannerly under the interested gazes of their friends and neighbours.

'On what sort of a husband you intend to make me, of course. If you're offering marriage *à la mode,* then I must refuse, for I couldn't live so, Charles.'

'Of course not. I'll never look at another woman if you marry me,' he declared as sternly as if he were about to go into battle.

She sipped her tea and leaned back in her seat, watching him with what she hoped was impenetrable composure.

'Well,' he conceded at last, 'I might look, but that would be as far as I ever went, and when I did it would only be to confirm I'd be taking the most desirable female of my acquaintance home to warm my bed.'

'And would you expect me to occupy a separate sphere to yours? I don't know that I could endure being immured in the drawing room, embroidering every night, while you con your accounts and discuss racing form with your cronies over the best cognac in our cellars.'

'Then I willingly undertake to include you in any and every dissipation I indulge in from now on, and you're quite welcome to the accounts—anything else?' he enquired rather wearily and Roxanne let the words she really wanted to ask hover on the tip of her tongue, then swallowed them down with another sip of finest China tea.

'Then, if you promise to allow any children we might have to be part of our lives, as well,' she went on gallantly, despite the fiery blush she was sure could be seen across the ballroom, 'I think we could come to terms,' she managed without even mentioning the possibility of a love match.

'They will be at the very centre of it,' he promised her huskily, and trust him to turn her practical attempts at laying down a contract between them into part of her seduction. 'Their begetting will be my finest endeavour yet,' he went on, his gaze ablaze with blue heat as he subjected her to a ruthlessly sensual scrutiny that left her in no doubt as to how much he intended to enjoy it.

'Let's put the cart before the horses, shall we, Sir Charles?' she asked in a voice she had trouble recognising as her own.

'Three weeks,' he told her implacably.

'Three weeks? That's hardly long enough to have a bridal gown made, let alone invite everyone who thinks they have a right to be at our wedding.'

'Three weeks,' he insisted. 'I'm not made of stone and much longer than that and I'll have to insist we make a start on those brats of ours without benefit of clergy.'

'I might have something to say about that,' she protested in a voice that didn't even convince her.

'I shall make quite certain you do,' he informed her arrogantly. 'You'll say "yes" over and over again,' he said, his voice a murmured promise as his eyes locked on hers with such complete certainty that she should be insulted.

'I haven't even said one very important "yes" yet,' she argued gamely.

'Then stop playing with me, Roxanne, and make me the answer we both need to hear.'

'What if one of us falls in love?' she finally offered, revealing the most important caveat of all.

'There's no such thing, and would you risk the rare accord we have with each other for such a fleeting mirage, Roxanne? I never could and promise I honour you above any other woman on this earth and always will do. I also want you unmercifully, so if you'd just stop thinking up obstacles and agree that we're perfect for each other, I'd be obliged to you.'

'You'd be obliged to me?' she echoed, torn between the terrible temptation of his offer and those seemingly careless words.

'Stupid of me,' he snapped, impatient with himself instead of her this time. 'I'll be honoured, triumphant and the happiest man in England, let alone Kent, if you'll just say that you'll marry me, Roxanne. I've never lacked the right words with any other woman but you, which is *not* be the best way to persuade you, now I think about it. But with you I can't find the easy phrase or casual kiss that might bend your will to mine—you're too important for that.'

It was as close as she'd probably ever get to a declaration of love from him, and Roxanne let herself consider whether she *could* live the rest of her life without hearing anything more. Considering the alternative, which was to refuse him and either live her life alone or marry another man solely for the pleasure of bearing children, she finally made up her mind that she could.

'Very well, Sir Charles,' she said rather stiffly, 'I will marry you.'

'Thank Heaven for that, then,' he said on a heartfelt sigh and immediately called for champagne and silence. 'It is my undeserved good fortune in introducing Miss Courland as my newly affianced bride,' he announced to all and sundry, before she could change her mind.

Chapter Fourteen

Once upon a time there was a foolish, romantic girl who dreamt her days away, longing for her fairy-tale lover who sailed the seven seas in search of adventure and booty, and she *knew* her wild sea-rover would come home and lay his hand and his heart at her feet one day. Which was why, Roxanne reflected, as she struggled against an odd sense of unreality that fitted fairy tales better than it did a sunny winter day, she was about to become Roxanne, Lady Afforde, and one out of the two would just have to do.

When she stepped over the threshold of Hollowhurst Church today, she would commit herself to being Sir Charles Afforde's lawfully wedded wife until death did them part. The very idea of death spun her back over those anxious years when she'd scanned the newspapers for reports of his dashing exploits and studied the lists of the fallen after battles at sea with heavy dread in her heart, then exultation when she didn't find his name.

Someone else's loved one, some other girl's hope of happiness, died that day and not Charles Afforde, so Mrs Roxanne Afforde lived on in her imagination. After she'd grown up and realised it was all a fairy tale, she'd still performed that ritual every time an engagement was reported, but never again had she dreamt her dream, and now it was coming true, after all.

'Have you still got my handkerchief for your something borrowed?' Stella asked anxiously as she scrambled down from the carriage to fuss over the precise arrangement of Roxanne's ivory-velvet skirts.

'Yes, Mama,' Roxanne replied with a grin at her nervous matron of honour as she managed not to fall over her fussing senior bridesmaid, '*and* the fetching blue garter your Great-Aunt Augusta presented me with last night.'

'Trust her,' Stella breathed with a sidelong look at the church as if she thought her formidable great-aunt might be able to hear her through stone walls several feet thick. 'But what about something old?'

'I wondered about wearing those comfortable old riding boots you're always nagging me about,' Roxanne teased, laughing as Stella was unable to resist peering down at her fine kid slippers, 'but I decided they didn't match and contented myself with Charles's locket instead.'

'A good choice, for I never knew him to so much as move without his mama's favourite trinket in his pocket until he gave it to you,' Stella said sagely, then scurried ahead to shoo the gaggle of little bridesmaids into the church porch ahead of them and out of a chilly December breeze.

Pulling her fur-lined cloak closer against it herself,

Roxanne followed her more sedately. She'd been surprised and touched by Charles's gift, astonished that he'd part with something so personal, so obviously precious to him, when he'd said not one word of love to her all the time they'd been engaged—not that three weeks was so very long in all conscience.

'I'm expecting too much,' she murmured and recalled Lady Samphire's advice to give Charles time to come to terms with his feelings for her.

'He ain't one to let on he even has a heart, m'dear, let alone wear it on his sleeve. Not that he ain't a sentimental idiot beneath all that devil-may-care insolence, you only have to look at the way he fusses over me to see that,' she'd concluded gruffly as she'd clung to Roxanne's hand with surprising warmth and strength. 'He won't admit he's capable of what I'll call romantic love for want of a better description, though. Deep down I think he knows he'll give his heart for all time when he finally does so and probably hand over his soul and his honour along with it, and he's far too guarded to give any of them up lightly. Are you careful enough to hold them safe for him when he does, Roxanne?'

'I'm a Courland, and we hold fast to what we love, my lady,' she'd asserted confidently, exhilarated by the thought that one day she might have the chance to guard Charles's love and treasure his honour after all.

Now she wasn't quite so sure, despite her ladyship's assurances and his promise of fidelity. What if he turned his eyes elsewhere, despite his vow not to? Nobody could regulate love and passion as he seemed to think he could, and she closed her eyes against the very idea of such a shattering betrayal, then blinked determinedly

and told herself not to be a pessimist. He was marrying *her,* wasn't he? He'd had most of the eligible young
ladies of the *ton* and a good many of their less respectable sisters among the *demi-monde* scrambling to snare
his hand or heart, and preferably both, over the years,
and he hadn't wed any of them. So, she only had to
walk up the ancient path ahead of her, past the leaning
gravestones and the hoary old yew tree she'd known ever
since she could first remember, and he would be joined
to her in an unbreakable bond.

'Am I expecting too much, Tom?' she asked her
brother-in-law as he waited patiently at her side, arm
crooked to encourage her to launch herself into the true
purpose of her wedding day so he could give her to her
groom and get out of this biting cold wind.

'You must expect it, dear Rosie. It's your right.'

'I don't see why.'

'Because you love him, and I believe he loves you.
Every bride in love with her groom must expect too
much of him on their wedding day. It's obligatory and
turns him from a boy into a man, irrespective of his
age.'

'Lord, when did you become so wise?' she asked
with such awe it reminded them both of a much younger
Roxanne and a time when he was her big sister's devoted
admirer and they both laughed.

'Your sister would tell you it happened the day she
wed me, but I argue it was the moment I married her
and finally realised what I was taking on,' he said
ruefully.

'Very well then, lead on, Oh Knowledgeable One,
and when I rue the day I let you guide me up this path
to meet my fate, I'll descend on you all at Varleigh

and declare it to be entirely your fault I ever found the courage.'

'No, you won't, for by that time you'll be wed, and every married woman on earth knows that when something goes wrong in her life, it's sure to be the fault of her husband.'

'So be it, then,' she said lightly and met his rather anxious look with a confident smile.

'You couldn't wed a finer man,' he assured her seriously.

'I know, so shall we get on with my wedding? Before he decides we're bored with the idea and have gone to Tunbridge Wells for a little shopping and the waters, rather than meet me in front of the altar and all his friends?'

'Aye, it's devilish cold standing here and I want to be back in that barrack you call a home with a hot toddy and my wife and family for comfort as soon as may be.'

'Come along, then, do,' she encouraged him in her best imitation of her sister Maria, and so they entered the church on a triumphant crescendo played by the village band.

With the braziers having burned all night and so many people crowded into such a small church, it was warm enough inside for most to enjoy the spectacle of Sir Charles Afforde embracing his fate at long last. The sight of him waiting impatiently for her at the altar, the winter sun gilding his dark gold hair to fairness and outlining his broad-shouldered figure in close-fitting dark blue broadcloth that nearly matched his eyes, reminded

Roxanne of her first glimpse of him across the snow and the shadows that fateful Christmas night.

Warmth caught at her heart, melted some chilly corner of it that was still sore with the thought that he hadn't known from that Christmas day on, probably by instinct alone, that they were fated to love and wed one day. Her breath stuttered, and she let some of her real feelings show in her eyes as she walked confidently towards him down the aisle. She'd waited so long for this day, and now it was come, it was just as wonderful as she'd always dreamt, even if he might never say he loved her. He felt something deep and powerful for her, it was unmistakable in the welcome and triumph and heat in his compelling eyes as he watched the heavy folds of silk velvet outline her supple figure as she walked, her cloak belling slightly out from her sides with the speed of her arrival, until she finally arrived, glowing and a little breathless, at his side with a radiant smile that, if she did but know it, took his breath away.

Pausing to remind herself there were others present to see them wed, Roxanne looked away from her groom to regard the posy of humble holly, ivy and hot-house camellias in her hand as if she'd never seen it before. Luckily Stella had her cohorts firmly in hand by now, so Joanna and Tom Varleigh's eldest daughter Julia seized Roxanne's bouquet, while Stella carefully turned back the bride's veil and little Roxanne Varleigh, her namesake and goddaughter as well as her niece, tottered only momentarily as she enthusiastically strewed the dried rose-petals from her basket now instead of when the married couple walked down the aisle together later because it seemed a good idea to her, which indeed it was. Consequently, Roxanne and Charles made their vows with the lingering scent of summer all about them and the sun casting golden light over them like a blessing.

'What an auspicious start to our married life,' he whispered, before he took full advantage of the vicar's permission to kiss the bride.

'Mmm,' she responded with her usual lack of words when at the mercy of even his lightest kisses. She really would have to develop some way of coping better with the world with her much-dreamed-of lover in it, when he might come upon her at any time and kiss her now they were married.

'Lady Afforde,' he said with a tender, rueful smile at his new wife, 'we really must put some work in on expanding your vocabulary.'

'Oh, but later, surely, Charles?' she gasped in shock at the very idea of what he might do to achieve that, and her husband gave an involuntary laugh that made her sister Maria's countessy nose twitch with disapproval and everyone else smile indulgently.

'Not too much later if I have anything to do with it,' he murmured in her ear before turning about to face the congregation with an openly satisfied smile on his handsome face.

'And how you expect me to make any sense of today with a threat like that hanging over me, I'll never know,' she chided as they climbed into the fine new coach he'd brought as one of his marriage gifts to her for the short drive back to the Castle.

'Tom warned me everything would be my fault from this moment on,' he said ruefully as he settled her skirts every bit as attentively as Stella had, but with a wicked smile that told her he was enjoying the chance to linger over the way the soft silky fineness of the best velvet available outlined her figure. With his bride now thoroughly discomposed, he sprang into the coach and sat next to her with a merry wave at the assembled villagers who hadn't managed either to squeeze into the church or be invited to their reception.

'He told me that as well, and he was quite right, too,' Roxanne informed him as she, too, smiled and waved at the many villagers and estate workers who'd turned out in the cold to line their route out of the village.

'In ten years' time, do you think we'll be as happily grumpy with each other as they are?' he asked as he took her hand in his, distracting her from being tearfully touched at the enthusiastic cheers as their coach went past by removing her glove so he could admire the broad gold band now joining the graceful diamond ring on her left hand. Perhaps reassuring himself he'd finally caught her? she wondered wistfully.

'I truly hope so, I'd hate to think we might become like Maria and poor Balsover,' she replied, distracted by his touch again. Now the carriage had picked up speed and the short drive to the castle left them a brief illusion of privacy, he held her hand up to catch the watery sunlight and it shot prisms of rainbow light from the stones in the ring she still couldn't believe was hers, made as it was to look like a trail of flowers that formed the most beautiful eternity ring she could have imagined.

When he was tired of admiring that fine piece of the goldsmith's art and the broad gold band wrought delicately with what she suspected were forget-me-nots, he silenced her altogether by lifting her hand to his lips and kissing her fingers one by one, until he finally went

back to her ring finger and took it into his mouth, his
blazing blue gaze explicit as he ran his tongue along its
fine-boned length until her eyelids went heavy and her
lips opened with an invitation that he took with ravenous
alacrity.

No matter how many times he kissed her, Roxanne
thought with dazed wonder, every time was a delicious
novelty. Then his mouth opened on hers and demanded
all she had to give in return, so she gave it enthusiastically. She was breathless and hot and shaking with suppressed passion and sweet, heavy-limbed anticipation of
their marriage bed when she finally realised the horses
had slowed and they were almost at the great doorway
of the oldest part of the castle, usually kept firmly shut
at this time of year to keep the draughts at bay.

'Why didn't I just abduct you and carry you off across
the Border so we wouldn't have to wait for half the
county to eat us out of house and home and toast us until
they're hoarse with my best champagne before we enjoy
our marriage bed, my lovely wife?' he asked her rather
unsteadily, and she was exultant that his hand shook
nigh as badly as her own when he leapt down from the
coach and held it out to receive hers, as if every move
they made today was significant in some way the rest
of the world couldn't dream of.

'I don't know, why didn't you?' she asked, clinging
to the support of his strong arm as they mounted the
steps like a king and queen taking possession of their
palace, made even more of a royal progress by the fact
that the castle staff were lined up there to bid them a
ceremonial welcome.

'Because they would never have forgiven me,' he
whispered in her ear when they finally reached the

doorway and she looked back at her old friends and a few new ones Charles had brought to Hollowhurst with him and smiled at them in rather a misty attempt at thanking them for helping to make her wedding day so special.

'Nor me,' she acknowledged unsteadily and blessed Charles's sure touch as he shook Mereson's hand while the butler wished them both very happy on behalf of all the castle staff, inside and out.

'Now let's all get in out of the cold and get on with making merry, shall we?' Charles asked as he shocked and delighted Roxanne by lifting her into his arms and carrying her over the threshold to the cheers of the staff, and the guests beginning to arrive from the church in their wake.

'Put me down, Charles,' she urged him, not quite sure her legs had the strength to carry her as he did so very slowly when they reached the great hall, and he gave her a decidedly wolfish smile. 'You're a very bad man,' she chided.

'Believe me, sweetheart, I could be a whole lot worse,' he replied with a wicked grin that dissipated some of her awe at the solemnity of what they'd just done and made her long to laugh out loud with sheer joy, after all.

'But not just yet, perhaps?' she replied with a siren smile.

'Not unless we want to be lynched by our staff and our guests, but later I'll have my revenge for every wickedly alluring glance and taunting smile, Lady Afforde,' he promised, and there was no mistaking the seriousness of his intent, despite the easy smile he turned on Maria and Henry Balsover as her sister insisted on entering the room first in deference to her rank.

'Happy?' Tom Varleigh asked when he stepped forwards to offer formal congratulations on a marriage he evidently approved of.

'Deeply,' she agreed, unable to care if Charles heard her admit it.

She *was* happy, after all, ecstatically so at the thought of what was to come tonight, although it was a little diluted by apprehension at the unknown. She knew with bone-deep certainty she'd never have been half as happy with any other man, however much he might have loved her. So, yes, she could admit to being happy, but luckily nobody had the temerity to come out and ask her if she also loved.

If they had, she must either lie and deny it, or tell the truth and cause Charles's eyes to cloud and his smile to waver as he faced the inequality at the heart of their marriage. Blinking tears away, she reminded herself how much she wanted this marriage and did it so well that by the time Charles removed her third glass of champagne from her hand with a shake of his head and a quizzical look she would have argued, if he hadn't whispered he wanted her in possession of all her senses later, so he could drive her out of them with something better than champagne!

After the wedding breakfast there was dancing and the Great Hall rang with music and laughter for the first time in years. Roxanne remembered a long-ago ball held here, when all she could do was observe from the minstrel's gallery as her bridegroom spun girl after girl about the ancient floor with laughing abandon. How she'd hated every one of them, including her sisters, that night. Yet now Charles Afforde was her husband, just as she'd sworn to herself he would be one day, when she was grown up and beautiful and he was loaded with honours and more handsome than ever.

'Our waltz, my lovely,' her handsome captain murmured in her ear with such intimate heat in his eyes while he watched for her blush that she wondered fleetingly if she might want to slap him if she didn't love him so much. 'And maybe we can escape this brouhaha once they're all fairly launched into the dancing,' he added, and was it any wonder she hadn't breath enough left to say yea or nay? He laughed at her confounded state and wrapped his arm about her as he urged her on to the dance floor. 'And pray don't leave me with a floundering bride in my arms as you did the night you finally agreed to all this,' he urged with a lordly wave of his arm at the assembled company, eagerly watching as the bride and her groom took the floor for their dance, their confirmation that this was their day, the start of their joint future.

'You can be very infuriating indeed, Sir Charles,' she informed him sternly. He nodded. 'And very highhanded.' Again that nod of wicked acknowledgement, but very little repentance. 'And as of today you are also *very* married,' she finished ominously, her dark eyes promising retribution.

'I *know*,' he replied with every appearance of triumph and how could she not be flattered and flustered as he held her even closer and their steps matched in a most disgracefully intimate dance the patronesses at Almack's would surely not have approved when they finally gave in and permitted the waltz to be performed in their hallowed halls.

Respect for their guests made them stay far longer

than they wanted to, accepting increasingly sentimental or raucous congratulations and dancing duty dances with the one or two who believed precedence triumphed over the sheer joy of a wedding. The early darkness of December had fallen long since, and the huge tree trunks burning in the vast fireplaces at each end of the hall had overcome the chill of the vast room. Even their indefatigable guests were succumbing to heat, champagne and happy exhaustion, when Charles seized his bride from a quiet coze with her eldest sister and Stella and whispered for her ear alone, 'I don't feel married enough yet, my lady, and it's time we did something about it.'

Heart racing, speechless with curiosity and desire, and a nagging jag of apprehension, Roxanne licked her lips nervously as she nestled into his embrace and watched his fascinated gaze linger on that action as if it was driving him demented, so naturally she did it again. He groaned and she felt the triumph of a woman who knew she was wanted above all others by a man she desired exclusively in return; thinking any deeper was banned tonight, and perhaps tomorrow and the next day as well.

'If you don't stop provoking me, I'll probably publicly embarrass you,' he grated out in a husky voice she hadn't heard before.

'How?' she asked interestedly, and he growled.

He really, really just growled at her like a hungry wolf, and she eyed him warily as she wondered, with a skitter of her heart that wasn't altogether fearful, if she really had provoked him beyond safe limits.

'Come,' he demanded savagely, but she excused him that when she saw what looked very like desperation in his eyes, and she let him draw her inexorably towards the door and the more shadowed part of the house, because she'd be a fool to do otherwise when she was finally at the end of an even longer thread of waiting and hoping than he was.

They heard a hue and cry behind them as the rowdier elements spotted their escape, but Charles's compelling arm about her waist urged her on and they sped along the corridor and darted through the door leading to the servants' stairs, just as the young men tore into the hall and demanded of Mereson where his master and mistress had gone.

'I really have no idea, gentlemen,' he insisted blandly, and Roxanne stifled a chuckle as she allowed Charles to tow her up the narrow stairs and out into the corridor that led to the master suite and safety.

'Remind me to double his wages,' Charles muttered as he scurried her along the splendidly carpeted hallway and, much to her astonishment, Roxanne found time to admire the many improvements he'd put in place since buying the castle.

'Hurry, my lady,' Tabby urged from the open door of her lady's bedchamber, and Roxanne finally felt the weight of her new position as she surveyed the comfort and elegance Charles had created within.

'It's so beautiful!' she gasped, awed by the transformation from dark and rather dingy chamber into a delightfully feminine bower.

'You can thank me later,' Charles said with a return of impudence and eloquence as he sent her a wicked smile and went to engage the locks of his chamber as well as hers, before anyone could run them to earth. Putting his head round the communicating door, he grinned at her, and she felt herself beginning to melt from the inside outwards all over again. 'Not much later, though,' he promised and left her to Tabby's starry-eyed ministrations.

Chapter Fifteen

Speechless for once, Roxanne sat and let Tabby remove her finery with relief, despite the fact she loved every stitch of it and would cherish her wedding dress until her dying day. The rhythmic stroke of the brush as her hair was released to cascade about her shoulders almost calmed her, but then she licked her lips and met her own eyes in the mirror and knew it was just an illusion.

She looked different, did young Lady Afforde. Like a woman awaiting something very significant and special indeed and not sure if she ought to embrace it. Yes, she told herself fiercely, this is what I always wanted, and she squashed the little voice that argued 'not quite', even as Charles strode into the room with a splendid dressing robe open to reveal he'd shed his coat and waistcoat and neckcloth and looked incredibly handsome in his ivory breeches and stockings and shirtsleeves. Tabby finished hastily and scampered out of the room with a cheeky grin that Roxanne promised herself revenge for, tomorrow.

'I've had enough,' her husband ground out concisely, tugging Roxanne into his powerful arms at last, as if he'd found the day as trying, and at the same time as joyful, as she had.

'Enough what, Sir Charles?' she asked with a provocative look into his stormy blue eyes.

'Fine clothes, champagne, relatives and friends, and most especially enough of your teasing, Lady Afforde,' he informed her in a driven voice as he lowered his head in a kiss that allowed nothing for maidenly modesty, but a great deal for the raw, undisguised passion that flamed into immediate life between them.

Luckily Roxanne was as impatient as he was and met his hot kiss with unguarded enthusiasm. Open mouthed, they clashed, took and drove each other mutually crazy. Best not to think that on her side she was crazy with love as well as desire, but Roxanne let her hands explore his strongly muscled shoulders and neck without the annoying restrictions of fashion and convention and ignored the inequality.

This, she decided as she breathed in the scent and sensation of bare, heated, satin-and-steel masculine skin, this was what she'd longed for all those long, frustrated, barren years while he'd been away. His tongue plunged into her mouth and she felt surrounded by heat and need, his and hers, and tipped her head further back to give him even more encouragement.

Unnecessary encouragement, as it happened, for his hands ran heat down her scantily clad back and neat *derrière,* as if he could hardly bear even the gossamer silk of her nightgown coming between the sheer luxury of skin on skin. It seemed that he already knew how badly she wanted him, she remembered, with a very small regret that she'd held nothing back that day when he taught her the breadth and depth and peril of truly adult passion in the castle gardens below their bedchamber windows.

And he'd taught her very well, she reminded herself as she carried out an exploration of her own and felt his tactile muscles tense and shift under her flexing, stroking, approving fingers. And it was mighty, the steely strength under his satin supple skin. He was a mature, dominant male, and how would her younger self ever have coped with so potent a lover? She would have improvised, Roxanne decided with a cat-like smile against the base of his throat. Now, how had her mouth got there? she wondered as she appreciated his unique charms with it, now it was somewhere so intimate, now this place was to be forbidden all other women. Fair enough, she decided, with hazy logic when his hands were wandering ever lower and driving her out of her senses with this dragging sensual curiosity and an almost painful need for the intimacy of his body where she suddenly knew she wanted him mercilessly, for she could never want another man after this.

'Don't wait,' she ordered between lips that felt stiff and swollen with needs beyond any words she had left.

'You're not ready for me yet,' he cautioned in a gravelly voice that made her feel even more urgent for whatever was to come.

'Damn it, Charles, if I were any more ready I'd burst into flames!'

'I like the sound of that,' he teased with some of his

old familiar lazy appreciation, belied as it was by the fierce burn of colour across his high cheekbones and the feral glitter in his burning blue gaze as he parted her now unbuttoned nightgown and pushed it down over her shoulders. 'How *risqué*,' he managed a little unsteadily as he paused to undo the beribboned bows among the frothy lace at each of her wrists; finally the insubstantial thing fell about her feet.

'I thought you'd like it,' she parried, resisting the urge to bring her hands up to protect her most feminine places from his very male gaze and watching it rove over her with lazy, unmistakable appreciation instead.

'I do, sweetheart, I most definitely do,' he replied and surprised her by stripping himself as openly as he had done her.

All the time he went about the task with fingers she thought enviably steady, he seemed to encourage her to feast her eyes on him just as he was feasting on her. It was so sensual, so open, so unexpectedly equal that her eyes grew heavy lidded and her tongue came out to lick suddenly dry lips and, instead of shying away with fear as she finally took in how powerfully aroused he actually was, she hoped she was making it as difficult to resist her allure as he was his emphatic masculinity. His manhood rose from his strongly muscled thighs in explicit demand and she found it oddly beautiful, the realisation coming over her in a moment of intense appreciation and arousal.

Maybe the gleam of feminine appreciation was obvious in her dark eyes, for he gave her a quick grin that reminded her of arrogant Captain Afforde, before his searingly hot blue eyes set that rake apart from her new husband. There was nothing carelessly guarded about this Charles Afforde, nothing deliberately held back and cynical, and she couldn't help but hold out her hands and smooth the satin-smooth skin, roughened by curls of dark gold hair on his powerfully muscled chest, with wonder.

'Charles,' she murmured as she stroked over his warm, very human skin with hands that wandered lower and yet lower, down over the hard packed muscles of his lean abdomen and even lower, until she held her breath and marvelled as he let her smooth the velvet hardness of his now even more awesomely aroused shaft, and she found it as wondrous under her questing fingers as she had under her voracious eyes.

'Roxanne,' he replied huskily, the rigid control he was forcing on himself beginning to show in the tension of iron-hard muscles as she let her other hand rove to explore his neat masculine buttocks and the mighty tension in his back, forcing himself to let her explore when she suspected he wanted to be inside her, possibly even more than she wanted him there. Only she didn't actually know the force and feel of a man inside her—no, not just any man, this man and only this man—yet could his need be any greater than hers? Probably not, but fairness made her acknowledge how awesome his control was, and how very far it outstripped her own.

'Yes,' she answered his demand with a whisper that seemed to fill the hushed room, blotting out the faint bubble of spitting sap burning from the fireplace as the seasoned applewood let out its steady heat, the whisper of a December wind outside the heavily curtained and shuttered windows and any noise the revellers might make below that was not held at bay by the mighty oak door of my lady's chamber.

'My Roxanne,' he asserted rather unsteadily, the very hint of a question in his gruff voice robbing it of the arrogance that once infuriated her so much.

'Yes,' she repeated unoriginally, but with a flush of fiery colour on her cheeks now and a challenge in her velvet-dark eyes that should inform him she wasn't going to suddenly shriek and run away in terror. 'Yes, yours; yes, your wife as of today; yes, I'm ready, and yes, I'll possibly expire of too much waiting if you don't hurry.'

Which seemed to do the trick, she decided in dazed appreciation as he launched himself at her, but even then he touched her heart by testing her earlier words and feeling for himself the moist, shameless heat between her legs, rendering them quite useless for their primary purpose of keeping her upright in the process. If she'd thought she was hot for his touch before, suddenly a raging need was roaring there, and she moaned and shifted to tell him even the intimate teasing of his long, strong fingers on her most secret feminine heart was not enough to slake this driving compulsion for more.

'Hurry!' she panted as she resisted his moves to walk her backwards to the bed and a more conventional coupling. 'No, I can't wait for that,' she ordered impatiently as she fought his restraining hands, prepared to climb up his heaving torso and drive them both demented with her inexperience rather than wait a second longer.

'It'll be too rough for a virgin,' he argued distractedly, but he must have been at the end of his self-control, too, for he shifted her so she came down on to his manhood, and at last she felt the smooth, hard heat of him enter her and gave a great purring moan of satisfaction.

'Oh, oh, Charles, oooh!' she praised and triumphed

all at the same time as she felt his mighty body tense and change to accommodate itself to her and to discipline himself enough so he could cradle her striving buttocks and restrain her as he felt her maidenhead beat against this hasty coupling.

Unwilling to wait while he played the perfect, gentlemanly lover, she confounded him by letting her legs fall just enough to breach that last, annoying barrier between them. Swallowing a cry at the sharp discomfort that was the end of her long wait for this night, she grinned into his eyes and experimentally flexed a set of muscles she hadn't known she had. Yes, she felt mightily stretched and just a little sore, but the hurt was fading already and it was all part of this glorious night, and there was no way she was going to let him treat her like spun glass just because he'd been annoyingly chivalrous and insisted they wait until their wedding night to do this at last.

'Oh, ooh, Roxanne!' he echoed, smiling impudently in reply as he thrust mightily within her to show her he was only allowing her to dictate anything about their first loving because he was a gentleman.

Her heart seeming to quiver in echo of her body as fire caught mercilessly once more. She leaned her forehead down to rest against his and watched his pupils flare and contract as she moved demandingly once more, suggestively wriggling her hips as if to remind him he was supposed to be the experienced one here. So he asserted himself by walking to the bed and manoeuvring her on to the high mattress under the splendid silk bedcover without yielding an iota of their intimate joining.

'Lie back,' he ordered, unclasping her clinging arms

from about his neck and spreading her very willing body against the velvet bedcover until she was lying with her arms over her head and her feminine core at the mercy of his full and dominant penetration, waiting on the explicit fire in his heated gaze.

Not that he showed her much mercy, she decided in a haze of sensual pleasure as he rubbed his palms appreciatively up her slenderly curved torso and spread them over her high and suddenly full and very aroused breasts and flexed them until she screamed with pleasure.

So next he bent to take one of her tightly budded nipples in his mouth, and the feel of it, the absolute pleasure of him inside her as he did so made her head thrash from side to side and soft little gasps urged him to rock that mighty body so they could climb even higher up this astonishing ascent to something, something beckoning and wonderful beyond words, she suddenly realised, as he abandoned her breast and took her begging, pouting mouth in an explicit, raw kiss and increased the pace of their striving bodies. Suddenly it didn't matter that she was splayed out under him, begging frantically in whatever ways she could for his absolute possession like a harem slave, this was all there was in life that really mattered, and whatever it was leading to, they were going there together. Abandoning any hint of subjection, she raised her knees and wrapped her long, limber legs about his waist, drawing him deeper, closer and faster into the now frantic rhythm driving them.

'Please, oh, please, Charles, I want everything now!' She wrenched her mouth from his to gasp a plea for him to tip her into this unknown glory that was suddenly so close she felt as if she could almost touch it. To end and yet never end this hot, stormy madness inside her as she strove with his driving, fabulous, oh-so-masculine body centred on hers toward a mystery she was desperate to solve.

'Soon, lover, very soon,' he promised before he took her mouth back to silence her, and his kiss was fire and a relentless, heavy beat of even deeper arousal as he thrust faster and deeper and she bucked under him, sensing that something glorious was coming, coming so close she could taste it. For a moment he rode her frantically, and she wondered if she'd ever achieve this beckoning wonder she'd somehow been promised, felt him convulse and hated him for not taking her with him, then at last there it was.

Or there she wasn't, rather. She was elsewhere, with him. She was him and he was her and they were more than themselves, outside here and now and at the very beat of life itself all at the same time. Great convulsions of glory and unutterable joy spasmed through her as he gasped and bowed and thrust into her, into them, again and again, and she felt his hot release even as her inner muscles worked round his shaft as if to hold them within this golden moment for ever, and him with it. Panting with exertion and feeling like singing or shouting with delight, she felt his weight rest full on her outstretched torso for glorious moments, and her arms came up in a loving reflex to hold on to the ecstasy they'd just given each other, even as he raised himself on his elbows and smiled down at her while he shook his head regretfully.

'I'm too heavy, my rosy Roxanne,' he murmured teasingly, even as his index finger outlined her chin and then her brow and down her nose to outline her lips, as if he couldn't get enough of her, the sight of her, or her scent or the touch of her soft skin under his questing finger.

She confounded him by opening her mouth and nibbling on that provoking digit, eyes watchful and ardent as she challenged him and shifted to show him she was quite happy between the softness of the mattress and the hardness of his fit, honed body.

'You didn't marry a properly shrinking young lady, I fear, Charles,' she teased huskily and hoped her half-lowered eyelids and invitingly pouted lips were enough to let him know she was very ready to do *that* again as soon as it might be possible.

'Well, that's good news, then,' he said conversationally and infuriated her by prising himself away from his bride, to stir the dying fire into new life and add a couple more logs to it before carefully replacing the fireguard.

'Not so far as I can see,' she complained and tensed for some hasty action as she refused to admit to herself that he looked like a fire-lit Greek god come down to earth from Olympus.

How could he be less eager to repeat that delightful seduction of each other's reeling senses and eager bodies than she was? Less caught up in the wondrous world he'd just created for them as lovers, then walked away from to attend to the everyday, even if it was to keep them both warm? She felt the burden of her love and his refusal to acknowledge he felt anything but desire and affection in return; after such exquisite pleasure, such transforming joy, she suddenly felt so lonely with her love for him.

Jumping out of bed and donning all her clothes before riding off into the night on wild young Adonis seemed a good idea all of a sudden, so she could put some distance between them as well and ride off the fury and ache of knowing that, yes, he wanted her as his bride and his lover, but not with the driven, helpless need she felt for him.

Yet she had to watch helplessly, because she couldn't trust her disobedient legs to even hold her up after that wondrously tender introduction to the joys of the marriage bed, and her new husband was striding about the room as easily as if he bedded formerly virgin wives every day of the week. Irrational anger and unwilling, merciless arousal at the very sight of him, so magnificent yet so separate, ground deep in her belly, even as she knew she was being unreasonable. Maybe he understood her better than she knew, for his expression was rueful as he eyed her warily, as if she might explode like an unpredictable firework any moment and he was judging which way to jump to get out of the way.

'I'd hate for us to argue so soon after you became my wife in *every* sense,' he asserted lazily as he strolled back to the bed and stood surveying her restless body and stormy eyes cockily, his manly grin as slow and appreciative and infuriating as he surely meant it to be. 'But, after that performance, I'll certainly never regret taking a dutiful little miss to my bed.'

'I'm *not* a dutiful little miss!' she almost shouted at him as she bounced up off the mattress and faced him on splayed knees with a militant frown and, she hastily realised, nothing else to dignify her protest with. She wanted him to be as shaken by that amazing consummation as she was, yet still his iron composure held and he shielded his most private thoughts from her.

'We certainly made very sure you're not a miss in any

sense of the word just now, my Roxanne,' he drawled and let his impudent gaze appreciate the effect her restless bouncing about had on her naked breasts, even as they betrayed her by visibly tightening and thrusting themselves at him in shameful argument with her brain, or most of it anyway, the part that wasn't as deeply in thrall to him as her wretched, disobedient body.

'And luckily I'd far rather have my wayward, headstrong wife than a pattern card of all the virtues any day,' he added, his eyes devouring her naked curves as she drew deep breaths to try to calm her temper and wondered whether to be furious or deeply complimented.

Whatever he needed to do to revive his passion for her had clearly been done, for there was no hiding his aroused state any more than she could conceal hers when neither of them had a stitch of clothing between them.

'Yes, you're quite right,' he observed as he took in her wide-eyed survey of his manly assets, and not even her simmering temper and this muddle of love and resentment and frustration fighting for supremacy inside her could overcome her appreciation. 'I'm clearly unable to keep my hands, or anything else of mine, off you for five minutes together, wife.'

'And fortunately for you it's mutual, or we'd have a reckoning for your insults right now instead of later,' she informed him as crossly as she could manage with a flush of excited anticipation burning on her cheeks and a gleam of wonder in her eyes as they roved over his body with admiration and avarice and a possession that he looked right back at her with interest. 'I believe the night is yet young, husband,' she murmured in what she hoped was a seductive husk that would remind him this was their wedding night, and therefore to be savoured and looked back on with joint and distinctly smug nostalgia during all the years they might have together.

And definitely not filed away among all the other nights he'd spent in other women's arms, she decided militantly, as she discovered much of her irrational fury was made up of jealousy. She reminded herself she had an advantage none of the others possessed: she was his wife and he'd promised to be faithful. All she had to do now was make sure he forgot the rest and stayed happy within that rash promise for the rest of their lives.

'I do believe you're right, your ladyship,' he drawled with a flattering intensity in his caressing gaze and stopped striding about the room displaying his manly attributes for her delectation and seduction, only to stand next to the bed and stare down at her instead.

Close to her, he was suddenly dangerous again, powerful and untamed and potent, and she swallowed a little nervously in deference to the maiden she'd been until such a short time ago. Then she recalled the wife and lover she now was and reached for the glorious reality of him and shamelessly plastered as much of her receptive body against his as she could physically manage.

'I'm always right,' she managed to assert, despite her tightening nipples and a shudder of pure delight he must be able to feel.

'So I'm content to let you believe, for now,' he murmured and surprised her by kneeling in front of her and pulling her across him so he would penetrate her only as her body adjusted itself to his rampant and eager shaft within her. It was gently compelling, urgently wanting on both their parts, but above all it felt deeply sensuous and caring as he fitted himself to her. 'Take it slowly, my darling, there's no hurry, and if we're to do this every night we must be gentle now, since it's all so new to you.'

'I don't care how it is, just so long as it is,' she admitted distractedly and felt his chuckle vibrate through her so intimately she wondered if it was possible for a woman to melt of pure desire and love.

'Well, I do,' he informed her with not altogether assumed sternness.

'Teach me then,' she responded crossly as he used his superior strength to gentle her frustrated striving and settle her into a dreamy, leisurely rhythm that none the less threatened to drive her slowly insane with passion and her absolute desire for more and more and yet more.

'Very well,' he murmured at last in reply to her demand. 'We've tried fast and furious, let's see how you like slow and sensuous and sweet.'

It was very slow and infinitely sweet as he showed her how the finest, most gentle of movements could drive a pair of lovers to the edge of insanity and then over it, into a satisfying and lengthy climax beyond even her wildest fantasies, now reality had so far exceeded any pale imitation of the truth she'd dreamt of before her wedding night.

And after that extravagant intimacy, that protracted loving introduction into the joys of the marriage bed, he watched her drift off into a sated, contented sleep and sighed regretfully before pulling the covers up round her and sliding out of her bed to resume his heavy silk robe and take one last, memorising, protracted look at his bride before he took himself off to his own chamber for the night.

Chapter Sixteen

A week later Roxanne wasn't quite so new to the delights of her husband's lovemaking, although he'd taught her more every night as promised, and she often wondered how any woman could ever be expected to actually sleep when there were such fiery glories to be experienced. All the same, she yawned over her luncheon, knowing full well that Stella and Lady Samphire, who'd driven over from Mulberry House where they were staying for now, were exchanging amused, indulgent looks across her weary head. Yet somehow she was struggling to feel as happy and content as such a well-pleasured new bride ought to. The urge to confide and even seek the counsel of more experienced ladies was strong, but she nobly resisted it.

Charles was an attentive husband, even during the day when there was little chance of anything more intimate between them than a lingering kiss, or a stolen embrace. He consulted her about estate matters and even took her advice when it didn't clash with his own views, and when it did they had a vigorous and enjoyable argument, and sometimes the day went her way and sometimes his. After simmering over his solution to a dilemma being favoured over her own this very morning, she'd stormed about the garden for at least half an hour before she forced herself to acknowledge he was right. Infuriating and inconsiderate of him though it might be, she couldn't hold it against him and would tell him so when he returned from the Home Farm.

Yes, Charles was a very good husband in so many ways, so why did she find it so disturbing, so distancing, that he'd never once spent the entire night with her? He always left her bed when she was asleep, so exhausted by his passionate lovemaking and her equally passionate reception of it that she couldn't stay awake to watch him go, however hard she tried. She'd done her best to tire him so much with her demands for the exquisite pleasure his body could give hers that he'd let go his defences and sleep in her arms for once, make himself as vulnerable to her as she seemed fated to be to him every single night. Yet fulfilment and weariness always defeated her and she'd never managed it.

No matter how many times they made love, no matter how many new ways he showed her for a man and a woman to couple and give each other glorious, heady pleasure doing so, he'd not slept with her. Not once. She sighed and regarded the beautifully cooked chicken and the warm, crusty bread roll spread with golden butter from Hollowhurst's own farm as if she despaired of them and not her guarded husband.

'Perhaps a rest would do you good this afternoon, Roxanne, my dear,' Lady Samphire suggested indulgently.

'Yes, indeed,' Stella said with a mischievous, knowing look that Roxanne shouldn't find irritating, but did so all the same. 'It'll never do if you fall asleep in your soup on your first bride visit tonight. There would be far too many ribald jokes over the port and brandy once the gentlemen were alone if you did that; poor Charles would be mortified.'

'Poor Charles, indeed! He'd be slapped on the back and congratulated on his startling vigour until he preened like a turkey-cock,' she replied irritably.

'Then I wonder at you for putting yourself up to make a fairground diversion of yourself, girl, when a few minutes of being sensible and actually sleeping when you seek your bed for once will prevent it,' Lady Samphire told her far less indulgently, and Roxanne thought ruefully that, if Charles ever lacked a defender in his besotted wife, he'd have one until she breathed her last breath in his grandmother.

'Quite right,' she conceded as she decided she'd probably be impatient with her herself as well today, if she didn't inhabit her own skin, so she smiled at the peppery old lady. 'I'll take myself off on that worthy errand as soon as you've told me what you're both intending to wear tonight, for I can't seem to relish my food today, however much Cook tries to tempt me.'

'Very well, then,' Lady Samphire observed with a sharp nod and bent a look on Stella that forbade her to comment on that curious fact.

* * *

'It's far too early to tell,' she warned her niece as soon as they were alone in the well-sprung carriage on their way back to Mulberry House.

'Of course it is, and I certainly had no intention of implying the dear girl could possibly be *enceinte* yet, they've only been married a week, after all,' Stella replied indignantly.

'The way they've be stealing off to their bed early every night to mate like a pair of lusty rabbits in the springtime, it'll be a miracle if she isn't before very long and you'd be a fool if you didn't suspect it. All the same, she don't need us watching her like hawks every time she pecks at her food or lies abed a little later than usual in the mornings. This is Charles we're talking about, after all, and anyone can see he's intent on seducing her whenever and wherever he gets the least chance to do so. Little wonder if the girl's at risk of becoming exhausted from his incessant attentions.'

'Lucky thing,' Stella said with a rueful look that admitted to her aunt she very much missed the joys of the marriage bed herself.

'Aye,' that lady agreed with a sigh, then shot her startled niece a militant glare. 'I may be old, Stella Lavender, but I ain't dead yet, even if I do have to rely on my memory to tell me Charles's grandfather at least had the good taste to lust after his wife when he recalled he had one.'

'If he'd had better taste, he'd never have left you alone long enough to risk another man noticing you were a neglected wife.'

'He knew I loved him too much to take comfort elsewhere, the rogue. I only pray Charles don't follow him in that as well as impudence and arrogance.'

Seeing a very genuine concern on her aunt's face, Stella considered such a notion for a moment and dismissed it with a decided shake of her head. 'Not he, Charles is more like you in character. He'll love once and always, and I think he's already done so, whether he admits it or not.'

'I truly hope you're right, but there's something holding him back from admitting it to himself or Roxanne, and it vexes me to know what. Anyone can see that girl's head over ears in love with the damn fool.'

Stella shrugged and was looking almost as troubled as her aunt when the subject of their anxiety breezed into their temporary sitting room before they'd hardly settled down for tea and a good worry, and he told them they looked like a couple of professional mourners at a wake.

'Cheek, my lad, that's all I ever hear from you,' his grandmama accused him stalwartly.

'Considering you'd very likely throw something at me if I informed you that you're the light of my life, Grandmama, cheek is my only option.'

'Don't waste your breath bothering me with such an untruth, when there's someone not so far off you should waste your cozening words on rather than me,' she said with enough seriousness in her brusque tone to make him frown.

'I'll not cozen my wife any more than I would you.'

'You're an idiot, boy,' the Dowager informed him wearily as she sighed deeply and looked her age for once, 'and likely to lose everything you hold most dear if you don't look into your heart and let someone else know what's rattling about in there for once.'

'Handing out advice, Grandmother?' he asked satirically. 'How very unusual of you.'

'No need to mock my natural wish to help those I love not to make a complete mess of their lives. I mean it, Charles, you risk far too much if you persist in refusing to do as I recommend.'

'So it's your wise counsel you're offering me and not royal commands for once, is it? That's a notable first, I must say.'

'I'm sorry I just told Stella you're a better man than your grandfather, because it's plain to me now you're as impervious to the finer feelings of those about you as he was. Well, go to the devil in your own way, then, and I wash my hands of the consequences, but disturb that poor girl of yours when she's finally getting some rest this afternoon instead of more of your rakish attentions, and I swear I'll swing for you.'

Saying which her ladyship swept from the room in a swirl of silk petticoats and indignation and marched off to pace her chamber out of sight and sound of the rest of her household.

'I'm not sure whether to follow her or stay and sympathise,' Stella said with a wry smile.

'Oh, stay, Stella mine. It seems I'm to avoid my lady's chamber when I get home *and* be at odds with my formidable grande dame, so stay and tell me I'm not quite as bad as I'm painted, before I sink any lower in my esteem and everyone else's.'

'You're well enough, but I wouldn't want you for a husband,' she told him bluntly.

'Just as well I never had the least inclination to stand

in a better man's shoes then,' he observed a little more seriously.

'Even if we weren't related, I wouldn't wed you, Charles. I value my serenity far too much.'

'Yet my wife seems happy enough,' he challenged, oddly stung by her implied criticism.

'Yes, but I made a love match, Cousin, so "happy enough" wouldn't offer the least temptation for me to risk my heart and peace of mind, even if either of us wanted me to.'

'Well, it does very well for me,' he defended himself dourly and strode out of the room without any of his usual meticulous courtesies and, instead of speeding home to his bride as he'd intended, rode off to inspect a faulty roof he'd meant to put off seeing until Roxanne was with him.

He was quite capable of running an even larger estate than this alone, after commanding a man of war for the last three years of his naval career, then his own squadron. And if Roxanne wasn't happy with their bargain she should tell him so, instead of leaving Stella and his grandmother to decide there was something amiss.

Charles brooded over his wife and his acres all the way to Deevers Farm and had to force himself to examine the gables and hips in the minute detail Deever insisted on when he was there.

It wasn't as if he was a domestic tyrant or careless of his wife's happiness, he assured himself as he finally made the journey home through the fading daylight of the December afternoon. He was a considerate husband who applied himself enthusiastically to satisfying her every desire, and he'd even ceded her some of his responsibilities. That was more of a concession than she knew, when he'd commanded a ship's company for more years than he cared to remember. Perhaps that was the problem, he decided with a sigh. He was used to command, and it was a solitary business. No matter how fine his lieutenants and warrant officers, a naval captain was isolated by the respect he must command if his ship was to be an effective weapon of war.

Yet he was at peace now and intent on building a new life, so *had* he set Roxanne at too great a distance? And if he went on doing so, might it prove dangerous or even disastrous? 'Yes' and 'perhaps' seemed to be the correct answers to those uncomfortable questions, but she wasn't the one complaining, so perhaps he'd not been wrong to give her room to live a life of her own, after all. They'd only been wed a week, every night of which he'd spent in her bed, proving to both of them she meant more to him than any other woman he'd ever encountered, in bed or out of it.

Even so, Roxanne had spent most of her adult life at Hollowhurst as companion and lieutenant to her great-uncle, then had taken Davy Courland's place while he evaded his responsibilities. She probably didn't know she was more crucial to him than any other female could be. She was four and twenty, but did that mean she was up to snuff any more than some little débutante, pitchforked from schoolroom to ballroom between one day and the next?

One Season in London when she was far too young to fit her exotic looks or passionate temperament had done nothing to tell her what power she might have over a man's imagination and ardour. His fists clenched at the thought of her discovering she could enthral other men with enchantress's eyes and a responsive, tactile body, when it had been formed for their mutual delight. But could any woman be so ignorant of her own charms and remain completely safe in mixed company?

Probably not, and then there were the wolves. More unscrupulous rakes than he'd ever been, waiting, hoping that he'd get her with child before the honeymoon was hardly over, so they could pounce while he complacently turned his back on his wife and preened himself on his own potency. His frown became a glower as he tried to get a vision of Roxanne being seduced by one of the scum who preyed on young society wives out of his mind. He'd kill the carrion who dared, then put a watch on his wife every waking hour of the day, while he kept her so occupied at night that she'd lack the energy to stray, even if he left her any will for it.

His expression was still formidable when he returned home with bare minutes to get bathed and dressed for a night of mild dissipation at the Longboroughs. Even so, he was ready to offer Roxanne his arm as they met at the top of the stairs like models for a marriage portrait. She was in her beautiful ivory-velvet bridal gown, as she was to be the guest of honour tonight as befitted any new bride in her first month of marriage, and he was tricked out like a dandy in his dark blue coat, gold-embroidered ivory-silk waistcoat and a cravat so exquisitely tied that young Longborough would probably long to plunge a knife in his back even more ardently than ever.

'Good,' his grandmother pronounced when she greeted them on entering the Longboroughs' drawing room, 'I despise this shabby-genteel fashion of gentlemen dining out in their riding breeches, or even worse, those new-fangled trousers instead of decent knee-breeches and silk stockings. I'd not put up with having the stables or barracks brought into my house, so why should any other respectable woman endure such cavalier treatment?'

'And it does show off a finely turned, gentlemanly leg so beautifully, don't you think?' Stella added with apparent innocence.

Charles was relieved to see a wicked smile crack through Roxanne's too-correct façade and reveal the woman he liked. Yes, the woman he liked so much. He raised one eyebrow at her in question, doing what Charles Afforde never did and seeking reassurance that perhaps he wasn't so hard to look upon, after all. She'd changed him, his passionate, headstrong bride, and he'd been more than ready to change after all, hadn't he?

'Yet one wonders what the gentlemen would think if we ladies went about flaunting our nether limbs as blatantly as they do?' Roxanne speculated mischievously, apparently not needing any more answer than the green glint he was sure must now be visible in his eyes.

How very satisfying that she only had to suggest such a fashion to have Charles looking as if he'd rather lock her in a cupboard than let any other man see her thus, Roxanne decided with a rather feline smile. The idea of another man seeing her dressed so made her shudder, but that was neither here nor there. Charles was jealous at the idea of other men leering at her legs and anything else on display in such a scandalous form of dress, and that was more than good enough for her.

There was no reason for him to know it, she decided vengefully, for in general he was altogether too sure of her fascination with him. He might own her body and soul in the eyes of the law, but there had to be some compensation for that state of wifely slavery, or there'd be no more wives willing to tumble into matrimony at the drop of the right man's handkerchief. No, she was his wife, and that counted. She raised her chin and met his eyes with pride and just a hint of desire in her own. If she ever managed to look on him with anything less, it would mean she was either very ill indeed, or more probably dead, but he didn't have to know that.

'Come and meet my sister and her husband, my dear Lady Afforde, if your husband can spare you, of course?' Mrs Longborough interrupted with an indulgent smile for what she imagined were a pair of true lovers.

'Oh, I'm quite sure he can,' Roxanne muttered darkly and went off to pretend to be delighted to meet Mr and Mrs Risborne, when she really wanted to have a furious, purging argument with her husband, largely because he was as handsomely self-sufficient as ever.

It went on in the same way for yet another week, this half-happy, half-terrifying state where Roxanne felt suspended between joy and the threat of something dangerous underneath the fragile surface of their marriage. Meanwhile, Christmas was almost on them, and she'd never felt less full of joyful anticipation of Christ's birth. Guilty at her lack of appropriate feeling for a season she'd always loved, she refused the carriage when Mereson offered it upon seeing her bundled up in a warm cloak, thick gloves and her stoutest boots against the gloomy cold of a day that threatened anything the elements might think up in their worst moods.

'No, a walk will do me good, and I only intend to

visit Mrs Lavender and her ladyship, Mereson. I dare say I'll be back before anyone misses me.'

'Sir Charles won't like it, Miss Roxanne; it looks as if it might snow.'

'I'm quite capable of walking little more than a mile, even if it were blowing a gale and snowing a blizzard, Mereson, and I'll thank you and my husband to remember it,' she snapped, giving up on getting in the mood for the season as she swept out of the house and strode toward Mulberry House as if her life depended on getting there at top speed.

'I'm so glad to see you, Roxanne,' Stella said gamely when her stormy-looking visitor strode into the room and dared her to comment on her flushed cheeks and generally ruffled state.

'I thought I might as well come and see what her ladyship wanted to discuss so urgently.'

'I don't think it was urgent, which is just as well considering Great-Aunt Augusta's dashed off to Westmeade to see Caro Besford. Caro and Rob finally have a son at last, Roxanne, isn't it wonderful?'

'Yes, indeed,' Roxanne agreed, but it didn't need her friend's over-cheerful smile and too bright eyes to tell her that accompanying her great-aunt would have been painful for Stella, now that she would never be a mother after losing the husband she obviously still loved very deeply. 'I'm so very glad.'

'So am I, truly, Roxanne, so please don't think I envy them. I do, of course, but not enough to begrudge them a moment of their joy. Apparently Caro sailed through her labour this time, and Rob's having trouble persuading her to rest, so I'll go tomorrow and spread our visits out.'

'I'll go the next day if it'll help, and Charles can escort me. If he's to be the child's godfather, he might as well start as he means to go on.'

'Famous, although if Great-Aunt Augusta doesn't set out early this afternoon she'll be staying there, for Simkins informs me it's sure to snow by nightfall.'

'So Mereson insists as well, and I suppose two butlers can't be wrong,' Roxanne answered, eyeing the heavy clouds.

'Anyway, I'm glad to be spared a walk to the Castle with your letter.'

'Oh, what letter's that?'

'Now where did I put it? Sorry, Roxanne, but my mother sent me one of her epistles this morning and I forget where I put the rest now.'

'Never mind,' Roxanne murmured, trying not to look as impatient as she felt, for nothing about her current state of unrest was Stella's fault.

'Ah, here it is. It looks as if it had quite a journey to get this far and I can only suppose it got lost somehow between here and the Castle since Simkins found it in with a box of ornaments in the lumber room nobody thought to unpack until today. I dare say it was slipped in there as you all left the Castle and someone forgot all about it in the excitement, for one or two of the maids are silly enough to forget their own names at times. Anyway, I thought you'd want to have it as soon as possible now it's finally found.'

'Thank you,' Roxanne managed as she recognised her brother's impatient scrawl on its best behaviour long enough to inscribe her former direction. 'It's from my brother and I'd dearly like to read it.'

'Considering he's your only brother and thousands of miles away, I'd be surprised if you didn't. Hurry home first, though, before this fabled snow can make it hard work for you, or Charles comes looking for you.'

'You're a good friend, Stella,' Roxanne told her sincerely, giving her a fierce hug before she turned face about and marched out again.

Chapter Seventeen

There was no chance of waiting until she was home to read Davy's much-delayed letter, and it wasn't even raining yet, let alone snowing, so perhaps the combined wisdom of Mereson and Simkins would be proved wrong for once. Undoing the seal with only just enough patience to make sure she didn't tear the paper, Roxanne hungrily read her brother's letter as she walked. It began with news that wasn't really news any more. He was married and delighted with his bride, who seemed to combine such beauty, charm and wit as to make her an almost impossible paragon, except Davy was obviously fathoms deep in love with his Philomena.

Luckily Roxanne allowed for that and was glad her brother had found such happiness. At the time she'd been hurt he'd sell Hollowhurst without consulting her, but it had brought Charles back into her life, so how could she wish it any other way? Except to have Davy and his wife living in the next county instead of half a world away, of course. Her steps slowed as she read her brother's account of the sale of his estates and his marriage.

It sounded as if Charles had been in New England much longer than she'd thought. Long enough for lawyers and bankers to exchange all that was needed to be exchanged, in fact. Six whole months, and he'd never told her much about even a week of it. Fool that she was, she hadn't taken in the fact that the sale of such a large estate must be a long and complex business, even between friends. Her heartbeat stalled, then raced as something about that sale struck her as out of kilter, a warning that came not a moment too soon when she deciphered the next few lines.

Now she halted at the side of the road and stared at Davy's letter as he told a truth that leeched away her every last hope of happiness. 'Don't hate me for selling my birthright, Roxie,' her brother pleaded as she read his words again and wished fervently her eyes had deceived her the first time.

'There's no man on earth I'd sell Hollowhurst to other than Charles Afforde. You ought to be heiress to everything in England that only held me back, yet I couldn't sign it over to you. Joanna and Maria would have been hurt and furious, and you *are* a woman, after all. Charles will be a better master there than I could ever be, but that wasn't the reason I relented and sold it to him.'

Roxanne gasped and turned ferocious eyes to the leaden skies, blinking furiously as she refused to cry but was tempted to scream and curse and rend her clothes because there was such pain raging inside her, desperate for an outlet. Instead, she forced herself to read on.

'I sold Hollowhurst to Charles Afforde because I

knew you wanted him more than any other man on earth. You're four and twenty now, Roxie, so please consider his offer sensibly and don't dismiss it out of hand. I made it a condition of sale that he propose marriage to you within three months of taking possession, so I know he'll do it soon. Don't spurn the chance of a happy marriage with him just because we arranged it between us. When he comes to know you, he'll love you, my dear sister, and it need be no more complicated than that.

'Forgive me, little sister, and wish me happy? Charles is the only man you ever showed any interest in marrying, so please do so, love, or I'll be haunted by regret for the rest of our lives.'

Forgive him—her wretched, conniving, managing, wrong-headed fool of a brother? How could she ever forgive him? Or Charles Afforde—her snakelike, worm of a husband, the man who'd promised to love and cherish her for the rest of his days, probably with his fingers firmly crossed behind his back? Oh, no, she'd never forgive either of them!

Charles finally appeared an hour later, looking so cold and weary that a concerned wife would have offered him hot punch and waited until he'd warmed himself with a bath in front of his dressing-room fire before she confronted him with his sins. Except that now nothing was as it had been just this morning. Her whole marriage was a fiction, so she'd no intention of playing the part he and Davy had scripted for her any longer. Seeing that she made no move to offer comfort or accept the kiss he might have placed on her wifely cheek with the least encouragement, he stood back and eyed her with that look of satirical interrogation she'd so recently found irresistible.

Refusing to look at him directly, Roxanne silently handed him her brother's letter and watched him register just what it revealed. Pain should be doubling her up, desolation robbing the colour out of her life, but just now she was too numb to hurt, too dazed to see anything as he bent his head but the dark gold hair that curled despite everything he could do to stop it, the sailor's lines about eyes more used to watching vast horizons than one perfectly discernible woman. Letting herself see him again, but feeling as if there was an invisible wall between them that might never be breached, she noted that the startling blue of his eyes looked as unique as ever, and she knew perfectly well that under his neatly masculine tailoring there was a magnificently masculine body.

Yes, Charles Afforde looked much the same as he always did, so why was her whole life tumbling round her as all she knew became untrue? Not a wild fiction, not even that. Just a small lie he'd allowed her to believe, probably out of kindness. A small but so important a lie, the one that had allowed her hopes and dreams instead of arrangements. The one that made a distortion of everything she'd ever wanted from this man.

'It's not what you think,' he told her gruffly, as if, just because he said so, Davy's words were unimportant.

'It's exactly what I think,' she assured him coldly, and that chill seemed to bite into her very bones now. 'At least David has enough honour left to tell me the truth.'

'You doubt my honour, madam?' he demanded as

if she'd accused him of the most heinous crime in the calendar.

'Oh, no, for it led you to cozen a superannuated old maid into thinking you wed her for the joy of it, didn't it? How could I doubt the *honour* behind such a noble action, Sir Charles?'

'Be damned to that,' he swore, running the hand not holding her brother's letter like a scroll of that precious honour through his hair and wreaking even more havoc with his fashionable Brutus haircut. 'Do you think I make love to you night after night because it's my *duty*, woman? You must be out of your wits if you think I've made it my pleasure and yours to seduce you in and out of our marriage bed, just because we're wed and making do with one another.'

'I suppose finding you can enjoy rather than endure bedding me must have been a pleasant surprise when you wed me to order.'

'Then you suppose wrongly.'

'Ah, you found it unpleasant, then? What a fine actor the London stage lost in you when you were born in a lady's chamber and not an actress's.'

'If I wanted to wed for convenience, there were heiresses enough, and land and fine houses to go with them. There was no need for me to wed a sharp-tongued virago to gain what I could buy easily enough.'

'Then why the devil *did* you marry me?' she burst out with the question she'd managed to keep inside for so long.

'Because I wanted to, because I wanted *you*,' he rasped, as if it cost him dearly to admit even that much.

Not because he secretly loves you then, Roxanne,

she acknowledged with a wince of pain he seemed to see, for he held out a hand as if appealing to her not to probe this wound any deeper.

'Because of my childish infatuation with you?' she asked relentlessly.

'No, not that, it was never about that. I wanted you from the moment I set eyes on you again, and you certainly weren't suffering from hero worship then. In fact, I began to wonder if I'd ever persuade you to marry me. But make no mistake, Roxanne, I wanted you mercilessly the instant you appeared out of the shadows that dusky night and, God help me, I still do.'

'My turn to be flattered,' she returned, cold to her very toes with the conviction that all she'd ever been to him was a warm body in his bed, wife or no.

'There's clearly no reasoning with you now; we'll discuss this once you're rational again.'

'No, we won't!' she shouted furiously as he refused to even take this terrible misery tearing at her seriously. 'I won't be soothed and petted into resuming the role of besotted wife and mistress to you, Sir Charles. Take yourself back to London where your dubious talents will be appreciated, and while you're at it, please take a woman into your keeping who *knows* she's only there to serve your more animal needs, for I want no more of them.'

At that, she turned to march out of the room and slam the door behind her, but he was too quick for her. Before she could head for the door, he grabbed her by the waist and spun her round to face him. Never before had she seen him so furious, his eyes hard and merciless as they bored down into hers, as if he could see into her soul and didn't like anything there.

'Do you not, Roxanne?' he snarled as if he'd been well beyond the end of his civilised tether even before she provoked him to dangerous fury. 'Now I beg to differ, Lady Afforde. I'd wager Hollowhurst Castle and all its lands and demesnes that you adore fulfilling my needs, especially the "more animal" ones. In fact, you'll cry out for them until you're hoarse before you leave this room.'

'I'd rather die.'

'No doubt,' he grated and seemed to find that silly little lie the last goad to lose hold on whatever restraint had held him back every other time they'd made love.

No, not love, she reminded herself sadly, even as his mouth ground down on hers in a savage demand and his powerful body pinned her against the oak-panelled wall with little consideration for her slighter frame and relative inexperience. They'd never made love and they weren't about to now, but lust, oh, yes, now *that* they were good at.

His hands were everywhere and she wondered ludicrously if he'd suddenly grown an extra pair, then she took in the way her ridiculous, disobedient body was writhing against the smooth old oak to assist his plundering and might have despaired if she wasn't beyond it. She heard the fine wool of her morning gown rip like rotten gauze under his impatience, listened to a curse that should have made her blush to her very ears when he encountered the petticoats she wore against the winter chill. If only she'd donned a sensible spencer instead of the voluminous shawl that was to have kept her warm, she might have had time to come to her right senses while he tore through that, but the fine Kashmir wool just slipped away and he reached his first target before she had time to even shiver at the loss of its warmth.

His large hands cupped her breasts emphatically, nothing coaxing or worshipping about his touch today. There was just lust, stark and searing hot in his examining eyes as he observed them rising high and rounded in his kneading, assessing hands. They shamed her by peaking and thrusting towards the rough seduction he'd threatened to strip her of her dignity with, or did they? Perhaps not, because by responding to him so eagerly, so blindly, wasn't she seducing herself and reducing his threats to humiliate her?

Perhaps, she answered herself, then decided she didn't care, as he concluded that part of her had been seared by whatever white-hot passion drove him long enough. Holding her against the now body-warmed panelling by her hips, he knelt at her feet, eyes lancing into hers with a terse demand she stay where she was. He positioned her carefully, as if watching her in thrall to this wild seduction pleased him nearly as much as the prospect of taking everything she had to offer, and perhaps a little more.

He used his thumbs to urge her legs apart, to reveal the heat and scent of a thoroughly roused woman with exploring hands as he drew them mercilessly upwards. Then, shockingly, he bent his head and licked and suckled and thrust his tongue into her most intimate centre until she forgot herself enough to let out a small, gasping scream that she muffled behind a hand that shook, but for the life of her she couldn't find the strength to reach down and push him away. He looked up with triumph and possession and need openly revealed in his wolfish smile and went back to demolishing every barrier, even a few she hadn't known she had.

He used a wicked, exploring finger to test her arousal once more, then followed it with too much knowledge of exactly where she needed pressure and where tantalising would do better. His mouth on her once more, he must have felt her shiver on the very edge of losing control. Again he lifted his head away and this time had the effrontery to raise one eyebrow at her as if they were engaged in trivial small talk.

It took a mighty effort, but she bit her lip and refused to plead as he'd promised she would. He grinned as if happy to push her even further and this time his tongue was less persuasive and more demanding and she no longer shivered lightly, but began to shake with racking shudders as she held back from the agonisingly wondrous edge of bliss with such an effort she wondered she was still conscious. Then one last butt of his golden head against the dark curls at the very centre of her and she screamed, she actually screamed with the power of her climax and a small part of her heard the pleas he'd promised she'd cry out leave her lips and despaired, even as the rest of her was racked with such pleasure that she couldn't have cared less about those betraying demands if she tried.

Maybe afterwards she'd have felt humiliated and terribly lonely, if he hadn't surged to his feet and joined with her as if driven by a lot more than revenge, just as a last powerful spasm of pleasure nearly rocked her off her feet. He forgot himself, just as she'd done, and took his wife in a heated, driven rush of need against the wall of her boudoir, in broad daylight. He forgot he was a gentleman, forgot he was anything but a man driven half-mad with wanting her any way he could get her. Amazingly, wild shudders of completion rocked through her irresistibly again, just as he gave a great wrenching cry and drove into her with deep, powerful surges of extreme pleasure, and his thrusts took them both to the peak of satisfaction and beyond.

For a long, precious moment all was quiet in the room, as if the labour of their breathing and lingering shivers of an ecstasy neither could resist feeling would keep everything else at bay. Her breath sobbed between lips that felt as if they might never speak sense again. Maybe in a moment she'd have to think, but now she put her energy into just breathing as she revelled in the undeniable. She'd done just as he said she would and begged, but he'd proven he couldn't keep himself separate and cynical from her while she did so. Yes, maybe he'd won on a technicality, but it wasn't outright victory, and hope was running strong in her. Such a glorious, unarguable tide of it that she had trouble concealing it from the stubborn, infuriating wretch.

'I beg your pardon,' he said stiffly when he finally seemed to notice he was still pinning her against the wall, the weight of his body still hard against and inside her softer one, and she wondered for a ridiculous moment if she bore the imprint of finely carved linen-fold panelling on her bottom.

'Don't,' she protested as he began to ease away from her, hating the chill of reality that was threatening now all the heat and sensual clamour were fading, along with some of her certainty that he felt far more for her than he ever could for a convenient wife.

'That was unforgivable,' he muttered as he pushed himself away and looked as if he was the one who'd just lost their sensual battle instead of her. 'I threw myself at you like a rutting bull, and I dare say I've hurt you.'

'No, you didn't hurt me,' she comforted him, even while her mind reeled at what they'd done. She felt as if she'd just become his lover or his mistress as well as his wife, but, in that case, why did it seem so wonderful? 'Nothing you did caused me pain.'

'But I've caused you more than enough anguish since I came here, haven't I, Roxanne?' he asked bitterly, setting himself to rights as best he could while he eyed her state of dishabille as if he dared not come near enough to help her attempts at tidying herself in case they seduced each other all over again.

It really was quite flattering to be considered irresistible by a man who'd flirted outrageously with some of the most beautiful women in Europe and beyond. He'd flirted and perhaps more with them, but, she reminded herself rather smugly, he'd wed her and then he'd made love to her as if driven to seduce her into thrall to him. Not that there was any need, when she was about as resistant to his charms as most of her sex not otherwise enchanted.

'My life has certainly changed since you came to Hollowhurst,' she admitted warily, 'but who's to say change is a bad thing.'

'I walked into your life, took your home and your occupation from you, and then manipulated your situation to suit my own convenience.'

'Oh, dear, so you did,' she agreed, without feeling in the least bit sorry that he'd done just that all of a sudden. 'Now whatever can I do to devise sufficient punishment for your perfidy, Sir Charles?'

'The dungeons, d'you think?' he mused, catching her

lighter mood as if he couldn't resist it, despite the fierce argument that sparked their stormy loving, and his and Davy's diabolical plot.

'Not nearly severe enough, considering they're now the wine cellars, and you'd probably enjoy yourself far too much down there. No, instead of so light a punishment, you're tasked to ride out to the very spot where we had our encounter on the beach that day and not to come back until you've sat out there in the cold and seriously considered the subject of marriages of convenience and how you truly feel about your wife.'

'Now that really is severe,' he joked, but she could see in his eyes that he knew how serious a quest she'd set him.

'I need you to carry it out, though, Charles, and not to come back until you've fought your demons,' she said lightly enough, but she let her eyes speak for her and hoped they were as steady as her conviction that love ran like a fierce undertow under their every word and action together since their wedding day and perhaps before. 'As I waited so very long for you, the least you can do for me now is to give me honesty.'

'I gave you that when I asked you to marry me,' he told her flatly, but this time she did what she'd just hoped he would and searched his gaze for a deeper truth.

Yes, it was there: a spark of doubt, a hint of uncertainty and the slightest suspicion of what looked like dread. For the latter she might well flay him with her sharp tongue now and again for the rest of their lives, but for the rest she made herself turn to look out of the window in case she weakened and just assured him her love would be enough for both of them.

'It'll be black dark by five,' she warned as if he hadn't spoken.

'I hate a nagging woman,' he muttered, but he impatiently ran his hands through his disordered hair and restored it to something close to normality for a man who'd just weathered a hurricane and stalked to the door, turning back to say, 'I'll probably be out later than five, so don't send half the neighbourhood to find me and see what a fool marriage has made of me, will you, wife?'

'Not if you wouldn't like it, dear,' she said in such a meek and mousy voice that he simply glared at her and frowned all the harder.

'Vixen,' he bit out and marched through the door before slamming it behind him, as if he needed that small release of frustration.

'Idiot,' she said fondly and set about the task of making herself fit to be seen again without letting her household guess what their master and mistress had been about.

She'd have to hide her ruined gown and smuggle it to the ragman herself next time he came. Time to worry about that when the time came, for now she'd have enough trouble convincing Tabby it was quite normal to change her attire halfway through the day, from the skin up, without the help of her maid, and she must bathe as best she could, too. Tabby might suspect what they'd been about for the last however long, but Roxanne refused to announce her enthralment to her husband if Charles was bull-headed enough to carry on insisting they shared a marriage of pure convenience.

Only half an hour ago she'd have turned on anyone who suggested her hope of a happy and fulfilled life at her husband's side were recoverable and snarled out a bitter denial. Yet her husband had just taken her as if she were an equally wild lover he'd dreamt of for many long months at sea, and now they had all those accumulated weeks of desperate ardour to slake on each other's desperate bodies. He'd just treated her like his whore instead of his wife, and contrarily his uncontrolled need of her had given her back hope. If the risk paid off, these half-wonderful, half-terrible weeks since their marriage would end and their real marriage begin. Of course if it didn't, she'd be far worse off than before, and truly trapped inside an arranged marriage.

Chapter Eighteen

Charles cursed all women and his wife in particular for at least the first mile of his solitary gallop to the beach. Then he added the other half of humanity to the mix when he thought of Davy Courland's ridiculous letter, and that occupied another two or three miles. At this rate he'd be in Rye or even Brighton by nightfall, and certainly not back at Hollowhurst where he wanted to be, but he checked Thor when they finally reached the shore, and he could spread a rug over the gelding's sweating sides and brood over dull, cloud-mirroring, grey-brown waves all the way to the horizon.

She'd been quite right to send him here to contemplate his sins, he decided grimly at last, not yet ready to forgive Roxanne for being Roxanne and not letting him hide behind the conventions and cowardly evasions any longer. The English Channel was as familiar and yet as resistant to any human influence as it always had been. Ever changing and at the same time unchangeable, and as much beyond the orders and purposes of a mere captain or even a commodore as ever. *And I'm still standing here, busily avoiding the conundrum my wife has set me,* he decided with a wry grin at the unresponsive waves.

Of course he could just turn about and go home, admit he loved her without telling her the rest and perhaps save his marriage, because he knew very well now that he did love her. He'd discovered it when he read that damning, infernally interfering letter of Davy's and thought it made an end to everything. The end of their marriage, of seducing Roxanne to their mutual pleasure night after night for the rest of their lives. Of the family they might have…Oh, just of everything that suddenly mattered to him so vitally. So why not just admit it and nothing more and hope their lives would go back to normal, to the very pleasant everyday they'd established between them these last three weeks of marriage?

Because she deserved more, he concluded with a heavy sigh and wondered if telling his story would produce the same result if he went back to Hollowhurst and told her he didn't love her after all and probably never would. Ah well, that would be a huge lie now he'd found out he needed her with him to make every breath he took worth taking, so if the truth produced the same result as an untruth, why not hand her that lie and watch all her hopes and dreams vanish into nothing? Because she'd see through it, he decided grimly, categorising himself as a coward for knowing that if he thought he could get away with it, he would indeed lie to his lady, his lover, in the hope a falsehood might wriggle him off the hook he richly deserved to hang himself on.

And how the *devil* had he been idiot enough to let himself fall in love with her? He'd promised himself he'd never do such a stupid thing after watching his friend Rob fall into the trap of loving a wife he'd sworn never to love or bed. Then, even with that stark example of husbandly lunacy in front of him, *he'd* wed Roxanne Courland and been ass enough to think he could emerge heart-whole from *his* marriage bed, even with her in it. Was any fool on earth as great a want-wit as Charles Afforde proved to be by thinking he could marry a woman like Roxanne and keep himself aloof?

Probably not, and so now he'd have to pay for his folly by confessing exactly what, and who, he really was. Little point putting it off, he thought gloomily. Testing his fate would be bad enough if he did it before all the reasons not to occurred to him; leave himself room to think, and he would probably ride off to one of the Cinque Ports after all and drink himself into a stupor just in case he could get away with being a coward again. Who'd have thought Charles Afforde, rake and cynic, would contemplate drinking himself into oblivion to escape telling his own wife what lay behind his bravado?

'Come on then, old fellow,' he murmured to his fidgeting horse as he turned his back on the rapidly calming sea at last. 'Let's get you back to your stable and arrange some comfort for you at least tonight.'

By the time he guided the weary beast back into the stable-yard it was pitch dark, and Charles could taste snow on the dying wind. As he rode, the whole of nature had seemed to fall silent around them in either awe or dread of what was to come. Now he thought about it, there had been a curiously yellow tinge to the leaden sky as it faded into dusk over the sea, but he'd been too occupied with his own thoughts at the time to notice, when getting home safely to Roxanne was suddenly more important than anything else in the world. She would see to fetching in firewood and distributing food to the needy before it was too late, and Charles thanked his stars for the wonderful wife he'd gained undeservingly. If he got this right, he'd have a wife at his back any man must envy him for the rest of their lives: a wife of rare beauty combined with her extraordinary strength of character and a unique mind.

Not that he ought to leave out her incredible body, he decided, as he contemplated all the other benefits of having married Roxanne with a wolfish grin while he saw to his horse himself and sent the stable-lads back to their wood chopping and water carrying. No, the endless exhilaration of wanting his wife and being wanted passionately back for the rest of their joint lives couldn't be underestimated, and he promised himself that from now on he never would fail to thank God for her every day.

Roxanne was upstairs, doing her best to reassure the housekeeper that the Castle could now withstand a siege from the weather as stalwartly as it repelled enemies hundreds of years ago. Even so, she couldn't resist looking out of the window so she could peer helplessly into the snow-blinding darkness outside and worry about her husband. He'd survived battles and terrible storms at sea, for goodness' sake, so why was she struggling with this sudden terror that he'd take a tumble from his horse and lie unconscious and in acute danger under a suffocating blanket of falling snow until morning? Common sense informed her he was perfectly safe, but that didn't stop her being furious with herself for sending him out into the early darkness of a December afternoon to consider his true feelings in the first place.

'And then there's all the pensioners, your ladyship,' the housekeeper carried on fretting as Roxanne listened with only half an ear. 'There wasn't time to fetch them all in from the more outlying cottages.'

'Then we'll have to rely on their families and neighbours to take care of them,' she pointed out firmly, as if all her attention was on the subject. 'It's just as well Sir Charles insisted on removing Mrs Bletter from her tumbledown old shack to one of the almshouses, is it not? She lived miles from anyone and would certainly be cold and comfortless if she'd stayed where she was.'

'I hope nobody expects thanks for that mercy, my lady. A more cross-grained, awkward old biddy than Dame Bletter you'd go a long way to discover, if you were silly enough to want to in the first place.'

'Yes, I dare say Sir Charles exerted all his famous charm to get her to move, but at least he put it to good use and we're spared worrying about her.'

'Roxanne! Roxanne, where the devil are you?' the masculine voice she'd been waiting so anxiously to hear again bellowed from somewhere close by and she felt a silly snap of annoyance at him that might disguise her huge relief from the suddenly amused housekeeper.

'As if you'd be doing anything other than setting the household in order at a time like this, Miss Roxanne,' Mrs Linstock said with an indulgent smile for the follies of gentlemen and her new employer in particular, who clearly hadn't been restricting his fabled charm to Dame Bletter.

'Here!' she went to the door and called before he

roused the household, who were much better occupied with the tasks she'd set them.

'Thank heaven—I thought I'd never find you.'

'Then you didn't look very hard,' she told him repressively and went back into the housekeeper's room to ask if there was anything else left for them to worry about before asking Cook and her minions to prepare dinner.

'Nothing at all, my lady, so I'll go down to the kitchens and ask her to do so now, shall I, your ladyship?' Mrs Linstock replied rather disobligingly, for Roxanne was suddenly very nervous indeed about what Charles had decided on what must have been a freezing cold beach and an unpleasant ride through the gathering gloom and the start of a snowstorm.

'Yes, indeed,' she just had time to agree before her husband's patience ran out and he grabbed her hand to tow her gently towards his personal sitting room, so at least it wasn't the scene of her most recent demonstration that she found him irresistible.

'Hadn't you better change and get warm, Charles?' she said hopefully.

'No, I've more important things on my mind, although thank you for the fire in my rooms,' he observed as he finally tugged her in through the door and eyed the cosy intimacy of it. 'It's just the place for a weary man to warm himself after a strenuous afternoon.'

'I had a strenuous time of it as well, you know.'

'I could see that, but I don't think you sent me off into the teeth of a blizzard to think about organising logs and bread for our pensioners.'

'That's true,' she managed meekly, wondering if she'd known what she was doing when she suggested he go and think about their lives together. He seemed to have concluded he needed to be a benevolent dictator and she didn't relish feeling like a rating under Commodore Afforde's command.

'Come and enjoy it with me, Rosie,' he demanded, using their still-joined hands to tug her down on to the thick Persian rug in front of the fire and she plumped down beside him as if her legs had suddenly become boneless.

For a long, precious moment he just held her, one strong arm hugging her close as warmth seeped into them both from the mesmerising flames, and some of the strung tension drained out of her.

'I want to tell you a story,' he began, and she wriggled restlessly. 'Don't you want to hear it?' he asked rather severely.

'That depends on the ending.'

'You'll have to judge what that is for yourself,' he returned, and she could have sworn he sounded nervous, but since when had mighty Captain Afforde succumbed to nerves in any form?

'Very well, you may continue.'

'Thank you, my dear, gracious of you.'

'Whatever you say,' she replied, stealing a look at his rather stern profile and fighting a strong desire to distract him by running an exploring finger over it and luring him into warming them both up very rapidly indeed. 'Just get on with it, will you though, husband, for I want my dinner.'

'Been busy, have you then, my Roxanne?' he said, the sultry memory of their vigorous loving in his half-closed eyelids and slow, sensuous smile.

'Yes, someone had to prepare your household to be snowbound for Christmas.'

'Our household,' he chided with a frown.

'Yours, ours, whichever. Now, are you going to tell me this tale or not?'

'Aye, I'd best before I lose my nerve for it,' he said with a suddenly very serious sigh and she nestled herself closer into his powerful shoulder and wriggled pleasurably.

'Just tell me,' she encouraged with a contented smile that should tell the great idiot she'd never flinch away from a man she loved so deeply as she did him, whatever he had to say.

'It all began one snowy Christmas,' he said very seriously and she had to control the leaping of her pulse and the ridiculous arousal of all her senses, for she knew perfectly well he meant that first Christmas they'd met, when she'd fallen headlong in love with him at first sight.

'For me, too,' she breathed and risked a look at his face, both mellowed and shadowed in the firelight.

'Perhaps, but this isn't half as pleasant a tale as yours, love.'

She'd have forgiven him everything and just contented herself with that one significant word if left to herself, but evidently he'd resolved to tell all and she must hear it, now she'd forced him to confront it, whatever 'it' might be.

'Anyway, I met a girl, not much more than a child really, and knew one day I'd come back and marry her. For all she thought herself grown up and insisted on staring at me with her heart in her stormy dark eyes, I decided she must be at least three years older before I didn't have to be an arrant rogue for marrying her and carrying her off to sea with me. I confess I didn't leave Hollowhurst in love with you, Roxanne, or think I'd even let myself love you when the time was ripe and I could wed you. I was four and twenty and knew with all the supreme arrogance of youth and privilege, that by the time I was three years older I'd be a captain and considerably richer. Life's always lonely as captain of a great ship, however sociable he might be, and heaven forbid I be confined to a mere sloop. *I* would command a frigate, then a man o' war.'

'Fair enough,' she interrupted, 'that's exactly what you did.'

'By good luck more than any outstanding talent.'

'That's not what I heard.'

'But you couldn't have listened with unbiased ears if someone paid you to, now could you, my passionate, partisan wife?'

'Never about you, but it wasn't only me who thought you a hero and a superb commander of men, Charles. The news-sheets were full of your dashing exploits and quite determined you were to be the new Nelson.'

'More fool them then. I knew enough of him before he was killed, for even a callow youth such as I was, to sense I was in the presence of genius. And I haven't the heart for battles not fought in a war, Roxanne, whatever small talents I might have. Once Boney was beat, all my famous fierceness and daredevilry went flying off my quarterdeck.'

'Which is perfectly acceptable, considering you had a castle to buy and a new life to live with me,' she said with a smile and a happy wriggle as she slipped off her shoes and flexed her toes so they could feel the fire's warmth properly and leant back against him.

'Fool that I was, I thought that when I reached New England on my discontented wanderings about the globe and met Davy there, that his dilemma solved mine and there was nothing more for either of us to worry about. He wished he could sell his birthright and I wished I could buy it. Simple enough, we both thought, as he trusted me to love and look after it as he somehow could not. Then he suggested I set his mind at ease about our whole bargain and wed his sister, and suddenly I could have my cake and eat it. So I promised to marry Miss Courland, if I could persuade her to have me, and that made our deal all the sweeter.'

'Very convenient,' she said in a cool, non-committal voice.

'It would have been, too, if I hadn't arrived here one dusky night and wanted you more urgently than any female I'd ever laid eyes, or hands, on.'

'It was more than hands you laid on me that night.'

'One almost-chaste kiss, and I dared not risk coming any closer, or I'd have done my best to seduce you right there and then.'

'Funny,' she murmured with a reminiscent smile, 'I don't remember it being so very chaste.'

'Wanton,' he accused, and his other arm came up to hold her closer, as if he revelled in their closeness nigh as much as she did. 'Now, where was I?'

'Seducing me in the twilight.'

'Ah, yes. It came as a terrible shock that you'd grown into a stubborn, capable and independent woman while I was away, as well as one of the most beautiful females I ever laid eyes on.'

'Come, Charles, we must deal honestly with each other now,' she scoffed and sat a little more upright in his embrace.

'Roxanne, I found your complete innocence of your own powerful allure exasperating and dangerous even before I got you up the aisle. Don't make me regret you weren't born with a squint or a wooden leg.'

'Nobody could be born with a wooden leg.'

'I dare say not, but you know very well what I mean.'

'I don't.'

'Then you should; you have the finest of finely made features, the most lusciously curved feminine body I was ever privileged enough to lust over and I could lose myself for hours in appreciating your hair, my dearest love. I love the look of it and the heavy silk feel of it between my fingers, under my hand, and I dare say the male half of the local population would feel the same, if they ever saw it down about your naked shoulders in a witchy web as I have. Of course, if any of them ever do, I'll have to kill them, then lock you up in the tower for the rest of our lives.'

'Harsh,' she murmured in what sounded even to her like a sensual purr rather than an indignant protest.

'But interesting.'

'Hmm? Well, maybe, but I believe you didn't sit me down all undignified and unladylike in this fashion to flatter me beyond reason, sir?'

'I can see I have a lot of enjoyable work ahead of me, convincing you that I speak only the truth, but for now let's get back to our sheep.'

'If you must, but if you truly love me I need nothing

more,' she said, turning enough to watch him with her feelings in her eyes.

'No, I need to tell you now, even if you've turned cat in pan.'

'Go on then,' she told him huffily as she swung back round to stare into the fire again.

In retaliation, he settled his chin on the top of her head and drew her back into his arms, so she settled into his embrace and finally let the tension drain from her muscles. There seemed no point fighting her compulsion to snuggle as close to him as possible, when he liked having her there nearly as much as she did being held as if she mattered.

Chapter Nineteen

❦

'It was after that joyous, carefree Christmas I spent with your family, which somehow makes the memory of it seem so much more shocking.'

Charles began his tale with his eyes fixed on the fire, but she could feel the tension in the tightly packed muscles of his torso and almost wished she'd never demanded he purge whatever horror haunted him and for so long had stopped him admitting he loved her just as surely as she did him. He needed to tell her and she needed to hear him out, however terrible his tale might be, so they could face it and defeat it, together.

'I rejoined my ship and found everyone fit to sail scrambling to get us to sea. As many ships as were even half-ready to embark were under orders to sail to Spain and pick up as many of Sir John Moore's expeditionary force as we could save from falling into Bonaparte's clutches.'

'I remember wondering if you'd got back in time to sail with your ship.'

'I'm not sure to this day I wouldn't rather have missed it. Anyway, we reached Vigo at last and discovered we were in the wrong place, and most of the army were waiting at Corunna while the French got closer with every hour that passed. We sailed off to find them in the teeth of a gale that seemed as if it would never give over, until at last we reached harbour and began to embark as many as we could carry. We took on men until it seemed as if one more might sink us, but I begged the captain to let me take one of the transports and collect any poor souls the French would capture if we left them behind and eventually he let me go.

'It was like a scene from hell, Roxanne, the beach covered in the corpses of their horses, the town with all its windows blown out from our army exploding its remaining powder. The people did their best to defend their town from the advancing French, and even the women braved the French fire to wave farewell at us from the rocks, but it was hopeless and we'd just taken off what few men we could and were preparing to return with them when a French battery opened fire. There was a great panic and some cut their cables without bracing their yards, so their transports ran aground and those poor souls aboard were either wrecked or drowned.

'Hardened to battle as I thought I was, it horrified me to choose between the wretched souls we already had aboard and those at risk of drowning or capture on shore. Still, the second lieutenant I had with me pointed out we must save what we had, so we were halfway back to our ship when we came upon a most pitiful spectacle of all. Apparently one of the men on another boat had smuggled his woman on board with him, disguised as a soldier of the 38th, although not particularly well, it must be said.

'On hearing the French shelling, she screamed and scrambled upright in her terror, so the master of the vessel took out his pistol and shot her, then calmly ordered her body thrown overboard. We saw it all from afar and were powerless to do anything, Roxanne, but I was bitterly ashamed to be part of the same navy that day. We found her floating in the water, but there was nothing we could do for her, she was dead as the poor horses on the shore. She looked to be Spanish or Portuguese rather than English, for masses of black hair floated about her and she looked almost peaceful, if you discounted the bullet hole through her heart. She was also heavy with child, which makes me wonder even more what sort of a wicked fool failed to note he had a pregnant woman on board and then shoot her as casually as I might a rabbit.'

'Oh, Charles, how appalling. No wonder if you were deeply shocked, and you were still so very young to see such a desperate sight.'

'I saw men blown to pieces in battle from the age of thirteen when I became a midshipman, my love, so I really can't tell you why this one affected me so. We never managed to track down the man who did it, and, even if we had, the Admiralty wouldn't have disciplined him. We had orders not to take camp followers, although many ignored them and pretended they hadn't seen the women among so many men, and most of them were a pitiful sight, grey-faced, starved and sexless after that terrible retreat. One dead Spanish girl shouldn't have meant much when we were carrying so many starved and hungry soldiers from a chaos of regiments, yet from that day on she haunted me as if I'd put that damned bullet in her breast myself.'

Roxanne slewed round in his arms and hugged him close, feeling him tremble at the memory of that day and cursing the callous, black-hearted rogue who'd shot a helpless girl for no real reason other than that he could.

'It wasn't your fault,' she informed him fiercely, kissing his lean cheek and horrified to feel the wetness of tears under her lips. 'You would have saved her if you could, and you'd never kill a woman, Charles, or a child.'

'Maybe not, although it's astonishing what men will do in battle. The wisp of a man who you expect to climb down among the ballast and cower there, despite the stink and the danger, will fight like a lion until he's hacked to pieces by the enemy or carries the day, and some great hulking bully of a sailor might just as easily break down and scream like a baby at the first sound of cannon-fire. I may never have been tested enough to know what I'd do in the grip of panic and the certainty I could die if I didn't strike out.'

'Don't be a fool, Charles, you've been in acute danger more times than I care to think about, and I would have heard if you went about screaming and striking out at the first vulnerable creature to get in your way,' she told him sternly. 'The public likes nothing better than knocking down this week a hero they made last week, so if you'd a cowardly bone in your body we'd both know it by now.'

'Not if you went about organising my defence, we wouldn't,' he told her with a wry smile she saw in the fading firelight as he disengaged himself long enough to add a couple more logs to the fire and watch them catch. Then he sank back on to the rug at her side and took her into his arms again, as if he needed her in them to be able to confess more. 'Shortly afterwards I began to have nightmares about her—she'd lie there in the water as she had that day and suddenly open her eyes accusingly. Funnily enough, she didn't seem any less dead as she watched me with hate in her eyes, as if I'd fired that shot and ended her and her baby's lives, but the worst part of it was she watched me with *your* eyes, Roxanne, and it was *your* wildly curling ebony hair that floated about her at the mercy of the current. Then sometimes she'd raise her hand and point at me with hate in her eyes and a curse on her pale lips.'

He paused, watching the flames lick over the new applewood with sombre eyes. 'I knew then that I wouldn't come back to Hollowhurst and claim you after all. I'd never risk taking you to lose your life at some stranger's whim on a foreign sea, maybe with my brat in your belly to rob me twice over of all that mattered in my useless life.'

'Oh, Charles, my love, I'd never think my life useless if I spent it at your side, however long or short it might be. Never think that, never!'

'I might dare to now, love, but I didn't then. I was a coward and all the more so when I woke one night and found I was wrestling with Rushmore, my personal servant, in my sleep, because he'd heard me cry out and come to see what was wrong and I thought I'd finally got my hands on that murdering bastard and could end my torment by avenging her.'

'No wonder he treats you with quite a ridiculous

amount of respect then,' she said, quite unimpressed by another reason he'd found not to be happy with her and not to come back and marry her, which seemed even more important, considering she'd spent nearly ten years being denied her wildest dreams.

'Just say I'm a coward, why don't you, my love?'

'No, for I never met a braver man, but you *are* a fool, husband. Do you still have these nightmares now, after ten years?'

'For the first few months after it happened I did, but in the last eight or nine years only the once, after that first night we met again. I roused Rob and Caro's household with my shouting in the process, and if Rushmore hadn't been there to cope with my ridiculous starts, heaven alone knows what I'd have done.'

'Did you try to attack him again, then?' she asked.

'No, he developed the knack of talking me out of my terrors after that first time, no doubt out of respect for his own skin if he didn't,' he joked weakly and she blinked back a tear.

'And apart from that time, you never had a repeat of your nightmare?'

'Not so far as I know, but d'you see why I dared not sleep beside you, Roxanne? Much though I'd like to sleep with you in my arms all night long and wake to you and everything you do to me every morning, so we can do something about it for once. I can't put you in danger.'

'Nonsense, do you think me incapable of doing what your manservant has learnt to and talk you out of it and back to sleep? Waking or sleeping, or even in the grip of your darkest nightmare, you could never hurt me, Charles, so if you dare to sleep anywhere but in my bed from now on I'll track you down to where you *are* sleeping and make your nights hell without any help from a long-dead spectre who never had any grudge against you in the first place. Is that understood, husband?' she ended briskly, believing common sense a far better antidote to his fear than the tears and sympathy she longed to pour out over him after his long thrall to a tragically dead girl he'd done nothing to harm and would have risked his life to save if he could.

'It is, wife, and how can I argue when all I seem to have done for the last few weeks is long to have you in my arms all night and at my side every waking moment of our days?' he responded with a boyish grin that made her heart wobble for a brief moment, then skip with joy, it was so like the one he'd entranced her with that first snowy night she had set eyes on him.

'And maybe we can do something about your primitive morning urges as well, husband,' she promised with a wicked smile. 'But one thing I can assure you of, Charles Afforde, is that if you don't share my bed from now on, I'll very likely come in one night and murder you myself. And I'll be awake while I do it, what's more.'

'In that case, I'd best keep you so content you'll only want to kiss me all night instead,' he jested feebly, but she knew instinctively he'd have no more nightmares of drowned women while she slept content and fulfilled at his side.

'Is the memory of that poor woman really the reason you made sure I took a violent disgust of you the one time I laid eyes on you during my come-out Season?' she asked as she sat up in his arms and glared at him accusingly.

'Of course. I knew there was no point trying to reason with you when your eyes were full of hero worship and your smile was warm as the sun rising over the Mediterranean on a July morning.'

'Horrible man.' She thumped a balled fist into his chest and heard the 'Oof!' of his protest with some satisfaction. 'You broke my heart, or at least I thought so at the time. I was seventeen and thought I loved you more than any woman ever loved a man.'

'But it mended.'

'I patched the poor battered thing up as best I could and went home to Uncle Granger and a life of single blessedness.'

'So did I,' he said virtuously and she thumped him again, a little harder.

'You raked and caroused your way round the world,' she accused and thought of those lonely years when the only news she had of him was Maria's satisfied letters, informing her that Captain Afforde was still busy flirting with all the most beautiful women in England whenever he was home on leave.

'I certainly appeared to, but I doubt if any man could satisfy as many conquests as rumour credited me with, or not without killing himself from the effort at least. I've led a far more blameless life than you'd credit, love. It's far easier to give a dog a bad name and hang him for it than it is to actually find out he's not as much of a dog as he appears. I made myself useful by helping on some deserted ladies' campaigns to make their husbands and lovers jealous and a lot more attentive as a consequence.'

'So you're entirely innocent of all the sins ascribed to you and have lived the existence of a monk for the last decade? Just how gullible do you think I am, Sir Charles?'

'Certainly not that gullible, my lovely, but whilst there have been a few women I liked and even lusted after and bedded to our mutual satisfaction during that time, I never even came close to loving one.'

'Well, you can stop looking so smug about it, you didn't think you loved me, either, until I made you stop and decide you might, after all, manage to do so, if you worked at it hard enough.'

'Oh, that wasn't anything like work, love, more of a poor, stupid, ignorant male's realisation he'd finally met his fate and stood no chance of escaping it this time.'

'How lovely to be a "fate", as if you can think of nothing more terrible than meeting me some dark night,' she said crossly.

'I forgot to add that I don't want to escape you this time, that being without you now would be an arctic waste of a life—in fact, no life at all.'

'Really?' Sitting upright enough so she could face him and look deep into his eyes, Roxanne closely examined his handsome features and most particularly his dark blue eyes for any sign of insincerity.

'I hope my countenance has the wit to tell you the truth of what's in my heart, Roxanne, for I love you to my very soul, and I'm afraid I always will.'

'Afraid?' she asked, mock-horrified even as brilliant joy sang in her own heart and probably shone betrayingly in her own eyes, as there was so much delight inside her fighting to express itself. 'You're afraid, husband?'

'Aye, wife, for a rake who's fallen so deep in love with his wife is such a bad example to all damn-your-eyes rogues who look to me as a model. They'll surely disown me now and drum me out of town.'

'Damn examples, Sir Charles, the ex-rake. Come here and kiss me.'

'Willingly, my sweet vixen, willingly,' he murmured, and suddenly speech was not only useless but deeply undesirable as he succumbed to the lures of true love in his wife's arms and seemed to find the experience of proving how fervently he returned her lusty passion for him matchless.

Epilogue

'So tell me again exactly why we're standing out here in the freezing cold, up to our ankles in slushy snow, Roxanne?' Mrs Thomas Varleigh quizzed her youngest sister.

'Because we're both ridiculously in love with our husbands,' Roxanne said, trying not to let her teeth chatter out loud and give Joanna an excuse to drag her inside to the comfort of a blazing fire and Mereson's delicious hot punch while they got warm again.

'True, although I'm still not quite sure my devotion to Tom extends to standing about in depths of the holly grove at midnight while my feet become strangers to the rest of me.'

'It did once,' Roxanne told her abruptly, trying hard not to recall she was four and twenty now, not a silly, over-romantic schoolgirl about to fall in love with the handsome outward image of a man, when the real, faulty, human one beneath all his flash and glamour and animal magnetism was so worth loving. Not that his very masculine, very superior good looks exactly repelled her, but they were a bonus, a wonderful addition to the man she adored, just as he adored her.

'I do remember that night as well, you know,' Joanna answered as if she thought Roxanne had claimed the monopoly on folly and needed to be told it was a family failing. 'Standing here with such hope and this odd, inexplicable ache at the heart of me I couldn't understand. All I knew then was that Tom was the only man who made me feel that ache and I couldn't imagine ever feeling it for anyone else. Come to that, I still can't,' she added ruefully. 'Even after nine years of marriage and three and a half children.'

'Three and a *half?*' Roxanne squeaked and even to her the sound rang loud on the still night air.

'Did I not tell you about that?'

'No, you didn't or I'd never have included you in this mad idea in the first place.'

'Just as well I didn't then, for I believe number four is perfectly comfortable where he or she is, and that I won't break just because I'm going to have another baby. Anyway, why should you two have all the fun?'

'It sounds to me as if you've been having some of your own.'

'You're just jealous, which is outrageous considering how late you and your captain rise of a morning nowadays, even when you have guests in the house to entertain at Christmas.'

'Guests who haven't been spotted at breakfast ever since they arrived, although I suppose you have some excuse if you're *enceinte.*'

'Thank you, but I'm past that stage now.'

'Goodness, when's it due, then?' Roxanne asked, rather alarmed she was so in love with Charles she hadn't even noticed Joanna's baby bump.

'May or June, so don't panic, I'm not about to drop it here and now.'

'But perhaps you'd better wait for Tom inside?'

'No, I've had three babes without suffering more than a couple of weeks of morning sickness; now I've finally managed to persuade Tom I don't need wrapping in cotton wool all the time, I'm not having my little sister take over where he left off. I'm very well and quite safe. If my feet were only a little warmer, I might even consider myself comfortable.'

'All right then, I'll stop worrying, but do you think it's really enchanted?' Roxanne asked with a sigh, so reassured about her sister's continuing well-being she went off at a tangent in pursuit of her own dreams.

'Is what enchanted? I don't want to give birth to a changeling.'

'Idiot, I mean this holly grove. Remember all the wild tales in the villages that it's the haunt of witches and their familiars?'

'Who's the idiot now? If you believe one word of that hoary old tale, then I'm calling a halt to this nonsense right now.'

'Of course I don't—well, not the bit about witches and their covens anyway. It just seems a little strange that all three of us stood here that night wishing for exactly what we've finally got, that's all.'

'That sort of enchantment I'm more willing to countenance then, although I'm not sure poor Balsover altogether deserves his fate at Maria's hands. Our illustrious brother-in-law would far sooner be at Balsover Magna among his acres and his horses than in London while she conquers the social world.'

'He loves Maria in his way,' Roxanne defended her sister's illustrious marriage, although she preferred piratical sea-rover baronets to earls herself.

'No doubt, but sometimes I wonder if she loves his title more than she does him.'

'Well, if I were Henry, I wouldn't risk playing host to any mysterious strangers who might be long-lost heirs.' Roxanne laughed joyfully and, since both of them seemed to have decided there was no point pretending they weren't here, Joanna joined in and they were both giggling like schoolgirls at the thought of their solemn and dignified sister being usurped by a rival countess when just then the jingle of harness finally reached their dark hideaway.

'Here they are at last—do you think they've been partaking a little too much of the Vicar's sherry?' Joanna asked as she strained her ears and her eyes through the now rather worn snow.

'No, he'll have hurried off to his vicarage to sleep. I believe he's expecting a busy day tomorrow.'

'Indeed, who'd have thought it, what with it being a Christmas morning and all?'

'Christmas morning, ten years on,' Roxanne managed with an infatuated sigh as Thor's rider became visible through the gloom at last.

'And this year at least I know you're happy as well.'

'Oh, I am, Joanna, I am indeed.'

'Wife!' a powerful bass rumble boomed out of the darkness and Joanna fluttered a quietening hand and hushed frantically.

'You'll wake the children,' she protested, stumbling out of her prickly hiding place and into her lover's arms.

'The nursery is on the other side of the castle and it'd take a cannon firing outside their bedroom windows to do that, so tired and over-excited as they are about tomorrow,' Tom assured his wife as he picked her up, kissed her soundly and threw her up into his saddle to carry her off.

'And what about you, wife? Have you gazed on your handsome husband from the gloom long enough, or would you like me to fetch a lantern so I can show you my best profile?' Charles said as he stood holding Thor and smiling as easily as the laughing young man of a decade ago had done.

'No, Charles, I'd like you to come in here and kiss me. Then you can take me inside so I can study your faults in peace and comfort.'

'D'you hear her, Thor? What a nagging wife I've wed,' he confided in his fell mount, although this one was far better tempered than the demon he rode in on a decade ago. He slapped the patient animal on his rump and Thor obediently trotted off to his stables and the oats Whistler had waiting for him.

'Are you never going to kiss me, Charles?' Roxanne said impatiently, for a cold wind had suddenly blown up, and it was dark, and she could feel a branch of holly dancing threateningly close to her face and she wanted it to look as perfect as possible for the best Christmas she'd ever had.

'I'm letting you savour the moment, love, so you can relive the full glory of my first sparkling appearance in your dull life.'

'Popinjay,' she scorned.

'Not a bit of it. My wife thinks I'm a hero, I'll have you know. Ever since I found that out, I knew we were made for each other.'

'Stop it,' she demanded, swatting him with the ancient muff she'd found in the attic for tonight's expedition.

'I will in a minute,' he promised, batting away that intrusive branch and standing very close to her. 'What a fine view you had of us that night; I dare say Tom and I would have felt self-conscious, while secretly preening ourselves like turkey-cocks, if we'd only known you were here.'

'It *was* a fine view, I'm glad I saw it.'

'Still, after all I've put you through these last ten years, love?'

'Always,' she promised with such heart-felt fervency that he kissed her.

And Sir Charles Afforde kissed his wife of just over three weeks with all the passion and sincerity fourteen-year-old Roxanne could have dreamt of, and an added undercurrent of sexual, sensual desire lay under his enthusiasm she certainly couldn't have conjured up then, all innocent and headlong in love with a handsome face as she'd been at that tender age.

'I'm glad you did, too,' he said, suddenly serious. 'Imagine how terribly empty my life would have been if I'd never laid eyes on you and married some poor echo of my fierce, brave love.'

'Although I'll try to if you absolutely insist, Charles, I really don't want to just now if you don't mind,' she said as she stood on tiptoe and kissed him in her turn, slowly, passionately and with deliberate, slow-burning invitation.

'No, to the devil with all my other possible wives, I love only this one,' he said huskily.

'Just as well….Now, about that hot punch and nice warm fire Mereson has arranged for us…'

'If he's half the butler I think him, our punch and that fire will be in our suite and Joanna and Tom's will be in theirs.'

'D'you know, I think he *is* the very perfect example of his kind and that you're quite right?'

'Of course I am, Roxanne, it's my mission in life.'

'When it took you ten years to come back and marry me? I rather think not,' she scoffed even as he decided to risk no more nonsense and lifted her into his arms for the short trip back to their castle, their home.

'I came back though, didn't I? *And* I managed to persuade your brother to sell me this millstone because you loved it so much.'

'Bah! You bought the castle and had to accept me as the millstone,' she argued gruffly, and there was still a trace of hurt in her voice, just a sliver of pain in her velvety dark eyes as he walked close to the lantern set burning above their door to guide benighted travellers toward a warm welcome, this night of all nights.

'If I had to choose between you and a pile of hoary old stones, my Roxanne, it would be you every time,' he assured her and kissed her under that lantern, perhaps because even Mereson allowed himself the occasional waggish moment and had caused a sprig of mistletoe to be suspended from the bottom of it, or perhaps he just kissed her because he wanted to, something he did rather a lot nowadays.

'And you for me, Charles, so you really didn't need to buy me a castle.'

'Damn, d'you suppose your brother will take it back?'

'No, I think you're stuck with Hollowhurst as well as your nagging wife.'

'Never was such a burden shouldered so joyfully, my love,' he told her and carried her over the threshold to find their household virtuously, even ostentatiously, in their beds, preparing for the most joyful Christmas Hollowhurst could remember in ten long years.

Not that the master and mistress of the house would have taken much notice if they'd all been up and dancing a jig, but as Charles insisted on carrying her up the stairs, protest how she might, Roxanne looked back to the great doorway of Hollowhurst and for a fleeting moment thought she caught a glimpse of a tall and still-straight figure much like Uncle Granger's standing beside it looking very pleased with himself about something.

'I love this wonderful old house you bought me so selflessly, and I love you, Charles Afforde,' she whispered in her lover's ear, then kissed him soundly when he would have put her down at the door of her chamber and reached down with the hand that wasn't feeling the suggestion of golden stubble on his lean cheek and undid the door handle for him.

'That's good to hear,' he managed, before walking into their fire-lit bedchamber and reaching behind his wife's temptingly curved back to shut the door on any interested spectres who might be listening or, heaven forbid, even watching Charles Afforde seduce his final lady love.

* * * * *